Tangled Tales
Julie Castle

Warning: Not intended for persons under the age of 18. May contain coarse language and mature content that may disturb some readers. Reader discretion advised.

Cover Art Design by: Kelly Moran/Rowan Prose Publishing
Photo Credit: Adobe Images
Editor: Shelly Small
First Printing
ISBN: 978-1-961967-41-0

Rowan Prose Publishing, LLC
www.RowanProsePublishing.com

Published in the United States of America

Tangled Tales (series) Reviews

"There was so much heat and passion, and just enough tension to keep you wanting more. This was the first time I've read Ms. [Castle's] work and I will be looking for more in the future. I enjoyed her sense of humor and her writing style." –Enchanting Reviews

"[Castle] takes a much beloved fairy tale and puts a modern spin on it with delightful results. This is a fun, imaginative tale with a bit of suspense which I'm sure readers will thoroughly enjoy." –Romance Junkies

"The suspenseful climax of the story is very well written and had me at the edge of my seat. I just could not put this story down and was very sorry to see it end." –The Romance Studio

"If this is what all her books are like, then [Castle] has a new fan in me. Now go out and pick up your copy today." –Fallen Angel Reviews

JULIE CASTLE
A Wolf's Tale
FAIRY TALES REIMAGINED: Red Riding Hood
Tangled Tales Book One

Chapter 1

❧⸻❦⸻☙

Mitchell Wolf sat straight in the swivel leather chair inside his run-down office at Wolf Investigations and gazed at the photograph Libby Sinclair had sent him. A summons from the society matron wasn't something a PI, who wasn't quite human, could ignore. She wanted him to go undercover and protect her granddaughter, Gina. Whom he thought didn't need protecting.

The Sinclair family matriarch couldn't possibly know about the debt his pack owed her clan, so why seek him out? Why not go to one of the high-priced, high-profile firms like Garret Lamont's? And she sure as hell couldn't be aware of his predicament, the key to his survival was tied to Xanadu, her castle on the hill.

Even now, he could feel the weakness creeping over him, the difficulty changing shape. He'd thought the family curse was just an alpha male's raving when his grandsire had told it to him, but when the stain appeared on his feet two weeks ago, he'd known it was all too true. If he didn't find the key to the Lupine Treasure in two weeks' time, a month from the time the stain appeared, he'd permanently turn back into a wolf and die.

He'd attempted to buy the estate through a third party, planning to tear the place apart stone by stone until he found salvation, only to be rebuffed. Just a few days ago, his broker told him there was renewed interest in selling but wanted to keep it very hush-hush. And now, Libby Sinclair had sent for him. It seemed like the answer to a prayer, but he didn't trust his luck. To have the solution handed to him in such a neat, if convoluted, package, made him wary. Suspicion was healthy as it kept his pack alive through the centuries.

The image smiling back at him from the photo was electric. The full-length photo of Gina Sinclair, taken at the pool, left little to the imagination. Twenty-eight years old with long red hair and sparkling green eyes that tilted up at the ends, she was a natural beauty. Her eyes held a teasing glint that stirred his animal senses, along with his libido, but he ruthlessly tamped the sensation down.

He'd gone too damned long without mating, making him vulnerable to a bodacious pair of tits. She was human, not his for the taking, he had to remind himself of that pertinent fact. Did Libby Sinclair have any notion of the beast she was unleashing with her request? No matter, he had to keep his head on straight, and his dick in his pants, it was the only way for him to survive.

Gina Sinclair cursed her poor time management skills as she tore down the lane on the back of her red custom-made Harley toward Xanadu, her grandmother's mansion. She took her family obligations seriously and she was late for a meeting with Gram's business manager, Harold Baker. She wrinkled her nose as she thought of him, finding his sudden urgency suspicious. All his moves lately had one aim: stick Grandmother in a nursing home and sell the estate. He wasn't fooling her one bit with his supposed concern over Gram's health in the somewhat drafty old manor house.

She was concerned, too, but not enough to push Gram out of the castle she'd moved into as a bride. Unfortunately, her grandmother's brother, Bart, seemed to agree with Harold Baker, so they were at a stalemate. As the three remaining members of the Sinclair dynasty, she thought that she, Gram, and Bart should stick together. Bart however, seemed too self-centered to care. She and Gram were made of sterner stuff, but was Gram strong enough to thwart their continued assault on the estate?

She slowed to turn into the gate, the bike bumping over the cobblestone drive, and winced as pain shot through her sprained ankle. It hadn't been back to normal since her fall two weeks ago. She'd tripped, rushing down the path from her cottage to Xanadu, and then there was her wipeout on the bike a few days later when her brakes failed. All in all, she seemed to be getting more accident-prone lately.

As she rode through the garden gate, she was sure she heard a wolf whistle. It so startled her, she slowed, and her bike sputtered to a halt as she looked around. No lascivious man was lurking in the vicinity. No hunky gardener, no cute pool boy, just her and the chipmunks. Too bad, it had been six months since her last date, and she couldn't even remember the last time she'd had sex, not that she'd ever found it that satisfying. Men were either after her for her money or put off by her somewhat un-conventional ways. A year ago, when Charles Roark, a family attorney and her sometimes beau, broke her heart, she'd concluded that romance wasn't in the cards for her.

Instead of romance, her focus had been all about her art as of late. Still, she could have done with a sexy distraction, she thought before restarting her Harley. She rode up to the house and came to a halt under the portico. Taking off her helmet, she shook out her tangled red hair in a last-ditch attempt to look presentable. It was then that she noticed her jeans were splotched with paint. She stifled a groan. Damn, it was too late to change. She'd been in such a rush to get to the art supply store after she realized her paints were ruined, that she hadn't noticed her disarray. How two hundred dollars' worth of oils and acrylics wound up being smashed by a packing box she still didn't understand. It didn't make sense but now wasn't the time to fret about it, as she had Grandmother's interests to uphold.

With grim focus, she rushed up the stairs. Having Harold Baker think her an artsy kook was probably to her advantage. That way, he'd underestimate her abilities to stop him. She let herself into the front door and brushed past Grandmother's butler, Frank Sloan, causing the formally clad older man to scuttle out of the way. "They here yet, Frank?"

"They're waiting in the study." He raised a brow making a tsk-tsk sound at her. "You'd better slow down, young lady, before you do more damage to that bad ankle of yours."

Nodding to appease his concern, she waited until she was out of his line of sight to sprint down the marble hallway to the study. More unofficial uncle than servant, Frank had been a fixture in her life since her childhood, reading her wonderful fairy tales and teaching her to ride a bike when she was five. She'd come here to live after her parents were killed in a plane crash when she was a baby, it had been a loving and happy childhood. She hated to think of the estate being sold to strangers.

The marble hallway she hurtled down gleamed with fresh wax, mak-ing for treacherous footing, which she realized too late. As she reached the doorway to the oak paneled study, and tried to slow down, her feet suddenly skidded out from under her. Arms flailing, she let out a cry of embarrassment as she tumbled into the room. Closing her eyes, she braced for impact with the floor.

Instead, someone reached out to pluck her out of midair. Bent backwards and held fast in strong arms, her eyes popped open, and she stared breathlessly into a man's warm brown eyes. The stranger's eyes were hypnotic, almost feral, and she could swear she saw plain unvarnished arousal in them, as he slowly looked her over. He wanted her with a raging passion she'd never experienced. It was a revelation, one that made her heat with embarrassment. More handsome than any man she'd ever seen, and wondered if she was only wishing his attraction as she licked her lips.

As he cradled her, she felt something funny happen to her insides—a melting sensation. Falling into his honey deep gaze, Gina's senses went into full alert. Her nipples tingled, budding as an electric sensation zinged through her, making the spot between her legs grow heavy with arousal. Astounded by her physical reaction, she let out a little gasp of shock.

His hands tightened around her, his mouth tightening into a firm line. Everything else seemed to slip away, Bart mixing himself a cocktail at the bar in the corner while chatting with Grandmother, Harold Baker opening his briefcase on the conference table. After a long moment, she remembered to breathe. Why didn't he say something? Instead of speaking, he set her, trembling, back on her feet with a slight shake of his head. Feeling quite unsteady, she blushed and looked away, trying to hide her strange reaction. Bart, nattily dressed in a blue three-piece suit, gave her a perfunctory nod from the bar. A former B-movie actor, he always did things with a dramatic flourish. Her grandmother's younger brother, they'd both been in the movie business decades ago. While Gram had achieved stardom before marrying and retiring from the profession, Bart worked as a B-movie actor until coming to live with them after Gina's grandfather died. Grandmother had welcomed him with open arms, but Gina had never been able to get close to him. She managed to pull herself together enough to walk over to give him the expected air kiss on the cheek. "Hello, Uncle Bartholomew."

"Hello, child."

She frowned. Gina was hardly a child, but refrained from pointing that out. The stranger's hot gaze was glued to her back, she could feel it burning into her. It made her tingle with sensual awareness. Trying to stifle her lingering primal response, she walked over to greet her grandmother. "Hi, Gram."

"Gina dear, you've been painting."

"I was, until I realized I was out of paint. I've just come back from an art supply run. Sorry I'm late."

"Nonsense, you're just on time, isn't she, Harold?"

"Of course, Libby," he parroted back, shuffling his papers.

Gina turned to look at him, hearing the resignation in his voice. Harold Baker was dressed in a three-piece suit, but she couldn't help noticing as he sat down that his socks didn't match, one blue and one black. She stifled a smile at the comical sight. It was gratifying to see him brought down a peg, even if he wasn't aware of it. Maybe there was trouble at home if his blue-blooded wife, Carla, had let him out of the house that way.

He'd taken a position at the head of the table, his papers spread out before him. She decided he looked just like the little kingpin he thought he was. He didn't like dealing with her, having her act as a buffer. Tough. Grandmother wasn't ready to be bundled off to a nursing home, or pushed out of the Sinclair Foundation, and any intimation that she was made Gina see red. She knew what lay behind it—money and power. Harold Baker wanted a free hand. Not on her watch, she vowed.

Leaning a bit on her silver-tipped ebony cane, her one concession to advancing age, Libby Sinclair moved away from Bart at the bar and walked toward the table. Resplendent in a purple caftan, her silver hair drawn back in an elegant chignon, she retained most of her movie star beauty. High cheekbones, tip tilted eyes, she carried herself with a regal bearing.

Baker hurried to pull out her chair. "You're looking well, Libby."

Libby smiled as she settled in her chair like a queen ascending her throne. "Thank you, Harold."

Gina couldn't keep her gaze from flicking to the new guy who took a seat at the end of the table. Who was he? One of Baker's hired guns was the logical and heartsick answer, pretty but deadly. Hadn't Baker already had a string of realtors and estate planners in here, what was one more? But this guy was different—she could feel it, even though she couldn't put a name to the sensation he caused inside her. He still hadn't said a word to her, and she was dying to hear his voice—would it be as compelling as the rest of him? He was eyeing them all with a brooding expression, but when he saw her staring at him, he smiled back at her. Dark and mysterious, he was fodder for a girl's fantasies, not that she needed much excuse to go there.

His eyes were the first things that drew her attention, warm and intense, they seemed to see inside her soul. His features were sharp, masculine and extremely attractive. His hair was dark and a bit too long, brushing the collar of his staid business suit. Even so, he didn't remind her of any businessman she'd ever seen. There was something that set him apart from the other men in the room—a fierce toughness that made her blood sizzle. Her gaze swept down to his sensual lips.

What would those firm lips feel like slanted against hers? Against her breasts, and lower? He'd probably give great head. Suddenly, his piercing gaze locked with hers, like he knew what she was thinking. There was just the hint of a smile on his sensual mouth. Damn!

She looked away, embarrassed and shocked by her wandering imagination. He was so stiff and formal, he'd probably never given head in his life. Strictly a missionary position kind of guy, a sheep in wolf's clothing. Telling herself anything else was just setting herself up for a fall. She tried to dismiss him as a secretary, and turned to look at Grandmother, who gave her an indulgent smile.

Baker sat down and turned to Libby. "Tell me, who is the young man you brought with you, Libby?"

So, Gram had hired him, not Baker, things were suddenly looking up. It put his presence into a whole bright new perspective.

Libby tilted her head, giving him a startled look. "If you'll recall our earlier conversation about the importance of doing an inventory for insurance purposes—"

"Of course, I remember, Libby, I just thought you'd let me handle it." Baker blinked and looked over at the stranger with an inquisitive glance. "I trust your qualifications are in order, Mister..."

Gina watched the stranger calmly give Baker a secretive half smile.

"He's Mitch Lamb," Libby cut in, calmly folding her hands, giving Baker her focused attention. "He's from one of the firms you recommended, Lamb Accounting. Do you have a problem with that?"

Baker's face turned red. "No, no, of course not. Mr. Lamb's firm does come with excellent references. We should be able to work well together."

"Good."

Mitchell Wolf sat back in his chair and wondered again how he'd gotten into this mess. He didn't enjoy playing games, but it was a chance for survival, even if it was a fool's errand. He gave the assembled group what he hoped was a non-feral smile. Well-played, Ms. Sinclair. They never saw it coming. It proved that Libby Sinclair, while suffering the frailties of age, had lost none of her business acumen. She thought that outside forces threatened her estate and her granddaughter, and she'd stop at nothing to protect both. Baker looked confused, and Bart looked bored as he downed his martini.

The granddaughter, Gina, looked troubled. Mitch's hot gaze focused on the rapid pulse thrumming in her tender neck, the perfect fit for a wolf's teeth. He could almost taste her allure from where he sat, floral, feminine, and enticing. More tomboy than siren, she was the type that didn't yet know her female power.

Mitch turned back to Libby, noting a mysterious twinkle in the lady's blue eyes. Was she just enjoying getting the better of Baker, or was she playing them all for fools? As he thought it, he rejected the notion. There was no way she could know him, and if she did, she sure as hell wouldn't have hired him. "I'll need full access to the estate, ma'am. A job this size will take some time. If you could recommend a good hotel nearby..."

"Nonsense, you'll stay on the estate. You can take Eden, it's the guest-house next to Gina's. She'll be glad to show you around, won't you, dear?"

He heard Gina's gasp. His quick gaze locked on the sway of her breasts under her pink tank top as she sucked in a deep breath. She wasn't wearing a bra. Her nipples were beaded, like ripe berries. His mouth watered as he thought about licking and nibbling her there, and everywhere. Her wide-eyed glance told him she'd noticed the direction of his stare. Tearing his gaze off her luscious tits, he turned his head to note Baker's smirk of satisfaction. He thought he'd finally gotten past the girl's defenses.

"Um, um, of course," Gina stammered.

"That's just fine then." Bart sat his martini glass down on the bar with a clink. "If you'll excuse me, Libby, I'm late for my luncheon appointment."

Mitch's gaze snapped over to the rotund older man. The man still dyed his hair jet black, a holdover from his acting days, he surmised. Mitch had taken the precaution of doing a light background search on the man, not that there was much to find. Plump, and a hanger-on, he favored showgirls and gambling, which explained his frequent trips to Las Vegas. He watched as Bart hurried out of the room, giving Baker a pointed look, which the business manager studiously ignored. Mitch cataloged the silent exchange for later.

Baker closed his briefcase and stood up. "Excellent, I'm glad things are going so smoothly." He slanted a sharp glance Mitch's way. "I'll give you my number, in case you need my help."

Mitch could feel Gina stiffen from where he sat, saw her watchful gaze narrow, and had to rein in his feral instinct to lash out at the man.

He was so close to salvation; he wasn't going to allow the stupid ass to muck things up. There was no need to fan the fire of Gina's doubts or blow his cover. "I won't need it," he bit out, his voice clipped. Baker frowned, then shrugged, packing up his papers.

"Fine then. I'll speak with you later." He walked from the room.

Out of the corner of his eye, Mitch watched Gina give her grandmother a what's going on look. Libby Sinclair's extracted promise of silence on his part had him in a stranglehold, so he couldn't go after this in an open, easy way. She was sure her granddaughter would refuse the services of Wolf Investigations. From this meeting, he had to agree. She was feisty, unpretentious, utterly beguiling. Yeah, he could just picture her shock if he blurted out, *I'm here to protect you. I'm also a werewolf and only a key to the Lupine Treasure hidden somewhere in Xanadu can save me.*

Libby smiled. "Gina, dear, I want you to personally show Mr. Lamb around and help him get settled into Eden. Give him all the help he needs."

Casting a furtive look back at him, Gina asked, "Are you sure about this, Grandmother?"

"Trust me, dear. I'd see to it myself but I'm late for an appointment with my designer for the Sinclair Ball."

Gina bit her lip, knowing she was sunk. Avoiding Mitch Lamb's appeal would be like the Titanic avoiding an iceberg—not bloody likely. She hadn't felt this flustered in years, and he damn well knew it. Even if he wasn't one of Harold Baker's spies, which she still wasn't ruling out, he was way out of her league. She didn't want to be just one more notch on his bedpost.

"Don't let Madeline wear you out," Gina responded, feeling her tension mount as she gave Grandmother a kiss on the cheek. She'd just try to stifle her feelings. Turning to walk away, she called over her shoulder, "Coming?"

Mitch hurried to catch up, startled by her abrupt flight. She was walking fast, no doubt feeling threatened. He couldn't blame her for running, besides, he enjoyed the chase. They reached the doorway at the same time, and Mitch managed it, so they collided. Time to reassert his presence.

Gina gasped, bouncing off him.

Mitch felt the contact deep inside and decided it had been a stupid move on his part. Her breasts pillowed against his chest, their crotches collided, and he felt sparks ignite deep inside him as his cock swelled. Just who was the predator here? He couldn't help feeling like the one caught in a trap, as he grabbed her around the waist to steady her.

Groaning as Gina's gaze locked with his, Mitch told himself to knock it off but couldn't. She had the deer in the headlights look again, the one that brought out the protective instincts in him, and he couldn't help focusing on the racing pulse in her throat. She was so cute; two fetching specks of pink paint dotted her upturned nose. Her fragrance, something light and heady, wrapped around him and he wondered where she applied it. How shocked would she be if he bent to sniff her, taste her? He stifled a growl as his cock twitched, growing stiffer.

"You can let go of me now, Mr. Lamb."

Gina's sweet voice only made him throb, kicking his arousal into overdrive. She felt it, he could tell by her quick intake of breath, but she didn't try to pull away, just kept a wary gaze focused on him. This was sweet torture. Too bad it wasn't the old days when storming a castle meant taking its women by force. Now a guy had to use subtlety, something he lacked. Not yours to take, he had to grimly remind himself. "It's Mitch," he corrected her, gently.

She licked her lips. "Mitch."

He set her back on her heels and reluctantly dropped his hands from her waist. She was delicate, human, no match for a beast like him. "Why don't you show me Eden?" he asked, finally finding his tongue. He looked over his shoulder to see Libby beaming at them and wondered what that meant. Apparently, she didn't have any idea of the damage he could do.

Gina turned and hurried out of the library. She led him to the French doors facing the courtyard, and then edged away. "The cottages are Eros, Eden, and the Rosebud—my studio. If you walk through the gate, you can take the flagstone path."

He watched her literally back away, his eyes narrowing. Why the retreat? Had she finally sensed his intentions? "Aren't you coming with me?"

She smiled. "I rode my bike."

Mitch felt instant relief, seeing her smile. "Your Harley." At his mention of her motorcycle, he saw her smile vanish, and felt a light dim inside him.

"How did you know about that?"

Suspicion was rife in her voice, and he didn't like it one bit. Stupid move on his part, letting her in on his inside knowledge.

She frowned. "Oh, right, Baker."

"I didn't say that," Mitch cut in, but Gina was already striding away from him, toward the butler he'd noticed upon entering. The man stood like a sentinel, eyeing him with suspicion—the old family retainer was no fool. There was something different about the guy, but Mitch was too focused on Gina to pay him much mind.

"Is there a problem, Miss Gina?" the butler asked, stepping into Mitch's path.

Blocked, Mitch suddenly had visions of tangling with the elder, something he didn't want to do, as the butler let out a sniff like he smelled something bad. He wasn't here to spill blood, but to save it. He stared down the man, but the butler didn't budge, even though his eyes widened as if he was startled by something.

Gina stepped back to touch the butler's arm. "No problem, Frank. Mr. Lamb will be staying at Eden while he conducts an inventory of the estate. I trust it's ready for visitors."

Mitch couldn't help glaring at her hand touching another man. He was jealous. It was stupid, he hadn't claimed her for his own, couldn't have her, but he couldn't stop the possessive feeling.

"Of course," the butler replied, stepping aside as he eyed him with new caution.

Mitch felt about as welcome as an ant at a picnic as they both swept him with troubled looks, but he stood his ground. He trailed Gina out the front door, not liking her sigh of displeasure.

Gina stalked toward her bike. "Gram isn't fragile or senile like your boss is intimating..."

So, they were back to Harold Baker being his supposed puppet master. "For the record, he's not my boss," Mitch cut in, stalking her. The assertion that he worked for Harold Baker bothered him more than it should. After all, he was here on an undercover mission, deception was par for the course. Didn't matter, he had to set the record straight. "It's common knowledge that you drive a motorcycle, Gina. Shocks some of the country club set, I'm told." She looked at him then, her smile warming him again.

She wrinkled her nose as she lovingly touched the motorcycle. "I know, according to Uncle Bart, it's not ladylike."

Admiring the bike's sleek lines, he stepped up beside her. Cherry red, it went with Gina's adventurous spirit and her fiery red hair. He cocked an intrigued glance her way, what would it feel like to have her stroke him that way? She was a breath away and watching him warily. His hands itched to reach out, touch her, and caress her. Instead, he stuffed them in his pockets. "Why don't you give me a ride?"

She blushed and looked away.

Idiot, he told himself, he hadn't intended the double entendre. The pretty human had a strange way of making him lose control.

Slanting a slow glance at him, she replied with a grumble, "I suppose there's little chance of getting rid of you."

Relieved that she was willing to overlook his blunder, he grinned at her sarcasm. "No chance at all."

She reached in her saddlebag to pull out a spare helmet and thrust it at him. "Here put this on."

Mitch noted the art supplies filling the other side of the saddlebag. She must have bought out the store. Of course, growing up rich, she doubtless didn't know the value of a dollar. His pack hadn't had that advantage, and he was glad of it. He knew the value of his possessions and he cherished them. Could the American princess climbing onto her Harley say the same?

His background checks on her hadn't turned up much. Never in trouble with the law, she'd studied art in Paris, and now worked as a commercial artist. Unmarried, she didn't have any romantic entanglements, at least none that he'd turned up. He suddenly found himself glad of that fact.

He watched her don her helmet, glad she was smart enough to wear it, and put on his. Having her follow simple safety rules made his mission to protect her easier, not that he put much stock in the assertion that she was really in danger. He'd already been told about a few accidents, which were probably only that. Until he had reason to believe otherwise, he'd go on that assumption. The fact it freed him up for his search bit at his conscience, but he salved it, knowing even half of his attention would be enough to protect her. Twice as strong as a mere man, even with his power waning, he felt up for the task.

That wasn't all that was up, Mitch thought with a groan as he climbed on behind and grabbed her waist as she started the bike. His hardness sandwiched between their bodies, he thought he was going to lose it.

She took off with a roar, and he held on tight swearing with every bump they clattered over. It was sexual torture and served him right for even fantasizing about poaching outside his species. *Some guy's going to marry her and keep her,* he told himself, *not you.*

If Gina felt the hard thump of his cock against her bottom, she didn't let on. Her moves were fast, but efficient as she drove them down the long driveway and onto the lane. They drove along the fenced wall surrounding the vast estate, to the rear, and turning into an open gate, drove to the three cottages clustered by the pool.

Mitch gingerly climbed off the bike, noticing the lack of security. It was the first change he'd make, and he'd approach Libby Sinclair about it the first chance he got. Having a few members of his pack standing by could only be of benefit to him.

He gazed at the three, fairy tale appearing, Tudor-style cottages, and the azure blue swimming pool beyond them. The estate was well named, Xanadu indeed, but he wasn't worried about finding paradise here, just deliverance from a curse. Mitch handed Gina his helmet, watching her stow it and then heft out the bag of art supplies. "Allow me to help you," he stated, snatching the sack from her and earning a look of surprise.

"Um, thanks, but it's not that heavy, I can carry it." Trailing after him.

Mitch kept walking toward her cottage at the end of the row. She was frustrated and a wee bit nervous, natural reactions to his morph from Baker's stooge to gentlemen. She didn't seem to know which to believe, smart girl. "Nonsense, and deprive me of a chance to prove my gallantry? So, tell me about Xanadu."

A few seconds of silence ticked by as she hesitated. "It's big."

"I can see that," he commented, not put off by her reticence.

She tilted a curious glance his way. "What do you want to know?"

"Everything." Noting the mingled curiosity and distrust in her face. "Who built it? How old is it?"

"It's ancient, the east tower dates to the old country. An ancestor, Darrin Sinclair, had it brought over and reconstructed piece-by-piece. It's said he built it for his lover. It's a wonderful place."

He could see her warming to her tale, and it touched him. "Why do you love it so much?"

"How could I not? It's my heritage, a part of me. Growing up in a fairy tale like setting has warped my mind, I guess," she concluded with a chuckle.

"I wouldn't say that," he answered, stepping closer. He saw her intake of breath as he invaded her personal space and moved in for the kill. "A place this old must have legends, secret passageways." He watched her for a guilty reaction, but saw none. Then she turned to smile at him, and his heart melted.

"Yes indeed, the Love Chronicles."

Love Chronicles, what the hell was that? He'd been hoping for a hint about the key to his survival. "What?"

"Love letters and poems written by an ancestor and said to be hidden at Xanadu. I used to search for them as a child but never found them."

He tried to hide his disappointment but saw awareness in her eyes that he was crestfallen. Since when had a human ever been able to read him? Since your powers were blunted, stupid, came the answer. "No secret treasure?"

She rolled her eyes. "Oh, God, you're one of them."

"Them?"

"We had a chimney sweep who dismantled it looking for a pot of gold, a maid who dug holes in the backyard, only to run off with a weird tale of werewolves stalking her. Not to mention, the score of alleged tradesmen who've cased the joint looking for the treasure. I'm telling you right now, it doesn't exist."

Treasure! He couldn't believe she'd just volunteered it that easily. "What treasure?" he asked, hoping it wasn't wishful thinking, and that he hadn't completely misinterpreted her words.

"The Lupine Treasure, said to 'deliver riches to he who finds it and cure beasties of their ailments'."

He felt time stand still as she quoted him part of the rhyme his grandsire had told him. "You don't say."

"I'm telling you this for your own good, treasure hunter, all I ever found was the scroll and it never led to anywhere."

"Scroll?" He could damn near taste it, salvation was so near.

"Come on." With a sigh, leading the way to her cottage. "I might as well show you so you can see for yourself it's a lost cause."

Mitch trailed after her, feeling like a puppet on her string. He waited while she unlocked her door and followed her inside. Standing inside her cottage, he looked around, too on edge to be soothed by her cheerfully decorated living room.

"Give me that." She took the bag from him.

Mitch watched her put it on the table and then walk to a bookcase. She came back carrying a rolled-up scroll. He could feel its power, smell the wolf bane it'd been soaked in to ward off vampires, but it was clear that she didn't perceive any of those things as she negligently thrust it at him.

"Read it and be gone."

He heard her bitter disappointment but tried not to focus on it. She thought he was only interested in the treasure. She was dead wrong, although she'd never know how he ached to take her. He unfurled the old document and read.

The Lupine Treasure is easy to find for those with a loving heart. All others beware, for danger lies there. It has the power to provide great riches to he who discovers it. A price above rubies, to he who finds the key to knowledge. It has the power to cure beasties that walk the night of their afflictions.

He looked up to see her watching him and handed it back with a smile. "It's a riddle."

"Know any vampires that might need curing?" she asked flippantly.

He raised a brow. Actually...but he wouldn't go there. "Vampires?"

"Creatures that walk the night."

"How about werewolves?" he asked, gauging her reaction. He didn't have to wait long to see her quick grin.

"Now you sound like Frank. He used to tell me fairy tales about them. I stopped believing them when I was five." She swept him with a curious glance, teasing, "Don't tell me you believe in those, too?"

"Of course not," he hurried to reassure her. "Speaking of treasure, I could use some help with my inventory."

"Why don't you ask one of Harold Baker's secretaries?" At his frown, she blushed. "Sorry, I guess that was below the belt."

"It's okay. I'm used to rough treatment." He saw her shock and cursed his loose tongue. If she were a she-wolf, she'd be snarling at him by now. Instead, she looked intrigued. Dangerous, he didn't want her probing into his secrets.

Chapter 2

Later that day, Gina stood on the ladder in the library helping Mitch catalog her great-grandfather's selection of Victorian erotica. First editions and extremely valuable, they made her blush, especially when she recalled sneaking in here to read them when she was fourteen. They'd been her introduction to sex. Naturally, the sisters at St. Agnes's Girls' School hadn't covered sex education.

She glanced down at him, sitting at a library table, his laptop open as he keyed in the entries. A treasure hunter, or Harold Baker's spy, he was now the picture of accounting efficiency. Had she only imagined his wolfish qualities? Maybe having him checked out was unnecessary, but it was too late to call it off, besides, she had to stay one step ahead of Harold Baker and his minions.

She'd called Charles Roark, family attorney and her sometimes beau, the second Mitch had left her alone in her cottage. Charles had readily agreed to check out Mitch's qualifications. She didn't like snooping, but sometimes, a little prying was necessary. There was more to Mitchell Lamb than met the eye, and she was determined to find out all his secrets.

Still, she couldn't help wondering how she'd gotten herself into this. Why was it that he got to sit down while she scaled ladders? Because she was only his assistant, so she did the grunt work. She was tempted to demand that he call in an assistant from his accounting firm. Two things kept her from doing so; first, a desire to keep tabs on what he was doing, and second, a crazy urge to be near him. It was nuts, he hadn't even kissed her, and only touched her to keep her from falling on her ass twice. Still, she was hungry for him, like a chocoholic for a candy bar.

"What's next?" he called out from below.

She reached out to pick up the next book and blushed, the classic S&M volume almost burning her fingers. This was forbidden stuff, even for a woman as broad minded as her. "Um, The Story of O," she replied softly.

"What?"

She peered down at him to see an amused look on his handsome face. From his smile, she could almost swear he'd picked up on her whisper. If so, he had the ears of a bat. Was he making her repeat it for his own amusement? Even as the possibility stirred her ire, a little thrill zinged down her spine as well. Her legs started trembling. "The Story of O."

He grinned. "It's a bit much for my tastes, too. Dominance has its place, mind you, but only accompanied by passion."

Dominance, huh? Shocked at the words coming out of his mouth and the gleam of his smile, she could only stare down at him. He had the most compelling eyes—hypnotic, sensual. Her body began to tremble again, and the room began to spin. With a shocked cry, she lost her grip on the ladder, dropping into a pair of strong arms.

"I've got you."

Gina didn't have to open her eyes to know it was Mitch. There was no mistaking his strong body, or magnetic aura. How had he moved so fast? Her eyes opened in time to see him bend to kiss her. She froze for a second as his sensual mouth slanted across hers, hot and demanding, and fire broke free inside her. It was what she wanted, what they both wanted. With a sigh of surrender, she opened her mouth for his surging tongue, hers mating with his. He was so savage, so elementally male; it couldn't have been any hotter. Her breasts swelled, pressing against him, and the spot between her legs grew dewy.

As if he knew her needs, he picked her up and carried her to the leather sofa, pulling her onto his lap. Gina whimpered, on fire as his big hand shaped her breasts through her top, teasing the nipples to hard beads of readiness. When he bent to take one in his mouth through the fabric, she let out a wild cry of pleasure, shocking herself with her primal reaction. His rousing cock swelled in response, growing hard under her bottom. She couldn't resist rubbing against it, earning a primitive growl from him and a nip to her nipple.

She whimpered at the brief pleasure-pain, but he quickly licked it away, making her squirm with need. His hand slipped up her bare leg and inside her shorts, until he was touching the hot place between her legs, caressing her through her panties. Gina gasped as his big finger pressed against her swollen clit and she came, muffling her shout of triumph into his mouth.

Another sound broke through, a tapping on the door. Mitch let out a pained groan, and Gina sat up, trying to rearrange her clothes. She wriggled off Mitch's lap, wincing as she heard him groan. "Yes," she called out.

The butler, Frank, opened the door and poked his head in. "I'm off now unless you need me. Your grandmother is dining at the club."

Gina couldn't stop the blush that covered her face as Frank took in her rumpled clothes in a glance, and then gave Mitch, who sat next to her, a pointed look. The butler was closer to her than her own uncle and very protective. "I'm fine, enjoy your night off."

She waited until the door closed behind him, before turning back to Mitch, already backpedaling, trying to put her aberrant behavior in perspective. Such animal passion was unlike her; she'd practically attacked the man. He was looking at her, his expression wary, watchful, and incredibly hot. She couldn't help feeling like prey in that moment.

The evidence of his arousal was plain to see, there was a huge bulge in his pants that made her blush. What did he look like under those pants? The thought so shocked her, she shot to her feet.

He still sat there, lounged, eyeing her with a predatory glint in his eye that told her he wanted to grab her and finish what they'd started. "Um, as you heard, it's the staff's night off. I'm afraid you'll have to find something to eat in town."

He raised a brow. "What about you?"

Stopped by his inquiry, she had no choice but to look him in the eye. Heat was there but something else as well, determination, she decided, feeling hunted. "I'll just scrounge something up here."

He nodded. "That'll work for me, too."

"I don't think that's such a good idea, after..."

"The least you could do is offer me dinner after ravishing me. It's common courtesy."

Gina frowned, realizing he'd be impossible to shake, that is, unless she found a way to put him off. Backing away past the table to the door, she stated, "At seven in the dining room." She turned and fled the room feeling his gaze follow her.

Mitch walked into the dining room a little before seven to find it empty. She wasn't going to stand him up, was she? Just the possibility made him tense. Then he noticed the two place settings and felt some of his worry release. His body was still charged from Gina's orgasm. God, to have the woman come apart in his arms had been mind–blowing and had damned near brought out his baser instincts. He hadn't been able to stop himself from touching her; she was just so damned irresistible.

Still on edge, he wanted nothing more than to watch her orgasm again, this time with his cock buried deep inside her. Walking around with a permanent erection wasn't an option if he wanted to find the key. The moment he touched her, his plans to keep his distance had been irretrievably altered. He'd just have to figure out a plan to get it all, life, and the girl, if only temporarily. She wasn't his kind, wouldn't want him if she knew, but would a dalliance be so bad? he wondered. Just then, he caught wind of her alluring scent and turned toward her soft footfall.

She walked into the room, wearing a prim gray dress buttoned up to the neck. Kryptonite against sex maniac accountants, he guessed, with a spark of wry amusement. He found the row of little pearl buttons a challenge, and he never backed down from a challenge. "Right this way, Mr. Lamb." She turned and led the way to the table.

When he held out her chair for her, she looked at him, startled, like she wasn't used to such courtesy. Were the men around here all blind to her charms, or just too damned stuffy? She sat and he scooted her in, loving the feel of her warmth brushing his hands. She trembled and he felt it all the way down to his cock, which started to spring to attention.

He let go of her chair feeling scorched and moved down to his before he could embarrass himself. Sitting down, he finally looked at his mostly bare plate—celery, a tiny scoop of rice, and bologna. He looked over to see that hers contained the same.

"I told you I was scrounging."

At her wry smile, he knew she'd done it on purpose. It wouldn't work, he was going to be her shadow. "I'm not complaining."

Chapter 3

Gina slipped down the path to the pool after midnight, Mitch Lamb still firmly on her mind. He was like a ghost lingering in her senses. She shivered a bit at the image that brought, goose bumps breaking out on her arms.

There was something otherworldly about him. Why did the man have to stick so close to her? Instead of getting angry at her efforts to push him away, he took everything in stride, even laughing at the skimpy dinner she'd served him. She'd hoped to cut down further group dinners. From his reaction, she knew it hadn't worked. It was enough to make her lose control, and that wasn't all. She'd come at his touch, how embarrassing.

His hands could do magic. Her body still tingled, her nipples budded, bare under her robe, and there was a longing between her legs that only the right man could fill. Mitch. She didn't want to desire him, but she'd never been this sexually aware of a man. He seemed to delight in pushing her buttons.

She had another button between her legs she'd like him to push again, she found herself blushing at the errant thought. Until she got Charles' report, she had to keep her distance. Even if Mitch could kiss her hot enough to set her body on fire, he might be the enemy.

The path was dark, but she knew her way by heart. The scent of the night blooming jasmine and narcissus led her on. She slipped through the pool's wrought iron gate and walked over to dip her toe in the water. Cool and refreshing. It was perfect.

Dropping her robe, she dove into the water nude. This was the wonderful thing about living on the estate—her midnight moon baths. She stroked through the deliciously cool water, swimming half a length of the pool before she got a feeling that she wasn't alone.

Gasping, she swam into something soft and furry over a solid body. It shocked her for a moment until strong male arms wrapped around her. Mitch! She knew it was him. He was imprinted on her senses. She smelled his cologne and the elementally male smell of him. "Don't scream," he whispered, his mouth inches from hers.

"I won't," she replied with a gasp, as his body rubbed against hers in the water. He was nude too, his body hot and aroused. Shocked and excited, she didn't try to move away, couldn't have even if she wanted to. Their legs tangled in the water; his rousing cock brushed against her sensitive mound making her moan. It was stupid, insane, but she stayed put, trembling on the brink from the erotic sensation as his mouth closed over hers.

He tasted wonderful, just like she remembered from the library. Her tongue flicked out to taste his lips. A sexy rumble came from his throat as her naked breasts brushed against his hair-roughened chest. Gina whimpered, her nipples impossibly hard, like diamonds teased to distraction by the pelt on his chest. She'd never gone in for hairy men before, but now she found it a turn-on. She couldn't resist rubbing against him.

He responded by slipping a hand around to cup one globe. His big fingers finessed the nipple, tugging on it, making it harder. Their lower bodies meshed as his erection nestled deeper between her thighs, rock hard, rubbing against her swollen clit. She cried out, shivering against him, ripples of ecstasy making her quiver. It'd been so long since she'd been with a man, too long, and even though she sensed danger, she didn't want to pull away. He let out a growl, sucking on her neck and Gina gasped. He moved against her, grinding against her, rubbing his manhood against her rippling pussy. She moaned, arching into him, and exploded, crying out at the night sky.

Panting, she was kept afloat by him as she slowly drifted back down to earth. Mitch's arms supported her, keeping her from going under as he swam them to the edge of the pool. Her head resting against his chest, she listened to his heartbeat slow in tandem with hers. Wow! She'd never experienced anything quite so wild or explosive. His cock, still rock hard, rubbed against her abdomen. Pulling back, she looked up at him in the dim moonlight trying to read his expression. His face in shadows told her nothing; only his body spoke to her. The pent–up tension running through him was palpable. What were his intentions? Was he Baker's spy, or a treasure hunter? She watched him frown, as if reading her indecision.

He took a step forward. "What are you doing here, Gina?"

She licked her lip, inching back, trying to maintain space between them. It was the only way to keep her from making the ultimate blunder of falling for him. "I could ask you the same thing. This is my pool after all."

"Sorry." Pressing her back to the tile wall. He didn't sound sorry at all, just satisfied, she decided, making for the stairs. But he wasn't satisfied, she reminded herself. A vivid example of his frustration was visible as he followed her up the stairs. She'd gotten her jollies by humping him again, almost attacking the man. Flushed with embarrassment, all she wanted to do now was run. "I wanted to cool off." He bent to pick up her robe.

Gina could feel his hot gaze burn into her, as he straightened to hand her the robe, taking in her nude body in the moonlight. His slow perusal made her burn, even more aware of him. He was still naked; in fact, she didn't even see a towel for him to cover up with. Had he walked down here nude from his cottage? The thought made her blush.

She didn't want to look at him, but didn't have a choice as she took the robe, he extended to her. Slipping into it, she was glad of the small barrier between them. Mitch's hot eyes had a way of making her lose control. It was too soon, she didn't go in for one-night flings, and he might be Baker's spy, all good reasons not to take this any farther. But damn, she wanted to. "Well, I'll leave you to enjoy your swim then."

"Go to sleep, little Gina," he called out after her, adding, "I'll be right next door if you need me in the night."

Chapter 4

Mitch stomped into Eden a few minutes later. He was frustrated, his cock full to bursting. He noticed a light on in Gina's cottage and thought about asking her to take care of it. Yeah, right. He was a hired hand, Baker's supposed stooge. He was good enough to dry hump but not to sleep with. He walked straight into the shower, turned it on cold, and jacked off under the stinging spray.

It helped for about two seconds. Stepping out of the stall, he wrapped a towel around his hips and went to the kitchen for something to eat. Supper hadn't been enough to keep a mouse alive, probably Gina's idea to keep him from sitting in on family meals again. He watched her living room lights flick off. *Sure, go to sleep while I've got a case of blue balls that would kill a gorilla.*

He was just putting away the juice when a scream tore through the night. Gina! Not stopping for his gun, he ran from Eden to the Rosebud and pounded on the door. After a moment, she came to the door. The same robe was belted around her waist, so he knew she was naked beneath it. He wanted to peel the garment off her but the sight of her eyes brimming with tears hit him like a punch to the gut. Tension making his shoulders ache, he stepped toward her, asking, "What is it?"

"Oh, Mitch," she cried, falling into his arms.

Mitch cradled her trembling body against his, with only her robe and his towel separating them, but suddenly, mating was the last thing on his mind. Ice filled him as he realized something bad had occurred, maybe another alleged attempt. Was his dismissive attitude about the threats wrong? "What happened?"

"M–m–my painting."

Taking a deep breath, inhaling her scent, he felt some of his fear vanish. She was only worried about a painting. "What about it?"

She pulled away and took his hand. "Come with me, I'll show you."

Mitch enjoyed the feel of her small, soft hand holding his as he followed her past her living room to her studio out back. The paintings on the walls drew his attention, and he couldn't help being charmed. She painted in a style that was completely her own, just this side of impressionistic. Gina was a gifted artist, not just a rich girl, he had to give her that. He turned around then and saw she was halfway across the room at an easel and watching him.

She'd picked up on his admiration of her art; he could read it in her soft eyes, her slightly relaxed stance, but then she looked down at the canvas on the easel, and grew rigid again, tears filling her eyes. He stalked forward to see what had her in such a state. As soon as he got close, he saw the cause. Someone had taken a knife and slashed the painting to ribbons.

"It was a commissioned work, a landscape for Dale Wallace at Wallace Oil, and almost finished. Damn it, how could this happen to me again?"

"Again?" He looked at her closely. This was something Libby Sinclair hadn't told him about. "Has something like this happened before?" He watched her fists ball at her sides.

"Not exactly. I had a sculpture smashed a few weeks ago. And I've had some paints ruined. That's why I went into town today, to get more supplies." She let out a heavy sigh. "I thought it was just a run of bad luck."

Was it Harold Baker trying to scare her off? He didn't like it one little bit. Even though it wasn't what he'd signed on for, Baker needed a second look. If Baker was guilty, he'd have one pissed off werewolf on his ass. "Did you report the incidents?" At the question, he watched her freeze up as if cornered.

She bit her lip. "I didn't want to worry…"

"Grandma," he concluded grimly, furious that she'd risk her neck so recklessly. She gave him a defiant look, then heaved a heavy sigh when he didn't back down.

"Yes, something like that."

The off-hand disclosure, coupled with the attempts on her life she didn't know he knew about, scared even a beast like him. He closed his eyes searching for patience, she needed a keeper, she needed a spanking for being so careless with her life, and she needed him. "Come on." He reached for her hand.

Gina held back. "Where are we going?"

"Back to Eden with me." He gave her a tug and she came along, sputtering objections.

"But I shouldn't, it wouldn't be..."

It sounded like she didn't want to be alone with him, didn't trust him not to try to jump her bones, and it irritated him. He might be a beast, but he wasn't a rapist. Still, she'd experienced enough traumas to make anyone paranoid, so he tried not to take her rejection personally.

He drew her out the door with a little squeeze to her hand that he hoped she found reassuring. "No hanky panky, Gina, I'll sleep on the couch."

As he walked her down the garden path to Eden, he smelled the intruder's scent. A cool focus of rage settled in him. The trail would be easy to follow, but first, he had to get Gina settled. She was calmer now, looking at him with more trusting eyes. It touched him more than he wanted to admit, but he told himself it didn't matter. When she found out what he really was, all bets were off, and she'd turn away from him.

He opened the door and stood back as she brushed by him, acutely aware of their near nudity. It would be so easy to peel off her robe, unfasten the towel around his hips, and take her to ecstasy—easy, but pointless. "Would you like anything before you go to bed?" She turned those elf green eyes on him, and he felt his dick begin to stir.

Blushing, she turned away. "No thanks, I'm fine."

"I'll leave you to it then, I'll take the sofa. There are pajamas in my top dresser drawer you can change into."

She nodded and hurried into the bedroom firmly shutting the door between them. He heard the lock click. As if that could keep him out if he was determined to get her. Fortunately, he had something else to focus his savage energy on, tracking down the intruder.

Lying in Mitch's bed, smelling his cologne on the pillow, Gina felt restless. Who would destroy art? *The same jerk who's been playing other nasty tricks on you.* Mitch was right, she should have been much more proactive about the threats. From now on, she would be. In trying to protect Grandma, she'd really done her a disservice by hiding the truth from her.

Who would have access to her studio? Mitch was the only new person here, but it couldn't have been him. First, he'd been trying to make love to her in the pool, and second, he'd be much more direct. He wouldn't sneak around to spook her. On a deep level, she trusted him. In the morning, she'd call off the dogs on Mitch. Having Charles check up on him was unnecessary. Would a person who'd so meekly sent her to bed alone be a threat? She didn't think so now. With that comforting thought in mind, she fell asleep.

Mitch slipped back out the front door, locking it behind him, and went on the prowl. The wind had shifted coming from the east, and he instantly picked up the scent. Running, he felt this world slip away, a dark swirl of motion, a flash of pain, and he changed. Bigger, stronger, faster, his senses more acute, he tracked his quarry. His sensitive nose sniffing out a scent he'd only sensed earlier. It was always like this, two sides of a coin, but not a whole being.

He ran full on down the hedgerow, his shape blending into the shadows, following the scent. In the distance, he saw a man almost to the gate, the glint of a knife in his hand. Mitch's night vision was acute as he chased him down. The man looked behind him at the last minute and didn't recognize Mitch. The intruder let out a howl of fear and slashed at him with the knife. Snarling, Mitch was on him, his rage a black cloud of emotion, growling at a quick flash of pain.

Lashing out, he sunk his claws into the intruder's leg, wishing it were his neck. One slash on the jugular and it would be all over. The flick of the bedroom light flashing on in Eden brought him back to his senses.

He rolled away, springing into the shadows. The intruder stumbled to his feet, and hobbled out the gate, running to a nearby car. Mitch stood there frozen, shocked by his blood lust. He hadn't been this out of control, ever.

It was Gina's doing, she was opening him up, changing him, and he wasn't sure he liked it. From now on, he'd be careful to rein in his emotions. Mitch watched the intruder drive away, hoping he'd scared the son of a bitch off permanently.

He went back to the cottage to stand watch over Gina, morphing back into his human form, dressing his nude body in pajama bottoms at the last minute.

Gina sat up in Mitch's bed, shivering. What on earth had made those sounds, a pained cry followed by savage snarls? They'd woken her with a start of fear. Was it the return of her intruder? Why wasn't Mitch saying something? Unless he was out there dealing with danger. Her heart sank at the thought. She slipped out of bed and put on her robe. It was no good cowering in her bed, she had to go out and investigate.

She hurried to the bedroom door and pulled it open, scanning the living area for Mitch. Sure enough, it was empty. Her heart sank. Was he being outside tangling with someone, risking his neck for her sake? Then the front door opened. Mitch came inside barefoot and dressed in his pajama bottoms. Where had he gotten them? His hair was disheveled, and he was holding his arm funny. "What was that?"

"Some night creature hunting in the dark, nothing for you to fret over." He winced, shutting the door.

"What's wrong?" Her gaze swept to the hand he held over his right forearm and his palm was stained red. Was he bleeding?

"Nothing, go back to bed."

"No." She stalked over to him, ignoring his attempt to brush her off. "Let me see.." She tugged his hand away from his arm and gulped. A three-inch gash went down his arm, blood trickling from it. "My God, you need stitches."

"Nah, it isn't that deep. Besides, I'm a quick healer."

She frowned at his cavalier attitude, typical man. "Come on." She pushed him toward the bathroom.

"Where are we going?" he asked.

"To play doctor," she replied, her sass returning.

"I like the sound of that."

"Now why doesn't that surprise me?" She walked up to the vanity and got out the first aid kit. Reaching for the bottle of rubbing alcohol, she gave him a glance. He was watching her as if she was fascinating him, hadn't he ever been cared for before? "Brace yourself, this is going to hurt a bit."

"Your touch will take away the sting."

Surprised by his suddenly poetic turn, she poured a goodly amount of alcohol over the wound, knowing she had to sterilize it. He didn't even flinch. She cocked a probing glance at him. "Aren't you human? What are you made from, pure steel?" She watched him tense.

"No, just flesh and blood."

She saw the shuttered look on his face and wondered about it. The man liked to keep secrets, but she wasn't about to back off. "Tell me what happened out there."

"I went out to look for your intruder."

"And found him," she stated, looking at his arm.

"He got away."

"Well thank heaven for that, he might have killed you." She dressed the wound with a bandage, noticing that the bleeding had stopped. He was a fast healer, just like he'd claimed. Smoothing the bandage across his rippling forearm, she peered up at him seeing the banked passion smoldering in his eyes. Her being quivered with excitement as she came to a decision. She reached up on her tiptoes and kissed him. He went still in her arms for a moment and then kissed her back with a hunger that made her tremble. Her body melted as he pulled her to him. He kissed her like he wanted to consume her, like he couldn't get enough of her, and she felt the same.

He broke the kiss to murmur, "Are you sure, Gina?"

"Yes," she replied, nibbling his neck and hearing him growl in response. His animal passion thrilled her, making her tremble. Her hands roved over him as he carried her to bed. He was like one of her sculptures come to life, only better—he was a warm flesh and blood man who wanted her.

And then he was standing her next to the bed. Her knees buckled when he nuzzled her neck while unbuttoning her pajama top. His hot lips skimmed along her neck, his hand cupped her breast, and she moaned, sagging against him. He peeled it off and laid her on the bed. Gina laid back, eyes shining as she watched him shed his pajama bottoms.

He was on her, one of his big legs laid over hers, holding her still while his hand slicked down to toy with her pussy. His big fingers rubbed her labia while her stiff clit sent sparks of pleasure through her, driving her wild. She whimpered as he pressed her clit, her pussy flooding with moisture. He was slipping his fingers inside her, one, then two, stretching her. She touched his cock, feeling the surging heat of him, testing him. He groaned, rippling against her.

"Stop that or I won't be able to wait."

"I don't want you to wait. I need you, Mitch." She gasped as he played with her clit. "Oh yes, there."

He growled, toying with her.

"Yes," she breathed, kissing his neck, even more turned on by his reckless passion. He wanted her so badly, he was shaking; she could feel the tremors coursing through his body. She was on fire, hot for him, but he seemed to delight in making her wait. Playing with her breasts, he tasted her, sucking on her nipples, making her arch against his hungry mouth, seeking more. "Oh, please, please."

"Soon," he replied, moving onto the other peak, drawing hard on her nipple, leaving it with his raspy tongue until she was quivering with pleasure. She now knew the meaning of domination; he was in charge. Two could play the teasing game. She reached down for his rampant manhood. He jerked in her hand, growing to an enormous size, hot and steely. With a groan, he slipped from her grasp and pressed a string of kisses down her body, stopping to leave her navel and then lower to her pussy. She cried out when his rough tongue licked her there, her head thrashing on the pillow. When he sucked on her swollen clit, she screamed ripples of orgasm sweeping through her.

He pulled a condom out of the nightstand, sheathed himself with it, and surged into her. Gina sucked in a gasp, amazed by the sheer size of him. "You're so big."

"Oh, babe, you're so perfect."

He started moving in and out of her. Gina moaned, meeting his thrusts, seeing stars behind her closed eyes. Her pleasure built, waves of ripples increasing where they met. If anything, he seemed to be getting bigger inside her. She didn't understand it as she gasped, her body pulsing as their bodies joined.

"Yes," she cried as he filled her. He rose on his forearms, changing his angle, and she wrapped her legs around him, making him slip deeper, crying out at the wild pleasure. "Oh yes, yes," she cried out as spasms overtook her, clamping down on him, making him growl. He stiffened, coming high and long inside her. Gina felt dizzy from the passion as her body quivered around him. She closed her eyes with a sated sigh as he rolled to the side and pulled her into his arms.

"You, darling, are the perfect woman."

Gina smiled at the compliment, feeling secure in the accountant's arms.

Chapter 5

Gina woke up the next morning, her back tickling, snuggled next to Mitch's heat. His big hand possessively cupped her left breast. Her nipple budded, tingled against his warm palm. She loved his hairy arms, legs, and chest, so sexy. His hunky body spooned against her; his semi-hard manhood nestled between the cheeks of her bottom. He was so virile, even that contact was arousing. He nibbled her nape making her sigh with pleasure and wriggle back against him.

It was true, she hadn't just dreamed it, he was her lover. In one short, delicious night, he'd managed to work his way past all her defenses. She'd slept with the hunky accountant, Harold Baker's supposed spy. It was a downer until she pondered on it a little more. Who said he was a spy? He was probably what he claimed to be, an innocent accountant caught in the middle of a family squabble. Until she had reason to believe otherwise, she was going to hang on to that positive thought. It was the only way to get through this and keep her heart intact. She rolled over, coming face-to-face with him.

"Good morning, babe."

"Um, good morning." She couldn't help being a little embarrassed, she wasn't used to awkward morning-afters. The covers had slipped down, and her eyes followed them, straight to his rousing cock. She couldn't help staring because she hadn't gotten a good look at the instrument of her pleasure last night. It was huge, like tanned silk over iron.

"I've got a present for you," he murmured.

She looked back up at his face, startled, and blushing "A present? What?"

"One guess." His voice was a low bedroom grumble as he rolled her onto her back and slipped between her open legs.

She smiled, eager for him as he entered her tingling pussy. He'd pleasured her repeatedly through the night, and she was amazed he had the stamina to do it again. "I love my present," she whispered with a pleasured sigh.

It hadn't been an extended erotic dream. It was real. He was real, very real, and he was all hers. Her arms wrapped around him, her fingers combing through the thick hair on his nape. He pulled almost out, and then surged back inside her, his shaft rubbing against her swollen clit. She whimpered at the sweet sensation. Gina felt the ripples begin inside the trembling walls of her pussy, turning into a tidal wave of orgasm as she clamped onto his thrusting cock. With a hoarse cry of triumph, he came, holding still and high inside her. Gina slowly came back to earth, he was still on her, in her, but he was holding his weight off her, so as not to crush her. After a moment, he rolled to the side taking her with him and rubbing her bottom. She snuggled against him. "That was…"

"Amazing."

"I was going to say wonderful, but amazing fits." He was the one that was amazing, but she felt every inch a woman in his arms. Their hands linked, her smaller one in his big one. She noticed the faded scars on his side. "What happened here?"

"A fight."

His matter-of-fact tone surprised her, he was a strong man, she already knew that. "I'm guessing that you won."

"I'm here to tell the tale." He teased, wrestling her to her back.

Gina looked down and saw the red marks on his foot. Kind of like a geometric design. "Oh my gosh, why didn't you tell me you hurt your foot last night?"

He glanced down and frowned. "No. I've had that for a while. I've been a bit under the weather. Sorry."

She could feel him pulling away from her and she wondered about it. Didn't he think she'd want him if he were less than perfect? He couldn't have been more wrong. She pushed herself back into his arms and relaxed when he held her. "I'm sorry to hear that."

"Thanks for the kind words. My pack tends to reject anything like this."

"Then you need to get some better friends."

He chuckled. "I'll tell them you said that."

"What do you have, one of those skin diseases?"

"No. It's a family thing, genetic." At her sigh, he brushed a hand down her back. "It's nothing for you to worry about, babe. I feel better this morning than I have in weeks. Your kisses must have restorative powers."

"There's more where they came from." She smiled and placed a butterfly kiss on his chest.

He gave her a hug. "Why don't you go start us a hot shower and I'll put on the coffee?"

Gina liked the idea. At least he didn't have any preconceived ideas of her making the coffee. "Fine." She slipped out of bed feeling his admiring gaze on her. She felt sexy, alive in the face of his appreciation. She walked to the bathroom door and gave him a coquettish look over her shoulder. "Don't be long, Mitch."

The heat in his gaze made her sizzle, her libido heating up again. The man was superhuman, never seeming to run out of steam. She walked into the bathroom and turned on the taps, glad of a little breathing room. It was all a bit overwhelming. Her love life was hurtling out of control, but she didn't want to stop it. She stepped under the spray with the comforting notion that at least she was going to be one satisfied woman while he was here. Maybe enough sexual healing to last a lifetime.

Mitch waited for the door to close behind Gina before rolling out of bed. Truth to be told, there was no way he could tear his gaze off her luscious ass. Some predator he was, he couldn't chew gum and walk a straight line in her presence. He stalked over to his cell phone and pushed a number on speed dial.

"Wolf Investigations, we'll howl for you."

Mitch wrinkled his nose at Michael's chipper voice. He wasn't feeling particularly chipper this morning despite a night of no-holds-barred, drop-down, drag-out sex. He was insatiable for the redheaded vamp in his shower. "Had a spot of trouble out here last night. The first thing I want you to do is call in Lash and Cairn, I'll want surveillance immediately until this is over."

"So, the grandmother's stories that the granddaughter was in danger were true."

"It seems so." Mitch felt a weight of guilt at the admission.

"What happened?"

"Some goon broke in her studio and trashed it last night."

"Did you catch a perp in the act?"

Thinking of his tussle in the dark, he felt his hackles rise again. "Not quite, but I got a piece of him. Should be enough for the trackers to follow."

"Do you mean you didn't get him? Boy, you're getting feeble in your old age." He gulped. "Oh, sorry, bro."

Mitch knew he felt bad for the unintended mention of his growing weakness. "Don't worry about it, Mike. I'm doing fine," he murmured realizing it was true. He was feeling stronger this morning. Maybe the knife attack had pumped him full of adrenalin, or maybe it was the result of a night of the most incredible sex of his life—more than sex—there'd been intimacy. It was an unknown factor in his species' mating rituals.

"Second, I need you to dig up anything you can on Harold Baker."

"Who's he?"

"Libby Sinclair's business manager, he's the one who I suspect secretly put the estate up for sale."

"Do you want me to continue negotiations with the Reno Holding Company?"

Mitch hesitated, he didn't need to buy it anymore, now that he was in and Gina had given him the first clue, but it might be the edge he needed to bust this case wide open. "Yeah, but drag it out. I want to give them enough rope to hang themselves."

"Do you mean you don't want to buy it? Lara's put together the financing."

Mitch smiled at the mention of his accounting wizard kid sister. "Don't need it anymore."

"Why not?"

"Gina gave me the scroll."

"She just gave it to you?" he stated with a gasp.

Mitch heard his shock and still shared a piece of it. Gina's generosity still had the power to stun him. "Yes, she gave it to me."

"Damn. Tell me about her. How does she fit in this?"

Mitch hesitated. "It's complicated."

"Complicated, huh?" Michael teased. "Keep your eyes on the prize, bro, and your fly zipped."

"And you keep your nose out of my business," Mitch replied with a snarl letting the good-natured jibe get to him more than it should. Taking a calming breath, he added, "I'm still head of this pack."

Gina rinsed off in the shower and let out a sigh of regret. Mitch hadn't joined her after all and what's more, she didn't smell any coffee. She stepped out of the shower, toweled off, and went off in search of her man. She opened the door to see him standing naked next to the nightstand, his cell phone at his ear. She couldn't help ogling his bare butt, he had the most powerful body she'd ever seen. However, she could tell by his rigid stance that he was tense.

"Don't question my motives, just do as I say, Michael." He snapped closed the flip phone, cutting off the conversation.

Gina's troubled intake of breath made him stiffen. He turned like he could pick up on her vibrations. His brow was furrowed, his gaze hard, but when it lit on her, she watched it first mellow, and then heat up. "Trouble?"

"It's no trouble at all," he replied, tossing the cell phone on the unmade bed and stalking up to her with a lascivious grin on his face.

"Who's Michael?"

"My pesky kid brother"

Gina let out a delighted laugh as he tugged her towel away, scooped her up in his arms, and carried her back into the bathroom. "I've already had my shower."

"I haven't," he stated, carrying her into the double stall. "You can wash my back." He bent to kiss her.

Gina sighed as his plundering lips slanted over hers, opening for his tongue. Her nipples beaded, rubbing against his hairy chest as he set her on her feet.

"Feel good?" he asked.

"I love your hairy pelt. It teases my nipples."

"I'm not teasing." Rubbing against her as one big hand slicked down her wet body to cup her mound and squeeze gently.

She whimpered, her knees wobbling, and leaned into his hand. He had magic hands; she'd realized that last night. As if he knew instinctually how she needed to be touched.

He picked her up, moist and ready for him, and lifted her onto his erection. She sighed, loving the perfect fit. "You're perfect."

"So do you like hairy men?"

"No." She felt him tense at her quick answer and realized she'd hurt his feelings. With a sigh of regret, she bent to nibble his neck, hearing him groan. "What I meant to say is I haven't till now, you've opened up a whole new world for me."

With a growl, he backed her against the marble shower wall, and surged into her. His movements, at first restrained, became fiercer, stronger, until she was moaning his name in absolute bliss. Groaning, pulsating, gripping his cock with her fierce orgasmic spasms, she came and passed out from the intensity.

A few moments later, she felt kisses on her face as cool water splashed on her body. She opened her eyes to see Mitch's worried face.

"You alright?"

She laid her head against his shoulder hearing his heart skip a beat. "Better than ever, thanks to you." She thought she felt him tense as he kissed her.

Chapter 6

Later that morning, Gina was cleaning up her studio. The shredded canvas was enough to pluck her out of the orgasmic cloud she'd been walking around in. It was a painting of Winslow Point, a beach area between Sinclair Cottage and the Winslow's old homestead. It would be a commission lost and dozens of hours wasted. Looking at the carnage made her feel queasy. How could anyone be cruel enough to destroy art? The incidents could no longer be ignored. Someone was trying to get rid of her. It was time to seek out some help.

A sound, a sense, made her aware that she was being watched. With prickles of awareness assailing her, she looked around for something to defend herself with. Her eyes fell on a pallet knife on her table. Scooping it up, she turned around. A man's shape moved out of the shadows. She let out a sigh of relief. "Uncle Bart, you about scared me to death."

"Really, Gina dear, you are getting overly emotional again." He brushed a smear of paint off his shirtsleeve and looked around her cluttered studio with a wrinkled nose. "I've been sent to remind you about your fitting this afternoon."

Gina rolled her eyes. The last thing she wanted at this moment was to get fitted for a costume for Grandmother's masked ball. A huge money-making event for local charities, Grandmother took great pride in hosting it. Would this really be the last? It saddened her to think that it might, if outside forces couldn't be stopped. "Thanks, Uncle Bart."

He stepped back, straight into an easel.

"Look out," she shouted, but it was too late. His heel caught on one of the easel's wooden legs and he tripped, arms windmilling as he fell on his elegantly dressed butt. Gina was both horrified and amused. She tried not to crack a smile as she murmured, "Sorry."

"You should be, I might have broken my neck." He scowled up at her from the floor. "Really, Gina, you need to clean this mess up. It's a fire hazard."

"That's what I was in the process of doing." She winced, gazing down at him nervously. He looked okay, but he was a well-known hypochondriac. If she weren't a relative, he'd probably sue her. Strike that, she thought watching him; a little thing like family loyalty wouldn't stop him from a lawsuit. She winced in sympathy for his ruffled pride. "Are you okay?"

"No. I was almost killed."

"Sorry." Again, wincing at the overstatement. First, her studio was trashed, and now she'd have to deal with Bart's soon-to-be-constant complaints. This would give him something to fuss over for weeks. What other disasters might fate heap upon her? Frowning, she decided she didn't want to know.

Suddenly Mitch appeared in the doorway to the studio. He looked from Gina holding the pallet knife, to Bart on the floor, and scowled, a nerve pulsing in his jaw. "What happened? Did this bozo bother you?"

"No," Gina cut in, wincing at Bart's reaction to the insult and the implied threat. She didn't need Mitch's protective instincts making things worse. One night of incredible sex did not make him her keeper. "I'm fine. Uncle Bart just tripped, that's all."

Bart frowned at him. "Are you mad, sir? Staff should concern themselves with the house."

Gina rolled her eyes. "He's hardly a staff member." She looked up at Mitch to see the appreciation in his eyes as he walked over to offer Bart a hand up.

"I don't need any help," Bart stated, trying to untangle his feet from the easel and stand.

"Up you go." Mitch tugged him effortlessly to his feet.

Gina's eyes widened; Mitch had to be incredibly strong. Bart wasn't exactly a lightweight. Once on his feet, Bart backed away limping.

"Was there something you needed from me, Mr. Lamb?" she asked Mitch, and tried not to blush at the sudden heat in his eyes at her unintended double entendre.

He smiled. "Yes, you promised to help me finish cataloging the books in the library. That is, after you finish with the police over here."

"Police?" Gina and Bart said in unison.

"Why the police, what's wrong?" Bart asked, looking at Gina for clarification.

Mitch shrugged. "Someone broke in here last night and trashed the place. I took the liberty of calling the police."

Gina's jaw dropped. How could he do that without consulting her? She didn't like his high-handed tendencies one bit. Besides, when did he have time? They'd been together all morning. Maybe he was simply trying to get a rise out of Bart. If so, it was working, Bart's face was tight with irritation. "When did you do this?"

"What kind of craziness goes on here?" Bart demanded.

Mitch ignored him and stepped closer to Gina. "This morning. I called a friend who's on the force. He'll swing by later to quietly take your statement. Don't worry, he understands the need for discretion."

Gina nodded as Mitch's hand touched her, feeling safe and trapped at the same time. Bart was livid; scowling at the two of them, no doubt upset he wasn't consulted. Was he worried about bad publicity?

Mitch looked over at him. "I don't take attempts on Gina's life lightly."

"Attempts on her life?" Bart's brow wrinkled. "Do you mean her spill on the bike?"

"For starters."

"That was just—"

"An accident," Gina put in weakly and watched Mitch shake his head. He didn't believe it and she was starting to have her own doubts. She watched Bart's frown fade and realized with a groan that it helped bolster his assertion that they weren't safe here in the country, damn it. It was one of his reasons for having them sell Xanadu.

Bart sighed. "I wish you hadn't done that, Lamb." He turned to Gina. "This proves what I've been saying. Our lack of security out here is a selling factor."

"I disagree," she cut in.

"No kidding," he muttered. "At any rate, it proves my point that we need to hire some guards, at least for the time being."

Gina frowned, not liking the idea. "I don't see any need to do that."

Bart shrugged. "Too late. I've already got Lamont Security on retainer. Now seems like a fortuitous time to tell you."

Gina watched Mitch grimace as the security firm was mentioned. Didn't he like them, or was his wound acting up? She turned back to Bart. "I don't think that's really necessary."

"Neither do I," Mitch muttered.

Bart frowned. "Well, I do." Bart turned to scowl at Mitch. "And I'll thank you to keep your opinions to yourself. I don't see that this is any of your affair, young man."

"I'm making it my business. Lamont is so big; this job is going to be a small one. They're liable to assign it a low priority."

Gina tensed as the men squared off and the situation threatened to get out of hand. The last thing she wanted was to make things worse or upset Grandmother. She reached out to touch Mitch's arm, feeling his tension. "It's okay. What's done is done. Mitch, I'll make your police report, and Bart, I'll put up with your security detail, if they don't upset Grandmother or interfere with the charity ball." She could tell that neither man was completely satisfied, but that was just too darned bad, it was time she asserted herself.

Mitch watched as Gina walked away for her fitting, climbing the staircase inside Xanadu. She was more formal with him since the showdown in her studio, no doubt annoyed with him for reporting the incident. Trev Stewart, deputy sheriff and one of his clans, would be discreet. What's more, Trev brought news that the trackers had followed the intruder's blood scent to a shack out by the beach.

While his few remaining loyal pack members went on the hunt, he realized he needed to get back to his search. The knowledge had to refer to the library, at least that's what he was hoping. He turned to go into the library, time to rededicate himself to his search. Sure, he felt revitalized now, but how long could that last? His gaze flicked to a secretary desk in the corner. He hadn't looked there yet.

He was combing through the papers in the bottom drawer when he felt a presence. Startled, he looked up at Frank Sloan, the Sinclair family butler. How the hell had Sloan snuck up on him? Maybe his hunter's instincts were blunted. The look in the butler's flinty eyes was guarded, suspicious, and why not? He'd caught him in the act.

"What happened last night?" the butler demanded in a quiet but insistent voice.

The question took Mitch by surprise. No 'what are you doing rifling through our desk drawers', just 'what happened'. His mind first went to the hot night he'd spent in Gina's arms, but he knew that wasn't what Sloan was asking about. He was asking about the break-in, but why? "Why do you ask?"

He raised a brow. "A couple of flatfoots are setting up two guard shacks, that's what makes me ask."

Mitch grinned at the old-fashioned lingo. So, Lamont's people were already here. Bart must have paid big bucks to get such speedy service. "Gina's studio was broken into last night." He watched worry pinch the old butler's face and shared his concern.

"Damn," Sloan muttered.

He watched the butler's knowing expression. "It isn't the first time, but I think you know that."

Frank cocked a curious look his way. "I suspected more was going on than just a run of bad luck."

"Right."

He gave a pointed look at the rifled drawer. "Mind telling me how you fit into this?"

"I'm an accountant," Mitch replied, sliding shut the drawer.

"And I'm heavyweight champ," Sloan cut in sarcastically.

Mitch sighed, time to come clean. "Libby hired me to look out for Gina."

Frank rolled his eyes. "Lord preserves me from meddling women. It's just the kind of harebrained scheme Libby would pull."

"You two go way back, don't you?"

"Since she and her husband married in the thirties. They're good people, the Sinclair's, well, most of them." He had to be referring to Bart. Bart's limp earlier had him wondering, although his senses told him he wasn't the man he'd savaged. Still, he felt off, his reactions blunted, since sleeping with Gina.

"Just what are your intentions, young man?"

Mitch felt like a kid with his hand caught in the cookie jar. To steal you blind wouldn't be PC, although it was true when it came to the key. "What do you mean?"

"About Gina."

Mitch felt his face flush as guilt washed through him. How did the man know? His intentions—he hadn't thought beyond lust. He noticed the butler's tension seemed to abate as he looked at him. Did it show? "I don't mean her any harm, if that's what you're asking."

"I don't want you to break her heart."

Her heart? His kind didn't think in those terms. Besides, since when had he had the power to do that? "Don't worry."

"There's more to you than meets the eye, Mr. Lamb, if that's your real name. I'm putting you on notice, break her heart and I'll hunt you down."

Chapter 7

Gina punched Charles Roark's number on speed dial while waiting for Grandmother's dressmaker, Marlene, to arrive. It was time to call off the background check on Mitch, a little leap of faith on her part. "Hello, Charles," she stated when he picked up.

"Gina, are you okay?"

She frowned. News of her break-in hadn't gotten out, she hoped. Maybe that detective Mitch had introduced her to wasn't so tight-lipped after all. "I'm fine, Charles. Why do you ask?"

"Then you'd better sit down, honey."

She frowned into the receiver. Why the dramatics and the pet's name? They didn't have that kind of relationship anymore. "What's wrong?"

"He's a fake, there is no Mitchell Lamb working for Lamb Accounting."

"What?" Gina shouted into the phone, then covered it up when the maid looked up. There had to be some rational explanation. Her knees grew weak, and she sat down. It was the last thing she'd expected to hear in Charles' clipped voice. Was he a treasure hunter who'd scammed them? It'd been done before, but not by him, she couldn't bear it.

"Settle down, honey. Want me to come down there and kick the bastard out?" he offered.

"No." Gina closed her eyes picturing the one-sided fight that would ensue. Charles, despite his eagerness to help, had no idea what kind of strong man he was talking about going up against. It couldn't be true, yet she'd thought that Mitch was holding back secrets, but what kind? If he wasn't an accountant, he was doing a good copy of one. It still left the question of what he was doing here.

"Fine, I'll step back for now."

Gina heard Charles' tension. He seemed even more upset than she, as if he had more at risk. Had he picked up on her personal interest in Mitch? Was he jealous? It was no secret that he'd been sweet on her in the past, but she'd set him straight that she wasn't interested. She simply didn't have romantic feelings toward him any longer. Was he making this up? Maybe having him vet her dates wasn't such a good idea. He might not be objective. "I'll do a little digging on my own," she stated, not wishing to elaborate as Marlene came into the room carrying a garment bag.

A few seconds later, she was standing in front of the pier glass in a blue satin ball gown like one worn by Marie Antoinette. The fussy dress really wasn't her style, but she didn't want to put a damper on the woman's excitement. "It's pretty," she murmured, lost in her own thoughts while Marlene pinned a loose seam. Usually, the ball was exciting, but not this year. She had other things on her mind, like the mystery man down in the library. Why the deception? He was almost done cataloging the books.

Tomorrow, he'd move on to the solarium. Soon, he'd be gone. If he'd lied about his identity, what else might he be keeping from her? Her heart sank and she sagged, yelping when she got jabbed by a straight pin. "Ouch."

"Mademoiselle must stand up straight," Marlene scolded.

Libby walked into the room and smiled when she saw Gina in the costume. "Gina dear, you do look a treat in that gown."

Gina smiled at her grandmother, breathing a sigh of relief when Marlene unpinned her. Gina slipped out of the gown and hurried to get dressed. She waited until Marlene was out of earshot before approaching Grandmother. Something had to be said. As usual, Grandmother picked up on her distress, her smile fading into a worried frown.

"Is there something wrong, dear?"

Gina bit her lip, wondering how to break the news that they'd been had. Recalling her night of bliss, she blushed. "Mitch."

Grandmother's tension eased as she smiled. "Oh yes, Mr. Lamb, what about him?"

"Yes, Mr. Lamb, if that is his name." She heard Grandmother's quick intake of breath and wondered about it. "I've been checking on his credentials and they don't check out."

Grandmother frowned. "His credentials? How?"

"Um, a friend of mine at the city hall."

"Don't tell me you wasted Charles Roark's time with this?"

"Guilty as charged. Don't worry, we're not being billed for it. He's doing it as a personal favor to me."

"It's not the cost I object to. Do you think it's fair to lead Charles on this way?"

"Lead him on?" she asked, biting her lip. It echoed her previous thoughts.

Grandmother patted her hand. "He's your date for the ball, isn't he?"

"Well, yes, but we've had a standing date for the past three years. We're just friends."

"You may think that, but trust me, the man is carrying a torch. He's not the man for you," Grandmother stated with a shake of her head.

"Let's get this back on track, about Mitch's lie."

"I know all about his background. Let me worry about his credentials, or lack of them. Has he done anything to make you think he might not be who he claims to be?"

What an odd turn of phrase. Grandmother wasn't usually given to riddles. "No. Not exactly." Did Grandmother suspect their affair? It was embarrassing to think it.

Mitch stood in the shadows unseen and felt ice encase his heart. Gina had checked on him. She hadn't trusted him. It was logical, but it hurt. And even worse, she had a date with some goon. Who the hell was Charles Roark? He morphed back into the shadows and walked back to the library, reaching for his cell phone.

"Wolf Investigations, we ain't just a wolfin'."

Mitch bit back a curse at Michael's flippant greeting. No wonder clients were few and far between. "Cute."

"Oh, hi, bro. What's up?"

"My hackles. Find out who's been investigating me and get my bona fides registered. It's throwing up red flags. You find anything on those searches yet?"

"Yeah, they're still chomping at the bit to sell. I did a bit of pushing on the seller's credentials and found out that Reno Holding Company was acting under Libby Sinclair's power of attorney."

Mitch raised a brow. "I think that'd be news to her."

"Kind of figured that. Do you think it's just a scam to steal our money?"

"Maybe."

"There's more."

"That beach shack is leased to the Reno Holding Company."

"Crap." Mitch suddenly had visions of things evolving out of his control. "Get all the proof together. I'll meet you at five o'clock outside the west gate. And watch out for Lamont Security, they just set up shop here."

"Right, boss, piece a cake."

Mitch pocketed his cell phone and turned away when he spotted it. The treasure is with the knowledge. It was what had caused him to hit the library first. Time was growing short, and so was his life, he had to find the answer soon.

The last section of books stood out from the others, catching his eye from this new angle as the afternoon sun shone across it. Why hadn't he seen it before? He walked up to it and pressed a volume back. With a click, it popped back open to reveal a hiding place, a wall safe. Rubbing his fingers together, he leaned in, morphing into his other shape to enhance his senses. He worked the dial, listening to the tumblers click inside. There were many reasons he was cut out for this profession, and this was one of them. It gave him an advantage. He got it open and reached in, his nails snagging several items.

Chapter 8

Gina walked back to the library; her mind still troubled over the conversation with Grandmother. Was Mitch something other than the meek accountant he claimed to be? Approaching the room, a sixth sense set her on alert as if something had changed in the atmosphere. Even though the rational part of her mind told her it was silly, the hair rose on the back of her neck. She tiptoed closer and in the shadows at the far end of the library, she thought she saw something that made her freeze—dark, covered with fur, like something out of one of Frank's fairy tales. Stress had her going bonkers. She closed her eyes, blinking it away with a strangled gasp of disbelief.

When she opened her eyes to look again, she realized it was only Mitch standing in the dark, the dying light casting strange shadows on the wall. As she approached, she noticed his hand shoved deep into the bookcase. So deep, she couldn't see it. She also noticed the guilty look on his handsome face. As she neared him, she saw that it was an opening behind the books, a wall safe, and he was elbow deep in it. She turned an outraged gaze on him. "You are one of those treasure hunters," she stated, her heart sinking. "How could you use me this way, you beast?" She watched him wince at the name, and then saw his expression mellow.

"Now, babe, don't fling words around you don't understand."

"Yeah right."

"I saw that one of the books was sticking out, opened it, and found this. He pulled out a handful of objects and handed them to her. "I was getting them out for you. Since you hadn't mentioned a safe, I assumed you didn't know about it, unless you were trying to hide assets from the account."

"I was not, and no, I didn't know about it." His story was fishy, but she looked down at the objects in her hand, intrigued, despite her anger. A bundle of letters, tied with a red ribbon, an old-fashioned brass key, and a jewel box. He'd found a treasure she hadn't believed existed. Now what, would he snatch it and run? Even as she thought it, she knew he wouldn't. She felt it, whatever was budding between them; he was in for the long haul. Besides, she'd found her treasure in his arms last night, she didn't want more. Ignoring the jewel box and key, she reached for the bundle of letters. She looked up at him to see him smiling with approval and thought about his alias. "Don't think this gets you off the hook. I've got some pointed questions to ask you."

He leaned back against the bookcase. "Fire away."

The letters were burning a hole in her hand. She itched to read them. The legend of the Love Chronicles had always been just that in her mind. One of the fairy tales Frank had spun for her during her formative years. Who knew they existed? And she'd be the first to read them, thanks to Mitch's snooping.

She looked at his wavering confident expression. Was she really prepared to question his honesty? Did she really want answers that might break her heart? Yes, damn it; she had to know the truth. "You're a fake, Lamb."

"You're right." He pulled out a business card and handed it to her. "Mitchell Wolf, Private Investigator at your service."

She glanced from the engraved card to him, shocked. "But how, why? Then this accounting pose is all a sham."

"No, ma'am, I'm quite a capable accountant. My sister owns Lamb Accounting. I sometimes work for her when I'm between clients."

"Your sister, huh?" Was he telling the truth, or was it another con? "Then why the fake name? And what's your connection with Harold Baker?"

"The alias is my sister's idea, and I have to agree. She didn't want her clients bothered by the fact they were rubbing shoulders with a PI. And frankly, it wouldn't be good for my image to be known as an accountant. And I personally don't have a connection with Baker. My sister's done the occasional freelance work for him."

"I suppose that makes sense," she replied, watching his tight shoulders relax as his tension ratcheted down visibly. He was worried about her good image of him; it was a balm to her heart and soul after Charles's intimations. She didn't care if he was a treasure hunter. "So, the tough PI is in reality a meek and mild accountant," she teased.

"Who told you I was a fake?" he asked, watching her face.

Hearing him parrot back her words made her blush. He couldn't have heard her conversations with Charles and Gram but somehow, he knew. "Um, a friend."

He raised a brow. "Your friend seems to have connections."

"He's an attorney, an old family acquaintance." She frowned at him, caught off-guard by his inside information. But she supposed it was a private investigator's job to dig out secrets. The profession fit his skills. "I asked him to check you out, if you must know." He smiled and she was surprised he took the news so well.

"That's okay. I'd do the same in your position. So, is he fixing to come in here with a writ and toss me out?"

She watched the light of battle in his eyes and the suddenly stiff set of his body. He'd give Charles a fight if he tried it. "No. He wanted to, but I stopped him."

"Sounds like it's personal to him."

She fidgeted as he focused on her lips like he wanted to kiss her senseless. It was so like Gram's contention that Charles had romance on his mind. She knew better, he'd dumped her a year ago, or did he? Charles' renewed interest had her wondering. "It used to be. It fizzled out a year ago."

He reached out to caress her face, saying, "So I shouldn't be jealous?"

Gina leaned into his touch like a flower to the morning sun. The thought that a hunk like him would be jealous over her was astounding. "No." She looked down at the objects in her hand, trying to change the subject. "So, what kind of goodies did you find?"

"You tell me," he replied.

She looked at the thick bundle of letters. "I'm hoping these are the Love Chronicles."

"What about the key and the box?"

She heard the coiled expectation in his voice and stifled a smile. It was a natural reaction, he was a treasure hunter, after all. "Who cares?" She thrust them at him. "If you want to go on a treasure hunt, be my guest."

Mitch breathed a sigh of relief as Gina freely relinquished the key. Life had played a funny trick on him, having him find it in her presence. She'd seen him for a microsecond, but her disbelief and his magic powers would mask the memory from her mind. He was just as surprised to find the Love Chronicles. He could see that she was burning to read them. Part one was over, he'd found the key in the library just as the scroll had said, but part two was uncharted territory. It would take time to search, time he didn't have.

In the meantime, he had to meet Michael. Mitch made his way out to the west gate to meet Michael, already speculating on what the kid had found, not that it really mattered anymore. He'd already found the key to survival. Now he had to find the lock it fit to.

He edged around the guard shack that had been set back in the trees. Bart's idea of keeping a low profile, he supposed. He wouldn't have done it that way. It made them less than useful. He saw Garrett Lamont, five foot twelve with a comb over, walk out of the guard shack and toward his car. Mitch eased back into the shadows and watched the man drive away in his caddy. This job was a feather in Lamont's cap, but he was doing a piss poor job. Mitch felt his protective instincts click into overdrive. Before he left, he'd make sure Gina was safe—it was the best good-bye gift he could give her.

He made his way over to a break in the fence. A gangly, half-grown timber wolf stood by a pine tree across the lane. More wolf than human, Michael reverted to a pure lupine form. Mitch stalked his way, noting the glint of an earring in his left ear. The kid didn't know how to keep a low profile worth a damn. He stalked over to him. "Some hunter's going to shoot, you idiot. I can see your picture in the Enquirer with a caption, 'Bigfoot captured'."

Michael morphed back into his human shape, a gangling eighteen-year-old with a punk haircut and earring. "I ain't no Yeti, bro, and those bozos never saw me."

"What'd you find?"

Michael smiled. "The Reno Holding Company has deep pockets, and lots of secrets. But ta-da." He conjured an envelope out of midair and handed it over. "Supposedly, it's run by a guy named Roy Clinton, but it has Harold Baker on its board of directors. We checked out Clinton, he's pulling down minimum wage as a janitor and he's been out sick for a week."

"So, Baker is the power behind the throne."

"Exactly. But it gets better, Laura checked into the Sinclair Foundation's books. They've been cooked. Baker's been bleeding the foundation dry."

It was what he'd expected to hear but it didn't sit well. What would happen to Gina and her grandmother? "Then they're broke?"

"Nah, I wouldn't say broke, just a bit overextended. Ain't it great?"

He frowned at Mike. "No."

"Sorry. I didn't mean to ruffle your fur, big brother. She gave you the scroll. I guess that makes her one of the good guys."

Mitch frowned at the half-teasing statement.

"Did you find the key?"

Mitch opened his palm to show the antique key and Mike whistled.

"Wow, so it really does exist."

It was so like Gina's words when she'd found the love letters, it was like a punch to the gut. "Now I've just got to figure out what it fits."

"If anyone can do it, you can, bro."

Mitch appreciated the vote of confidence even if he thought he didn't deserve it. So far, he'd done nothing but screw up. "What about the beach shack?"

"Type O positive blood. Baker's A negative so we know it wasn't him. I'm still trying to find out the janitor's blood type."

"I already figured it wasn't Baker, I didn't recognize the guy. Keep looking, I don't have much time left, and I want to make sure Gina is safe."

Gina carried her treasure back to the Rosebud, curled up on her bed, and opened the first letter. Something was strange—there were holes in it, almost like claw marks. Moths? With a shrug, she opened the hand–calligraphic sheet.

My Love,

It is so long since we have last lain together. A week seems like a century. Do you miss me? Does your heart ache for me? Does your body burn for my touch, my taste? I ache to lick you all over, to taste your essence, the heart of you.

When we meet again, I will take you to our bedchamber, and not let you out for a week. I will kiss you all over, worshiping your beauty with my mouth and make you do the same for me, make you do all the things that you profess make you blush and giggle at the same time. I burn to have you take my manhood in your sweet mouth. To feel your teasing touch drawing the passion out of me and giving it back tenfold.

Your lover, D

Gina lay back with a sigh and closed her eyes, drifting off to sleep. She woke when hot lips pressed down hers. Mitch! As his clever hands opened her blouse, it almost seemed like the love letter come to life, but better, because it was Mitch. She moaned as his mouth found her nipple drawing on it, teasing it to aching need.

"Did you enjoy your letter, my love?"

"Umm," she said as he moved to suckle the other breast. "It was all about this and more."

"You don't say."

He was already undressing her, moving down between her legs to lick her there. "Oh yes," she sighed quivering as his hot breath blew against her swollen clit. It was stiff, standing out like a sentinel, her pussy rippling with need. He teased her labia with his tongue, then drew them into his hot mouth, making her scream with pleasure as her hips arched off the bed. He growled and pushed his tongue into her quivering vagina repeatedly until she was a mindless thing, only feeling, needing completion.

Her fingers tangled in the luxuriously thick hair on the back of his head as she trembled on the brink. When he pulled out of her pussy, she let out a wail of protest, but he ignored it, moving to take her swollen clit into his hot mouth. Gina shook at the sheer erotic beauty of it. He suckled the turgid nub, flicking it with his tongue, nipping it lightly and then sucking again. Wild, Gina arched her hips off the bed as she came. He was still kissing her gently as she came back to earth. He kissed his way up her body licking her navel, which made her giggle. When he lay down beside her, she curled into him, spent. His erection rubbed against her thigh, igniting the spark in her imagination. She wanted to taste him. She pushed him onto his back and reached for his cock, bending toward it.

"Don't, babe, you don't have to..."

"I want to." She'd never given oral sex before, but she meant every word. She burned to pleasure him that way. Flicking out her tongue, she swirled it over his erect penis. He tasted wonderful, salt over his sweet passionate flesh. She licked at its red head and down his stiff shaft making him groan. Emboldened, she took him into her mouth with a sigh, loving his growl as she sucked on the head, slipping down to take him as deep as she could, moving with a rhythm that was instinctual. She cupped his balls in her hand, hearing him groan as she sucked harder. His whole body seemed to tighten, his thighs and abs rock-hard.

"Stop, I'm going to..."

She kept at it, wanting to experience it all, loving him with her mouth. As he jerked inside her mouth, he seemed to grow bigger. And then he came. When she finished, she moved up to kiss him, then lay in his arms.

"That was mind-blowing, babe."

"For me, too, Wolf. I've never..." She went quiet as he stroked her tenderly.

"Thank you."

Chapter 9

Mitch went on the hunt while Gina was busy painting, trying to replace the commissioned work that had been slashed. He had to find out what the key fit and he was running out of time. He made his way to the little-used east wing. Even so, it was gleaming. He started downstairs, prowling though the wine cellar. No doors for his key to fit to. He went upstairs to walk through the rooms, a music room and solarium, nothing.

Climbing to the second floor, he walked through bedrooms and baths, but the locks all looked modern. The key couldn't possibly fit them. A spiral staircase to the turret beckoned. He climbed the stairs and found himself facing a heavy paneled door. He reached out to try it, finding it locked.

Taking a chance, he tried the key in his hand. It slid home with a click. He held his breath and turned the key, pushing the door open. He walked into what was a bedroom. No apothecary with a potion for him to take, no magic amulet, just a bedroom. But what a bedroom—huge and opulent with items that dazzled the imagination. A big four-post bed stood in the middle of the room. He walked over to find it freshly made, and cushiony, with a red velvet throw. What surprised him most was what looked like manacles at the posts. He turned to see a spanking bar and several old and dusty spanking implements. Someone had been into S&M; probably the same guy with the first editions.

He couldn't help smiling as he walked over to it. How shocked would Gina be if he bent her over and paddled her lush bottom? He'd been reading the Love Chronicles at night while she slept, wanting advance knowledge of what she'd be reading, wanting to please her. The third installment contained references to B&D. It would give her a little taste of wildness without being wild. The search had been a bust, but somehow, it didn't seem quite so important now. This might not be a bad way to spend his last few nights as a man.

Gina worked on her painting, adding the final details to the landscape while Mitch lounged on her futon in the corner. Thanks to photographs she'd taken that day, she was able to recapture the scene. Ripples on the water under a cloudy sky, and three men sunbathing on the beach, it had been such an incongruous sight that it had captured her imagination.

She usually was uncomfortable working in front of others but not with Mitch. Somehow, he brought out the best in her. She glanced over at him, typing on his laptop. He seemed to want to spend every minute with her, but in a way, he was withdrawn. Something was bothering him, maybe the end of the job. It was bound to affect their love affair. "Mitch."

He looked up at her, setting his laptop on the coffee table. "Yes, babe."

She put down her brush and walked up to him. "What's bugging you?"

He pulled her onto his lap. "Tell me again about this Charles guy who's taking you to the dance."

She looked at him, startled, she'd already told him about Charles but hadn't shared the news that they had a standing date for the ball. How did the man learn all her secrets while she knew none of his? "What do you want to know? It's not a real date, only a social obligation." At his gimlet stare, she relented. "Okay, he may still have feelings for me, but it's not mutual."

"You sure about that?"

"Positive." Gina's face colored, she wasn't used to juggling two men, not that it was what she was doing. "I was infatuated with him once, but it's all over now. You're jealous, Wolf."

"Guilty," he replied, not backing down. "I don't want to see you stuck with some loser who'll hurt you."

"Thanks for worrying about me, but as long as you're around, who'd dare?" His hug tightened around her, and she winced. "Easy, Wolf."

"Sorry." He loosened his grip.

He cares. She wanted to shout it from the rooftops. Instead, she reached up on her tiptoes to kiss him. His lips softened under her onslaught. "I want you to come to the ball, please say that you will."

"I'll come," he murmured nuzzling her neck. "I'd better let you get on with your work."

"How about if we take a picnic lunch?" she asked, wanting to be near him. "I can whip up a few sandwiches and be ready in half an hour."

"You finish cleaning up in here, and I'll make the lunch. Deal?"

"Deal." She gave him a kiss and stood up, watching him venture off to the kitchen. There was a renewed spring in his step, and she knew her openness about Charles was responsible. Gina picked up the phone and dialed Charles' number. It was time to clear the air.

"Gina."

His quick pick up startled her. "I hope I'm not bothering you."

"No. I'm always available to you. What's wrong? I'm on my way over to the estate to get your grandmother's signature on some documents. I can be there in five minutes to eject that guy."

She stifled a groan at hearing that he was coming. It was a good thing they were going on the picnic—it would keep some space between Mitch and Charles. "Nothing's wrong, and no, I don't want you to come eject him."

"It's like that, is it?" he grumbled.

Gina closed her eyes, how had he picked up on that? "I was calling about the ball, to tell you that I'd prefer to go solo this year. I wanted to let you know early in case you wanted to bring a date." She listened to his sigh and knew Gram had been right, Charles was still carrying a torch; she hadn't meant to hurt him.

"My cell phone's cutting out, so I'll have to cut this conversation short."

Gina hung up to the tune of static. Weird, there was a tower only a mile away.

She couldn't help worrying that this wasn't over by a long shot.

Chapter 10

She cleaned her brushes, put away her paints, and went in search of Mitch. He was standing in the kitchen packing a picnic basket. She walked up and kissed him.

"What's that for?"

"Just you being you. No games, just what you see is what you get." She felt him stiffen for a moment, then relaxed and hugged her back.

"That's me, good old reliable Mitch Wolf. I'm almost finished here. Why don't you get us a blanket and I'll pick up a few special items from Eden and meet you out front."

Gina went back to her bedroom to pick up a blanket, then turned to meet Mitch out front. She stepped out the door in time to see Charles striding up the walk to the Rosebud and stifled a groan. Tall, thin, and perfectly groomed, she suddenly wondered what she'd ever seen in him. From his sandy brown hair to his light blue eyes, he was ordinary. He certainly couldn't hold a candle to Mitch Wolf.

She should have known he wouldn't take no for an answer. His brisk stride told her he meant business. Just then, Mitch walked out of Eden with the picnic basket in arm. She saw him stiffen as he saw Charles and stifled a groan. This was not good. Both men drew to a halt, eyeing each other with disdain. Oh, no. She ran out to try to avert trouble. "Charles, what are you doing here?"

Charles stepped away from Mitch and reached over to kiss her cheek, which brought a growl from Mitch. "I came to try to talk some sense into you."

She scowled, hating his superior tone. She wasn't some little wallflower he could keep dangling on a string anymore. "I already told you I'm going with another date this year." She could see Mitch's startled smile at the disclosure, and it bolstered her confidence.

Charles shook his head. "Forget the inappropriate escort, how would that look to our supporters if you go with him?"

So that was it, his pride was hurt that she'd been the one to reject him this time around. Mitch didn't even bat an eye at the insult and her estimation of him went even higher. He certainly wasn't afraid of the high-powered attorney. Mitch intimidated Charles without saying a word. It was an eye opener. "I'm not going to let what other people think affect me anymore."

"We always act as co-hosts to take the burden off your grandmother." Charles sighed, his expression downcast. "Don't forget, I'm the council for the foundation."

Now he was trying to lay a guilt trip on her, he'd used it to get his way before, but no more. She walked around him to link her arm with Mitch. "I'll save the first dance for you, how's that?"

"It'll have to do." He then asked, "What are you wearing?"

"I'm going as Marie Antoinette." She watched Charles's eyes narrow as he nodded.

"I'll go as King Louis. It will help maintain continuity with past years."

"Perfect casting," Mitch muttered.

"Splendid," Charles stated, kissing her hand. He nodded at Mitch. "Wolf."

"Roark."

Gina walked up to Mitch feeling the waves of anger pouring off him as he watched Charles walk away. He was jealous, she realized. She touched his hand to regain his attention. "You've nothing to fear from him."

"Fear?" he asked.

She saw him savor the word as if new to him. A big guy like him probably didn't have much to be afraid of, but she sensed his fear of losing her.

"Has he been calling you, putting pressure on you? Say the word and I'll make him back off permanently."

"No. He just happened to be on the way over here with papers for Gram to sign when I called him to tell him our date was off. As you can see, he doesn't take rejection very well, but he sure as hell can give it out," she grumbled, thinking of the way he'd dumped her last year.

"What do you mean by that, what did the bastard do?"

"Let's just say he's the kind of guy who takes you out, says he's going to call and never does. Apparently, I wasn't sexy enough for him," she replied, thinking of the silicone–enhanced blond she'd seen him out with a few weeks ago. She looked over at Mitch to see him looking in surprise at her, as if she'd lost her mind.

"You've got to be kidding, babe. You are without a doubt the sexiest woman I've ever seen. You personify romance."

She blushed, warmed by both his words and the hot gaze he pinned her with. He meant every word; she could feel it. "Thanks. You're the only man I want to be with, so let's not waste any more time talking about him."

He kissed her, making her toes curl. When he broke the kiss, she tugged on his hand pulling him toward the south lawn. "Come on." When she started to lead him into the woods, he held back.

"I'm not sure we should go out this far."

She looked over her shoulder seeing his watchful gaze scan the woods. "What are you worried about, wild beasts?"

"How about the security patrol?" he asked with a frown. "They might think we're intruders and shoot us."

"They are awful, I agree. A—they don't seem to make patrols, and B—I don't think they're armed. I'm not worried; you can protect me from them, or anything else we might meet out there." She led the way through the trees to a clearing. Lush grassland, surrounded by trees and wildflowers, this was her secret place as a child. "It's a perfect place for a picnic, don't you agree?"

"Very pretty." He looked around the parklike clearing amid the woods.

Gina kissed him, and then pulled away as her stomach grumbled. "I'm hungry. I'll spread out the blanket while you unpack the goodies. She spread out the blue blanket on the ground. Her eyes lit up at the array of treats he laid out. It was enough to feed an army. She grinned when she watched him pull out a bottle of bubbly and two champagne glasses, his provisions from Eden, no doubt. She reached for a thick turkey sandwich as he popped the cork. They ate in companionable silence.

Then sitting back, enjoying the day, Gina saw a movement in the forest. "Oh look, there's a dog." Gina stated, looking at the shaggy beast, which looked back at her. She saw Mitch stiffen beside her, heard him mutter a swear word, and decided he was worried about her.

"He's harmless. Here, boy," she called out to the big canine. As it came near her, her eyes widened. It was like something out of a fairy tale, a half-grown wolf. With an earring. She did a double take at the silver stud in its ear. It came up to her and licked her hand, and she scratched it between the ears. She could swear it was smiling, laughing at Mitch. "I think he likes you."

"The feeling isn't mutual," Mitch grumbled.

Startled by his negative reaction, she turned to see the wary look in Mitch's eyes as he watched her pet the wolf. "Mitch Wolf, I never took you for a snob, just because he isn't a pedigreed dog."

"He's half wolf, Gina," Mitch cut in.

"I know," she replied, thrilling at the admission. "Isn't it wonderful? I love wolves. He's obviously someone's pet, look at the pierced ear. What kind of moron would do that to one of God's creatures?"

"Good question."

"Are you hungry, boy?" she asked, reaching for the spare sandwich. She handfed the wolf, smiling as he politely ate out of her hand. She looked up to see Mitch watching her, concerned. "See, he's tamed." The wolf stuck his muzzle in her champagne glass to lap up the bubbly. She laughed. "He likes it."

"He shouldn't, he's underage."

"I don't think that applies to wolves." She laughed at the disgruntled look on Mitch's face and stood up. "I'll take him back to my cottage and feed him."

Mitch stood gathering up their things. "You know what they say about strays, feed him once and you'll never get rid of him."

"So, who says I want to get rid of him? I like wolves, remember?"

"Just don't forget that they're wild things, they'll turn on you in an instant. We'll take him to my place."

They walked back to the cottages, the wolf walking between them. "I think I'll call him Spot," Gina stated, looking at the black spots on the wolf's paws.

"Nice name, but I think goofball fits better."

"Be nice," Gina scolded with a smile. She gave Mitch a lingering kiss. "I'm late for a fitting with Gram's dressmaker. In the meantime, you two can get better acquainted."

Mitch quietly shut the door in Eden before turning on Michael. "What is the hell do you think you're doing?"

Michael morphed back into his human shape and went to sit on the sofa. "I came to deliver a message. Nice girl, by the way, I can see why you love her."

"Who says I love her?" He frowned at his kid brother. "I'm a wolf. Love isn't in my vocabulary." Even as he said it, he knew it wasn't true, at least on his part. He loved her. "So, what's the message?"

"We located the janitor. He's in the hospital with severe dog bites. Oh yeah, and I checked those power of attorney papers Reno Holding claims to have, they haven't been filed yet."

Mitch felt everything coalesce as Michael mentioned the power of attorney. The papers Charles Roark was bringing Libby to sign. Could it be? "Crap, she might have just signed them."

Just then, a gunshot coming from the general direction of the mansion caught both of their attention. Gina was going there for a fitting; ice chilled his heart. "Gina," he gasped, running out the door. Michael morphed back to his wolf form and followed him. They tore inside Xanadu and found Gina standing in the foyer, shaking, a pin-sized hole dotting the wall next to her head. Mike and Mitch both growled. Mike bolted back out the door running after the shooter's scent while Mitch pulled Gina into his arms, covering her with his body in case she was still a target. "My God, woman, you could have been killed. Who shot at you?"

"I don't know. I just walked in the door when something came whizzing by my head through the open door."

Mike's fierce snarl, and another gunshot in the distance, made her tremble in his arms. Mitch went cold, torn between two worlds. A moment later, Mike came limping back, whimpering, a clatter of footsteps behind him as a security guard ran after him, gun drawn. Mike whirled around growling at him, before collapsing.

Gina pulled out of his Mitch's arms and turned on the guard before he could. "What in the hell do you think you're doing?"

Mitch snarled, advancing on the man.

The guard turned pale and backed away. "I was only doing my job. Mr. Sinclair told me to watch out for varmints. He was attacking some guy."

"Your stupid ass," Mitch stated with a snarl. "Who the hell was it?"

"He didn't do it," Mike replied telepathically before collapsing.

Mitch froze, if it wasn't this trigger-happy amateur shooting at Gina, it meant there was someone gunning for her.

"I don't know, didn't recognize him," the security guard stated, backing away. He turned and ran out of the room.

"You can run but you can't hide, asshole, you're fired," Gina shouted after him. She turned to look at Mike lying on the floor bleeding and ran over to him, pushing Mitch out of the way, wailing, "My wolf's been shot."

Fast footsteps behind them made Mitch turn with a snarl, flickering between his two selves as he lost control of his rage. When he saw it was Frank followed by Libby, he was able to turn off his instinctual response but not before he saw the awareness in their eyes. They'd had a brief glimpse of the real him. Gina's back was turned, she hadn't seen, would the others give him away?

Libby pushed past Frank. "What happened?"

"Get a vet," Gina replied. "My wolf's been shot."

Mitch saw Gina glancing up at his reflection in the mirror, while Frank went to phone for help. He saw confusion and distress in Gina's expressive eyes. Had she seen his uncontrolled change, the flicker that showed he was losing his powers? Before he could say a word, Libby was gently pushing him aside to hand Gina a wool throw. Gina gently wrapped it around the wolf, earning a lick to the hand and a weak flop of his tail. Mitch's heart sank, as he couldn't face losing his brother.

Frank came bustling back into the room. "There's a vet at the Sweeny stud farm, he'll be here in five minutes."

They were the longest five minutes of Mitch's life as he watched Gina sit on the floor cradling his brother's head in her lap.

A few minutes later, the vet arrived, harried, and rumpled from a night tending to a foaling mare, and Mitch stepped back and let him work. The vet dug a slug out of the wolf's shoulder, and Mike didn't even bare his teeth. "There's something strange about your new pet," Lyle Haskins stated, looking up at Gina, who was standing in Mitch's arms.

"You mean the earring?" she asked.

Mitch stiffened, waiting for the answer that might damn him. He couldn't help tightening his hold on Gina, earning a curious look over her shoulder at him.

"No." Lyle frowned. "He's not a dog."

"I know that."

Mitch felt the tension roll off him. He and his brother weren't being unmasked, yet.

"It's illegal to keep wolves as pets," Lyle pointed out with a frown.

"But I..."

Wanting to ease Gina's distress, Mitch frowned back at the vet. "You can make an exception for Miss Sinclair, can't you? Besides he's with me, not her, and he's not a pet." He suddenly felt invincible as Gina looked up at him in gratitude.

"If he's not a pet, what is he?"

Mitch felt the vet's watchful gaze on him. "Part of an animal sanctuary."

"You got a license for this sanctuary?"

"If pressed."

The vet finished bandaging up Mike's arm. "You've got all the answers, don't you?"

"I try to." Mitch stepped forward, watching the vet give Mike an injection. "How is he?"

"I gave him an antibiotic to prevent infection," he replied, getting to his feet. "He'll be fine. The bullet didn't hit anything vital."

"Thank God."

"Gina, dear," Grandmother stated. "Why don't you show the doctor out?"

Mitch watched Gina usher the vet out, knowing it was time to lay all his cards on the table. He turned to see Libby and Frank looking at him with worried eyes. "You know about me."

"Yes," Libby voiced, and Frank nodded.

"How long?"

Libby patted him on the hand. "I've known all along, that's why I sent for you, Mitchell Wolf."

"I, of course, was the last to know," Frank added with grim humor.

"Hush," Libby scolded.

Mitch tried to wrap his mind around the fact they knew and still welcomed him, hadn't tried to harm him. "How did you know?"

"I'm a Sinclair, my husband told me all about our link before we were married. I know about the fealty, the curse, and your quest. I've known for years you'd come. I just never thought the cursed wolf would be after my grandbaby. But when Gina was threatened, it seemed like fate was pushing us toward the same goal."

He decided to ignore that. "Then your husband was…"

"No, he was completely human, just like Gina and me."

"But why?"

"Took you long enough to get here, boy," Frank grumbled, morphing into a gray bearded timber wolf. Mitch stood there looking at the wolf elder in shock. How could he not have sensed this? His powers were more degraded than he'd realized. "Does Gina know?"

Frank shook his head no. "Mind what I said, break her heart and I'll fire a silver bullet through your ass."

Libby nodded. "You're going to have to tell her."

After the vet left, Gina walked back to see Grandmother, Frank, and Mitch talking in hushed whispers. Something odd was going on here. They were arguing. "All right, you three. Tell me what's going on."

Mitch looked at Libby—a promise was a promise, she wouldn't give his identity away—and he couldn't tell Gina why he was here. And even though he knew he'd have to eventually; he couldn't bring himself to tell her his identity just yet.

Libby stepped forward. "I hired Mr. Wolf to protect you."

Gina's jaw dropped as she looked at her grandmother. Oh, God, that wasn't why he'd stuck like glue to her side, was it? She couldn't bear it if their love affair was just a sham, built upon his need to keep tabs on her. Distressed, she grumbled, "I don't need it."

Mitch frowned. "You were just shot at."

Gina scowled back at him. "By a trigger-happy security guard."

"We don't know that. What about the guy Spot was savaging?" He gazed intently at her. "It's not a chance I'm willing to take."

"You're willing?" she muttered, her eyes narrowing. "Like you make the rules around here?"

"When it comes to keeping you safe, yeah I do."

Questioning his motives, the way she felt forced to, the last thing she wanted was for him to give her orders. It smacked too close to Charles' manipulation.

"Children," Libby cut in. "We're all after the same thing here, Gina's safety. So, settle down, the both of you."

"There's something else that's come to my attention. I'd been planning to tell you privately, Libby, but now's as good time as any." He pulled an envelope out of his back pocket and handed it to Libby. "You're being robbed by Harold Baker."

"What?" She took it.

"Embezzlement, slow but steady, to the tune of millions. He's set up a dummy corporation and is siphoning off funds." Mitch frowned, explaining, "Even though you didn't hire me for that purpose, something he said got me wondering, so I did a little digging. I wanted you to know before you lost..."

"The estate," Gina finished grimly. "Thank you."

"Don't thank me, I'm not that innocent." Her praise made him uncomfortable, she didn't know he had his own agenda. He'd found the key, but to what purpose? He was still a doomed being.

Libby sighed. "I'd better call the police to report Harold Baker's thefts."

Mitch turned to look at her. "Hold off on that a few days. I want to set a trap for him. It'll give me time to reel him in and catch all the members of his pipeline."

"In that case, I'd better consult with my attorney."

"About that, I was just coming to ask you about the papers, he just had you sign. They weren't power of attorney papers, were they?"

Libby shook her head. "Why do you ask?"

"The Reno Holding Company has put feelers out about selling the estate. I know because I was offered a chance to buy it. They claim to have power of attorney to act on your behalf." From the shocked looks on Libby and Gina's faces, he knew it was news to them.

"Good heavens," Gina gasped. "I suspected he was a crook, but I never expected this."

Libby shook her head. "How could he think he could get away with it? Even if I was out of commission, Gina would fight him."

"Exactly," Mitch stated in a grim tone. Glancing from the shocked look on Libby's face, to the wary look on Gina's, he knew they got the unspoken message. Gina's life was on the line.

Libby nodded. "You have carte blanche to act on my behalf to bring these dastardly criminals down. Just please be aware of the value of who's in your charge."

Mitch gazed at Gina, his eyes brightening. "Rest assured that I do. She has a price higher than rubies."

Chapter 11

Mitch caressed Gina's back in bed. Things would be coming to a head soon. The trap was set, a buy would be made, and the cops would get whatever scraps of the bastard that was left after he got through with him. But first, he wanted a day off, bliss with Gina. It would keep him going during the dark days to come. "Want to see what I found in my treasure hunt?"

She rolled over to smile at him. "Don't tell me that key actually fits a lock around this place."

"Sure does." He jumped out of bed, threw on his clothes, then leaned back against the dresser to enjoy the extreme pleasure of watching Gina dress. He loved the way she wiggled into her panties, then put on her sundress, buttoning up the little buttons in front. His gaze flew to her cleavage, and he started getting hard. She slipped into sandals and walked to the dresser to brush her long red hair. He smiled and took the brush from her hand. "Allow me."

"Be my guest," she whispered with a laugh as she turned her back to him so he could brush her hair.

Mitch groaned, stepping close enough to her to feel her heat, indulging in her intoxicating aura. He slowly drew the brush through her tresses, his crotch rubbing against her sweet ass.

"Keep that up, and we'll never make it out of the bedroom."

He backed off, knowing she was right. He had greater treasures for her to see than those in this bedroom. He laid her brush down and took her hand. "Come with me."

Gina wondered about the twinkle in Mitch's eye as he led her by the hand out of Rosebud and across the courtyard to Xanadu. They walked through the foyer, Mitch nodding politely to Frank, and quickly moved on to the east wing. The entire section was older than the rest of the house, having been brought over from Europe. Other than the music room, the space was little used. They walked down several corridors until they got to the steps to the turret. It was always kept locked and impossible to break into; she knew because she'd tried it when she was twelve, breaking off a nail file. Did the key he found open the door? "Where are we going?"

"You'll see." Mitch pulled out the old key and stuck it in the lock. It turned with a click.

Gina held her breath, wondering what was inside. She followed him into the room and realized immediately that it was the Love Nest mentioned in the Love Chronicles. She could tell by the furnishings. The four-post bed, the rack, the spanking bench. Her cheeks flushed as she recalled the steamy letter she'd read.

She looked over at Mitch. He was standing back, watching her with an anticipatory glint in his hot eyes. She felt her pulse skip a beat while her pussy grew wet. Was she ready for this? Hell, yeah. She walked up to him smiling and knelt by his feet. "Be gentle, my Lord."

Mitch grinned down at her. "Just who's in charge around here? Sometimes, I feel like you're leading me around by my dick."

"Then you'll just have to tie me up and spank me for my disobedience." She watched his eyes flare and realized that on some level, it wasn't a game. Even so, she didn't want to get away.

"Undo my pants," he demanded.

Gina obeyed, her cheeks flaming. His rousing cock sprang free, growing before her eyes.

"Pleasure me with your mouth. Show me how contrite you are."

Gina's tongue flicked out, sweeping around his cock's head before she opened her mouth and took him in. Going down on him this way was both embarrassing and exciting. His hands tangled gently in her hair, and he thrust first slowly and then deeper into her mouth.

He groaned. "That's it, sweet baby."

Gina took him deeper, her own sex growing wet and needy. Her whole being seemed focused on his rampant cock. It slipped wetly between her lips, so big, she could hardly hold him. And then he came spurting into her mouth.

When he was done, she looked up at him expectantly. If anything, his gaze was hotter. She saw his penis stiffening again.

"Good girl, now up and strip."

Gina shivered a bit at his commanding tone but hurried to obey. Standing, she slipped out of her sundress and panties. She looked up at him, feeling shy suddenly.

"Undress your man," he stated with a growl.

She did, unbuttoning his shirt and pushing it off his shoulders. Then she knelt to take off his shoes and pants, anything to avoid his gaze. He was watching her as if he were trying to memorize her. It was a bit overwhelming, reminding her that this idyll was temporary. He was naked now, his rousing cock in her face once more. But instead of ordering her to blow him, he held out his hand and she took it, standing. He led her toward the spanking bench and her footsteps faltered.

"I'm going to paddle you now, Gina. Do you know why?"

"It turns you on."

"That it does, but it's for taking risks with your life."

"Risks with my life?" She frowned at him. "I'm an adult. I can take care of myself."

"No. In here, you're my little love slave and you're about to be paddled."

"But what if..." They arrived at the padded wooden bench, and she noticed what looked like a brand-new red paddle. He'd been reading the Chronicles; he knew what she'd read. "You planned this." He gave her a kiss that curled her toes.

Pulling back, he murmured, "I wanted to fulfill all your fantasies. Enjoy your spanking."

She bent over the bar with a sigh of surrender. "Okay, spank me, my big, strong sex god." She shivered with pleasure when he rubbed the leather against her out-thrust bottom. She was so aroused, her body humming with desire. It felt so good when he pressed the paddle against her mound, she moaned with pleasure.

"Six strokes," he told her, pulling back the paddle. "One."

Gina yelped when the paddle swatted down, causing more heat than pain. She braced herself for the next blow.

"Two."

Swat, the paddle caught the bottom of her cheeks, and she went up on tiptoe, crying out in surprise. He pushed her back down on flat feet.

"Three."

She gasped, her whole pussy trembling from the sting.

"Four."

She moaned, her mound rubbing against the bar.

"Five."

Ripples rushed through her pussy, her body on the brink of orgasm.

"Six."

Gina cried out, starting to come. And then he was behind her, rubbing her hot bottom with his big hands, then entering her pussy from behind. She moaned as he started to piston in and out of her, hotter and harder than ever before. Ripples tugged him inside, shards of pleasure shooting through her with each stroke of his cock. Her orgasm built, waves of ecstasy as she screamed out his name. He growled, holding still as he came high and hard inside her rippling pussy.

When they finally made it to the bed, she found it had been made with fresh linens, sweetly scented. She luxuriated in it and the cushy mattress. She snuggled against him. He kissed her and she fell asleep.

Mitch was lying there, loving the feel of Gina in his arms, when a cry of alarm from Mike came to his mind telepathically. Mitch. It's going down early. I need you now, come quick. Instantly alert, he lightly kissed Gina's shoulder using what remained of his power to put her into a trance. He didn't want her anywhere near what might be going down.

He slipped from the bed; the trance he'd induced in her would give him time to do what he needed to do. But was it enough? She was just foolhardy enough to go running into danger if he didn't prevent it. For insurance, he pulled out the restraints from the four posts. The old pulley system still worked remarkably well but he'd made a few modern adjustments. Like soft fleece so it wouldn't mar Gina's wrists. He clapped the irons on first one wrist and then the other, stopping to softly kiss her pulse points. He moved down to fasten the irons to her ankles, holding her spread-eagled and left the room, taking the precaution of locking her in. No one would get to her here.

Mike was waiting at the bottom of the stairs in human form. He had a white bandage sticking out of his T-shirt's sleeve. "Took ya long enough."

"What's going on?" Mitch asked, cutting right to the chase.

"Baker called. He's agreed to proceed with the sale since we offered him an extra finder's fee."

Mitch grinned coldly. "Greed will make you stupid. Where is he?"

"He's at his Reno Holding Company offices on Lakehurst Avenue. We have an appointment in half an hour to sign the papers and bring him the cash."

Mitch morphed himself into a business suit, along with a briefcase stuffed with cash and Mike did the same. Mitch raised a brow at Mike's Nehru jacket but didn't comment. "Let's go." They hopped into Mike's car and soon, were standing outside the office building. Trev was standing there in his trench coat looking nondescript as usual, if one didn't look into his piercing blue eyes. Around the corner came Cairn, in biker's black leather, and Lash, on their Harleys. The wolf pack was enough to scare any crook to death. Mitch nodded at them, glad of the backup, not that he thought he'd really need it. "Let's do it."

He and Mike walked through the doors of Reno Holding precisely on time, Trev trailing in behind them. Cairn and Lash would stand guard outside. The receptionist, a bubbly blond, smiled up at them and Mike returned her toothy grin. "We've an appointment with Mr. Baker."

"Oh yes, you must be from the Wolf Corporation. Come this way." She ushered them into a conference room, Mitch and Mike went to flanking positions on either side of the table. Trev waited by the door. They didn't have long to wait; a few seconds later, Harold Baker came through the door carrying a file. He gave Mitch a long look. "Do I know you?"

"Not likely," Mitch replied.

With a shrug, Baker walked to the head of the table and sat down. "Did you bring the cash?"

"Did you bring the bill of sale?"

"Right here," he replied opening the file.

"Ditto," Mitch stated, opening his briefcase while Mike did the same. He watched Baker's eyes light up, his fevered gaze flicking from one cash stuffed briefcase to the other, both were filled with stacks of hundred-dollar bills.

He licked his lips. "Fine. Let's get on with it." He extracted a document from his file and scrawled his signature on it, then thrust it at Mitch. "If you just sign on the dotted line and initial here and here, Xanadu will be yours."

Mitch's hand tightened on the pen. "Just like that?"

He nodded, gulping as his gaze strayed to the money. "I'll have the old lady and her pain-in-the-ass granddaughter out by Monday."

Mitch picked up the document and turned to Trev. "Got enough?"

Trev's eyes flashed fire as he nodded, saying, "To hang him? Hell yeah."

Their meaning took a while to sink in, but in a moment, Baker shot to his feet sputtering, "What is the meaning of this?"

Mitch turned on him with a growl, his shape flickering back and forth from man to wolf with his uncontrolled rage. "Sit your ass back down before I forget myself, gut you, and leave you bleeding to death, you bastard. It's no less than you deserve for going after Gina."

Trev walked forward to read him his rights. "You have the right to remain silent..."

"You do and I'll kick your ass," Mitch cut in.

"What the hell are you?" Baker shrieked in a high-pitched terror-filled voice.

Mitch leaned in, wanting so bad to put the bastard out of his misery. Knowing Gina wouldn't want him to spill blood if he didn't have to, he managed to rein in his fury. "Your worst nightmare, you embezzling asshole—a pissed-off werewolf accountant."

Baker's eyes widened, "Mitch Lamb."

"Got it in one. You made a fatal error when you tried to kill Gina. I tend to take attacks on my woman personally." Mitch felt Mike and Trev's attention flick to him with the admission that she was his, but he didn't care. For as long as he had left to walk this earth, he wanted to let the pack know she was his woman. They'd offer her their protection after he was gone.

Baker's eyes widened. "Are you crazy? I didn't try to kill anybody."

"Nice try," Mitch snarled. "Keep that up and you won't make it to the police station."

"It's true," he wailed.

"Where were you yesterday around one p.m.?" Trev cut in.

"In divorce court. Go ahead and check, I might be a thief but I'm telling you I didn't try to kill anyone. You've got the wrong man."

"Tell us about Roy Clinton."

"Do you mean my janitor? He's on vacation," he looked away, adding, "I don't know where."

"Right," Mitch replied sarcastically, not believing a word of it. "We followed his blood trail that led to your hunting cabin. He's in the hospital with severe wolf bites. Care to join him?" Mitch finished with a snarl.

Baker turned pale. "Okay. So, he went a bit too far. He was just supposed to play a few tricks, scare her off. I have nothing to do with attempted murder. I'm telling you the truth. My ex-wife is bleeding me dry in the divorce settlement. I was going to make one last big killing and get out."

Trev slapped handcuffs on Baker's wrists, making him squeak with alarm. "Then the power of attorney..."

He cast a fulminating look at them all. "I tried. The old biddy wouldn't sign it."

"And your partners?" Trev prompted.

"Partners?" Baker asked evasively.

Mitch felt a vast sense of relief as Baker was led away in handcuffs babbling incoherently about werewolves and accountants. He still believed that Baker was behind the attempts on Gina's life—he might not have pulled the trigger, but he paid for it." He turned to Mike saying, "I've got to get back to Gina."

"Go, we'll mop up things here."

Gina woke, noting long shadows on the wall. She peered up at the high window to see that it was getting dark outside. She tried to move and couldn't, something held her fast. She looked at first one wrist and then the other to see them locked in what looked like old metal handcuffs lined with soft fleece. She tried to move her legs to find they were in restraints, too. How dare he? Role-playing was one thing, but he was taking his pose as a dominant master too far. She arched, irritated, frightened, and heard a sound. She watched the door open.

Mitch walked into the room carrying a covered tray. "Good, you're awake."

"What is the meaning of this?"

He set down the tray and opened the cover. "Refreshments for my little sex slave."

Gina's stomach grumbled as she smelled the savory aroma. She had missed lunch. He sat her up propping pillows behind her head, but he didn't let her loose. "Aren't you going to release me?"

"I haven't decided yet."

Gina suddenly knew what it meant to be under someone's control, but something inside her let go. She knew she could trust him. And it was kind of kinky to be tied up like this. He hand fed her tidbits and she devoured them, looking deep into his eyes. When he introduced a blindfold, she giggled, going still when darkness fell. Now it was all about sensation—taste, smell, touch. Only she couldn't reach out to touch it, she had to wait for his pleasure.

Something soft brushed her lips and she opened them. He popped a sweet strawberry in her mouth, and she ate it, smiling. Then he popped a piece of chocolate into her mouth. It melted on her tongue, and she sighed, savoring it. She felt the bed sag as he climbed onto it next to her, and in a moment, something hard touched her lips, salty, with his scent, she knew without looking that it was his rampant cock.

With a welcoming sigh, she flicked her tongue out to taste him, hearing his male sigh of pleasure. She opened her mouth and took him in, suckling him as he made love to her mouth. She was on fire. Her body ached for his possession. She sucked all the harder, making him groan.

He pulled out of her mouth and fit himself between her spread legs. He thrust home. Gina moaned, wanting to hold him, wrap her legs around him, but she couldn't when restrained. He rose on his arms, deepening his angle of penetration, and thrust deep, making love to her. Gina cried out as he plunged deeper, her vaginal walls tightening around his thrusting member. Ripples tugged at him, sending waves of pleasure through her body. "Yes," she moaned as a wild orgasm built, her pussy clinging to his cock, contracting. "Mitch, oh God, Mitch," she cried out, coming.

"Sweet Gina," he groaned, thrusting deep once more, and pouring his sensual tribute into her as he came.

Chapter 12

Gina dressed for the costume ball, glad that Mitch was going to attend. They'd taken pains to keep their affair private, but she had a sneaking suspicion that others might have guessed. That was why she was still going to let Charles be her dance partner. Mitch was not pleased but he'd grudgingly acquiesced. She glanced at her image in the mirror.

She'd rejected the intricate ball gown in favor of a costume. Little Red Riding Hood all grown up. The form fitting green dress matched her eyes; it was cut low displaying her cleavage, nipped in at the waist and full over her hips to swirl around her calves in a handkerchief hem. It left no doubt of her sexuality, this week with Mitch had made her blossom. She put on a red cloak with a hood and picked up a wicker basket she'd filled with flowers and a few goodies. Would Mitch get the play on his name? She only hoped it wouldn't offend him.

Biting her lip, she left the room. The party had already started, and she was late, as usual. She walked out of Rosebud and over to Eden to collect her beau. Before she could knock on his door, it opened. He leaned against the jam looking her up and down. She thought he looked drop dead gorgeous in his tux and suddenly felt underdressed. "Little Red Riding Hood, get it?"

"Oh, I get it."

Hearing the tension in his voice, she worried she'd gone too far. "Sorry, I didn't mean to offend you."

"It's okay, you're Red and I'm the big bad wolf, and I get it." He smiled. "Never let it be said I don't have a sense of humor."

She let out a sigh of relief, her tension abating. It was going to be all right. He shut the cottage door and took her arm. "Shall we?"

"I've got something to tell you first."

"What?"

"Harold Baker has been arrested. He was caught red-handed trying to sell Xanadu. I wanted you to be the first to know."

She smiled, hugging him. It was the first bit of good news she'd had in a while. "What a relief." She frowned at his tense expression. "Who told you, and why don't you look happy?"

"I've got a friend in the department, remember?"

"Oh yeah, the guy in the trench coat." She thought back to the officer who'd come out to take her statement after her painting had been slashed. With a gasp, she turned to Mitch. "Did he admit shooting at me?"

"He claims he didn't have anything to do with the shooting. When you were shot at, he was in divorce court."

"Carla's divorcing him!" Her eyes widened at the shocking news. "He never said a word about it. That might explain his sudden need of money."

"Yeah. He did admit to having an employee slash your painting and play other tricks on you. He was trying to make you run. In short, that's why I'm not happy. While he might not have pulled the trigger, he could have paid someone to do it. Until I know for sure who's after you, I'm going to stick like glue to your side."

"Sounds good to me, Wolf." She took his hand, leading him out the door. "Come on, I want to dance with you." They walked hand in hand past the pool toward the manor house. Sounds of the orchestra warming up drifted in the summer air and the moon was high. Gina squeezed Mitch's hand, feeling relaxed and ready to face the future. She wanted to dance under the full moon. Instead, she let him hurry her toward the house. She wanted to assist Grandmother with any last-minute crises.

Mitch watched Gina in Charles's arms as they danced and felt his blood boil. The guy couldn't seem to tear his gaze off Gina's breasts. Just barely able to control himself tonight, he didn't need that kind of prod to make him change. Changing too soon would ruin everything.

She sure as hell wouldn't want him if she knew the truth. The costume had been like a punch to the gut when he'd seen her. He'd almost lost it but then she'd smiled up at him nervously and his heart had melted. She was the key to his other half, even if she didn't understand that.

A noise caught his attention. He looked to the French doors to see Michael standing there in wolf form. Silver eyes gleaming in the moonlight, Michael was staring at him through the window. Mitch hurried out into the garden and walked behind a potted palm. "What are you doing here like this?"

Mike changed into human form, wearing jeans and a navy T-shirt. "Don't sweat it. The stiffs dancing in the other room didn't even notice me, you know I can blend into the background. A natural tracker."

Mitch shook his head. "You don't have to quote me your résumé."

"That her in the Red Riding Hood getup?"

"Yes."

He tipped back his head and howled with laughter. "How ironic."

"Keep it down, will you, before one of Bart's security details takes a pot shot at you again."

"Never gonna happen, bro. Besides, the two I saw were kicked back in their guard shack having a beer."

"Nice." Mitch said sarcastically, having his low estimation of Lamont's Security confirmed. "So, what's up?"

"Besides, like I said, the shot that hit me came from some other guy. Tall, sandy hair, fast on his feet."

Mitch looked at Gina dancing in Charles' arms and got a sinking feeling. The description covered about half the male population, including the guy who was whirling her around the floor. "My God, how could I have been so blind?"

"What?" Mike hissed.

"Take a good look at the jerk she's dancing with."

Mike turned and looked. "Well, damn if it ain't him." He started forward but Mitch grabbed his brother's arm stopping him. "Not here, too public. Let me get him alone and I'll..."

A howl caused them both to fall silent.

"It's Cairn," Mike hissed. "Something's wrong."

"I know, I can feel it too." Just then, their attention was caught by a sound from the cottages. Michael held a hand to his ear, then turned to Mitch.

"Crap. Someone's breaking into your lady's cabin."

They both turned and went on a run. Mitch could feel his body break free as he morphed. A stinging pain followed by power and freedom.

His senses acute, he could smell the intruder, feel his rage. He'd fallen into his trap. There was something personal involved, he sensed.

They ran past the guard shack. He could hear a boom box playing, men's laughter, and wanted to savage them, for their careless disregard for their job. What if Gina had been here alone, vulnerable? It chilled him and made him coldly angry.

Rushing forward, he smelled smoke before he saw it, billowing from Gina's cottage. He and Mike separated, going for the separate entrances. Gina's front door was ajar, and Mitch burst through it, with a growl.

Bart was setting fire to a canvas; the copy Gina had made of the one that had been slashed before.

Mitch snarled and hit him like a linebacker, rolling him to the ground, going for his throat. Bart shrieked, trying to get away. Michael got him by the leg.

Gina ended the dance with Charles just as she heard a wolf howl. Spot! Was he in trouble? "If you'll excuse me."

Charles took her arm. "What's your hurry, honey?"

She frowned at the endearment and the firm grip on her arm. He wasn't taking her rejection well at all but the need to check on Spot superseded her need to get free of him. "I need to check on my wolf."

"I'll go with you."

With a frown, Gina headed across the terrace toward Rosebud. Charles still clung to her side, but she barely paid him any mind. Spot had been better, healing since being shot. Had he somehow gotten worse? And then she realized Charles hadn't been a bit surprised that she had a wolf, how did he know about it? A whiff of smoke caught her attention. Approaching Rosebud on a run, low growls accompanied by a man's scream made her shiver. Was the same culprit attacking Spot?

"Oh no," she cried, dashing through her front door. Bart lay on the floor pinned by a large wolf, while Spot took hold of Bart's sleeve, trying to pull a torch out of his hand. Her studio was on fire, the canvas she'd just finished burning, and a torch was still in Bart's hand, as he flailed trying to get away. It took her an instant to realize Bart had set it ablaze, but why? She ran to put it out before the whole place burned down.

"Let it burn." Charles pulled a sword from the scabbard on his costume.

She gaped at him for a second in complete shock. "Why?"

"Let's just say I don't want that picture to get out. It might send someone to the slammer."

She suddenly realized the sunbathers had a strong resemblance to the trio, Baker, Bart, and Roark. They didn't even like each other, why were they meeting? To cheat Gram was the answer. "Too late. If you're talking about Harold Baker, he's already there."

"You're lying," he hissed.

She watched the larger wolf turn as Spot held down a weeping Bart. His eyes were brown, hypnotic just like Mitch's. Instinctively knowing the wolf was on her side, she knew she had to keep Charles distracted. "You, Bart, and Baker were trying to get Gram to sign a power of attorney paper. When that didn't work, Baker decided to just take the money and run. No doubt by now, he's turning state's evidence against the lot of you. She looked over at Bart. "Aren't you going to save your partner?"

"And take my eyes off you, no. Besides, the stupid ass is expendable. Let the wolves have him. It'll keep them occupied and be my alibi. One slice to your jugular should do the trick. They'll put it down to the mauling and finish what I started with the smaller one."

"So, you're the one who shot Spot," she spat out, seeing the wolf silently coil up ready to strike.

"Spot," he stated with a chuckle. "That's cute. What is it with wolves anyway?"

"I'm coming to find out they're a lot more honorable than some humans," she replied as he tilted his head, and she inched to that side to give the wolf more room. He nodded his head, startling her. "My question to you, Charles, is why'd you have to pull the lovelorn act on me?"

He sneered. "Damned near worked, didn't it?"

"No."

"Mitch Wolf is an incompetent fool. Where is he when you need him?" he asked, with a dry chuckle.

The wolf leapt, hitting Charles, and knocking him to the ground. The sword flew out of Charles's hand and Gina ran to pick it up. He grabbed for her foot, and she struck—slicing his arm with the sword as the wolf pinned him to the ground and sunk its teeth into his throat. Charles let out a strangled wail and stopped struggling.

Thundering footsteps outside alerted her to the security crew's arrival, late as usual, and she watched in a daze as the wolf let go of Charles's neck letting him breathe again. Suddenly, he turned into Mitch, still holding down his prisoner. He turned to look at Gina.

Gina saw the pained look in his eyes, the same eyes as the wolf's. She couldn't quite take it in, it was like one of Frank's fairy tales about werewolves come to life. There weren't any such things as men who turned into wolves a rational part of her mind said, but she'd just seen it.

"Gina, babe, I can explain..."

The security crew burst through the door.

Gina watched in shock as they took Charles and Bart away. Mitch was standing there watching her and she couldn't look at him, instead, she petted Spot, who'd come to lie by her feet, his watchful gaze following the men out the door.

Mitch stepped toward her. "Gina, look at me."

She looked up at him, seeing real fear in his eyes.

"It's true what you just saw." He took a deep breath, looked deep in her eyes, and stated, "I'm a werewolf."

"It can't be true, I'm hallucinating."

"No. It's real, as real as this." He touched her face, then bent down to kiss her, sweet and light. He turned to go, saying, "Even after I leave, my pack will give you, their protection."

Gina sat there watching him go, her heart in her throat. She didn't want him to leave, but he was already gone. It couldn't be true, but it was. Deep down, she'd known that Mitch had a secret, but this? Spot stood up and ran after him. Quick footsteps gave her hope until she saw that it was Frank.

"Are you okay, Gina girl?" Frank asked.

She shook her head, tears pooling in her eyes. "No."

"I said that wolf if he hurt you, I'd kill him."

"He didn't hurt me, I hurt him," she voiced, demoralized, then picked up on Frank's words. She looked at him. "You know he's a..."

"Werewolf," Frank cut in. "Yeah, I do. So does your gram. Our clans have been linked for centuries."

Startled, she watched Frank transform into a wolf. The funny thing was it wasn't all that shocking. She had vague memories of childhood glimpses of his wolf persona as he'd read her fairy stories acting out the parts. It was a delight for a four-year-old. A little part of her had always known but refused to believe. "Please tell me everything. I need to understand, so I can understand him."

"I owed a debt to your grandfather. I've been here to protect you all these years. Now it's Mitch's turn," he stated, adding softly, "if he survives."

"Then this is only a job to him." She wanted to cry at the thought.

"Wake up and smell the coffee, girl. He's crazy about you and what's more, he needs you. He's going to fade away if you don't save him."

It couldn't be true, she didn't want it to be, but she knew Frank would never lie to her. "The curse?"

Frank nodded. "He doesn't have much time left."

Why had she let him go? Agony swept through her as she thought of a future without him. She had to go get him, but where had he gone? The Love Nest? "I think I know where he is."

She tracked him toward the house. Suddenly, Spot was blocking her way. Instinctively, she knew he was one of them. "Out of my way, whoever you are."

Spot bared his fangs, then morphed into a human. "Why should I, Gina?"

"Because only I can heal him. I know that now." She looked at the gangly teen and saw his grudging admiration.

Gina headed into the house praying that he'd head for the Love Nest to die. She walked up the turret stairs and saw him lying on the bed; he'd turned back into a wolf. Magnificent but shaking. He seemed to be unconscious, refusing to rouse. She got in bed with him and curled up next to him, petting him. "I need you more than life itself, Mitch, please don't die on me." There was no response.

She sobbed, curling up against him. Her tears trickled onto his fur, and he breathed, letting out a sigh. She could hardly believe it, but it gave her hope that she had the power to revive him. Stroking his fur cuddling up with him, she opened her heart to him. "I love you, Mitch."

She felt him change in her arms, turning back to his human form. Soon, she was caressing warm skin. He moaned, and she kissed his shoulder. "I love you, Mitch."

He moaned, rolling over to face her. His eyes popped open.

Gina felt his warm gaze all the way down to her toes. He was her wolf, and she loved him. "I love you, Mitch."

"I love you, too, sweetheart." He kissed her.

Gina reveled in the hungry, toe–curling kiss. When she drew back, she looked down at his bare feet to see the red marks gone. "I think we found a way to break the curse."

"Not we, you, and I thank you for it. I owe you, my life."

It reminded her of what Frank had said about Mitch taking over and she couldn't help but frown. "No. I don't want a wolf that stays with me out of gratitude."

"Gratitude doesn't even come close to describing my feelings toward you." He bent to nibble her neck. "Try love, passion, commitment."

"Good," Gina replied with a purr as the pack surrounding the estate set up a howl of approval.

JULIE CASTLE

Cindy Revisited

FAIRY TALES REIMAGINED: Cinderella

Tangled Tales Book Two

Prologue

Up above, Imogene sniffed back a tear, her silver wings fluttering. "Oh, my stars, it's worse than we thought, girls."

The members of the fairy's circle looked down through the heavens at their fairy goddaughter, Cindy Taylor, and sighed. After watching Cinderella, she'd been their charge since she called to them when she was six.

Agatha handed her a lace handkerchief. "Now, dear, don't get weepy on us. She hasn't had the right opportunities for romance. Blot your eyes before you cause a flood."

Hilda scowled. "Aggie, are you knocking my love spell?"

"The pigmy goats drank the enchanted water, not that handsome vet," Agatha pointed out. "Now her dude ranch is overrun with the little buggers. As our sex expert, you've been spectacularly unsuccessful."

"As a head fairy, you should have given me better intel." Hilda turned to Imogene for support. "Am I right, Imme?"

"Now, ladies, I'd say there's plenty of blame to go around." Agatha sighed. "Let's focus on helping our fairy goddaughter. Have faith, ladies. I have a plan. I'm bringing in an outside consultant."

Chapter 1

"It was a total flop, Dora. At this rate, I'm never going to get laid," Cindy Taylor grumbled, mucking out stalls.

Dora backed away from the flying manure, her nose wrinkling with distaste. "Do you mean he didn't even give you a good night kiss?"

"Nope, I'm still un-kissed and un-everything else," she replied, hitching up the strap on her bib overhauls. She tucked a tumbledown strand of red hair up under her cowboy hat. Her best friend shook her head. Dora was the picture of loveliness with sleek black hair cut in a bob and fashionably dressed in designer jeans that enhanced her petite curves. They were worlds apart, but a friendship beginning in kindergarten could withstand her lack of style. For the past six months, since she'd returned to save the ranch, Dora had been trying to help her get laid. So far, nothing had worked. Bless Dora for sticking with it.

Still, she didn't have time to mope. Since her father's sentencing for tax evasion, she was all that kept the ranch from bankruptcy. At least he'd had the good sense to put her in charge in his absence. Her stepmother, Cordial, and airhead eighteen-year-old stepsisters, Tiffany and Brandy, didn't know a thing about ranch management and didn't want to learn. So, Cindy had bitten the bullet, closed her art studio in Taos, and come home to help, not that the other's appreciated it. She hadn't done it for them. She'd made the sacrifice for her dad, and because she loved the ranch that'd been in her family for generations. All the other women cared about was that the money kept rolling in, and there was precious little of that.

"So where are the three witches?" Dora asked, gazing up at the big ranch house on the hill.

"Cordial hasn't made an appearance yet today. I think she's sleeping in."

"More like sleeping it off," Dora muttered.

Cindy chose not to comment. Her stepmother had been acting differently lately, more standoffish, and spiteful than usual. And her teenage stepsisters had turned into self-indulgent brats while she'd been away. "Brandy and Tiffany are probably primping for the dance tonight."

"And you're up to your ankles in horse shit."

"And your point is?" Cindy asked wryly.

"There's something wrong with this picture. At least say you're going to the dance tonight."

Cindy shook her head. The Policeman's Ball was the high point of Cider City's society year. Held at the newly constructed Hyatt Regency, it would no doubt hold the cream of the local stud crop. While she ached to find the right guy to make her a woman, she couldn't bear the thought of another dud on such an evening, especially not one on such a grand scale. "I can't. I don't have a thing to wear."

"No problem. I have a stylist..."

"I don't want to hear it," Cindy interrupted yet another pitch for the makeover she desperately needed but couldn't afford.

"Word has it the elusive JT Randal might make an appearance," Dora stated with a conspiratorial grin. "How can you stand to miss it?"

A little thrill went through her at the bad boy's name—grown man now, she amended. It'd been twenty years since he'd roared out of town on the back of his Harley, which would make him in his late thirties. An experienced man of the world, a risk taker, now he had what it took to introduce her to sex in a big way. Her mouth curved in a secret grin. He was probably big all over. She saw Dora watching her with a smirk, no doubt guessing the way her dirty thoughts had wandered.

They'd both had unrequited teenage crushes on the hunk. She'd kept track of him through the news like everyone else, a successful businessman, while others on Wall Street had dubbed him the Barbarian. The name fit. He'd always had a primitive streak. Now that his father was ailing, the prodigal was expected to return, but she'd never put much stock in rumors. Besides, having the two of them double team her would be disastrous. It'd been hard enough repelling Silas Randal's attempts to steal the ranch out from under her. "As far as I'm concerned, he can stay away."

"Now Cyn, don't be so pessimistic. Old man Randal didn't say for sure your ranch was on the chopping block, did he?"

"He didn't have to. His slimy personal assistant, Dwain Hawkins, didn't pull any punches. You know what he tried to pull."

"The man tried to romance you; you kicked his ass and set the goats on him. You've got to stop doing that if you want to attract a man."

"So, I didn't fall for his sudden fatal attraction for me. I'm too smart to buy the bill of goods he was selling. Besides, when he touched my boob, he asked for it. The scrawny jerk thought he was god's gift to women. I did all the other females in the valley a favor and set him straight." She knew exactly what kind of lover she craved, and he wasn't anything like the smarmy Dwain Hawkins. Tall, dark, dominant, but with a playful streak; now that was for her. The fact that it fit JT Randal's bio to a 'T' was only coincidental.

"I can't give you an argument there. I hear Hawkins had been making a pest of himself at half the ranches in the valley, trying to gobble them up."

"See what I mean. The Double T Ranch would give Randal Industries direct access to the railroad for shipments, and everybody knows the old curmudgeon Silas Randal is itching to expand his business. Hawkins is his henchman, he's willing to kiss you, or cheat you, at his boss's say-so."

"Are you still getting the seemingly anonymous, obscene letters?"

"Feast your eyes on the latest," Cyn replied, pulling the typewritten note from her back pocket."

"*...someday soon, you will know what it is to feel my touch. I have the patience and intelligence to tame a wild bitch, like you and bring you to heel. You'll moan with ecstasy as I shove my giant cock down your throat, inch by inch. Don't try to run...*"

"He certainly has an inflated picture of himself." Cindy's eyes rolling to the back of her head. "Turn it over and read the secret message."

Dora flipped it over. "Good grief, they've scrawled it in lipstick."

"Yup, it's like the other secret messages."

"*Run you stupid, pigheaded girl, while you still can. This may be the last warning I'm able to give you.*"

"Hmm, it seems you have a friend trying to warn you off. Or maybe Hawkins has a jealous girlfriend."

"I doubt it. Can you really picture him with a girlfriend?" she asked, her nose wrinkling in distaste.

"No. So maybe you should run, and your old man should give in to the pressure from RI, and sell up," Dora told her sympathetically. "It might be the best solution for all concerned. Your father's never been all that good at ranching from what I could see. Then you could get away from this mess and get a life."

Cindy blew her a raspberry. "Hell, I'd settle for a love life but I'm not running, and my dad is too good at ranching, when his hearts in it." She pocketed the note, telling herself it was true. "And don't you dare tell him about these notes. He's got enough to deal with getting through the next three months till he's released, and besides…"

Dora held a hand up to forestall her. "Fine, I give up. At least say you'll reconsider going to the dance."

"Maybe." She really wasn't up for another unkissed evening. And she really didn't own anything fancy enough for the formal event.

"I'll be watching for you, just in case," Dora stated, going to her car. "And if you're worried about running into JT Randal don't. After all, what would a high-powered industrialist be doing at the Policeman's Ball?"

"True." Cindy sighed as she watched Dora drive away. She had a sneaking suspicion Dora wouldn't take no for an answer. Stretching the kinks out of her back, she went to finish her chores, unloading the bags of goat chow. The pygmy goats had one hell of a love life, reproducing like crazy. Too bad, she couldn't say the same. When she finished, she walked to her cabin located next to the bunkhouse, going through the dude ranch lobby to her digs. What she needed was a pint of rocky road to cheer up her pity party.

Suddenly there was a tap on her door. It could be Dora with a suggestion for another god-awful blind date, or more likely one of the steps with another dress crisis. Stitch the hem, iron the gown, or get out a stain, her money was on stain at this late hour. She threw it open to find three short older ladies carrying makeup cases, standing in the lobby. Were Avon ladies going out in gangs now, she wondered with a smile? "I think you want the big house, ladies."

"No, Cynthia Jane, we're here to see you."

"Really?" she asked, shocked.

"Of course, we're your Fairytales makeover team. Just think of us as your Fairy Godmothers."

"But I didn't order a makeover, and I certainly can't afford one."

"My dear, it's already taken care of."

Cindy felt a small stirring of hope grow inside her. This must be Dora's surprise birthday gift she'd been hinting about. *You're going to love it, Cyn.* The tiny ladies beaming up at her were certainly loveable. She read their gold embossed nametags, Agatha, Imogene, and Hilda, and smiled. "Ladies thank you; I think you came in the nick of time."

She stepped back to let them inside. Then, around through the lobby, came a troop of hairdressers and technicians. "So many of you?"

"Of course, we give deluxe service. Just put yourself in our capable hands."

Cindy put troubling thoughts out of her mind, and did just that, letting them treat her to a spa oil bath and massage, softening her work-roughened skin. A pedicure and manicure came next. She looked down at her pink toenails and smiled, feeling sexy and feminine. When she slipped into the hairdresser's chair, and looked at her tangled, limp ginger hair hanging down her back, she let out a sigh. "I think it's hopeless."

"No dear," Agatha stated. "You just haven't had anyone to show you what to do with it."

How did she know that? Her mother died when she was born and she'd grown up a tomboy, looked after by Pedro and Juanita while her father grieved. When the stylist turned her hair from a tangled mess to fiery waves of copper and gold, cascading around her shoulders, she couldn't believe her eyes.

"It's lovely" She shook her hair, watching it shimmer and catch the light. She looked at the beaming trio, her Fairy Godmothers. "How can I ever thank you?"

"Go to the dance," they replied in tandem.

Now, how did they know about the dance? Or that she wasn't planning on going? Dora must have tipped them off. "I can't. It's formal, and I don't have a thing to wear."

"Not to worry, my dear." Imogene going to a large suitcase.

Cindy watched curiously as she opened the suitcase, an aura of gold light radiating out of the deep case, refracting rainbows on the paneled walls. Gasping with wonder and surprise, Cindy watched Imogene reach inside and pull out a gorgeous turquoise blue evening gown. The princess style dress, shot through with gold threads, would make her the bell of the ball. "It's beautiful."

"It matches your eyes," Imogene pointed out with a tender smile.

Cindy gazed at her reflection in the mirror, realizing they were right. The expertly applied makeup she wore, played up her eyes and her full lips.

"This should get his attention," Imogene stated, with a giggle.

"Him?" Cindy asked.

"The man of your dreams." Imogene blushed.

How did they know she had sex dreams? Dora certainly wouldn't have told them about her secret erotica library.

Hilda smiled, and walked over to the case, shooing Imogene aside. "My turn." She winked at Cindy and pulled out lingerie. She watched as Hilda reached into the case and pulled out a rainbow of different colored sexy lingerie. She picked a matching gold lace bra and panty set out of the pile and held them up. "Try these tonight to light his fire."

"Those might just do it." Cindy grinned, wondering if they had a little love potion number nine in that magical case of theirs.

Chapter 2

An hour later, Cindy entered the ballroom at the Hyatt Regency. Her wary gaze immediately shot to her stepmother, holding court with a group of her country club women friends. An ice blonde, in a tasteful black gown and pearls, Cordial still resembled the beauty queen she'd once been. It didn't take much looking to spot her stepsisters out on the dance floor. They were the center of attention in their faux designer pastel gowns, Tiffany in pink and Brandy in baby blue. Blonde, bubbly, as long as they got what they wanted, the twins were stunning with their fair-haired beauty.

When Cordial glanced at her, Cindy went stiff as a board, fearing exposure, afraid that she'd be unmasked, and laughed at. But her frosty stepmother looked right through her without even a hint of recognition, and she let out a sigh of relief, knowing that she was home free. Cindy's tense posture relaxed, and she smiled as she scanned the crowd. First, she had to find Dora and thank her for this life-altering makeover. Then, she was going gunning for big game, the perfect man to make her a woman.

Dora breezed by her on Jim Carol's arm as she left the dance floor. She parted from him with a giggle and headed for an empty back booth. Cindy rushed over to her knowing her friend wouldn't lack for dance partners. She slid into the bench seat across from her, and flashed Dora a giddy smile when she did a double take. It confirmed Cindy's thought that she looked completely different, almost unrecognizable from the old Cindy. "Hi there. I came."

Dora swept an impressed gaze over her. "Cynthia Jane Taylor, my heavens, is that really you?"

"Shh," she replied, looking around to make sure they hadn't been overheard. "It's really me, and I'm trying to go incognito for the night. So far, it's working, so please don't blow my cover. Call me Cyn, okay?" The alias just popped into her head. It fit for the adventurous woman she wanted to become. She sure as hell needed a new identity to pull this off. Dora's nod and approving smile made her feel much more confident in her ability to get away with her deception.

"The queen bitch didn't recognize you?"

"Looked right through me like I was glass. Isn't it great?"

"Terrific. For once you can let down your hair, literally." She looked at Cyn's tresses. "You're going to have to tell me who styled you."

"As if you didn't know." Cyn smiled, adding, "How can I ever thank you?"

"For what?" Dora's brow wrinkled.

"The makeover. The Fairytales team was fabulous. You went way overboard for my birthday present, but I loved it."

"But I didn't. My birthday gift is tickets to the Chippendales show. I was going to give them to you at our annual birthday lunch tomorrow."

"Well, if you didn't send them, who did?" Her puzzled gaze locked with Dora's. "Cordial?"

"Yeah right. The Queen Bitch only thinks of herself, and you know it. She probably doesn't even remember that it's your birthday next Saturday."

"You're right." Cyn sighed, regretting once more their lack of warm family ties. Dora was so lucky, growing up with four siblings and loving parents. "I wonder who sent my Fairy Godmothers to me, then."

"Fairy Godmothers, you say?" Dora smiled, adding, "Maybe somebody up there likes you."

Cyn thought about her charming, little Fairy Godmothers, their magical bag, and smiled, letting herself believe the fantasy. Tonight, felt like a night to suspend disbelief. "I think you might be right."

Dora ordered them chocolate martinis from a passing waiter.

Cyn nodded in agreement when Dora ordered her one. It was a night for new experiences, even though the cocktails were expensive, and decadent. Cyn smiled at the waiter when he brought their drinks and was stunned to see him give her the eye.

"Here's your money." Dora slipped him a twenty. She smiled when his gaze strayed back to Cyn. "I was going to suggest we find you someone to try your womanly wiles on, but it looks like you don't need my help."

"I'm not so sure about that." Cindy blushed and took a sip of the luscious chocolate confection. "These are wonderful."

"Told you." Dora smiled. "Don't worry about handling men, Cyn. All you must do is bat your eyes and they'll fall at your feet."

"Sounds messy," Cindy replied, and laughed.

"So then kick their ass and set the goats on them, you're good at that."

When Dora's date came back to claim her for a dance, she smiled. "Go ahead and dance, girlfriend. I'm man shopping."

Dora chucked. "Yell, if you need advice. Otherwise, I'll meet you at the Coffee Cup at noon tomorrow for lunch."

"Okay," she murmured, and scanned the crowd. Cindy noticed she was attracting some embarrassing attention of her own. Interested men were giving her the eye. She blushed clear down to her toes, not knowing how to flirt. Besides, none of them seemed right. She didn't want permanence, didn't have time to devote to a relationship. She wanted a fling, the right man to finally make her a complete woman.

She let out a sigh of regret, conceding that it might not be in the cards tonight. Still, she wouldn't get down, she'd waited until the age of twenty-eight to have sex, another loveless night wouldn't kill her. The makeover would be the start of a whole new her. She could be a rancher in the daytime and a sexually adventurous woman at night, with at least some semblance of a love life.

A burst of masculine laughter from the bar made her breath catch in her throat. She thought she recognized that sultry laugh, even though it had been years. It couldn't be. Her gaze went to a tall, dark, hunky male with his back turned to her at the bar. The coloring was right, and he had the best butt denim ever covered in his jeans. Her fascinated gaze ran up long legs, to longish black hair, curling over the collar of his black leather biker's jacket. JT Randal. She knew in her heart it was him and smiled as a thrill zinged through her. She still thought he had the best butt she'd ever ogled. He was standing with Mack Walsh, owner of a seedy erotica shop, and Zane Redcloud, a hunky Native American cop. What a testosterone packed trio, but she only had eyes for JT.

She trembled, her body heating. Apparently, the unwritten dress code didn't mean a thing to him, he hadn't changed from earlier. It smacked of JT Randal's rebellious teenage behavior. And then he turned, the breath caught in her throat, as his identity was confirmed, conclusively. She vividly remembered his whiskey dark gaze, the sultry shape of his hard mouth, and the scar on his chin that set him apart as a tough guy. He looked right at her; and she creamed, her sex instantly responding to him. Devastating, sexy, powerful, and normally way out of her league, he was any woman's wet dream...certainly hers, and she wanted him bad. A buzz went around the room as the others speculated about his identity. How could they not remember him? He was one of a kind, unforgettable. But she wasn't above capitalizing on the situation. It gave her the first shot at him.

"Will you look at that lowdown biker scum," Cordial hissed in a brittle voice that carried. "You'd think they'd bounce riff raff like that out of here, dressed as he is."

Cyn tuned out her stepmother's catty drone, as eligible women's heads all turned to ogle him. She groaned, the younger women didn't find his lack of decorum a turn off, quite the opposite in fact. About half the herd headed out on the dance floor to shake their booties at him, responding to his hot good looks. A moment later, her stepsisters were in the front of the pack on the dance floor, shimmying to a fast dance beat. Well, hell, seducing him suddenly didn't look very probable. She stared at JT, noticing Zane and Mack elbow him in the ribs, teasing him. No doubt, this mass hysteria happened all the time to a hunk like him.

As if JT felt her stare, he turned to lock gazes with her, and she forgot to breathe, as she fell into his amber depths, her nipples beading. "Perfect," she whispered, and he grinned, like he'd read her mind. It sent a jolt of heat straight through her, curling her toes in her high heel evening slippers.

Jake Randal went still, his cock swelling behind his fly, his pulse thudding as the fiery little redhead gave him a hard on from across the room. Damn, suddenly all he could think about was plunging into her until they were both spent, and then taking her over his knee. He'd bet she'd like that, a little kink. He watched her blush, as her gaze focused on the bulge of his cock. Oh yeah, she knew what she wanted—him. An incongruous mixture, innocent and seductress, she had the power to turn him inside out with a sultry glance. Which persona was true, he wondered? He aimed to find out.

His gaze swept from her twinkling eyes to her full mouth, to focus on her ample cleavage, displayed by her pretty, low cut, gown. The same

color as her stunning eyes, turquoise, reminding him of the Mediter-
ranean. He swore as he saw her nipples beading through the silky
fabric, as he stared at them. Responsive little minx. They'd be more than
a handful for him to enjoy, and he had big hands. Beside him, he knew
that Mack and Zane were going on point, giving her the eye. He cut them
a quick repressive frown, warning them off, already feeling possessive.
They smirked back at him, knowing he had it bad for her. He ignored
them, glancing back at her, glad that she only had eyes for him. "Who
the hell is she?"

"Damned if I know," Mack muttered beside him. "But if you don't
make a move soon, I will."

"Ditto," Zane agreed.

"Not a chance in hell I'd allow that, gentlemen," Jake stated with
wry self-humor, as he picked up his long-necked beer off the bar. The
mystery woman had him anywhere she wanted him, including flat on
his back as she rode him until she came. He watched her nibble her
full lower lip and peek back at the growing bulge of his cock behind the
placket of his jeans. "Later." He started heading toward her.

"The poker game still starting at midnight?" Mack asked.

"Nope," he mumbled, walking toward her like a moth to the flame.
"I'll call you later." He hadn't planned to make an intimate connection
tonight. He'd come to meet with Mack about quietly locating the new
headquarters for Scion Enterprises in the back of his erotica shop. And
he'd needed to get Zane's take on his suspicions about North Star and
the losses at Randal Industries. Hell, he was on an undercover mission,
but all sense of caution flew out the window as he strode her way.

Cyn tingled as JT came to her. He moved like he looked, raw male power,
a dominant aura that made others clear a path for him. *How did a
woman go about seducing a man like him? What was she going to say to
him? Hey, big boy, want to make me a woman?* He'd run a mile, probably
in Brandy or Tiffany's giggly direction. She took a calming breath as he
closed in on her, swamped by his primal brand of leather and hot man,
as he stepped up to her table. The man was just plain edible.

Her heart fluttered as she gazed up at him, struck again by his height.
Did she want a man she had to look up at? Hell yeah. He seemed to take
up the entire space, his legs brushing hers, and everything else seemed

to fade away. Really, what kind of man wore jeans and biker leathers to a formal dance? The kind of maverick she wanted to teach her about sex. As if sensing her thoughts he flashed her a bad boy smile, his eyes twinkling. He leaned in close to say, "Hello, love. What's your name?"

She got lost in his whiskey eyes, watching the irises contract. "I'm...um...Cyn."

"Mind if I join you Sin?"

"Y...yes, of course, please sit down." She let out a started gasp when he nudged her over, sitting in the booth beside her, instead of going on the other side. Maybe seducing him wouldn't be so hard after all.

"The name's Jake Randal, Sin." His long, thick fingers curling around the long neck bottle he carried.

She couldn't help staring at his hands, recalling what they said about big hands, big feet, big cock. Was it true? She tried to peek down at his lap surreptitiously to check, hearing him chuckle in response. So, he'd caught her at it. He'd know exactly how to use his big hands to bring her to unknown peaks of ecstasy or perhaps paddle her. Did he even like kink? There was only one way to find out, she decided, looking him in the eye.

He smiled, setting down his bottle of beer, and reaching out to take her hand. "Want to dance, sugar?"

She shivered with delight when JT's hand enfolded hers, making her feel petite in comparison. His hand was still cold from the beer, and the chill made her sex creamier, while she let out an involuntary gasp. His touch was better than she'd imagined, and they were only holding her hands. His fingertips were callused, rough from hard work she supposed, wondering once again what he'd been doing since he'd left town. Whatever it was, it hadn't been easy.

JT's fingertips brushed the pulse point on her wrist and lingered. "Your pulse is racing," he stated, giving her a tender smile. "Do you live up to your name, SIN?"

"It's spelled C–Y–N actually, but yes, I know how to be a bad girl, especially with the right man." Her gaze darted down to his impressive bulge. He was obviously huge and hard for her, definitely the right man. Face heating at her own boldness, she looked up, giving him what she hoped was a confidant smile. "Actually, I want more than a dance from you. I'd like to seduce you, JT. Would you please take me to bed?"

She watched his eyes smolder at her request and his mouth kick up in a sexy grin. A glance at his bigger bulge confirmed it. Wonderful! She'd made the right choice. He wanted her as much as she wanted him.

JT edged nearer, his thigh pressed against hers. "You don't beat around the bush, do you...ah, Cyn? Now, I'm not easy, but I can be had, with the right persuasion."

Burning where their thighs touched, she pressed her leg a little tighter to his, the side of her breast against his chest, and barely held back a whimper. "I've been aching for you all my life, JT." She gazed up at him, studying the startle look in his eye, the slight flush on his tanned face. Whatever he'd been expecting her to say, it hadn't been that. The fact he was just as affected by their contact soothed any lingering fears. "I don't have time to play games."

"Neither do I," he replied, his voice a husky bedroom rumble. "I'm sold. I'd love to take you to bed, sugar."

The pet name flowed over her like honey and made her nipples tighten, the space between her legs melted, her sex growing wet. "Wonderful." She nudged his hip, trying to get him up so she could take him away, and saw his mouth twitch as he went. Was he laughing at her? He stood and reached out to take her hand, his hot eyes burning her, and she suddenly didn't care if he found her eagerness amusing. She couldn't hide it; she was on fire for him. Taking his hand, she let him pull her out, her knees wobbling as she stood. JT caught her, letting out a chuckle, his arm going around her waist, as he pulled her to him. She burned, pressing tight to him. Across the room, Dora gave her thumbs up. A glance at Cordial found her stepmother scowling at their public display of affection, as Tiffany and Brandy stood behind her scowling. They were a united front of disapproval. She didn't care.

"Who the hell is that cheap slut?" Cordial snapped at Tiffany.

"How should I know, mother? Some out-of-town bimbos I suppose, seeing that she's with him," Tiffany bit out.

Brandy gave her a dismissive gaze. "Who cares, he's too old for me anyhow."

"Yes, and his taste is definitely poor," Cordial agreed.

Cyn was too bemused by Jake's proximity, to care about their catty remarks. As far as she was concerned, they could all go jump in the lake. She smiled at Jake, and taking his hand, turned to head for the door. JT fell into step beside her, possessively looping a long arm around her waist to steady her. A sensual shiver shot through her at the contact, as he pulled her tight to his side. He must have felt her tremor, because he squeezed her waist, his fingers splayed on her ribcage, the breath catching in her throat as her pace faltered.

"Easy, sugar." He escorted her out of the ballroom. "Just one step at a time to paradise."

Cyn breathed deep, trying to stay calm. He was right. Step one was accomplished, she'd seduced him. Now she had to figure out where to take him. The night ahead held promise, and risk. She couldn't very well take him back to the ranch. JT clung possessively to her waist, as if he didn't want to let her get away. He didn't need to worry she wasn't going anywhere without him. Step two was about to begin.

Gazing up at him as they exited the ballroom, she focused on JT's sensual mouth. What would it taste like, feel like, skimming along her tender skin? When he drew her down the hall and into the cloakroom, she went eagerly. Alone time was just what she needed to carry this off with any sense of confidence.

"I'll go secure us a room," she stated, opening her clutch bag, to look for her credit card. Jake went standing stiff and quiet in front of her. She glanced up to see that he was frowning at her. What was wrong? They couldn't go back to her place, or his bungalow, it left the hotel, anything else would be too awkward. One thing she wanted to avoid at all costs were awkward morning-afters. It would be embarrassing checking into the hotel without luggage, but she could handle a little embarrassment.

He stepped closer, pressing her back against the rack of coats, demanding, "Why me, Cyn?"

So that was what was bugging him. It amazed her that a hunk like him would have any doubts about why a woman wanted him. He sounded hesitant, she decided, and he looked a little concerned. He was probably used to gold diggers trying to trap him. He needn't worry about that with her, she just wanted someone to deflower her. But she couldn't tell him that. "Because you're the man of my dreams," she replied, meaning every word. She watched the corners of his hard mouth kick up in a grin and breathed a sigh of relief. The first crisis averted.

"I'm glad you think so."

"I do."

"Well then." He pressed closer, his body brushing hers. "First of all, it's Jake not JT. Nobody's called me JT since high school. Second, I'll take care of the room, I'm no gigolo," he continued, taking the credit card out of her hand, putting it back in her purse, and closing it with a firm click.

Sensually overcome as he brushed against her, hot and demanding, she tried to focus on her objections. It might hurt his pride if she paid for the room, but letting him pay, ceded some control of the evening, his seduction, to him. Did she want to allow that? The hard length of his cock pressed against the juncture of her thighs, and she moaned, rubbing against that emblem of his masculine prowess. What was the big deal if he paid?

"Okay," she gasped, "If it's that important to you. You can pay."

"Good girl," he stated, leaning into her.

Cyn whimpered as her breasts pillowed against his chest, her nipples budding. His warm hands skimmed up the sides of her bodice, making her shiver with desire as they came to rest on either side of her breasts, his thumbs stopping, teasing, inches from her tingling nipples. She arched, trying to make him touch them, and hissed when she succeeded. All they did was land square on each bud, but she panted as her nipples throbbed with heat, waiting breathlessly for him to do more. "I'm not a girl, I'm a woman," Cyn argued. He smiled, his thumbs tracing teasing circles around her tingling, jutting nipples. Her head tipped back, as a needy moan poured from her lips.

"I love that sound, Cyn." Taking advantage of her open throat, he bent to nuzzle her, giving her a love bite, before moving on to nip at her earlobe. "In the bedroom you're a girl, my girl, and I'm in charge, right?"

"Yes, you're most definitely in charge in the bedroom," she gasped, swamped by erotic sensations, as she whimpered, pressing closer to his heat.

Sucking on her earlobe, he murmured, "Excellent. I've already got a room." He then pulled a key card of his pocket.

Well, why hadn't he said so in the first place? Because he'd taken for granted that he'd supply the room. He was trying to take charge in his alpha male way. She could forgive him, this time; after all, she was getting what she needed from him. Licking her lips, she focused on that sexy mouth of his when a troubling thought hit. "Why do you have a room? Could it have been any woman bedding you tonight?"

His eyes crinkled as he smiled. "Bedding me, that's precious." At her frown, he gently cupped her cheek, saying, "Relax, sugar. I was going to have a poker game after the dance. I called it off the minute I saw you. It couldn't have been anyone but you bedding me."

She glowed, relaxing. "Good, because I want exclusive rights to you tonight."

"That can be arranged. Are you ready for me?" he asked, rocking his pelvis against her.

She hesitated, hoping she wasn't manipulating him. "I don't want to push you into doing something you don't want to."

He cocked his head, watching her. "If you're wondering, I haven't been with a woman for over a year." He smiled, rocking against her again. "As you can feel, I'm primed and ready."

"And not taken," she added.

He chuckled. "You got that right, sugar! I'm not taken." He backed off, and took her arm, escorting her to the elevators saying, "This way."

His domineering tendencies gave her a little thrill. She might not want to live with them, but she could put up with them for one hot night. The compensations were obvious, she decided, slanting another intrigued look at the bulge in his pants, she could hardly wait to taste him. She sighed, instantly missing the feel of his erection pressed against her needy sex. "Don't forget, Jake, you may be in charge in the bedroom, but I picked you, so I'm in charge of the rest of the night."

"Great, you can order room service for me in the morning."

Up above, the fairies broke into applause. "We did it." Imogene crowed.

"I told you," Hilda whispered with a smile. "My lingerie will clinch the deal."

"Don't be so certain," Agatha replied, calling for caution. "This is just the beginning for these two. Free will and a clash of strong personalities still stand between them. Even though they're fated to be together, things could still go wrong."

"Oh dear. What are you sensing?" Imogene wrung her hands.

Agatha sighed, closing her eyes. "Danger—disapproval—but most of all, jealousy."

Imogene winced. "I don't like the sound of that."

"We'll just have to be on our guard," Hilda cut in. "And maybe a little spot of my love potion wouldn't hurt."

"No," Agatha forestalled her. "That's what got us in trouble with the pygmy goats. Anyway, look at the two of them, so in tune with one another's bodies. They don't need it."

Hilda smiled as she watched Jake pull Cyn close as he walked her down the hall to his room. "I think you may be right, Aggie."

Agatha nodded. "Of course, I'm right. For now, let's draw a veil over the proceedings, and allow the lovers to get to know each other. If we get into trouble, we can always call on our old friend, Eros."

Chapter 3

Jake tried to walk steadily, as he whisked Cyn down the hall to his suite. It wasn't easy with a hard-on the size, and strength, of a giant redwood. She turned him on like no other woman ever had. Lucky for him, he'd booked the room, because he didn't think he could wait. Cyn was driving him wild, her sweet seductive essence ensnaring him, making his cock throb, as it was squeezed in his suddenly too tight jeans.

Hell, everything about her was a turn on, from the sly needy looks she kept shooting at him; to the sexy way, she bit her lip, when he caught her at it. Her extraordinary tip-tilted, turquoise blue eyes were vaguely familiar, but he was too far-gone to care. He hadn't been this horny, or led around by his cock by a female, since he was a teenage boy. He was a man now, and dominant in the bedroom, but here he was, about to make love to this beauty at her beck and call.

He pulled out his key card and stuck it in the lock, glancing at her nervous expression. He noted her blush, and tensed, hoping she hadn't changed her mind. "If you want to back out, sugar, this is the time. Otherwise, I may not be responsible for my actions." He watched her shiver, and tried not to grin with relief, at the hot look in her eyes. She was trying out a walk on the wild side, and he meant to deliver.

"I don't want to back out. I want you," she replied, gazing into his eyes.

Jake burned, as her turquoise eyes ate him alive. He held the door open for her, and she rushed inside. He couldn't take his eyes off her as she stood in the suite's sitting room, watching her like the predator he was, trying to figure her out. One minute she was rocking his world like a trained courtesan, the next, she was a blushing virgin.

He closed the door, leaning against it. She trembled, looking back at him in seeming wonder. Surely, he wasn't the first to be with her, but she had the skill to make him feel like her first. He shrugged out of his leathers, conscious of her fascinated gaze on him. Maybe she liked bikers? He stepped toward her, and to her credit, she held her ground, her defiant little chin in the air, even though she looked like she wanted to bolt. The hell with trying to figure out her game, he needed her.

He stepped into her personal space, feeling drawn to her, and she gave him a smile of sweet surrender. He wondered at her vulnerability, as he pulled her into his arms. Her quick intake of breath, the way she melted her sweet body against his hard throbbing one, drove the thought from his mind. One thing she couldn't lie about was her physical reaction to him.

He stroked her back, her budded nipples pressing into him, as she rolled her hips against his cock. He reveled in the signs of her feminine arousal. He pulled back to look at her, confirming the heat, in her astounding turquoise eyes. "Want to take this into the bedroom, sugar?" he asked, giving her one last chance to back out, even though it would kill him.

She nodded, nibbling her lower lip. "I wouldn't have invited you to take me to bed if I didn't want you. I'm not a tease, Jake."

He smiled, relief surging through him, as his cock swelled even more. It would have been hard as hell to let her go, but he'd have managed it somehow. "Glad to hear it," he stated, wrapping his arms around her waist, to sweep her off her feet, and carry her into the bedroom.

Cyn clung to him, with a shocked gasp. "You do have cave man tendencies."

"Any complaints?" he asked, smiling at her when she shook her head, her eyes shining with delight. He sat on the edge of the bed and put her on his lap, her legs straddling him, her gown going up to bare her damp, panty covered sex. It pressed provocatively against his raging cock, making him groan. "Well, you've got me where you want me, Cyn. Now what?"

"A kiss," she replied, gazing at his mouth, and leaning forward to brush her lips across his.

"Oh yeah," he muttered, deepening the kiss, nipping her bottom lip to demand access to her sweet mouth. She opened with a gasp, and his tongue surged inside, tasting her sweetness, mingled chocolate, and woman. Her tempting breasts pressed against him, like twin laser beams burning into his chest. He groaned, his hand slipping down between their bodies to cup her mound, making her gasp as she wriggled her lush, seductive, ass on his lap.

"Like that, do you?" he asked, with a low masculine chuckle, loving the sound of her pleasure.

He did it again and she pulsed hot and damp against his hand, dampening it as she cried out. He growled, unzipping the back of her dress, lowering the bodice to bare every creamy inch of her breasts. Her strapless gold bra pushed them up for his delectation, and he stared at them for a heartbeat, savoring the sight. Her unvarnished arousal was a turn on, her luscious globes trembling, as she gasped for breath. Hell, he felt as if he had run a marathon too, his heart was thudding like a crazy snare drum.

Intrigued, he rubbed his thumbs against her nipples, visible through her bra, and watched them jut out, just begging for his attention. Who was he to turn down such an invitation? "Beautiful," he growled, pinching the buds, rolling them between his thumbs and forefingers, tugging on them as she let out an extended whimper of need. Cyn pressed her needy sex, tight to him, dry humping him, the pressure giving him blue balls, but he didn't care. He couldn't resist doing it again, murmuring, "That's it, Cyn, give me all your passion."

"Oh yes," she gasped.

He bent to lap at her nipples through the bra, and she went wild, arching into him, crying out. His hand slipped down between their bodies, inside her panties, to find her stiff little clit. He pressed, and she screamed, riding his hand. "That's it, sugar, fuck yourself on my finger." She shuddered, coming in his arms, crying out his name. Jake held her dazzled. "Easy, sugar. This is only the beginning."

Cyn sagged against him, breathing hard.

He reached back to unhook her bra. "Is this what you want, Cyn?"

"More than you could possibly know," she answered, leaning back to unbutton his shirt, trying to strip him. His shirt buttons popped, pinging onto the carpet. "Oops." She giggled at her lack of finesse.

"Easy." Taking her hands, he pushed them behind her rolling his hips, giving her a little taste of restraint to see how she liked it. She ground against him, her eyes hot and defiant at being thwarted, almost unmanning him. "My little hell cat," Jake growled. He transferred both wrists to one hand and cupped her mound with the other. Her eyes snapped fire at him as she wailed, arching against him. He let go of her wrists, learning what he needed to know, she liked it hot.

He picked her up, reversing their positions, to lay her down on the bed, while she let out a needy whimper. "Reach up and grab the headboard," he commanded. "Don't let go until I tell you to," he continued, watching her stunned expression. She smiled, her eyes gazing into his, as she reached up and grabbed the spindles of the headboard. He groaned as the position thrust out her tempting tits and pushed up her dress. He quickly stripped off her panties. "Now spread your legs for me, Cyn, show me what you want. He groaned when she obeyed him, parting her long legs to show him her perfect, pink, wet sex, her swollen clit. God, but he wanted her.

He lay down beside her, and she let out a shuddering breath, as his fingers traced a path down her slick sex, to home in on her swollen clit. She cried out, closing her eyes, arching off the bed, as he played with the sensitive nub. "That's it, Cyn. Go wild for me."

Jake kept his thumb on her clit, and slipped one finger into her tight wet heat, before his little finger ghosted her anus. She quivered, as if startled by the dark caress, and then moaned, as he fucked her that way, her body clutching at him. When he couldn't take it anymore, he unzipped his pants and settled between her warm thighs.

His throbbing cock rubbed against her creamy sex, and she arched up, trying to complete their union, still clutching the headboard. He backed off an inch, seeing her mew of protest as she grumbled, her eyes squeezed shut. He wasn't going to let her reduce him to just some blind, anonymous, fuck. "Look at me, Cyn," he demanded. He watched her eyes pop open, and smiled when her steamy, pleading, gaze locked with his. That was more like it. "Do you want this?" he asked, rubbing the head of his swollen cock against her clit, making her hiss with pleasure.

"Yes," she replied, with a needy moan.

Satisfied, he groaned, trying to slow down and make it good for her, as his cock pressed tight against the pulsing entrance to her cunt. She murmured, flexing her hips up at him, but he clamped down on her hips, determined to control the pace, and give her the restraint she desired. She glared up at him and he smiled, slowly entering her, beads of sweat breaking out on his brow, as he gradually pressed into her tight cunt. She winced, crying out in pain, and bit her lip. He froze in place, poised at the barrier of her cherry, feeling like the biggest fool in the world as he gazed down at her and cursing at her guilty expression. Now he knew why she'd seemed too innocent. The question was why she'd come onto him, like asking men to bed her was old hat. "This is your first time," he bit out the gritty statement.

"Um, yeah," she stated, biting her lip. She wiggled against him and tried to pull him closer.

He clamped down her tempting hips. "Why me?"

"I already told you. You're my dream man. I wanted it to be special," she explained, tears misting her eyes.

He groaned in sexual agony as he took in her frustrated gaze, her hands still clutching the headboard. His stupid cock aching for him to finish what he'd started, but he needed answers first. He was too smart not to smell a trap. "What are you trying to pull Cyn, if that is your real name?"

The suites door flew open, Mack and Zane entering, laughing as they talked.

"Where you at, Jake?" Mack called out.

"The bedroom door's shut, and the light is on inside the room," Zane chimed in. "Ten to one he's with that sexy redhead."

"Well, give Detective Zane Redcloud a gold star for the missing redhead, and poker buddy, investigation," Mack commented.

"Up yours," Zane laughed out. "You deal."

Jake closed his eyes, praying for patience, while Cyn looked stricken underneath him, and let go of the headboard with a blush. He'd told them the game was off. At least he thought he had. He was too wrapped up in Cyn, the temptress, to recall the details. He glanced down at Cyn's blushing face, needing answers, as she went rigid beneath him. He wasn't bloody well going to get them right now. He bit out a curse, calling out, "Stay out there, you two knuckleheads."

He glanced back down at Cyn, saying, "Don't move. I'll take care of this interruption and be right back. Then we'll talk. You've got a lot of explaining to do." He rolled out of bed, feeling her fascinated gaze on his cock, as he tucked his throbbing member back in his jeans, and zipped up with a wince.

"Ouch, I bet that hurts," she whispered with a wince. "It's so big." She flicked a regretful gaze back up to his eyes. "I wish I'd been able to taste you."

He groaned, closing his eyes, trying to talk his twitching cock into behaving. "You're killing me, Cyn," he muttered, before turning to head out into the sitting room and get rid of the guys. He didn't share women anymore, hadn't since high school, and he sure as hell wasn't sharing a choice morsel like his Cyn. He turned to soak in her seductive charms one more time. She was still sprawled out the on the bed, looking like a fiery sex goddess. Her red hair spread out on his pillow, her skirt pushed up around her hips, and her beautiful tits bared. They were like tempting strawberries waiting for him to feast on them. This wasn't over by a long shot. "Don't you dare move, you hear me?" he commanded, and smiled when she reached up to grip the headboard. She'd be the perfect lover, if she wasn't trying to lie to him.

Cyn nodded, watching Jake leave her with a regretful sigh, her heart aching, along with her throbbing pussy. Step two hadn't gone off as planned, in fact, it was a total disaster, and worst of all, she was still technically a virgin. At least he'd made her cum, twice. She closed her eyes, murmuring yummy sounds, as she thought about his talented hands. Too bad, he'd been perfect, he was perfect. She'd seen him tuck that hard monster back into his pants, and wince when he'd zipped up. He had what it took to satisfy a woman, and he knew what to do with it. Would he want to try again?

She listened to hearty male laughter in the next room and blushed, praying the joke wasn't on her. No. She sensed he was an honorable man, wouldn't have let herself bed him if she'd believed otherwise. But she couldn't meekly let him order her around. Stay put indeed, she couldn't risk being seen. She let go of the headboard and rolled out of bed. Straightening her clothes, she found her bra under the bed, wondering if the Fairy godmothers had an out clause, something about turning back into a pumpkin at midnight.

What was Jake telling them, and why were they still here? More importantly, what the hell could she say if he came back to demand answers? An honest affair was impossible given her present situation. It was time to make a clean getaway while she still could, she decided, looking at the patio door. Where the hell were her panties? She scanned the room one more time, then gave it up, and tiptoed to the door. She slipped outside, giving the closed door a wistful look. It'd almost been perfect, but she knew the value of a strategic retreat.

Chapter 4

Jake rode his Harley down the long, dusty driveway at sunrise. He'd spent a sleepless night after Cyn had run out on him. The bed had smelled like her perfume and her sweet arousal. Who the hell was she? At least he had one clue, the gold panties in his top pocket. Now all he had to do was find the girl that filled these, he decided, with a wry humor.

Before he could concentrate on finding her, he had business to take care of. His audit of Randal Industries had turned up some improprieties. It was the reason he'd slipped into town unannounced. His father had been pragmatic enough to give him carte blanche. Of course, stopping for a drink with his buddies had threatened to blow his cover. It was worth it, it'd brought him Cyn.

He gazed at the antebellum house on the hill. It was splendid, and might just be the natural place to relocate his Scion headquarters. By contrast, the dude ranch area he pulled up to was shabby. It confirmed his intel that the ranch was in financial trouble. He cut past a broken-down pickup truck, and skidded to a halt.

Cyn, toting a large gunnysack almost as big as she was, took one look at him, tripped, and fell on her delectable ass. The feed sack toppled, ripping open. A second later, there was a thunder of little hooves. Jake did a double take when a heard of pygmy goats ran at him, weaving around his bike. He dismounted, chuckling; things were looking up.

Gazing at Cyn, her red hair flowing around her, dressed in jeans and a tan blouse buttoned all the way up, probably to hide his hickey, he stated, "We meet again, Cyn." He felt sucker punched, his body tightening with desire, his heart beating faster, as Cyn stared up at him, mouth agape.

Cyn groaned, gaping at her lover of last night, as the pygmy goats feasted on the spilled grain all around her. He looked even yummier and more dangerous this morning, stubble covering his chin, and the dark look in his eyes. It made her toes curl inside her cowboy boots. She pushed Curley and Magnolia out of the way, so she could get a better look at him. How the hell had he tracked her down? "It's CJ, and you'd better get out of here, all I have to do is scream…"

He reached down, and jerked her to her feet, pulling her into his arms as he smiled. "You were saying?"

"Scream…" she gasped, leaning into his sensual body, as she gazed at his heartbreaker's smile. Lord, if he told her to grab a hold of her headboard so he could ravish her, she'd probably do it. She needed deprogramming, fast.

"Go ahead." Lowering his head to kiss her. "I remember that you're a screamer."

She moaned, as his mouth slanted over hers, going up on tiptoes, kissing him back. Her body instantly aroused, transported back to last night's earth shattering rendezvous. He'd been masterful, sexy, alluring, and all hers; and she ached for more. And she'd never got to taste him. To make up for it, she nipped his lower lip, and he growled into her mouth.

"CJ, you want us to move the…damn it, how'd these goats get loose again?"

Cyn pushed away from Jake as her ranch foreman's voice broke through her lust-fogged mind. She gazed up at Jake, blushing at his sultry, knowing, look. "Don't think you're going to get around me with sex, JT Randal."

"I wouldn't think of it," he commented back as he patted her gold panties in his pocket.

She noticed them, and blushed even harder. Good grief, he'd found them. She'd been forced to run off without them last night. She spun around, just as Pedro came around the corner. The older foreman and father figure to her, noticing her telltale blush, gave Jake a penetrating stare. "You okay, Cynthia Jean?"

"I'm fine."

"I was just checking in," Jake interrupted.

She shot him an annoyed glance over her shoulder. He might be the boss in the bedroom, but this was her dude ranch. "Sorry, our last room is full up, for two weeks as a matter of fact." She heard Pedro's gasp at the lie, but didn't back down. If she and Jake stayed together, she'd screw him blind within a week.

"I know. My secretary Mona made the reservation for me."

Cyn swallowed hard. Her luck couldn't be that bad. She only had one reservation, a Mr. Smith, for two whole weeks, an unheard of occurrence for the no frills dude ranch. It wasn't him; she decided, crossing her fingers. She slanted a suspicious look his way. "Mr. Smith."

"That's me."

"Damn," she muttered. She had to admire the smooth way he told the bald-faced lie. She'd never learned the knack herself.

"Ditto, sugar." He hoisted his duffle bag out of the Harley's saddlebags. "Show me where to bed down."

"I'll take care of these critters," Pedro stated, shooing the goats back to their enclosure.

And I'd better take care of mine...

"If you'll follow me, I'll check you in, Mr. Smith." She led the way into the dude ranch's office, in the front room of her cabin, and went behind the counter, ever aware of JT following her. His scent, his proximity, was intoxicating, doing crazy things to her libido. She could bottle the sex pheromones he gave off and make a million bucks, she thought, with a secret smile. Her nipples tingled, beading, making her grateful she was wearing a loose blouse, which she'd had to button all the way up, thanks to his love bite. He was a wild one, and she'd be a fool to trust him.

She turned to find JT had stopped to admire a painting on the wall. It was one of hers. An impressionistic landscape, and she held her breath. Would he like it? And why did it matter to her if he did?

"Lovely." He stood there gazing at it.

Her heart skipped a beat as he stopped to absorb the painting. It was like he was drinking up part of her essence, her unique view of the world that made her paint. He actually liked it. Her mouth curved into a satisfied smile.

"Who painted it?" JT asked, staring at the painting, absorbing it.

"She's a regional artist," Cyn murmured, her face heating.

"I'll have to look her up."

"I'm afraid that would be difficult, her studio's closed." The determined look Jake turned on her, made her quiver inside. She licked her lips. It the way he looked at her last night when he was ravishing her, she remembered every sexy detail.

He gazed back at the canvas, looking at the signature. "CJ McCall. You?" he asked, giving her a slow, appraising glance.

"Yeah, I painted it. I'm a commercial artist. McCall is my mother's maiden name. I use it professionally." She motioned toward the register, trying to rush him along. She so didn't want to talk about her wishes, or failed aspirations, couldn't risk letting him know her that deeply. "If you'll just sign here, Mr. Smith."

"So, why'd you stop?"

She frowned as he leaned casually against the counter. There had to be some way to rush him. "Duty," she replied in short. "I was needed at home. But it's only temporary. And I haven't stopped completely."

"Until your dad gets out of prison."

She bristled at the statement. How did he know that? "You're pretty well informed for a man who's shirked his duty for ten years."

"I keep informed, especially when it has to do with Randal Industries."

"But it doesn't. The ranch isn't for sale, Jake. I told it to that slimy Dwain Hawkins, and I'll tell the same to you. If that's your reason for pursuing me, you might just as well turn back around. It didn't work for him, and it won't work for you."

"Hawkins has bothered you?"

She rolled her eyes at the understatement. "Yeah," she stated sarcastically. "You ought to know his techniques. He's working under your marching orders."

"Not until next week, when I take on temporary management of RI. It's a duty thing," he replied with wry self-humor. "Right now, I'm on vacation."

"Right." She didn't believe a word of it. He didn't strike her as the laid back type. "One tip, you might want to tell him to lay off the strong-arm tactics," she commented, watching Jake go rigid.

"Strong arm tactics? What did the bastard do?" he asked, in a deceptively quiet tone.

The flash of cold fury in his eyes startled her. It seemed like he really cared. She couldn't let herself believe that. "First, he tried to romance me, in a creepy, all hands sort of way. When that didn't work, he threatened me. Still is, indirectly."

"How?"

She reached under the counter and brought up the sheaf of poison pen letters, fanning them in front of him. "He's been sending me love notes."

"Damn. You sure it's him?"

"He isn't stupid enough to sign them, but who else would bother? I'm basically invisible around here." His doubtful look fed her fragile feminine ego. "Of course, he's already got Cordial wrapped around his little finger."

"The haughty ice blonde, dripping with pearls."

Cyn leaned forward. "Most of them are fake. She's had to sell off her jewels to support her lavish lifestyle. She's looking for a rich husband for her daughters, beware."

He grinned. "Thanks for the warning. Does that include you?"

"Hell no, I'm only a stepdaughter and an arty, weird, one at that. And no, I'm not looking for a husband. You're off the hook, stud. Staying here would be stupid. Once she realizes who you are, the girls are going to come gunning for you. If I were you, I'd run a mile..."

"I think I'll risk it," he interrupted, taking the key to bungalow six out of her hand.

"It's the last log cabin on the right." She pulled away. "You should have everything you need."

"I hope so, because I'm really hungry. Room service?"

She chuckled; he really did think he was back at the Hyatt. "No. The hands start work at dawn, and get breakfast at six. If you care to join in the work, I'll feed you. Otherwise, I'd recommend the Coffee Cup Café; they make a mean eggs Benedict."

"Think about it. I might just let you taste me," he called over his shoulder, swinging out the door.

Cyn watched him go her eyes glued to his very sexy butt. It was on. She'd like to take a bite out of that ass.

"CJ, I want a word with you." Cordial stepped up behind her.

Cyn jumped a mile. How had the woman snuck up on her? She'd been too busy ogling Jake, that's how. What was her stepmother doing slumming down in the bunkhouse, and at this hour?

Cyn turned around, bristling when Cordial raked her new look with a shocked and disgruntled scowl.

"Now I know what happened to my stylists."

Cyn had forgotten about the missing stylists, lost in lust with Jake Randal. If she'd actually poached her stepmother's stylists, it'd been in a good cause. But deep down, she believed there was a more mystical explanation. There was something magical about the godmothers showing up when she was in desperate need of them. "I don't know what you're talking about."

"Right." Cordial's eyes narrowed. "Watch your step missy. I can kick you off of these grounds."

The threat was laughable. Who'd do the work if she were gone? "And do the grunt work yourself? I think not," She bluffed.

"Is that who I think it was?" Cordial asked, glancing in the direction of the black Harley Davidson pulled up in front of bungalow six.

Boy, her stepmother didn't miss a thing. "I don't know, who do you think it is?"

Cordial's eyes narrowed. "Don't play games with me, young lady. I won't have that motorcycle bum staying here, you should have seen him last night, rubbing shoulders with his betters."

"He's not a bum," Cyn automatically jumped to his defense, and bit her lip when Cordial gave her a suspicious look. "He registered as a Mr. Smith, and paid in cash up front, so he's no vagrant."

Cordial laughed bitterly. "You really are an innocent. Mr. Smith, you say?"

"That's right," Cyn replied with certainty, trying to calm her down. Jake couldn't afford to have Cordial run her usual credit check on him. He was under an assumed name for a reason.

"Did he give you any idea what he'd doing here?"

"He's here on business."

Cordial frowned. "Monkey business. Smith is obviously an alias. Did he give you any hard clues to his true identity?"

"Nothing rock hard." Cyn smiled, thinking of his cock. "But he might give it to me later."

Chapter 5

Jake Randal parked his bike next to his father's Caddy in the near empty Randal Industries Executive offices parking lot. He'd never wanted to come back, now he had no choice but to take the helm of the ailing company. Just as he thought, his workaholic father was here early, defying his doctor's orders. Some things never changed.

In his teens, he'd done everything to rebel against the future that had been mapped out for him. He'd left home at eighteen, and knocked around the world, joining the military, getting an education in jungle warfare and army intelligence. It had prepared him well for the cut-throat business world. He'd managed to fight his way to the top of the business world, and now he was back to square one.

The good thing was that Scion Industries was thriving, and could operate anywhere he chose to move. The bad thing was the less than pleasant task of taking Randal Industries apart to put it back together again on a solvent basis. He'd planned to lay low, and wait until the audit and investigation were complete. Lull the crooks into a false sense of security. Cyn's leveling about Hawkins' behavior had changed all that. Action was called for, now.

He headed towards the security guard, recognizing Tim Bailey, a long time Randal Industries employee. It took a few minutes for recognition to spark in the older man's eyes.

"Good gosh, is it you?" Tim asked with a grin. "The rumors were right, you've come home."

"Yeah, I guess it blew my cover when I stopped in at the dance."

"People were arguing whether it was you or not. Most of them didn't think so, but I knew you straight off, when I saw you on the back of that sweet ride."

"Yeah, I had it shipped in along with the rest of my gear."

"So, you're here for the duration?"

"As long as the old man needs me."

"Good on ya. There wouldn't be a personal reason for you sticking around, would there?" he asked with a smile. "I heard tell you scorned the local girls, and left with some gorgeous redhead."

Damn, the local rumor mill had lost none of its fervor. However, he didn't like thinking of Cyn being whispered about. "You heard that, did you?"

"Yup. Some stranger in town, they said. A mystery woman."

"And I intend to keep her that way," he replied a bit gruffly, relaxing when the man nodded. He'd keep business and pleasure separate. At least Cyn's name hadn't been grist for the rumor mill, yet. He knew what it felt like to be whispered about, and he didn't know if Cyn could handle it. Her panic when he found her this morning was troubling.

To change the subject, and take his mind off troublesome thoughts of Cyn, he glanced at his father's Caddy. "I see pop is here, burning the early morning light."

Tim sighed. "Yeah, he is. Your mama would kick his ass if she knew."

Jake chuckled, thinking of his fierce, five foot nothing, mother laying down the law. Grown men knew enough to get out of his petite mother's way when she was on the warpath. "How long has he been doing this?" He stood implacably while Tim hesitated, obviously trying to balance loyalty with concern. "Don't worry. I'm not going to tell Mom."

"I don't like to squeal, but he needs to slow down." Tim shook his head. "It's been about a week, while your mother is in Chicago for a showing. He told me he's trying to stay one step ahead of things. Apparently, there's some trouble brewing. Rumor has it the companies about to go bust."

"Don't worry. It's not going to happen. I've got everything in hand."

"Have I got your word on that?" Tim asked.

"Definitely. I know who's been sabotaging operations, and I'm going to shut them down," Jake stated, coming up with plan B on the fly. If he couldn't afford to bide his time because of danger to Cyn, he'd flush the bastards out.

"You want me to keep it confidential?" Tim asked.

"Hell no, go ahead and spread it around," Jake replied, seeing the comprehension in Tim's eyes as he walked away.

He walked down the quiet corridors toward his father's corner office, and went in. Silas looked up from the spreadsheets he'd been reading; a glass of whiskey at his elbow, and a cigar burning in the ashtray. He glanced at Jake, his eyes warming, before he frowned. "So, it's true, you're home."

Jake smiled a little, seeing through his father's bluff. He didn't like being caught breaking doctor's orders. "Isn't that against doctor's orders? What would Mom say?"

"You'd damned well better not tell her. This is the only time of day I can indulge my vices." He pointed to the bottle of Scotch on his desk. "Want one?"

"No thanks." Jake took the bottle away, carrying it back to the wet bar, and putting it in the cabinet.

"Well hell, boy. I don't need you preaching to me, too. Heard you made a spectacle of yourself at the dance, and insulted some of our local belles. That's no way to gain local favor, or get their land for our expansion."

Jake studied him, noting that while his dad was a little pale, he'd lost none of his vigor. At least he knew he could handle some direct questions that needed to be asked. "And screwing the locals out of their land is a way to gain local favor?"

Silas scowled at him. "Who the hell said that? Did that information come from your fancy bean counters, or that nosy PI you hired, because it isn't true. Forensic audit, my ass; I never cheated anyone in my life, boy."

"I know you haven't, personally." Jake pulled the preliminary audit and Investigator's reports out of his duffle bag. "Take a look at these," he stated, handing the reports over to his dad.

Silas glanced at the cover sheets. "You didn't have to hire them to find out we're losing money. I could have told you that. We're being run out of the market by bigger companies, that's why we need to expand operations."

"No, you're losing money because someone is embezzling. You're being taken by a ruthless con man and he's setting you up to take a fall with these bogus land deals."

Silas leaned back in his chair, to pin him with a frown. "Bogus land deals?"

"The ranches you've been buying up..."

"What about them?"

"North Star Developments has used extortion to obtain them on your behalf. The man behind it is a first class con man."

"Extortion...now hold on there, boy..."

"I've got proof." Jake cut in. He pulled out the threatening note Cyn gave him. "Here's a little sample."

Silas read it, his brow furrowing. "This doesn't mention North Star, or Randal Industries. What makes you think it has anything to do with us?"

"I got it from Cyn Taylor."

"That redheaded broad, with the hot temper. You can't believe a word she says. Why, do you know what she did to Dwain Hawkins? She damned near killed him."

"And do you know why? He put the moves on her, hard. She kicked his scrawny ass, and set the goats on him."

Silas hooted with laughter. "The hell you say. He never told me that."

"He wouldn't."

Silas shook his head. "It doesn't add up. The times I saw her, she was a drab little thing, hardly a beauty like her sisters. What man would try to romance her?"

Jake tensed at the slur. Cyn hadn't been kidding when she said she'd been invisible. Were the men in this county blind? "Watch your tongue, Dad."

Silas pinned him with a slow, sly look, and nodded. "So that's the way the wind blows. She's the redhead you picked up."

Jake gave his father a focused look, remaining quiet.

"Is that where you're staying?"

"Yeah, under an assumed name, for now." Jake waved his hand at the reports. "Those are your copies, Dad. Take them home, read them, and start following doctor's orders for god's sake."

"You expect me to go home in the midst of this," Silas questioned, a frown deepening the furrows in his brow.

"You need to rest up, if you're going to retake the helm of the new improved Randal Industries." Jake watched the startled, but excited look his dad gave him, confirming his thought that his father wasn't ready to retire.

"Then you don't want to stay? Your mother and I were kind of hoping you'd settle down here."

"I'm moving Scion headquarters back home to Cider City. Maud, my Gal Friday, is flying in today. I'm assigning her to you temporarily. She'll be our go between."

"Good god, you can't assign that harpy to ride herd on me. I'm a sick man."

"Yeah right," Jake replied, looking at the two fingers of Scotch in his father's glass. "Here's how it's going to play out..."

Cyn walked into the Coffee Cup Café at noon, carrying Dora's birthday gift. She spotted her friend at the counter, and hopped onto the stool next to her with a grin. This getaway was just what she needed after the twin distractions of flirting with Jake and fending off Cordial. "Happy birthday."

"Same to you." Dora gave her new jeans and blouse a pleased look. "I'm glad to see the makeover continues."

"Thanks." Cyn stated, preening a little. "That's not all that's continuing."

"You're still seeing JT!" Dora gasped.

Cyn nodded, a thrill surging though her at the thought. He was her very own stud if she wanted him. Who was she to turn that down? "He's my Mr. Smith."

"Get outta here," Dora exclaimed, her jaw dropping. She leaned in to ask, "Does Cordial know?"

"Not yet. She thinks he's a motorcycle gang member or something, and here for monkey business."

Dora chuckled. "How right she is. I bet you two had a laugh when you figured that out last night."

Cyn's face heated.

"You didn't have another un-kissed evening?" Dora asked with a frown.

"I had a half-kissed evening."

"Oh, good gravy, why?"

"We were interrupted by his friends, Mack and Zane, and I panicked and ran. Imagine my chagrin when he showed up at the ranch this morning with my panties in his pocket."

Dora hooted with laughter. "You didn't leave them behind!"

"Oh, I did. I was in a hurry to get out of there before he came back and demanded answers. If you ever faced down a frustrated, aroused man, who'd just found out the woman who'd seduced him was actually a virgin, you'd understand. I ran like a scared rabbit."

Dora let out a sigh. "Boy, you do have the devil's own bad luck when it comes to men. But you say it continues. Tell me more, girlfriend."

"He says I can taste him."

Dora giggled. "What are you going to do about it?"

"What do you think?"

Chapter 6

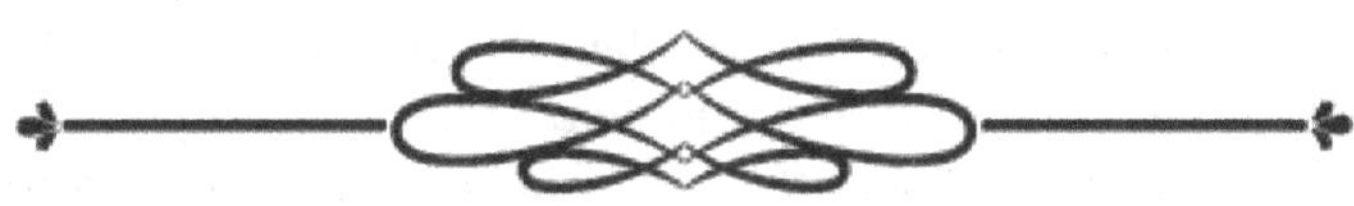

Jake opened the door to his bungalow after eight that evening, tired and horny, and hoping to see Cyn lying naked in his bed. He flipped on the light switch and looked around, his shoulders sagging when he saw no sign of her. He should have known it wasn't going to be that easy to snag the shy filly.

Thoughts of her had kept him going through this crappy day. After the stormy meeting with his father, and picking up Maud from the airport, he'd settled into his office behind *Branded,* and got down to business. He called Zane to tell him about the obscene letters Cyn had received. He suspected that Dwain Hawkins was responsible, the same man he suspected had been bleeding his father dry for months to the tune of a million dollars. The guy was slippery, covering his tracks well. It was the mark of a professional con man. Now all he needed was proof. If he made a move against Cyn before that could be uncovered, Jake would come down on him like a house of bricks.

Jake shrugged out of his jacket, tossed it on the bed, and saw the book lying open on his pillow. His cock twitched when he saw the title, *Bound to Serve.* He grinned, relief surging through him, melting his fatigue away, as he scooped up the erotic romance novel. Cyn had accepted his invitation, in her own unexpected way. He scanned the first chapter...

"Condor caught Bridget disobeying him. He left the document in plain sight to test her compliance. She'd defied him, as expected. The instant she sensed his presence, she looked up at him, giving him the guilty blush of a kid caught with her hand in the cookie jar. An instant later, she was smiling at him, unapologetic. His heart skipped a beat while his cock stirred.

"A private island, huh? I'm not surprised."

Her instincts were sharp; he had to give her that, but he was keeping her in the dark for a reason. She'd want to take over. Hell, she threatened to take over him, and it couldn't be allowed. Not on his watch.

Bridget clutched the file, gauging Condor's unyielding expression. She wouldn't have to resort to subterfuge if he'd share the info, like a normal agent. His brooding expression told her to save her breath. Wary, she watched him roll up his sleeves and sit down on a jump seat.

"Kick off your shoes, take off your jacket and piece, and come here." He patted his lap.

She gulped; he couldn't mean to actually take her over his knee. The flight crew might overhear. "No."

"You did agree to be trained. You'll take it over my knee."

She stood there, both shocked and aroused. If she balked, he'd replace her. The thought made her kick off her pumps. Her toes curled into the carpet, as she gazed at the masterful look in his eyes. Almost without thought, she took off her blazer, reminded of her bold stripping in the director's office. His interested gaze only made her hotter. She removed her gun and holster, disarmed in more ways than one. Maybe doing him would give her clarity. She walked toward him. "You don't have to do this. I'm a quick study. I can fake it."

He smiled. "I can't. Every minute you delay is a demerit."

So, he strove for reality on assignment. The knowledge should have stopped her cold. It didn't. She rolled her eyes. "What are you, one of the nuns at grammar school?"

"And did they paddle my little hellcat?"

"No. Nobody ever dared paddle me." One look at his laughing eyes told her he was daring.

Condor smiled and crooked a finger. "Come."

The demand was calmly voiced, but there was steel behind it. Just the thought of stretching out across his hard lap made her heart trip. He didn't reach out to grab her; it would have been easier if he had. "Fine, train me, Dino," she muttered, carefully draping herself over his lap while her face burned. His cock was semi-erect under her. Bridget gasped at the unexpectedly erotic feel, and arched away to break the disconcerting contact. Condor pushed her back down.

"Uh, uh."

He lifted up her skirt and she went still, mortified. Oh no, she was wearing her pink lace panties; fine lingerie was a weakness of hers. Who knew, when she'd put them on this morning, that she'd be draped over Condor's knee?

"You've so much to learn, Kitten." He rubbed her ass through her panties. "And there's not much time to teach you."

Bridget burned where his big hand touched her. Her sensitive pubes pressed against his hard leg, her pussy wet with need. She held her breath. He kept caressing her through her panties. Tears, she put down to nerves, sprang to her eyes. She blinked them away. Focus. She couldn't let him undo her with a single touch.

"Tell me, Kitten, why are you being punished?"

The amusement in his tone made her mad, even as his big hand caressing her bottom made her aroused. "Because you're a dinosaur." His chuckle was like warm honey.

"No, because you disobeyed me and snooped at the file," he replied, fingering the waistband of her panties. "Say it."

He'd probably left the damned file out on purpose to trap her, and she'd fallen for it. It didn't say much for her instincts. She let out a sigh of frustration. "I disobeyed and snooped."

"And are you sorry?"

"Will it keep you from spanking me?"

"No."

"Then, no, I'm not sorry." She'd gathered valuable information and if it cost her a red ass, so be it. His wicked chuckle made her stiffen, a moment before his big hand smacked her bottom. She bit back a cry, shocked by the stinging heat, but not wanting to alert the flight crew.

"Count the spanks for me, Kitten."

"No," she gasped, incensed by the outrageous demand.

"We go to five, honey, now count."

His big hand came down on her right cheek and she gasped as her stiff clit rubbed against his leg, "One."

"Very good," he praised.

She actually melted at the praise, how sick was that? He spanked her left cheek, and her stiff clit bumped up against his leg. She bit back a whimper. "Two."

"Ttt-three," she wailed when he smacked her another quick blow. Not two more, she'd either come or cry, either of which would be humiliating. She wanted to move, but couldn't make herself.

The leather pants she was lying against were warm, and Condor was even hotter. She groaned as his rousing cock pressed against her. Her sex pulsed, growing wet while her bottom burned. "Four," she gasped when his big hand landed again.

"Five," she gasped as he caught her from the bottom, barely holding back a moan.

Stunned, she lay molded to him, on the verge of orgasm, while he rubbed her hot bottom. She couldn't resist leaning into his arousing touch, even while her face burned with embarrassment. The eroticism of being turned over Condor's knee was deep and disturbing. Assertive as she was, that she could be broken by it, stunned her. She quivered, needing him to finish what he'd started. Condor's cock was hard below her, his breathing rapid. His hand rubbed lower. She whimpered when he cupped her mound.

"Good, you're wet," he stated.

His reserved tone broke through her sexual heat. Burning with need, she throbbed as his hot hand cupped her sex. Just a little more pressure and she'd come. If only he'd finish it, it might help her refocus. She arched against him, and he swatted her mound.

"No."

She bit back a raw sob at the quick sting; he was nothing but a tease. He pushed her off his lap.

Sprawled on the floor in front of him, she boldly gazed up at him. His eyes were a deep brown, speaking of arousal.

He frowned. "I'm going to teach you your basic submissive position now. Up on your knees, legs apart, palms resting on your thighs."

She tried to do his bidding.

He looked her over, approvingly. "You are a quick study. This is submissive position number one. Of course, you'll usually be naked and open to me when flowing into it."

Her eyes widened when she visualized the scene. Naked and open, huh? Taking him might let her refocus on her goals.

"Now up and strip."

He was going to take her, after all. Thrilled, she sprang to her feet, a bit unsteadily, her heart racing. Condor reached out to steady her. His big hand circling her arm, made her lean toward him. He gave her a tight frown and let go. With trembling hands, she unbuttoned her silk blouse and slipped it off, reveling in the fact that Condor couldn't keep his hot gaze off of her. Emboldened, she unzipped her skirt and let it fall to the floor..."

Jake grinned. It seemed his student wanted to try some spice and he was happy to deliver. He liked his couplings with a little kink. Hell, she wanted to taste him; his cock throbbed as he remembered her words. At the rate things were going; he'd have blue balls within the week. He strode over to the phone and dialed zero, waiting impatiently for his lover in training to pick up. She answered on the third ring.

"Hello," her voice was low, hesitant.

His cock swelled behind his zipper when he heard her sultry voice. It was like he was one of Pavlov's dogs, drooling after her. "I'd like some room service, Cyn."

"But I told you..."

"Special room service," he explained, hearing her sexy, quick intake of breath.

"Oh."

The shock and excitement in her honeyed voice made him leak pre-cum, as his cock twitched behind his fly. This was going to be good. He ached to be her guide in the bedroom, but he was going to call the shots, even if it killed him to slow things down. "Coming?" he asked, worried she might back down.

"Yes."

He smiled when she clicked down the phone in a hurry, thanking his lucky stars that she wanted him as much as he needed her. He put down the phone, and pulled out a straight-backed chair, positioning it in the perfect place for her spanking.

Cyn walked the distance from her cabin to Jake's bungalow, keeping a wary eye out for Cordial. The lights were out in the big house, which meant the girls were out on the town. Most people probably were on Saturday night, but Jake was saving the night for her seduction. Her heart raced at the thought, she ached to finish what he'd started. She still couldn't believe she'd had the moxie to present him with her wish list, in the form of one of her favorite erotic romances.

Her palms were damp on the wicker tray she carried. It was a good cover in case she was observed, and she figured he might be hungry. Knowing it was beyond her to play it cool, she picked up the pace, hurrying to his door. A warm night breeze blew the skirt of her sundress around her legs, as she stepped up onto his porch. When he swept the door open before she could knock, she sucked in a startled breath. "You were..."

"Waiting for you? Always, sugar."

Cyn's hungry gaze swept over the chiseled planes of Jake's handsome face, before drifting to focus on the manly bulge in his jeans. It was just as huge as she remembered. Licking her bottom lip, she gazed back up at his reckless heartbreaker's smile, and creamed. He still looked delicious, and slightly dangerous to her, but she noticed signs of fatigue on his face. He'd had a hard day. "If you'd rather take a nap first, I'd give you a rain check."

His low chuckle made her toes curl inside her sandals.

"Not a chance." He glanced down at the tray. "What'd you bring me, sugar? Or is this just window dressing to hide our rendezvous?"

"Actually, it's a little bit of both. Cordial is having you watched. But I thought you might be hungry, so I brought you supper." She watched his sultry smile, melting her where she stood, as her sex tingled.

He took a deep whiff. "Fried chicken and biscuits."

"And apple cobbler," she stated, self-conscious. It was just ordinary food, but his tender smile told her he was taking it as special.

"You're beautiful, and you can cook too. I'm a lucky man. Where have you been all my life, Cyn?"

"In the barn or the studio." She blushed. "And there's a treat for us...for later. If we do anything, that is," she added, feeling out of her depth.

"Believe me, we're going to do something," he replied, stepping back to let her in. "Come inside, and put the tray on the dresser, sugar. Good as your cooking smells, I'm sure you're far more tasty."

Trembling, she did as he said, his body heat igniting her libido as she brushed past him. She somehow managed to make it to the dresser without dropping the tray. His sexy chuckle made her whimper.

"You are good for my ego, baby," Jake murmured.

And he was good for her once sleeping hormones, Cyn decided, laying the tray down on the dresser. She slowly turned to face him, her nipples budding.

This time she intended to see him naked, no matter what. Jake leaned against the closed door, watching her with the steamiest look in his eyes. Her sex rippled in response. She couldn't resist another peek at the growing bulge inside his jeans.

"Come here, sugar," he demanded, quirking a finger at her.

She noticed the chair he'd placed in the middle of the floor, the novel she'd presented him with lying open on the bed, and bit her lip. He'd read it. She walked toward him, conceding there was no going back. Looking deep into his warm whiskey eyes, she decided to nibble her way from his chin to his toes, paying extra special attention to the manly parts in between.

Jake smiled, sitting down on the straight back chair, and patted his lap. "You'll take it over my knee."

He was going to spank her. Her tummy quivered, and her pussy clenched, as she stepped into his space, her thighs pressing against his powerful legs. She'd asked for it, but was she ready for a fantasy to become reality? Looking into the teasing depths of his eyes, she saw arousal and affection, and let her last fears go.

"I've got ya," he commented, taking her hand, and rubbing his thumb over her wrist.

Cyn melted while he maintained a firm, yet tender, grip on her wrist. His hand was big, easily encircling her wrist, and she felt small and protected by contrast.

He smiled, and tumbled her down over his lap.

She went over his knee with a gasp, shocked, and turned on, as her belly and thighs made contact with his firm lap and the harder bulge of his cock. "But I wanted to taste you," she gasped, as a delaying tactic.

"All in good time, Cyn. You placed yourself in my hands, and you're going to get it." He flipped up her skirt, baring her panty-clad bottom, and she felt heat rush through her. It was a good thing that she was wearing one of her sexy fairytale undies. The pink lace panties were probably a bit tame for a man of Jake's sophisticated tastes.

"God, you're so sexy," he stated, spreading his palm out across her bottom.

Cyn felt a flutter of excitement and alarm at the size of his reach, as the heat of his huge paw seeped through her silk panties. They weren't much of a barrier. She'd fantasized about this, but would the real thing be as good? She trembled, her nipples budding, achingly hard inside her bra, her stiff clit jutting out, throbbing. She moaned as it pressed against his thigh. When Jake raised his palm and gave her a quick smack, she whimpered at the sting and speed. "But I wasn't ready..."

He swatted her again, this time a little harder. "Ready now?" he teased.

Cyn's sex creamed. "Oh my god, yes," she gasped.

She trembled as he rained teasing blows across her bottom, and arched up, hoping for more. He was toying with her, making her ache for a harder paddling. "Please," she wailed. He stopped, and she let out a sob of frustration.

"Want more?" he asked, toying with the waistband of her panties.

She wriggled, trying to inflame him, and nodded.

"Say it."

"Please, I want more."

"More, what? Do you require a proper spanking, Cyn?" He fingered the lacey waistband, his fingers venturing beneath, to scorch a path over her stinging ass. "Do you want me to pull these pretties down?"

"Oh, yes, pull them down." She arched into his touch when his hot fingertips touched her bare flesh. "Spank me properly."

"Excellent." He pulled her panties down to her ankles.

Hobbled as the panties tangled around her ankles, Cyn felt the restraint deep inside, and it only served to turn her on more. Her sex wept for him, trembling as the resistance increased her excitement.

"What a good girl." He spanked her harder.

She whimpered with need and arched up, taking them as foreplay. "I'm a woman, not a girl," she insisted, remembering their discussion at the ball.

"You're a girl in the bedroom." He caught her on the bottom of her ass with his open palm, driving her into his thigh.

She cried out with delight. Her stiff clit rubbing against his hard thigh, making her hungry sex spasm.

"Like that, do you?" he asked, pleased, doing it again.

She shrieked with pleasure. "Yes," she admitted, shuddering, the contact with her clit increasing.

"Now be a good girl, and reach down and play with your clit, Cyn. I want you to come while I spank you."

Embarrassed by the sultry command, she hesitated, even while she ached to obey.

"Now," he commanded, his open swat catching the bottom of her ass harder, driving her higher.

She gasped and did as he said, her hand rushing to her clit, while he heated up the spanking, catching the bottom of her ass over and over again, making her moan. Her body tightened, and her sex spasmed, her ass throbbing as she came with a shriek. Her hand fell away from her clit. Jake's hand replaced it, his rough fingertip pressing her clit, his fingers filling her cunt, his little finger dipping into her juices and pressing into her anus. She gasped, as he loved her that way, wringing out and extended orgasm, which tore through her until she was limp. When it was over, she lay across his lap, totally drained.

Jake pulled her up, taking her into his arms, rocking her. "We have to set a few ground rules, Cyn."

Cyn leaned against him, loving the low rumble of his voice, his racing heartbeat, and his manly essence. His cock was still rock hard under her hot ass, reminding her of what they'd just done, and what was to come. "Rules?"

His hand cupped her breast. "Un huh, three little rules. First, I want you naked and ready for me when I say so."

Her nipple beaded as he fanned a fingertip over the tingling peak, making her gasp. They were still fully dressed, if you didn't count her panties about her ankles. She was putty in his hands, and she wouldn't have it any other way. Nibbling his ear, as he gave her nipple a little pinch, she complained. "That's barbaric."

"Welcome to the Stone Age, sugar," Jake stated, unbuttoning the row of buttons down the front of her sundress. He peeled the garment open to expose her full breasts encased in a pink lace bra that matched her panties. "Second, I like the sexy underwear, and the dresses. You'll wear them for me."

"No," she replied, rebelling. She'd never taken well to being told what to do. "JT, in case you haven't noticed, I do ranch work."

"It's Jake or sir when I'm disciplining you. When we have our sessions, you'll comply."

"Or?"

"You'll get lots more spankings."

Cyn's bare bottom burned against his lap. "Like that's much of a threat. I loved it, and you know it." She snuggled closer, saying, "I've got a demand of my own."

"Such as?" he asked.

"I get to taste you soon, and then as much as I want."

He groaned, his hand slipping under her skirt to touch her wet sex.

Cyn cried out when Jake's index finger homed in on her stiff clit. He pressed the sensitized nub and she moaned, instantly throbbing with arousal again. He tweaked it, and she muffled her cries against his broad chest, as she came. When she recovered, she peered up at him. "If this is how you conduct your negotiations, no wonder you're known as the Barbarian."

He chuckled. "I'm a man who knows what he wants." He kissed her. "Third, you'll be bare and open for me when I need you."

Her eyes widened as she gazed at him. He wasn't kidding. "Another Stone Age thing?"

"You got it, sugar." He spread her legs, his little finger probing her ass. "Oh, and fourth...we need to keep your tight little rosebud lubed for my cock."

Her breath caught, as both her ass and pussy quivered. She'd been afraid the prospect of anal sex would turn him off. It was in chapter six of the book she'd given him. "We do?"

"I'll insist on it," he replied, kissing her hard.

Cyn gave herself to him, kissing him back. His tongue slipped inside her mouth to mate with hers. When the kiss ended, he stood up, and set her on her feet. She was secretly thrilled by his Stone Age demands. A hot and heavy affair was just what she needed. Her feet were still tangled up in her panties, and she fell against him, wrapping her arms around his neck.

"I think that's a yes," he commented with a laugh, his arms going around her.

"Oh yeah." She leaned against him, listening to his heartbeat race. At least she knew she wasn't the only one affected by this lust.

"My own present to unwrap."

Cyn's heart skipped a beat. "So, what's stopping you?"

He smiled, and pushed the dress off her shoulders. It fell, pooling at their feet. "Some things are better taken slowly."

Cyn burned when he looked at her. "But not me," she complained. She grabbed his belt undoing it, pulling it off him. "Are you going to tie me up sometime?" she asked, running the leather through her hands, and giving him a challenging look.

"Would you like me to?" he asked, watching her.

"Maybe," she replied, but her face flamed. "It's in chapter eight."

"Knowing it's coming might spoil the experience."

She gazed up at his mesmerizing face. "Not with you, cowboy. Nothing could be too tame with you. You're still wearing too many clothes," she complained.

He smiled. "So, strip me."

It was all she needed to hear. She stepped forward, forgetting her hobbles, and gasped as she teetered off balance.

"Easy love." He reached out to steady her. "Let's finish you first."

"You wouldn't have spanked me so hard if you wanted easy." She burned as she kicked off her panties, enjoying his sexy grin. He was getting off on her eager delight for him, and she didn't mind a bit. Feeling like a predator, she backed him against the dresser. His eyes twinkled, as she started to unbutton his shirt.

"Hungry, are you?" he teased.

"You ought to know, you started the fire." The last button slipped out of its hole, and she opened his shirt to ogle him. His well-defined muscles, tight male nipples, and six pack abs were irresistible. She leaned forward to lap at one flat brown disc, it beaded under her tongue. Yum, he was delicious!

He groaned, shrugging out of his shirt.

She licked a path to his other nipple, then sunk down to taste his six-pack, and dip her tongue inside his naval. She swirled it around making him growl and jerk. He was ticklish there, excellent. She did it again, distracting him as she unzipped his jeans. His growl made her glance up at him for approval. The heat in his gaze made her cream. Trembling with excitement, she tugged down his pants and his erection sprang out at her. He was going commando.

Cyn gazed at his cock for a heartbeat, admiring it. It was huge, long, thick, and heavy enough to hang down at his thigh. The red head was blunt and mushroom shaped. Her cool fingers ran down the hot silky length of him, and he hissed, his cock's head rising up. A drop of pre-cum beaded on the slit. She leaned forward to lap at it and sighed with pleasure, feeling Jake shudder. Suddenly she found her female power. She lapped at his slit again, loving the salty male taste of him, as he leaked more cum, making him groan.

"Lick the head," Jake ordered.

She didn't need further urging as she swirled her tongue around his cock's hot velvety head, stealing another drop of cum off the slit.

"Shit," he bit out trembling. "Suck on the head."

After another lick, she opened her mouth and took him inside, only able to contain a little. The erotic feel of his hard throbbing cock inside her mouth was addictive. She sucked, and both her hands wrapped firmly around his shaft. He hissed, his cock twitching under her ministrations. She could feel him tightening getting ready to come, and her pussy quivered with excitement. She wanted it all.

"That's it, sugar, give it up now."

She gave him a mew of disappointment, her mouth still keeping him. He gently rubbed his thumb over her cheek. "Now," he stated gently.

Reluctantly, she let the head slip out of her mouth, giving his cock a final lick of departure. He drew her to her feet, and pulled her into his arms. Cyn went with a hunger, burning as his mouth claimed hers. Then, he carried her across the room to place her on the bed. He came down on top of her, and she welcomed his weight—the promise of his possession.

He broke the kiss to string a line of kisses down her throat, over her collarbone, to one hard nipple. He took the bud into his hot mouth drawing on it, making her squirm with need as she felt the pull deep inside her. Then he moved onto the other, teasing her to distraction, drawing the sensitive bud hard into his mouth, making her cry out. Arching up, into his hot mouth, she ran her hands over his back.

He moved on to scatter kisses down her abdomen, and she burned. When he moved down, settling between her spread legs, she couldn't help blushing. Her breath caught in her throat, and she tried to pull him up, to no avail, Jake would not be moved.

"Let me."

When his hot tongue rested against her swollen clit, Cyn's eyes rolled back in her head, and she let out a shriek. It was that earth shattering. Pushing her hungry sex against his mouth, she was lost to ecstasy. Jake began to lap at her, his tongue teasing her, before pressing into her quivering pussy. She rolled on the bed, but his hands reached up to hold her hips fast. There was no getting away from the pleasure he was making her feel, and she didn't want to escape, as she throbbed with arousal under his rough and talented tongue.

He'd already made her come so many times, but she felt the pressure build inside her again. He took the bud of her clit into his mouth, and drew on it. Cyn exploded, her sex convulsing, empty. Jake surged up her body and thrust into her in one quick motion. Cyn cried out at the invasion. As he finished taking her virginity, Jake sealed her mouth with his, silencing her cry.

He lay still, breathing hard on top of her, his body tense as he waited for her newly opened pussy to become accustomed to him. She closed her eyes, feeling stunned by the sensation of his huge cock filling her. Her after spasms rippled, making her gasp, and him growl. She smiled up at him and rocked against him, only to feel his huge cock delve deeper inside.

"Easy babe, take it slow." He slowly started to withdraw, and then rock back into her.

Cyn arched up to meet his strokes, taking more of him. He was huge. Her eyes widened with surprise. "More," she moaned, as his hot cock filled her. He rocked into her, harder and deeper, until they both gasped. "Oh yes." She wrapped her legs around him, forcing him deeper, and wincing, but not letting him go.

He lost control, surging into her, again and again, until she tightened, coming, shouting his name. He surged into her once more and exploded, coming hard and fast, tight against her cervix. When Jake eased off her, pulling her close, Cyn snuggled against him, sated and dazzled. It was everything she'd dreamed of.

Chapter 7

Jake stroked Cyn's supple back, enjoying the feel of her soft curves tucked tight against his body. It'd been a hell of a day, and she'd made it brighter. He held her close, feeling possessive. "Come on," he stated, rousing her, forcing himself to let go of her breast as he rolled out of bed. He gazed down at her, flushed from their lovemaking, and knew he was a lucky man. He bent to scoop her up.

"Where are you taking me?" she asked, clinging to him.

Jake felt honored by the affection, and trust he saw in her eyes. At least she trusted him in the bedroom. "You'll see," he replied, shouldering his way into the bathroom with her snuggled in his arms. Her breasts tantalized him, the nipples hardening, rubbing against his chest, and making his mouth water with the need to taste the strawberry tits. Hell, she'd tasted sweet all over. But he knew her first time would make her sore, and he wouldn't abuse her trust, no matter how horny they both were. He switched on the large walk-in shower, making the shower a little cooler than he liked.

He had a sneaking suspicion ice cubes in the North Pole couldn't cool him off when Cyn was with him. "I must say, you do run a first-class operation, Miss Cyn. The double shower with the body sprays was a stroke of genius."

"Cordial actually kitted this dude operation out before she lost interest, and I came back to take over."

"That's right, you didn't always live here." He recalled her talk of duty.

"I actually used to have a life, at least kind of, if spending hours cooped up in my studio counts."

"Oh, it definitely counts." He was pleased when she smiled.

"I'm glad you think so," she purred, rubbing her cheek against his shoulder.

"Well, my dad always thought being artsy was a bit weird, and according to Cordial, I'm an embarrassment to the whole family. I'm usually spattered with paint, or dirt from the ranch."

"Forget them. I like you best when you're spattered. Like, that dirt on your nose when you bumped into me was cute." He was warmed when she beamed up at him.

"Thanks."

"So, tell me more about your stepmother," he commented, trying to get more information out of her. He had a suspicion she was linked to North Star, but no proof.

"I don't want to talk about her, okay?"

"Okay." Jake stepped them under the spray. He set aside his line of questioning, and instead, luxuriated in the sensual feel of the woman in his arms, as water cascaded over and around them. She closed her eyes in seeming bliss, his cock stiffened again, and he groaned. Would he never get enough of this redheaded siren? Probably not, he decided, letting Cyn slip down his body to stand before him.

"That's nice," she whispered, rubbing her nipples across his chest.

He spread his feet shoulder's length apart, and pulled her wet curves into his body. "Oh yeah," he agreed. "Now behave, you're sore, and we can't do anymore tonight." Instead, she shimmied against him making him crazy. Reaching behind her, he gave her a sharp spank, so he could think. She pouted, blushing, her body radiant. Her lush lips were tempting him. He was in deep trouble. "Behave now, so I can wash you."

"Yes sir," she replied unrepentantly.

He soaped up a washcloth, and swirled it over her lovely body, paying special attention to her tempting tits, watching them tremble, as she inhaled a shaky breath. He rubbed the terry cloth over her nipples, and they beaded, as her knees wobbled. She moaned, leaning into him.

"No fair. How come you don't have to behave?"

"Do you want me to stop?" he asked, stilling the washcloth.

"No. Please don't stop." She pressed into him.

"I won't," he commented gently, and then turned her around, and spread her feet apart.

"Let's scrub that saucy bottom."

"I'd rather have you take it. I won't be sore there."

He smiled at her eagerness, his heart tripping a beat. She was hot, adventurous, and altogether perfect for him, but she wasn't ready. He teased her tight portal with a soapy finger. "All in good time. Arch your back, sugar."

"But when?" she asked.

He bit back a groan as she pushed her cute butt out at him, and slipped a finger inside, making her gasp. "Fuck yourself on my finger. Try it out." She froze for a minute, and then arched back riding his finger, her tight back passage pulling at him. He groaned, his stiff cock bobbing. She moaned, arching her back to give him better access. He restrained himself. If he spanked her, he'd fuck her. Instead, he reached out to adjust the body spray, aiming it at her stiff clit. She let out a cry, her backside clutching at his finger, as she came. He supported her when her knees wobbled, his finger coming free of her ass. He held her tight until she came back to earth.

Cyn turned to lay her head on Jake's shoulder, enjoying his touch, the slippery feel of his body against hers. She'd wanted a dream lover, but he was way beyond her expectations. "That was—"

"Sexy," he filled in.

"Earth shattering." She lapped at his nipples, drinking a droplet of water off his skin. His cock pressed hot and hard against her slick thigh. "It's your turn," she stated, stepping close enough to let his erection slip between her thighs. It rubbed hot and tantalizing against her mound.

"No." He pulled back. "You're too sore."

"So? Spank me later," she replied, taking advantage of his retreat, by fisting his cock. He growled, thrusting into her hands, while he scowled at her. She wrapped both hands around his hot crock to hold him. "Let's see if water power works on you." She took the handheld spray, and aimed it at his cock while jacking him off. He groaned, and his balls grew tight against his body. She watched, fascinated and, playing a hunch, aimed the spray at them. Jake hissed in reaction, his cock leaking pre cum. "Interesting." She was pleased with her experiment.

"Stop teasing the bear," he groaned, but throbbed in her gasp. Cyn laughed, and kept fisting him harder, as she moved the spray to his anus. He shook, letting out a roar, and spurted. "And I think we just found the sweet spot," she commented, crowing with delight.

"Don't get any ideas," he growled, his cock spurting.

Cyn sank down to capture him in her mouth. She drew on his cock, taking it deeper in her mouth. She sucked, breathing deep, felt him tremble and give her everything he had. She drew on him, draining him, and licking him clean. She looked up to find Jake looking at her with wonder.

He pulled her to her feet "Where did you learn that?"

"My personal library. You're the first chance I've have to put it into practice." His gaze smoldered at the last statement.

"And I'd better be the only."

His possessive statement thrilled her, but she wasn't fooling herself that she could keep him for long. When news of his return got out, every eligible woman in town would beat a trail to his door. How could she compete with that? She saw his irked expression and knew her silence bugged him. Good. It might be good to keep him guessing. Her eyes widened when he slapped off the shower, growled and bodily pulled her out of the shower.

"Now get this Cyn. I won't share you with anyone. You're mine," he insisted, bending to kiss her.

"I'm yours," Cyn whispered with a sigh, as his mouth claimed hers. She rubbed her tingling nipples against him, drawn into his possessive embrace. His tongue swept into her mouth mating with hers, as his hands swept down her slick back, to cup her ass and squeeze. She moaned pressing tight to him, her sex throbbing, as his cock stirred.

He broke the kiss to rub his manhood against her. "You belong to me Cyn, say it," he hissed.

"I belong to you," she agreed, with a pleasured whimper, rocking against him, watching his whiskey eyes darken. When he set her back on her heels, and reached for a towel, she let out a whimper of complaint. His stern glance silenced her as he dried her off. It felt surreal to have him pamper her, take care of her, spank her, but he did it so well. Rubbing a towel over her hair, he made her scalp tingle as he was touching her, then he finger-combed her red hair back behind her ears.

He smiled, seeing her dazzled gaze, bent to give her a quick kiss, and a teasing smack on the bottom. "Play time is over, sugar. Now let's eat, and talk."

Cyn blushed. She didn't particularly want to talk. He wanted to know things she didn't like to talk about. Like her fucked up family dynamics. Nevertheless, she took his hand, and let him waltz her back into the bedroom. Gazing at the rumpled bed, she ached to be back in it with him. Things were so simple when they let their bodies do the communicating.

"Have a seat and I'll get your supper," she stated, and smiled when he did. He couldn't question her with his mouth full. She turned to see him sitting on the bed, sprawled naked against the headboard like a male centerfold. She'd love to paint him that way, she decided, walking over to put the tray on his lap. She watched him lift the lid, heard his stomach growl. "You really are starved."

"I worked nonstop, and didn't have time to eat."

"That's not good for you. If you wear yourself out, you'll be no use to your father."

He looked up at her, and gave her a concerned, half smile. "Ditto."

The barb hit home. She'd been running herself ragged, and they were still losing money. At the rate she was going, she didn't know which would be depleted first, the ranch, or her. "Try my chicken then. At least it never killed anybody."

He patted the spot next to him. "Join me."

"Trust me, I wouldn't poison you," she teased, but eagerly climbed into bed next to him, and nibbled a drumstick. She snuggled as close as she could, shivering with delight when the curve of her hip pressed his, and the side of her breast brushed his arm.

"Not even after what Dwain Hawkins did to you?" Jake teased. "He works for Randal Industries after all."

The reminder made her frown. Jake might be a dreamboat, but he did employ a creep, or at least his father had. "I might consider slipping him a laxative, but not you."

"Thanks for the vote of confidence." Jake chuckled, and bit into the chicken.

Now that she'd told him about Dwain's behavior, would Jake take steps to stop him? She knew for a fact hers wasn't the only ranch he was using dirty tricks to get. She'd hesitated to tell her father about her concerns, not wanting to bother him. After all, what could he do behind bars? Now she might have to enlist her dad's support on his next visitor's day. Cordial rarely went there so there was little chance of running into her.

Jake dug into the food with gusto. "This is as good as it smells. Thanks for feeding me."

"You're welcome." She glowed, gratified to watch Jake polish off the rest of the chicken. He split a biscuit topped it with butter and honey, and lifted the morsel to her lips. She smiled, nibbling at the sweet treat, touched, and thrilled by the gesture as he handfed her. "Yum," she moaned out, licking honey off her lip.

"Allow me." He leaned forward to lick off the honey.

She trembled, as his tongue swept over the sweet spot, and then he slowly kissed her.

He broke the kiss, murmuring, "You are just as sweet as you look." Sobering, he continued, "We need to talk, Cyn," and watched her frown.

"About what?"

"The mess you're in. Tell me about Cordial, the ranch, and what Hawkins did to you." He watched her frown deepen. "Tell me about the letters."

"I really don't want to talk about them." Cyn replied, with a sigh.

"If it's coming from one of my people, I need to know."

Cyn sighed, and backed down. "I suppose you're right. Although, I can't say for sure who's sending them. They're anonymous, like I suppose all poison pen letters are, and obscene, talking about his giant cock, and intellect. Saying he's going to tame me. Some of them have scrawled notes on the back, in lipstick, telling me to run. I think maybe he's got a split personality or something."

"Did you report this to the police?"

"I didn't want to bother them with his lunatic ravings. The man is harmless, just annoying. He's never actually made good on any of his threats, and by the way, rumor has it, I'm not the only one getting them."

"I'll kill the bastard."

She smiled. "Don't bother, he isn't worth the effort. As you surmised, things are bad. My fathers in prison and my stepmother is being a royal pain, especially since we have to economize. She'd love to sell off and move to greener pastures. All I'm trying to do is hold the ranch together until my dad gets out, three months from now. As for Hawkins, he can go piss up a rope, I'm not about to sell the ranch."

"How long has your family owned it?"

"Generations. My great-great-grandfather founded the ranch."

"It's nice to have roots, I suppose." He was disturbed by the thought of walking away from his family all those years ago. He should have come back more often. Of course, he and his father had butted heads, and he'd had to grow up, establish himself. Now that he'd come home, he intended to make up for lost time, put down roots, mend some fences.

"You don't have any," she inquired, looking at him and then blushed. "Oh, excuse me, I didn't mean to..."

"Don't worry about it. It used to be true. But now I'm back, for keeps."

"You are?" she asked, nibbling her lip.

Was she worried she was going to be stuck with him? He didn't like the thought. "You don't have to worry about Dwain Hawkins anymore. I plan to fire him as soon, as I gather enough incriminating evidence against him, and turn him over to the law."

Her eyes widened. "So, he is doing something criminal?"

"He's formed a land management company called North Star. He's gobbling up the property for himself, cheating the sellers, and my father, and will probably skip town. I had a hell of a time convincing my father to let me play this out. He can't reconcile himself to the possibility he was conned. I'm trying to trick Hawkins into revealing his accomplices, whoever's backing his operation."

"Your father didn't take it well after all."

"No." He admired her sympathy for his dad, who'd tried to steamroll her, and admired her heart. "His pride is hurt more than anything, but he's a pragmatist. Eventually he came around. One trait we share is that we don't like to be cheated."

She smiled, leaning into Jake. "Thank you, thank you for taking care of Hawkins. It gives me one less battle to fight."

"I could help you…"

She pressed a hand to his mouth. "No, I can't allow that. I didn't sleep with you for that reason."

Jake nibbled her palm, making her gasp, stopping her protest. He'd act in her best interests whether she liked it or not.

Chapter 8

Cyn woke early the next morning, snuggled up to Jake's hunky body. His hand cupped her breast, making the nipple bead against his warm palm. His hot, steely erection, pressed into her bottom. *It wasn't just an erotic dream. They'd actually made love, repeatedly.* The thought made her smile. She pressed back against him, humming with pleasure as his cock slipped between the globes of her bottom, growing harder against her. He was going to open her there; she could hardly wait for him to take her ass.

Smiling, she glanced at the window, and gasped when she saw the sunrise. Good gravy, she hadn't intended to stay the night. Jake's cover was sure to be blown if she exposed him to more scrutiny. After last night, she fully understood his need for secrecy, and it was actually in her best interest to play along. If she made their affair public, Cordial would come nosing around. And the woman had spies, she knew at least one of the hands reported back to her. If one of them saw her leaving Jake's bungalow at this hour of the morning, it would be all over the ranch by noon. She simply couldn't risk it. And a selfish part of her wanted to keep him all to herself for a little bit longer. The minute his return was noted, Jake would be hit on by anything in skirts.

She glanced at the clock, and relaxed back against him when she saw it was only five thirty. Easing back against his sexy, hard body, she let out a pleasurable murmur. The lazy hands weren't up yet, and Pedro wouldn't be here for at least half an hour. There was time enough to linger, to revel in their newfound intimacy. Time enough to snuggle, before she had to sneak back to her place, and pretend she hadn't spent a lusty night in a guest's bed. She wiggled her ass against Jake's tantalizing morning erection, tempted to jump his bones while he was dozing, and let out a hiss of pleasure when it brushed against her sensitized mound. She did it again, and again, dry humping him, as he grew harder and bigger. The man had the most amazing cock. He let out a growl, his hand tightening on her breast.

Cyn bit back a moan, freezing as he woke, her nipple jutting out against his palm, her stiff clit tingling against his hot cock. She shouldn't start anything she didn't have time to finish. Sanity returning, she flicked another regretful glance at the clock. It was time to leave before she woke him up, it would be easier that way. With a sigh of regret, she pulled back the covers, and prepared to flee. Jake's hand tightened on her breast, holding her fast.

"Where do you think you're going, sugar?"

Oh lord, he was awake, but for how long? Was he aware that she'd been humping him? She prayed not, even as she thrilled to his sexy bedroom rumble. Sighing, she couldn't resist pressing her bottom a little tighter against his throbbing cock, gasping when he angled it to press directly against her clit. Jake growled, and teased the jutting nub repeatedly, with slight flicks of his hips.

"Sugar, any time you want me to pleasure you, all you have to do is ask," he stated, pinching her nipple.

Cyn whimpered, her nipple aching, her body tightening inside, her wet sex throbbing as her clit rested against his hot cock. The heat of him against her needy sex made her melt, turning to putty in his capable hands. "I have to get up, shower, and dress for the workday," she complained halfheartedly. "Otherwise..."

"The others will know we've been together," he finished grimly. "You ashamed of me, sugar?"

She heard the hurt behind his gruffness and placed her hand over his big one that still cupped her breast, to keep it in place. "It's not that. It's just that what we've shared is so special. I don't want to let the world intrude just yet. And you're trying to go undercover. If I get caught in your bed, it's going to start all kinds of speculation about you. You said it yourself; you need to catch Hawkins, before we go public." She relaxed when she felt his rigid body calm down, and he thrust his erection against her, teasing her to madness.

"What am I going to do with you?" he asked, pinching her nipple again.

Cyn moaned at the pleasure, and cried out, arching back against him. She gasped with delight when he entered her from behind, thrusting home in one swift motion. "I've got a few ideas," she replied, her heart skipping a beat as his cock surged, hard and huge, inside her, filling her needy sex completely.

"Good." He pulled out, and slammed back inside her, his hand tightening on her breast, as he thrust into her hard, again and again.

Cyn sobbed with pleasure as she met his thrusts, completely under his spell. He was all she wanted, or would ever need. She knew it as he mastered her completely.

"Just remember that you're mine," Jake commanded, pulling out to surge back into her.

"I'm yours," she gasped, crying out with ecstasy as his cock filled her. Her body tightened, her sex rippling, and she came, crying out his name.

Jake shuddered, surging back into her and coming with a growl, high and hard inside her, as he held her tight.

Cyn's racing heartbeat gradually slowed in tandem with Jake's, as he whispered soothing sounds, sweet nothings into her ear. His big hand slicked over her shoulder, to graze the side of her breast, and skim over her hip, bringing fire in its wake. Hell, she didn't want to go, instead, she wanted to turn around and taste every luscious square inch of him. When he finally let go, easing away from her, she felt the pang of separation deep inside. A part of her didn't want this idyll to end, ever.

He gave her a light swat on the bottom. "Go, or I won't be able to keep my hands off you. And for the record, it doesn't matter if my cover will be blown, but I won't ruin your reputation."

Cyn got out of bed, and turned, sweeping a fond gaze over the hunky male length of his magnificent body, wondering if a little scandal would be so bad. Jake looked sleep-rumpled, irritated with her, and slightly dangerous with his stubble and sexy bedroom eyes. The masterful, predatory look in his topaz eyes made her toes curl in the thick carpet. He was certainly scrumptious. She hadn't meant to infer that she was ashamed of him, or the fact that they'd lain together, but he seemed to be taking it that way. She'd have to deal with his bruised ego later, that is, if there was a later for them.

Deliberately breaking their awkward morning-after eye contact, she turned to gather her scattered clothes, all the while conscious of his brooding gaze on her. Good grief, he'd strewn them from the pulled out chair where he'd taken her over his knee, to the bed. She approached the chair, her knees going weak as she looked at the innocent looking piece of furniture. She'd never get over the shocking delight of being spanked by Jake Randal. Her face heated with embarrassment as she picked up her dress and bra.

Clutching the garments in her hands, she cast a furtive glance at the bathroom door. She could duck inside to dress, but she knew that would be the chicken's way out. Jake was watching her, his gaze feeling like a physical caress. Instead, she laid the clothes on the chair, and turned to smile at him. The hint of a smile curving his hard mouth told her that her boldness pleased him. She slipped on her panties, arching her bottom out to tease him, and was pleased to hear his breath go out in a gasp. Smiling, she patted the panties into place, and reached for her bra. She slipped it on, leaning forward to push up her breasts, running her hands over the sensitized curves. She shimmied into her dress, and turned to him. "Want to button me up?"

She bit her lip as she listened to Jake track over to her. God, the man moved like a sleek jungle cat, or a street fighter. She shivered down to her toes as his hands closed over her shoulders. He tightened them a moment, and she leaned back against him, with a pleasured gasp. He reached around her to do up her buttons; his hands sliding up her body to cup her breasts. His fingertips fanned over her nipples making her gasp.

"Don't tease me sugar, unless you want to go over my knee, and then back into my bed all day."

The rasped words shocked and pleased her. The seduction was a two-way street, at least she knew he wanted her. "Sorry sir," she teased. "You'll just have to paddle me for it later."

"Don't tempt me, bad girl," he stated, and zipped her up.

She picked up her sandals, and turned to meet his masterful gaze. "What are you going to do today?" she asked, hoping she wasn't sounding desperate. She'd die if he up and moved out.

"I'm going into the office later. I've got some research to do, and I have to set up operations for Scion."

"Oh yeah, where at?"

"I've leased office space in the *Branded* building."

"Oh gosh, you mean where your friend's sex shop is?" she asked, shocked.

"Want me to pick you up a present?" he asked, smiling.

"Another book would be nice," she replied, reaching for the novel she'd lent him.

"Leave it, sugar. Like I said, I need to do research." He smiled. "We won't want to run out of material."

"Somehow, I don't think that's going to be a problem with you."

"Nice to know I meet your expectations," he commented, his sultry gaze lingering on her face.

She wasn't sure if he was teasing her or not. "You've been absolutely perfect, Jake."

Jake watched Cyn go, when he really itched to pull her back into bed. She was like a fire in his blood. He wanted everything from her, but he'd settle for breakfast. He washed up, dressed, and rolled out for chores twenty minutes later, fully intending to stake his claim, and make sure Cyn didn't wear herself out with work at the same time.

Jake approached Pedro. He noticed two other hands, one older and grizzled, the other young, blond, and lazing around, joking.

"Well, Mr. Smith, I'm surprised to see you up and about at this hour," Pedro stated with a grin. "Is there something I can get for you, Hombre?"

Jake met the older man's steady brown eyes. He was protective of Cyn, which was good. "Cyn told me that if I worked, I'd get breakfast. Any objection?"

"Cyn, huh?" He went back to the tack. "Not as long as Miss Cynthia Jean's okay with it. Any trouble and I'll bounce your ass out of here, I don't care who you are."

Jake nodded, watching the flare in the older man's eyes. The man was sharp, had already figured out who he was. "Fine by me."

"You could go feed the goats; they're bleating their asses off, and then muck out the stalls." Pedro turned to scowl at the lingering young blond cowboy. "If you don't have anything to do Chance, I'll find you something."

Chance froze, and speared them with annoyance. "No sir, Mr. Orlando, I was just going."

"Sorry I'm late." Could be heard as Cyn walked into the barn.

Jake's cock twitched as her sultry voice washed over him, reviving his morning hard on. Cyn froze in her tracks when she caught sight of him, and blushed. He watched the blush go down her face and followed it to the V of her t-shirt, recalling that she blushed all over. He smiled. "You promised me breakfast if I worked."

"So, I did," she replied with a twinkle in her eye. "You help with morning chores, and I'll go organize breakfast. I hope you like it hot."

"You know I do. The hotter the better, sugar." His eyes glued to her sultry sway as she hurried back to the bunkhouse.

Half an hour later, Cyn handed Jake a platter of huevos rancheros she'd liberally loaded with peppers, and gasped, when his fingertips brushed her wrist. Jake's sultry look was enough to make her knees weak, darn the man. She'd wanted to avoid making their affair public knowledge, at least for now. She was acutely aware of the curious stares of the ranch hands sitting at the other end of the table, watching this tableau, but she couldn't seem to control herself.

Jake kicked out a chair. "Sit down, sugar."

"Yeah, CJ, take a load off," Pedro stated.

She sank into the wooden chair, feeling gratitude that Jake was taking care of her, and consternation that he thought he could order her about in her kitchen, in front of her men. She gleefully watched the man she adored help himself to the eggs, and take a big bite, waiting for him to yelp and reach for his water. She'd made the dish extra spicy to teach him a lesson. Instead, he quirked a startled brow at her, a grin twitching his manly lips.

"My favorite, Cyn," he commented, looking deep into her eyes, adding, "most cooks don't put in enough heat."

"Uh huh," she murmured, melting where she sat as she watched him savor her cooking. Everything about him was erotic.

"Eat," he commanded, looking at her empty plate.

How could she eat when her hormones were boiling over? Still, knowing they were being observed, she helped herself to the eggs and took a bite, wincing when the heat burst on her tongue. She reached for her water, her mouth on fire, hearing Jake's low chuckle. Caught in her own trap, darn it.

"Too spicy?" he asked innocently.

"I can handle it," she replied, making herself eat another small forkful. Once she got past the heat, it was actually tasty. Slanting a curious gaze Jake's way, she found his sultry gaze on her mouth. Time seemed to stand still.

Pedro cleared his throat, then stated, "Well men, work's a waiting, we'd best get at it."

Cyn blushed, grateful for the interruption. The hands weren't used to her dressing in anything but shapeless work clothes. The past couple of days had been an eye opener for them, and she didn't want to add fuel to fire their gossip. Trembling inside, she watched the corners of Jake's mouth kick up in a sexy grin. He knew exactly what she wanted, him.

"I'll be out directly," Jake replied, his eyes still locked with Cyn's. "First I think I'll have a second cup of coffee."

"Not necessary, Señor. You've paid for your breakfast."

"I believe in an honest day's work. I'll finish my chores before I go into town on business."

"Later," Pedro commented, following the hands out the door.

Cyn smiled, finding herself suddenly alone with Jake. She stood up and sauntered toward him, mischief on her mind. "I wonder how you would taste with strawberry jam," she murmured aloud. The determined gaze she focused on him, made him flash her his bad boy smile, the one that made her weak in the knees.

He reached out to snag her wrist, tumbling her down onto his lap. She landed with a moan, when she felt his rousing cock under her bottom. He growled and bent to kiss her, his arms wrapped around her. Cyn sighed with pleasure as his hard mouth slanted over hers, his tongue surging into her mouth. She plastered herself tight to his powerful chest, her breasts aching, the nipples budding like jewels against him.

The slam of the screen door barely registered in her sex starved brain. A gasp made her frown against Jake's lips, and break the kiss to look up. Brandy stood there, dressed in a red bikini, her shocked gaze locked on their clinch. Jake went rigid, his arms tightening around her, when she started to wiggle off his lap. Cyn stopped trying to get away, the cat was already out of the bag, and turned an irritated look on her stepsister. "Did you want something?"

Brandy smiled, flicking her long blond hair over her shoulder, as she gave Jake a flirtatious look. "Mother said you had a guy you were keeping all to yourself, CJ. That biker from the dance."

"So, you came to see for yourself?" Cyn filled in.

"Did not, I just came to tell you I'm going to a pool party at the Billing's Ranch. While I'm out make sure my room is cleaned properly. It's in a terrible state."

"Don't you have a housekeeper to take care of that?" Jake asked.

"She's cut back on the staff, so she can pick up the slack," Brandy snapped. "Besides, nobody does hospital corners like CJ."

"Ah," he stated.

Cyn frowned, irritated that they were talking about her like she wasn't there. She'd cut the house staff down to try to save money, and she didn't appreciate Jake knowing the embarrassing details of her dysfunctional family situation. "No," she replied, waiting for her refusal to sink in, as Brandy preened before Jake.

"What did you say?" Brandy asked, her jaw dropping.

"I said, no. I am not your maid. Clean up after yourself. You're going to have to do it when you go off to college."

"A lot you know. I'm blowing off school to knock around Europe with Tiff on our gap year. Then I'm going to snag a rich husband."

"Not on my dime, you're not."

Brandy glared at her, and then focused on Jake. "Hello Mr.?"

"Smith," Jake stated, without inflection.

Cyn watched their interaction, unable to look away. Brandy was about to hit on him, even while she was in his lap. She recognized her seductive sway, as she leaned across the table to shake his hand, giving him a view of her cleavage. She'd known she'd lose him, but she hadn't thought it would be so soon. But a glance at Jake told her he wasn't interested, he kept his eyes on Brandy's, a scornful look on his mouth, refusing to shake her hand.

Brandy pulled it back with a moue of disappointment. "You look good enough to eat, Mr. Smith."

"I'm not on the menu," he voiced, dismissively.

Cyn coughed, choking back a laugh.

"Just make sure my bedroom is cleaned properly this time, Cinders," Brandy snapped, storming away.

Jake scowled as the screen door slammed, and the manipulative brat stormed out. Cyn's back was rigid, but her hands were trembling in her lap. He recognized that she didn't want to show weakness in front of the girl. He smoothed a comforting hand down her back. "You were magnificent."

"Do you really think so?"

"I know so." He picked up his coffee cup, and held it to Cyn's lips. "Drink it, I think you need it," he ordered.

Cindy took a bracing sip. "Thanks."

"You're welcome. What are we going to do about them?" He knew the minute he'd said it he'd miscalculated, by her frown.

"Nothing, they're my family, I'll..."

He bent to kiss her, silencing her objections. He couldn't stand back and watch her get hurt. He groaned as his mouth slanted over her soft lips and she breathed a sigh of surrender into him.

"What that," Cyn murmured, when Jake broke the kiss, hearing buzzing.

"Who cares," he replied, nibbling her ear. "I'll pick you up tonight for a moonlight supper."

Up above, the fairies scowled as they observed Chance eavesdropping on the loving couple.

"That nosy young cowboy is back, Aggie," Hilda shouted.

Agatha rushed to the circle. "Persistent bugger, isn't he?"

"We ought to drop a thunderbolt on his ass," Hilda voiced, with a fierce scowl.

Imogene fluttered up. "Or maybe a flock of woodpeckers could dive bomb him. I've got a woodpecker spell we could use."

"No," Agatha stated, pointing her wand at the beehive under the eaves. "Bees are much more affective in cases like this."

The enraged bees flew out of the hive, flying in a line straight towards the lurking cowboy. He let out a yelp and took off running, heading for the creek.

The fairies laughed as he dived in headfirst.

"Serves you right, you dirty bugger," they shouted, their voices echoing in the wind through the treetops.

Chance resurfaced and darted a panicked glance around the woods for the voices, angry and confused.

Cyn went out to the mailbox that afternoon, her heart sinking when she pulled out yet another obscene note. The man just didn't give up. She tore it open and froze.

...Cyn, you stupid, cheap, lying slut. I put you up on a pedestal, and you're no better than a common whore, letting him spank you and sucking Jake Randal's cock like you couldn't get enough. Yes, I know who he is, and what you did, and I'll make you both pay...

She crumbled it up, sickened to realize that Hawkins had been watching she and Jake in bed, their private intimate moments. How did Hawkins gain such easy access to the ranch? She knew that Pedro was on alert for him, as was she. She sagged against the post, her strength ebbing, and then straightened. For all she knew, he could be watching her now. She wouldn't give him the satisfaction of letting him see her crumble under the pressure like this. The sick bastard had gone too far. The time had come to report him to the police.

The sound of footsteps behind her, made her tense, adrenalin kicked in as she spun around, flowing into a karate pose. Cordial gave her a startled look, her thin lips tightening.

"Are you completely insane?" Cordial snapped, stepping back a pace.

"No, just partially," Cyn replied with a smirk, at her stepmother's offended glower.

"What have you got there?" Cordial stared at the crumpled note in Cyn's hand. "Not another alleged, obscene letter?"

"Now, how did you know about them?" Cyn asked, instantly on her guard. She'd deliberately kept quiet about this, not wanting it to get back to her father and worry him needlessly. Only Juanita and Pedro knew, and she'd made them promise not to tell. She watched Cordial gulp, hesitating.

"I heard you talking to Juanita. It's a fine state of affairs when you'll go to a maid with your problems, and not me."

"Yeah right. Like you give a damn," she stated sadly, shocked to hear Cordial sigh.

"We've never been close, I admit, but I don't want to see anything bad happen to you." Her gaze went back to the letter.

"Don't worry about it. I'm not going to let some maniac's ravings bother me and run. I'm going to be just fine."

"About that, I think it would be better if you did run," Cordial commented, wringing her hands, before looking around nervously. "Go back to Taos before you get hurt."

"Why? What do you know?" she asked, hearing a note of panic in Cordial's normally cultured voice.

"I know that you're playing with fire, messing around with Jake Randal in his bungalow last night. Letting him spank you, for pity's sake, have you no pride?"

Cyn's jaw dropped. "How did you...?"

"Please, it's all over town."

Cyn didn't believe that. Brandy would have been all over Jake this morning if she knew his identity. Cordial's sudden knowledge, on top of the threatening letter, added up to a chilling picture. Her stepmother wasn't the type to window peek, but wouldn't be above employing a spy. Chance for instance, he seemed especially close to the girls. "Just keep your nose out of my business, Cordial, and we'll both get along."

Chapter 9

Jake leaned back at his desk, in the back office connected to *Branded*, eating lunch. With his wireless business, he could work anywhere, and he found the privacy back here advantageous. It was the main reason he'd sought Mack out at the dance two days ago, and it'd brought him Cyn. It also didn't hurt that he had easy access to sexy books to increase Cyn's erotica library. He dropped his sandwich, picked up *Bound to Serve*, and continued reading, his cock swelling. He had to shift in his chair to try to accommodate his discomfort. Good lord, she was going to kill him with blue balls.

...One look at Lola's glare as Condor hustled her out of there told Bridget she was in deep trouble. The reaction was instantaneous, but she wouldn't have done it if she hadn't been so on edge. Condor's tight grip on her arm told her he was worried, too. She had to trot to keep up with his long stride as he marched her across the grounds toward their bungalow. "I'm sorry, but he..."

"Not another word," he mumbled, opening the door to their bungalow. She tensed when he leaned forward, seemingly to nuzzle her neck.

"The place is bugged, and you've been very bad. So, for god's sake be good and obey my every command."

Bridget digested that disturbing news as he pushed her inside. She'd been bad and she was about to get it. The bugs she'd already figured on. *Knowing they had an audience gave her a little thrill. She eagerly brushed up against his hot body, on fire despite the knowledge they were watched. When Condor's lips brushed hotly over hers, she sighed with pleasure leaning into him, loving the hard feel of his body against hers, the surge of his cock against her naked belly. She still ached to see it, taste him. When he broke the kiss, she saw need, regret, and resolve in his stormy eyes. She was in for it, and her butt heated in anticipation as she blushed. She watched him wide-eyed as he walked over to what she'd guessed was a spanking bench. He crooked a finger.*

"Come take your punishment, kitten."

Bridget found herself moving forward, both embarrassed and turned on. She was so on edge and the sultry look on his stern but handsome face only added to her discomfiture. She bent over the padded bar wincing when she saw him pick up a red paddle. It was going to hurt worse than the spanking. Would it make her just as randy, she wondered, as Condor stepped up beside her. His big hand smoothed her hair back, and she bit back a needy sigh, trembling with need.

At least he didn't need to strip her tonight; she was already bare ass naked for him, and vulnerable. His hands swept in a loving caress down her shivering back, to cup her outthrust bottom. Her knees wobbled and she sagged against the bench, her pussy wet. "Tell me, why are you being paddled, kitten?"

"Because you're too mean to fuck me," she snapped. His warm laugh made her even more furious.

"You haven't earned that pleasure yet. You were very disobedient today, kitten."

She sniffed, crushed by the crisply spoken rebuke, her emotions on edge even though it was playacting. It was true in a way, she had messed up, and almost blown her cover twice. As an agent, she never made stupid mistakes like that. But he had her so achingly turned on she couldn't help it.

"You'll take six strokes of the paddle, and don't you dare come, you're being punished."

The paddle smacked down on her bottom, and she moaned at the mingled pain and pleasure, her ass heating. He was such a bastard.

"Good girl."

He smacked her and she lifted up on her toes, moaning.

"Down," he said, pushing her back down.

Bridget sagged against the leather padded bench, tensing as he swung the paddle again. It hit and she screeched, her pussy quivering. She couldn't take three more without coming, but she had to try.

He smacked her harder and her sex convulsed as she started to come.

"No."

She managed to pull it back, listening to his voice.

"Five."

The paddle smacked her left cheek, and she moaned, her ass and pussy on fire.

"Six."

The paddle smacked her right cheek, and she let out a helpless whimper on the edge of orgasm. She heard the loud rasp of his zipper being pulled down, and moaned needful and desperate for him. It might only be simulated sex for their possible audience, but she welcomed it.

Condor trembled, pressing up against Bridget's hot bottom. His cock was hard to bursting and he rubbed it teasingly against her wet mound, her needful sigh like music to him. She was creamy, hot, and perfect for him. He fought back his instincts and fit himself between her trembling thighs, simulating the act he burned to do, pretending to make love to her. Bridget sobbed with pleasure as his hard cock rubbed against her slick pubes, bumping against her stiff clit. She came, crying out her passion, and he bit back a pained groan, her rhythmic spasms torturing his rigid cock.

As she came back to earth, he pulled back and zipped up, still hard as a pole and unsatisfied. It wasn't about the mission anymore for him; it was about them. Bridget straightened up, turning her sultry, tear-filled eyes on him, and he folded like a deck of cards. His expression hard as the bulge in his pants, he scooped her up in his arms and carried her into the bathroom. It was the only place to give them a hint of privacy. "Turn on the shower." He ordered.

She did, and he set her inside the stall, stripped, and joined her. His hungry gaze stroked her as he stalked her toward the corner. She looked a bit nervous, he decided. "I don't like an audience," he stated, backing her into the shower. Growling, he bent to kiss her.

Bridget moaned as his hard mouth claimed hers.

Condor reveled in the feel of her damp body rubbing teasingly against his hardness. Her nipples beaded tighter against him, burning him like two laser beams. She rubbed them against his hair-roughened chest, whimpering at the sparks of pleasure the simple action caused. His big hands cupped the globes of her bottom and squeezed gently, feeling her sex cream against his abdomen, feeling her quivering with need. He lifted her up, and settled her over his erection.

Bridget sighed with pleasure, wrapping her legs around his hips as his hot, hard cock filled her.

Fully enclosed in her heat, he held her still, savoring the moment. But his tight body wouldn't let him. He started to move, his body tight with leashed energy, and felt like their hearts were beating in tandem. Hell, it was the most erotic thing ever. This was a hell of a lot more than an ordinary mission, but he pushed the thought away. He couldn't afford to care too much. He locked gazes with Bridget's passionate dark eyes. She shivered with delight, completely surrendering to him.

He groaned, accepting her sweet surrender, his grip on her ass tightening. He could swear she could read his thoughts as she clung to him, her pussy clutching at him. Her sweet moans were music to his ears. He backed her against the shower stall's marble wall, under the showerhead, and thrust deeper. Contracting, she exploded, waves of orgasm sweeping through her. Condor groaned and thrust high against her cervix pouring out his tribute. She laid her head on his broad shoulder, savoring the afterglow. His pulse was slowing back to normal and he held her tight. The tender intimacies of his touch made tears of bliss mist her eyes.

"This changes nothing," he whispered into her ear...

Jake put down the book and eased back in his chair, running baseball stats in his head to fight his hard on. Cyn had the kinky, soulful, sexuality of his dreams, and he could hardly wait to see her tonight. He'd planned something special, and private, indulging her need for secrecy.

"Hey buddy."

Jake looked up in his open doorway to see Mack standing there, two steaming cups of coffee in his hands. "Hey, I was just..."

"Reading," Mack finished with a smirk, as he glanced at the erotic romance novel. "I brought you a boost of caffeine."

"Hand it over." Jake leaned across his desk to take the steaming aromatic brew. There was no way he could stand up to reach for it, and show Mack how affected he was by the book. It wasn't just the steamy novel; it was the thoughts of doing those same things to Cyn. All he had to do was pick up a paddle from the store, and then he'd...

"Earth to Jake, are you in there, pal?"

"Man, you've got it bad," Mack stated, spinning around the chair in front of Jake's desk, and straddling it. "It must be the mysterious redhead."

"Smart ass," Jake replied, but there was little heat in his voice.

"So, I take it you caught up with your runaway lover."

"Yeah, you could say that," Jake answered, adding under his breath, "Now I've just got to figure out how to keep her."

Mack glanced back at the book. "It can't be. The woman that bought this novel is five foot two, a cute brunette, with sparkling green eyes; not a stacked redhead."

Jake arched his brow at the stacked redhead comment, recalling Mack and Zane's heated reactions to her that night. He didn't want competition, but he knew they wouldn't really poach, even though they'd shared lovers in the distant past. "Okay, I'll play along. What are you now, psychic?"

"Nah. *Bound to Serve* is one of the books I sell in the shop, a best seller. The cute brunette brought a slew of them a month back. Her name's Dana something, I think."

"Dora," Jake corrected him. "My woman's best friend."

"You know her? The sly minx always comes in on someone else's shift. How about an introduction?"

"How about a favor?" Jake shot back at him.

"Just ask, and it's yours."

Jake got back to the ranch at quarter to six, his plans for the night finalized. He was going to do his damnedest to bind Cyn to him with sex. He had a few sexy surprises in store for her. He'd only made it through a third of the book she'd lent him, and he was intrigued. He stalked up to bungalow six and entered, stripping off his leather jacket, and unbuttoning shirt, on his way to the shower. Thinking of Cyn as he'd left her this morning, a blushing, bewitching delight, made his cock swell. Her red hair tousled around her pretty heart shaped face. He was falling for her hard, and they'd only just begun.

A knock on the door stopped him in his tracks, halfway to the bathroom. Cyn! His cock throbbed as he thought her name, swelling to painful proportions inside his jeans. He smiled. It pleased him that she was early, proving that she was just as anxious to be together as he was. She could wash his back.

He strode back to the door hungry for her, and pulled it open. Brandy stood on his doorstep, and gasped, taking a half step back when she saw his scowling face. Damn it all, she was the last spoiled brat he wanted to see. She blinked her false eyelashes at him and smiled, recovering from her shock, as she took a step forward, deliberately stumbling, and falling into his arms.

"Oops," she stated with a giggle. "Excuse me, Mr. Randal. I never will get used to these new stiletto heels. Although they do make my legs look sexy, don't you think?"

So, she knew who he was, which probably meant big mama did, too. The word was out. They'd better damned not make trouble for Cyn. Jake scowled at the blond bombshell wannabe plastered to his chest, his hard-on shrinking like a popped balloon, and tried to peel her off him. It wasn't easy, she clung to him, digging her long nails into his skin. Damn it all, Cyn had been right, they were after him. The little, would be Lolita, was wearing full makeup, including false eyelashes, which she batted up at him as she gave him a calculated smile. Her cloying perfume made him gag, being potent enough to drop a cow, making his nose twitch. He managed to back her out the door, and slam it shut behind him. "Why are you here, Brandy?"

Her pleased gaze swept up at him. "You remember my name. Most boys can't tell me apart from my twin sister."

Oh brother. "You've got a mole on your left cheek. Don't take it personally. I'm a trained observer; I make it my business to notice things."

"I'll just bet." She traced a path down his chest with one sharp nail. "I've got another mole. Wanna see where it is?"

Annoyed, he clamped his hand over her probing finger to stop it from drifting towards his crotch. She misinterpreted his touch and grinned, her glossy red lips curving into a triumphant smile. The girl was out to try her seduction skills on some unwary guy, but it wouldn't be him. "No. I was just about to take a shower, and you're interrupting it."

"I could wash your back," she replied, licking her lips.

Cyn walked down the path to Jake's bungalow, ready for their date. She'd seen his bike pull in, and couldn't wait for him to pick her up. She had important news for him. His return was out, and she'd been open about their affair. She knew it would please him.

She turned the corner and saw Brandy in Jake's arms. His shirt was hanging open, her hand touching his bare chest, his hand over hers in what looked like a tender moment. Cyn stopped in her tracks, gasping with shock, as all her sultry hopes and dreams fizzled while she glared at them. How could he cheat on her with Brandy?

Jake heard her, looked toward her and scowled. He pushed Brandy's hand off his skin. "Cyn."

Brandy flicked her a victorious smile and Cyn glared back at her. This was no doubt payback for refusing to clean her room this morning. This kind of vindictive, childish behavior she could expect from the immature young woman, but Jake? It seemed so out of character for him. How could he have cheated on her so blatantly, knowing she might catch him? His outraged expression as he met her glare was confusing and only fed her anger.

"Did you need something, Cinders?" Brandy asked.

"Not a damned thing from you," she replied flatly, waiting for Jake to say something, at least beg her forgiveness. His closed, rather hurt expression, made her gut twist, along with her aching heart.

"Good, then why don't you get out of that ridiculous dress, put your farmer clothes back on, and give us some privacy. We want to be alone."

Cyn's spine went rigid, her chin rising with quiet outrage. She wouldn't give them the satisfaction of seeing her cry. "Don't let me interrupt." She turned on her heel, and rushed back to her apartment.

"Damn it all," Jake stammered out, giving Brandy a wide berth as he sprinted down the stairs. He was well and truly pissed. Cyn shouldn't have believed the ridiculous set up. It was ludicrous to think he'd prefer Brandy's blatant charms to hers. Still, she'd taken the first opportunity to flee. He stepped down the path after Cyn, but Brandy grabbed his arm, stopping him.

"Where do you think you're going? I'm not done with you yet," she asked, her green eyes narrowing.

He directed a forbidding scowl at her hand lingering on his arm, and she took her hand off his sleeve. "I'm going to retrieve my woman. Go practice your womanly wiles on some other unsuspecting guy, jailbait. I'm not buying."

"Well," she hissed, stamping her foot. "You won't get me by playing hard to get, Jake Randal. Don't expect me to fall for this lovelorn act either; I'm too smart for that."

"Believe what you want, little girl. I've got a much more important woman to deal with, and she's waiting for me," he snapped, turning away as Brandy glowered at him.

"Come back here," she demanded, with a screech. "You're not the type to let that old maid lead you around by your cock," she shouted after him.

"Old maid," he grumbled, his eyes narrowing, as he realized what kind of underhanded warfare they'd put his woman through. "Little brat, Cyn is more of a woman than you'll ever be," he stated, as he stalked away.

"You're up to something, JT Randal, and my mom is going to find out what it is. Just you wait and see." Brandy yelled back at him.

Chapter 10

Cyn slammed into her cabin, walking through the lobby and into her living space, blinking away the tears misting her eyes. How could she have been naive enough to think she had what it took to hold on to a man like Jake Randal? She'd known he was way out of her league when she'd seduced him at the ball. But Brandy? How could he cheat on her with the stupid little brat?

Brandy had gone after him mostly for spite of course, getting revenge for this morning. It only pointed out the futility of trying to get her to grow up and learn to stand on her own two feet. Damn it all, she should have expected something like this when Cordial revealed that she knew Jake's identity late this morning. Instead, she felt sucker punched, standing here sniffing back tears like a fool.

The lobby door opened, and she froze, her heart stopping. Please don't let it be him, she pleaded, silently. I can't take the humiliation, the pain of losing him. When she heard his distinctive, fluid, hunting footsteps cross the lobby floor she groaned. Why hadn't she thought to lock it? Because she'd simply thought he wouldn't pursue her. Why the hell had he, after she'd caught him red-handed? She tensed, her spine stiffening, her chin rising defiantly. If he thought he could sweet-talk her into continuing their affair, he was dead wrong.

As the connecting door to her apartment opened and closed, she turned to face him. He stood a foot away from her, his relentless hooded gaze locked on her. One thing she could say about him, he could be very focused. But so could she, and she chose to focus on his betrayal, as all her hormones went on red alert. His jaw was tight, his whiskey eyes clouded with hurt. She sucked in her breath at the startling sight. Why should he look so upset? She was the one who'd been wronged. "What are you doing here? Shouldn't you be *negotiating* with Brandy?" He closed in on her, his scent, his magnetic presence wrapped around her, making her shiver right down to her toes, despite her justifiable anger. Stiffening her spine, she glared up at him.

He kept coming, closing the gap. "No. I'm not interested in Brandy, or anything she has to sell. I thought I'd made that clear earlier, when I held you in my lap. It seems you need convincing."

Cyn shivered, her nipples tingling, and retreated, backing up past the kitchen island and into the dining nook. She wouldn't back down from her justifiable outrage. She couldn't afford to if she wanted to come out of this with her heart and pride intact. "Could have fooled me, the way you were wrapped all over her."

"It was the other way around, sugar. If you'll think about who was touching whom, you'll figure that out for yourself."

"Yeah right," she commented, inching back, reliving the appalling incident in her mind. Jake backed against his door, Brandy grinning like a cat with cream, as she leaned into him, her hand on his chest. It was true, Brandy had been the one with her hands on him, but he hadn't tried very hard to get away. "You're strong enough to push her back. You didn't."

"I repeat. I'm not interested in Brandy."

She backed away out of sheer self-survival, and wound up in a corner, trapped between the dinette table and the counter. Damn the man! He'd confused her so much he'd thrown off her sense of direction, turning her on at the same time. Her pulse was racing, but not from fear, she still wanted him, bad. She couldn't deny her arousal, their deep sexual connection.

"You're just using this incident to drive us apart because you're afraid of what you feel," he stated, leaning into her.

The accusation struck a little too close to home, and she glared up at him, his body heat making her flush. "That's not true."

"Prove it," he commanded, with a half–smile, his hands braced on the wall on either side of her head, holding her trapped.

Cyn burned, spellbound and needy, her gaze locked with his tempting, teasing dark one. How could she have come to need him so much in this short a time frame? It wasn't fair, because it made her vulnerable. "How on earth could I prove it?"

"Kiss me. If I don't rock your world, sugar, you can go back to hating me."

That kind of teasing statement was probably guaranteed to get him back into her bed, darn it. Damn, but she wanted to taste him. Her defenses crumbled as her nipples tightened and her lips tingled. "And if you do?" she asked, intrigued, in spite of her self-protective instincts.

"You'll find out," he stated, with a smile.

The sensual promise, coupled with his sultry smile, made her shiver with delight. What other sexual tricks did he have in his bag? One little kiss wouldn't hurt, and it would settle things in her mind. She leaned forward, her lips pursed, and frowned when he didn't immediately bend to kiss her. He wanted to make her work for it. She went up on tiptoes, and brushed her lips against his hard sexy one, moaning when she tasted him, only it wasn't as good when he didn't cooperate.

She whispered, "Come here, you," against his lips, wrapped her arms around his neck, and pulled him down to kiss her properly. He went with a growl, his mouth slanting over hers. He nipped her lower lip, and she opened for him, shivering as he took her mouth. Oh yeah, this was what she craved. He wrapped his arms around her, pulling her into his aroused body, and thrilled at her ability to turn him on. Whimpering, she rocked her throbbing sex against the rock hard bulge of his cock. Tonight, she wanted to see it, taste it.

She trembled when his hands slid down to cup her buttocks and squeeze. She rocked against the ridge of his cock, sparks going through her. When Jake flipped up her skirt to give her five sharp spanks, she whimpered and melted against him.

"We're exclusive. Never forget it again," he punctuated the last word with a spank that caught her on the bottom of her ass."

"Yes, sir," she gasped, her legs quivering as she went up on tiptoes again.

He smoothed her skirt down, and kissed the teardrops off her cheeks. "No more tears." He turned her towards her bedroom. "Pack an overnight bag. I'm taking you away from this mess."

"But the chores, I can't just leave."

"You've got hands, let them work a full day for once. I guarantee you Pedro would like to crack the whip on them."

"So, you've already spoken to Pedro about this?"

"We've talked. He wants you to cut back, is afraid you're hurting yourself. So am I."

It touched her to have both big men worry about her. It was true Pedro had been trying to convince her to cut back for weeks, and she hated to worry him. She hesitated, sorely tempted to chuck it all, and run off with Jake. "I'll give you tonight, I can't make any promises beyond tomorrow."

"Tonight, you're mine mind, body and soul," he stated, watching her pack.

And heart, she thought silently as she zipped the duffle bag, adding the latest obscene letter to the stack of clothes. She'd already accepted that she was in love with Jake, knowing full well he was only thinking of this as a summer fling. It didn't matter. She'd take him any way she could get him. At least he was trying to take care of her, in his own gruff alpha male way. For all his breeding, Jake Randal was still rough around the edges, and it excited her.

She walked outside with him, locking her door behind her. Instead of feeling like she was abandoning her post, she felt light and bubbly, like she was running away. Only Jake could affect her this way. Slanting a glance at his hard body, she could hardly believe she'd agreed to go away on a fantasy overnight with him. Her body tightened with anticipation, and her sex got creamy. She already ached for him.

He looked perfectly at home here on the ranch, in his biker leathers and boots, even though this had to be foreign territory to a sophisticated man of the world like him. Jake seemed to dominate whatever setting he was in, especially the bedroom. That thought made her tingle, as she licked her bottom lip. His steamy gaze locked on her, and she smiled, her heart racing.

"Ready?" he asked, holding out his hand, his gaze holding hers fast.

"Always," she murmured sinking deep into the whiskey depths of his masterful eyes, her nipples beading inside her bra, her lips tingling as she gazed at his. She was dying to kiss him again, needed to taste him. She took a half step toward him, his sheer magnetism pulling her toward him, like a moth to a flame. He was liable to burn her up, but what a spectacular way to go.

"Just a little warning, sugar," he stated, with a smile. "I read chapter seven."

Cyn stumbled, her knees going weak as his teasing statement sunk in. *Chapter seven; oh god!* Jake instantly reached out to steady her, his big hand clamping around her bare upper arm. She let out a needy gasp, her body turning to pudding. She was so melty, he could eat her up with a spoon, and by the wicked gleam in his eye; he knew it. He only had to touch her, and she was on fire. Jake gave her a bad boy smile in response, his rough fingertips stroking her skin.

Was she ready for chapter seven? It contained ultra hot scenes, paddling, and two men. Oh my! Truthfully, she couldn't foresee wanting any other man in her bed, or watching her have sex, but it was intriguing. Her heart skipped a beat at the thought. It couldn't be, Jake struck her as very territorial, the kind of alpha male that did not share his toys, despite his wicked, hell raiser, reputation as a youth.

"I'm starved for you, sugar." Jake reached out to take her bag out of her limp fingers.

Cyn let it go, glad he'd grabbed the bag before she dropped it. Stunned and turned on, she didn't know how to react to his brazen statement. "Me too," she murmured, it was the best she could come up with.

"That's sweet," he replied, skimming his hand down her arm to take her hand in his.

He gave her hand a little squeeze, and Cyn all but fell into a puddle at his feet. He knew she was nervous, and was trying to soothe her, how perfect. She squeezed his hand back to show him she was fine, and tried to give him a serene smile in return.

"Let's get this show on the road before you chicken out on me."

Smart man, he could read her emotions so well. "I'm ready to go," she commented, determined to hang onto her sophisticated pose. Truth be told, even though she was a little nervous, she was eager to be with him. To hell with whoever disapproved. She was starving for him too. She went on tiptoe to kiss him. Jake's mouth slanted over hers, his arms wrapped around her, pulling her tight to him, as his tongue mated with hers. The world became a rosy glow behind her closed eyes, as she indulged in a taste of Jake.

He was absolutely, positively, yummy, and as his cock grew hard against her mound, she whimpered, leaving him no doubt of her need for him, and she arched against him. Leading him back to her bed was sounding better and better all the time, to her sex starved body. Instead, he broke the kiss, setting her back from him. She let out a disgruntled grumble of complaint, frowning at him, to see his hard mouth twitching with stifled laughter. He was getting off on driving her crazy, darn him. "Stop playing hard to get," she stated, stomping her foot.

He tipped back his head and laughed at that, then reached out to snag her arm when she moved away miffed. "Honey, I can be had any time you say the word. You've got me walking around with a hard on half the time."

"Really?" She looked down at his bulge for proof. It pleased her to no end that she affected him that way. "I thought it only happened when we kissed."

"Sugar, it happens every time I think about you. Satisfied?"

"Uh huh."

"Good. Let's go." He took her arm and steered her towards his waiting Harley.

He was in a hurry for her, an excellent sign. Her sex fluttered, as she cast a sidelong glance at him, growing creamy for him. God he was sexy. Come what may, she'd chosen who she trusted, and she wouldn't look back. She'd as good as severed ties with Cordial today, and she didn't regret it, even though she knew there was going to be hell to pay later. Taking away something Cordial wanted was never painless. Cordial desperately wanted Jake as a son-in-law, just not married to her artsy spinster stepchild.

She wasn't thinking in terms of matrimony. She just wanted to have a hot and heavy affair with Jake Randal, get through the next two months until her father was released, and go back to Taos with some warm memories. Although, there could be more, Jake said he could work anywhere. Maybe he could move Scion headquarters to...

No! She absolutely wouldn't let herself go there, wouldn't torture herself with what might be. She'd just enjoy this to the fullest. At least Jake was taking care of the other thorn in her side, Dwain Hawkins.

She stood still, bemused, as Jake put on her helmet, tucking her hair back away from her face. Riding a motorcycle was another new experience tonight. Maybe she should have worn slacks, but it was too late now. Besides, pressing her thong-clad mound against Jake's ass was an intriguing thought. She watched him stash her duffle in the saddlebags, put on his own helmet, and mount the bike.

Cyn felt heat rush through her as she watched the utterly male movement. Her mouth watered. Prying eyes were probably watching, but she didn't care. Let 'em look, she was through kowtowing to Cordial and her ilk. Jake looked at her, and she slipped onto the back of the bike, gasping when her freshly spanked bottom touched hot leather.

"Put your arms around me, sugar, and hang on tight."

Cyn leaned into him, gasping when her stiff clit bumped against him, and her sex pulsed against the vibrating seat. Oh lord, it was going to be pure pleasure riding with him. She bit back an orgasmic moan, as a spasm went through her.

Jake let out a knowing chuckle, saying, "Enjoy it babe, it's one of the perks of riding with a bad boy."

After the kiss, and spanking, she needed to come—bad, and his words threatened to push her over the edge. She plastered herself to his back, her arms wrapped tighter around him, murmuring, "You are a wicked man, Jacob Randal."

He chuckled when her hands drifted down to his erection, and she gasped. "I'm glad I live up to my bad reputation, Cyn."

Cyn closed her eyes as Jake drove them towards town. All sensation seemed to be focused in her vibrating mound. She whimpered, her sex spasming. It was on the tip of her tongue to ask where he was taking her, but she wanted to prove that she trusted him. Her trust seemed important to him. Besides, she was too distracted by lust to think straight.

"You're dying to know where we're going, aren't you, sugar?"

"Of course not, I trust you," she stammered, squeezing him tighter, making him groan when she accidentally squished his erection too hard. Damn, but he could read her like a book. He knew her so well; her mind was spinning with the sexy prospects ahead. *He'd read chapter seven... she knew what that meant.* "Ah the hell with it. Yes. I admit that I'm curious, but it's not because I don't trust you."

"I appreciate that." He reached down to slide her hand off his package. "Keep that up, and I'll be out of commission."

"Sorry," she replied, with concern and moved her other hand up off his bulge. Having him not able to perform would be terrible.

"No problem," he chuckled, pulling up to *Branded.* He drove around to the rear parking lot, parking next to a big, black SUV.

Chapter 11

A tingle went through her as she gazed at the intriguing erotica shop. Were they picking up some sex toys? This was also new territory. She knew for a fact that *Branded* did a booming, if clandestine, business. Jake turned off the bike, and turned to look at her, with a focused intensity that made her toes curl in her pumps. He'd picked the perfect place to amp the heat. A shiver of sensual anticipation went through her. "Just what do you have up your sleeve, for me, Jacob Randal?"

He grinned, taking her hand and placing it on the burgeoning erection under his jeans. "Don't you mean what have I got in my pants for you?"

"Oh yeah." She caressed his steely length, thrilled to feel him harden under her touch. "Let me at that bad boy," she murmured, reaching for his zipper.

"Later." He reached out to still her fingers before she could strip him. "Our first stop, a private after hours, tour of *Branded*."

So, he wasn't just rushing in to pick up some toys. Cyn cast an intrigued, if wary, glance at *Branded*. She couldn't take much more stimulation without climaxing. Jake was going to tease her until she came, she could tell by the wicked look in his eye. He was watching her, trying to gauge her reaction. "Sounds lovely," she replied, with a little sigh of surrender, reacting to his steamy gaze, as she dismounted, took off her helmet, and handed it to him. She couldn't back down after her talk of being bold, and she didn't want to.

"That's my little, fantasy bad girl." He leaned forward to give her a slow, hot kiss.

Cyn's heart was beating faster when he broke the kiss and stowed the helmet away. She watched his quick focused motions knowing he was hungry for her; it gave her a little thrill. She leaned towards him like a flower to the sun, and he turned to catch her around the waist, tugging her bodily to him to hold her intimately as he nuzzled her nape.

"You are making me hard as a pole," he stated, rubbing his erection against her.

Cyn whimpered, her sex pulsing as his hardness tantalized her. "I know, thank you."

He growled, grinding against her. "Never doubt your power over me again."

"Never," she repeated with a gasp, as her body caught fire. She knew he could smell her arousal, when she glanced up to see his hard mouth kick up around the edges, she was already so turned on, totally wet and needy, how could she handle more? "I'll get you for sexually teasing me like this, Jake Randal," she whispered into his ear. His sexy chuckle made her cream even more.

"I'm going to paddle you for that, sugar, and soon."

"Promises, promises," she complained, rocking her hips against his solid erection, making them both groan. "Why don't you just take me back to good old bungalow six, and fuck me till I can't stand up straight?"

"Enough," he boomed, giving her bottom a light spank. "Stop trying to provoke me."

Cyn bit back a moan, as his hand lingered on her ass, and he stroked her bottom through her clothes. She leaned into his strength, inhaling his masculine scent, overdosing on his essence.

"Come." Setting her back on her heels, and taking her arm.

If only she could. She was achingly close to coming and he knew it. Still, she followed him on wobbly legs to *Branded's* solid metal, back security door. Jake punched out a security code on a keypad to gain entrance, and opened the door for her. She let him usher her inside and glanced around curiously. A closed door with *Scion Inc.* printed on masking tape was on the left side of the back entry door. *Branded*, what she could see of it through the safety glass door was on the right. Jake really did have an office back here. Why would an upscale businessman choose to work in such obscure setting? It would be a great place to lie low. It reinforced his claim of a quiet undercover investigation of North

Star Enterprises, and Dwain Hawkins in particular, and soothed any remaining doubts.

He noticed the direction of her stare. "If you need me during the day, come here."

"A little afternoon sex on your desk," she teased.

"Anything you want, sugar." He brushed her hair back off her face.

A heat wave rushed through her, as he touched her, and she couldn't help leaning into his strength.

Jake opened the glass door to *Branded*. An overhead bell tinkling in the empty, but still lit, store.

"Looks like you're right. This is a private tour. No customers but us." She walked inside, relieved to see they were alone.

"Sure thing, sugar. Mack and I do little favors for each other from time to time. The front door is locked, and Mack will be set up for our private showing."

Knowing that his hunky friend was in on her debauchery even if he wasn't here made her sex clench. She gazed at the exotic wares, feeling a new sense of naughtiness, taking in the Aladdin's Treasure Chest of Erotic Merchandise. The fairytale godmother's magic bag had nothing on this. She wanted one of everything. Just the possibilities to rock Jake's world intrigued her. Her dazzled gaze flicked from the lingerie to the vibrators to what looked like paddles and floggers.

Oh my...

"Are you ready to shop, bad girl?" Jake asked, coming up behind her.

Cyn leaned back against him, her pussy throbbing, as she pressed her hot ass against him, loving the feel of his erection pressing into her. "Oh yeah, I'm more than ready, Jake."

"Excellent," Jake broke the contact to pick up a basket, and thrust it at her. "We'll need to get you a wide assortment of toys of course..."

"Of course," she murmured clutching the basket, not knowing what to grab first.

"This way," he stated, edging her to the left.

Cyn frowned as he directed her to a rack of stubby, funny looking dildos. Then she read the labels—butt plugs. Her face heated as she took in the wide variety of sizes. "So many."

Jake grinned, and pulled three off the rack to add to the basket, explaining, "We need assorted sizes to get you ready for my cock, because I'm kind of big."

"Believe me, I noticed." She watched him pop two tubes of flavored gel into the basket.

"The lube goes with them. I want your rose nice and creamy for me, just like your cunt."

She moaned, spasming where she stood, as he talked dirty to her. She hoped that he'd make good on his promise to take her ass. So far, he'd been nothing but a tease.

Jake eased her away from him. "We need to get some edible love gel so you can taste me."

Now that got her attention. She looked at all the flavors, picked out strawberry and coconut, added them to her basket, and glanced at the tantalizing bulge in his pants. He was going to let her taste him—she could hardly wait.

Jake grinned, letting her ogle him for a moment, then took her elbow and led her to the display of vibrators. He leaned back against the wall, gazing at her with curiosity. "Pick two, sugar. I guarantee you that you'll like it when I use them on you."

She didn't doubt it for a minute. Cindy stared at them for a moment, her eyes widening at the diversity, as she checked out natural veined lifelike models, to neon colored ones, with intriguing clitoral bump outs. They came in all shapes and sizes. Running her hands over them, made her feel sultry, and ache to come. One even had double prongs. With her sex, wet and aching, she grabbed a large red one, labeled "The Stud", thinking it almost matched Jake's cock. Then she went for a smaller duck shaped one for bathtub fun.

"Excellent choices." Jake picked out a little one from the end of the rack.

She made a moue of complaint. "It's so small," she whispered. "It's for your ass," he replied, stroking her bottom through her clothes, his hand shaping the globes of her ass, before venturing in between...

"Ah," she blushed. Cyn gasped, her legs shaking as he teased her with his hands. If only he'd pop some batteries in her stud...or better yet unzip his pants. They were alone, nobody would see.

He gave her a playful swat, and steered her toward the racks of lingerie in a rainbow of different colors. "How about some nice lingerie?"

"Lovely," she whispered, looking at the beautiful assortment. She popped a black satin garter belt and matching fishnet stockings into her basket. They reminded her of something a film noir fem fatale might wear, and Jake liked them, she could tell by his pleased expression. "I'll model them for you."

"How about these, too?" He held up blue satin crotchless panties and a matching cut out bra.

Her eyes widened when she looked at the adventurous lingerie. They were like something out of a fifties men's magazine; they were perfect. "I think they're barely legal, and just what I need," she replied, with a matching grin.

"Not to worry, I have a friend on the force." He added the bra and panties to her basket with a wink.

Cyn quivered inside when she imagined herself modeling them for Jake. Alone in his bedroom, he'd take her over his knee, and spank her until she came. She squeezed her legs together at the randy thought.

"Let's go try out the paddles for size." He steered her toward the display.

Cyn throbbed as he walked her around the corner and she caught sight of the spanking bar pulled out from the wall, and red paddle already laid out on top of the padded leather bench. *Oh my, this was it.* She shivered with delight, both turned on, and embarrassed, as Jake reached behind her to unzip her dress. He licked her nape, flicking her dress straps off her shoulders one by one, as Cyn moaned, having to fight from coming. She had to wait. The dress slid off her with a hiss to pool at her feet, leaving her standing in only her underwear. Her nipples went instantly stiff, along with her clit.

"I promised you a paddling." He nibbled her ear.

Cyn whimpered with need as his warm breath stirred the tendril at her sensitive nape. He could be such a tease. Why did he prolong this aching need? He moved back, and she cried out, bereft.

"Take off your bra, and panties, sugar, and bend over the bar, if you want the paddle."

Trembling with need and apprehension, she bit her lip, and reached back to unhook her bra. It came loose, and the sound of Jake's rasping breath made her giddy. She slowly lowered the garment, teasing him, hearing him growl, and let it fall. Then she reached for the waistband of her thong, slowly inching it down the curve of her ass before stepping out of them. She smiled and picked them up, draping them over the end of the bar, saying designingly, "Another souvenir perhaps?"

"Don't press your luck sugar, or my patience. Over the bar now."

Cyn draped herself over the padded bar all joking over, and gasped when her abdomen pressed against the leather. Her ass was arched out toward Jake, exposed, and her breasts dangled, hanging free. She gasped when Jake ran a hot caress over her flanks, straightening her form, arching her ass out a little more. He toed her feet apart with a light nudge of his cowboy boots, and she moaned, her sex fluttering. When he laid the broad leather paddle against her ass, letting it rest there, she closed her eyes with a moan. He lifted the paddle, and she started to tense, but he brought it down so quickly with a teasing smack he caught the bottom of her ass unprepared. She yelped, as heat bloomed in its wake, and opened her eyes. Mack was leaning against the counter watching her, a steamy look in his eye. She gasped. "He's..."

"Watching you get it, bad girl."

The paddle came down with another teasing smack. She whimpered, needing more to come. Her sex rippled, her nipples budded tight, her breasts jiggling.

"See how hot you're making him?"

"Yes," she voiced with a squeak, watching Mack unzip his pants, and pull out his already stiff cock, to jack off. She couldn't look away from the sight, as Jake reigned teasing smacks against her ass. Mack's twitching cock was almost as big as Jake's, hard, and red.

"Now, smile for him Cyn. Show him that you like being watched while you're paddled," Jake ordered. "She's not doing it," Mack stated, giving her a shrug as Jake laid into her harder.

Moaning, her sex spasming, Cyn froze, gasping out, "I can't," her breasts jiggling as Jake heated her ass with the paddle. Mindless with need, she cupped her breasts playing with the nipples and spasmed as Jake landed a blow to her mound. She watched Mack's cock twitch, beads of sweat breaking out on his brow. Then Jake let up, she whimpered in protest, on the edge of coming. "Oh please..." she sobbed.

"What do you want, Cyn?" Jake demanded.

"Please spank me some more, sir."

"In front of Mack?"

"In front of the whole town. I don't care."

She locked sultry gazes with Mack, seeing his understanding smile, and smiled back at him.

"She's being a good girl now," Mack called out.

Cyn let out a sigh of surrender as Jake started spanking her harder. She was lost, moaning as her sex tightened and her pussy quivered. Her clit rubbed against the bar with each spank, and she came with a scream, as Jake continued to spank her. When her after-spasms ebbed, she opened her eyes to see Mack tuck his hard on back in his pants with a wince. He walked over, the bulge under his pants was huge, his gaze hot.

"Only for you, pal," he commented to Jake, giving him a high five, as he walked behind her. Jake went to the front and handed him the paddle.

Jake caressed her breasts, pinching her nipples. "Stay down, sugar," Jake commanded, gruffly. "You're not done yet."

Cyn moaned, wondering if she could take much more, as he rolled her sensitive nipples between his thumbs and forefingers, tugging on them, making her gasp with strong after-spasms.

"That was hot as hell," Mack stated, touching her stinging bottom. "And so is your ass. He gave you quite a paddling, didn't he girl?"

Cyn gasped, unable to stop leaning into the other man's caress. She nodded.

"Answer him, sugar," Jake ordered.

"Yes, sir," she gasped as Jake pinched her nipples, and Mack traced the spank marks on her throbbing ass. She wriggled, unable to stay still as her arousal returned tenfold. She moaned with need, completely sensitized, trusting them to give her as many orgasms as she could handle.

"I want your mouth, sugar," Jake demanded, unzipping his pants, as Mack touched the paddle to her bottom.

She whimpered, knowing what was coming, pushing back against the teasing paddle, and gazed hungrily at Jake's magnificent cock. He was already rock hard for her, the head a velvety purple-red, a bead of pre cum glistening on the slit. She moaned and flicked out her tongue to lick it off, hearing him hiss with pleasure. She swirled her tongue around the velvety head, toying with the loose flap of skin underneath, connecting the head to his long thick shaft, making Jake moan.

With a groan, she opened her mouth, and Jake slipped the head of his cock into her mouth. She murmured with pleasure, suckling on him, making him hiss, and thrust into her a little more. Emboldened, she took him deeper into her mouth, as he gently cupped her cheeks with his hands. Mack drew back the paddle, giving her a light smack, and she gasped, gagging a little, as Jake's cock went deeper.

"Easy, girl," Jake commented, caressing her stretched cheek with a gentle stroke of his thumb. "Time your movements with his spanks."

She moaned, doing just that, as Jake surged into her mouth time and again, Mack kept up a driving rhythm. She whimpered, aroused on both sides, as her body tightened once more. Her pussy rippled, her stiff clit rubbing on the bar. To come for another man seemed wrong, even though it felt so good. She tightened inside, holding back to the point of pain. Jake thrust into her, toying with her nipples.

"Come for him, sugar, I know you need to."

She sucked him harder, shaking her head a little, her body quivering as her clit burned. Jake came, spurting into her mouth, and she suckled him dry, draining him, needing to pleasure him.

Mack stopped spanking. "She's not coming for me, you lucky SOB. It's you she wants."

She lay limp and painfully aroused against the bar, Mack's hard on inside his pants rubbing against her ass.

"He can give you more," Jake stated, still caressing her breasts.

It felt good, and hell, it was just like the book, but it wasn't right. "No. All I want is you."

Jake felt the tension in him uncoil, as he met Mack's envious, but understanding gaze. He wouldn't have trusted any other man with this. He couldn't risk losing Cyn.

"I'll go ring this lot up and give you lovebirds some privacy." Mack picked up the basket, and walked away.

Jake gazed down at Cyn, still draped over the paddling bar, her nipples stiff as rubies, her sex hot and aroused, her ass rosy, her face blushing, and his cock swelled. Only she could get him hard this fast. He walked behind her, rubbing his cock against her outthrust ass. She moaned, and arched back against him. He slipped into her wet sex, and took her hard and fast from behind, his balls quickly tightening, as her cunt tightened, milking him.

She cried out as she came, and he drove into her.

Jake groaned, coming inside her. Draped over as they both gasped for breath, he thanked his lucky stars, he'd found Cyn. He eased away and pulled her off the bar, and into his arms. She pressed against him, spent.

"That was hot," she murmured, nibbling his jaw. "And very naughty."

"I agree." He cupped her hot ass and squeezed a little, adding, "But you are a bad girl." She flashed an amused and needy look up at him, and his cock started to swell again. Hell, he had to get her out of here before he screwed her again. That, he wasn't letting his old buddy in on. They'd shared women in the past but not this one.

"Time to get dressed." He helped her into her bra and dress. He picked up her panties from the end of the paddling bar, before she could reach for them, and tucked them in his top pocket.

"Are you starting a collection?" she asked, with a twinkle in her eye.

"Yeah, they're addictive, I just can't get enough. Any objection?" He watched her reaction. Instead of trying to brush him off, she smiled. He felt the connection where he lived; acknowledging that he was good and hooked, and that he liked it.

Mack grinned as they walked toward the register, and handed him a large shopping bag. "I added the paddle and a few other goodies. Don't worry about paying, I'll run you a tab."

"Later," Jake replied, taking the bag in one hand, and Cyn in the other. He rushed Cyn out the back door, eager to get her to bed. "I think well take the SUV, there's more room."

Chapter 12

"Why do we need more room?" she asked with a bemused smile. "Are we going parking?"

"You'll find out," he replied, pulling her duffle out of the bike's saddlebags, and throwing it in the back seat along with the *Branded* goody bag. He turned to look at her. She was watching him with a bemused expression, and he knew what a lucky guy he really was. He opened the door and grabbed her, lifting her inside. Smiling at her startled gasp.

"More of your Stone Age behavior."

"That's right. Welcome to my world, sugar." He buckled her in, closed her door, and rushed around to get behind the wheel. "This won't take long," he stated driving away. "We're not going parking. I just didn't want you to catch cold with no panties on." He winked, making her blush. He could hardly wait to bed her properly. Cyn's hot reaction to the paddling had him throbbing behind his fly. He drove through the property gates, pulling into the long private drive leading to a cottage alongside the lake. Tall garden walls and the rural setting insured privacy.

"It's a little slice of paradise." She looked out at the rustic cottage and beach.

He smiled pleased with her stunned reaction. He wanted to give her the sun and the moon, every sensual pleasure she could dream up, and some she didn't anticipate. "Glad you like it, sugar. I haven't been here for years, but I called the staff to make sure it was made ready."

"It's lovely," she commented, with a tranquil sigh, as her curious gaze scanned the wooded grounds.

"The fence surrounding the property, and its isolated location, should insure our privacy, for now." He watched her blush. She'd liked being watched and touched by Mack, but he was glad she didn't want another man inside her.

"Good. Because, boy, do we ever need privacy tonight. I'm going to enjoy tasting you, and..."

"Hold that thought." He grinned at her sudden boldness, turned off the engine, and exited the vehicle, to go around and help her out. He opened her door pleased that she sat there and waited for him. Her hot eyes were practically eating him up, making his hard on throb behind his fly. Maybe if he bought some baggy pants, he'd survive this, he thought with wry self-humor. As it was, he was going to have the worst case of blue balls in Texas history. He tugged open her door and reached for her, ignoring the hand she held out to grasp her around the waist and drag her out.

She sucked in a shocked gasp and melted against him as he pulled her onto him. His stiff cock twitched when the seductive witch purred as she brushed against him, and her luscious tits pillowed against his chest. His heart was beating like a drum, his cock throbbed in tandem. Letting out a growl, he bent to claim her mouth. His tongue snaking into her mouth to mate with hers, as she kissed him back. He broke the kiss with a rumble of approval. She was perfect for him, and he'd known it from the beginning.

He pulled back to rake her tantalizing body, and seductive smile, with an admiring gaze. "I approve of the dress, love." Touching her pretty dress's print rayon skirt. He could smell her cream, as she leaned into him with a needy gasp, while his hot palms ran over her even hotter bottom. He cupped the round globes of her sexy ass, delighted to hear her gasp. "The thong was a great idea, love. You obeyed my instructions," he stated, giving her another squeeze. "But did you lube your tight little ass for me?" he asked, the corners of his hard mouth kicking up in a smile as he pulled back to see her blush. He loved it when she blushed for him. "Did you obey me?" he asked.

She nodded, trembling, as she nibbled her lower lip.

He bit back a groan, and skimmed his hand over the sultry curve of her ass. He'd loved that she'd worn the thong, and matching satin bra. He grinned and flipped up her skirt to check, his hand caressing her freshly paddled bottom. It was still a little warm, and blushing. She moaned, her knees wobbling, and sagged into him. He laughed, catching her; his whole body primed with need, as he caressed her bare bottom.

Tracing the crease between the round globes of her bottom teasingly, he murmured, "Very nice indeed." He gave each cheek a teasing spank, loving the way she gasped and pressed against him. "You have the sexiest ass, Cyn, it just begs for my spankings and my cock to open it. Is it lubed for me?" he asked circling the puckered orifice with his fingertip.

"I used some baby oil," she replied with a gasp. "I felt extra naughty when I did it for you.

"Bad girl." He chuckled, loving her whispered confession. "We've now got something better than baby oil. Let's open our bag of toys and use the strawberry lube." He reached around her for the *Branded* bag. He watched her blush as she flicked a fascinated gaze over the contents of the bag. The paddle lay inside, along with some nipple clamps, a slave collar, blindfold and handcuffs. "Mack was generous," he commented, pulling out the flavored gel.

"Bend over the fender, precious. I'm going to lube you properly, and get your ass ready for my cock."

Cyn bent over the warm fender, her sex quivering, her face heating as Jake flipped up her skirt. He'd already claimed her panties and had them in his top pocket so there was no barrier. Standing half naked in the setting sun was shockingly erotic. Cream of arousal misted the nest of curls covering her pussy and ran down her thighs, as Jake ran his big hand over the outthrust curves of her ass. She moaned, pushing back at him, silently begging for more. She craved his touch. She was hot, and ready for him now.

His blunt fingertip suddenly circled her anus with a cool gel, making her gasp with shock, but she didn't pull away. Then something firm pressed against her pulsing orifice and eased inside. She whimpered at the invasion, her ass and pussy rippling in reaction, even as her clit throbbed. He pressed it a little farther inside her clutching bottom, and she arched back at him, while she gasped at the invasion. It wasn't warm like his delightfully naughty finger had been last night, and it sure a shooting wasn't big enough to be his magnificent cock. It was one of the butt plugs. "This is your smallest butt plug, Cyn," Jake voiced firmly. "I'm using it both to discipline you and to stretch you for my cock.

The word discipline made her tighten against him. It'd looked so small but now felt so big stretching her tight bottom.

"Relax," he commanded, rubbing her bottom softly. "Only a little more to go."

She didn't normally take well to discipline, but she relaxed at his touch, and he slipped the plug the rest of the way inside. She burned, seeming to be spread wide, but she knew it was tiny compared with his cock. As her ass rippled on the device, she couldn't help rolling her hips in arousal.

"Tight?" he asked.

"Yes, and naughty."

"Well then, it's just the thing for you, bad girl," he commented with a chuckle, wiggling it.

She gasped, moaning when he fucked it in and out of her a few times. She met the thrusts, her sex quivering.

"Excellent," he whispered, pushing it back in place.

She gasped in protest. "You're not going to stop now," she wailed. "I need more. I need the real thing. I want you to open me."

"I'll take your ass, when and if I decide that you're ready for it," he replied, straightening her up and turning her to face him.

She thought about digging in her heels, mad at him for making her wait. But in the end, she turned and fell into his arms with a needy sigh. He could be such a control freak. "You're mean," she complained. He spanked her left cheek, and she gasped as the plug moved inside her. She let out a helpless whimper under his hands, craving more. But he let her go, and gently set her back on her heels.

"Dinner is waiting." Jake taking her arm and leading her to the cottage.

She bit back a gasp, every step setting off sexual tremors inside her. She looked around the cottage impressed. The table was laid beautifully, and wonderful aromas wafted out of silver chafing dishes.

Jake smiled and led her toward the table. "I promised you dinner. Smells good, doesn't it, love."

"Delicious." She asked, "How did you do it?"

"I had it catered in. Mack set it up for us. He's a gourmet cook. Don't worry we've got the place to ourselves."

Just what surprises did he have up his sleeve? She gazed at his implacable expression, her body pulsing with desire, her ass rippling on the teasing butt plug. Good grief she hadn't known *Branded* sold them before their private showing, having sent Dora in to buy her contraband.

Cyn watched as Jake smiled his heated gaze, running over her like a hot caress. He knew what he was doing to her, how hot he was making her, and this was only the beginning. She smiled, licking her lip, hoping to provoke him into ending her misery, and watched his eyes darken with lust. Nice. Now if she could just seduce him...

"Sit," he told her, pulling out a chair.

She sat with a sigh, and then gasped when her ass touched the cool wooden seat, sending quivers through her.

He chuckled. "Relax and enjoy the sensation," he ordered, going to the chafing dishes to fill her plate. He walked back to place the plate in front of her before filling his own.

The food smelled delicious, but she was too aroused to eat. She watched every move he made, her sex creaming while her ass quivered. Her clit thrust out, seeming to throb in time with her racing pulse. Cyn bit back a moan, trying to sit quietly in a ladylike manner on her chair.

Jake sat down and gazed at her. "Eat, sugar, you'll need your energy to go toe to toe with me later."

She picked up her fork at his bidding and nibbled at her chicken and veggies. Watching him eat was even a turn on she decided, as she watched him savor his food. Would he savor her later?

Jake sat back, sipping his wine, and quirked his finger. "Come."

Cyn managed to get to her feet, biting back a gasp as the butt plug moved, making her pussy and ass quiver. It was pleasurable torture, and he knew it, based on the smile on his face. How many women had he trained? Strike that, she didn't want to know. Locking gazes with him, she started toward him. She was going to taste him all over this time.

Jake held out a hand to halt her. "That's far enough, sugar. Strip for me, Cyn. Show me what a bad girl you are."

Cindy stood frozen for a minute, her face heating.

"Want your present and your paddling?" he asked, his brow arching.

"Yes." She was already on fire for all he might give her. Her face heating, she reached for her zipper and turned her back to him, slowly lowering it. She wouldn't be the only one teased tonight. She looked over her shoulder at him and peeled off the dress, lowering it slowly to bare her bottom. She let it drop to pool at her feet. She turned, locking gazes with him, his sexy smile making her want to brain him, and fuck him at the same time. Instead, she ran her hands over her breasts, cupping them in her hands, offering them to him. She fanned her nipples through her bra, making them hard, thrilled when she saw his gaze darken with lust.

Her fingertips circled her budding nipples. Jake's breathing grew ragged. Oh yeah, she was turning him on. She reached for the bra's back clasp and unhooked it, shimmying out of it. The fire in Jake's eyes made her pant.

"Pinch your nipples for me," Jake demanded.

She did, and whimpered at the small-mingled pleasure and pain.

"Good girl," he praised.

"Kick off your shoes and come here," he ordered, patting his lap.

She stifled a moan and walked over to him. He ran a hand over her body, pinching her nipple. He pulled her onto his lap, astride him, her open pussy brushing against his slacks, her breasts pillowed against his chest, her ass rippling on the butt plug. Jake smiled and kissed her.

"I heard it was your birthday. Open your present."

She picked up the gift-wrapped package, tore off the gift-wrap, and saw a jeweler's case. What on earth? It was too big to be a ring, not that she expected one.

"Open it," he requested, toying with her nipples, lengthening them.

Stifling a pleasured moan, she opened the box, to find two jeweled clips.

"They're your nipple clamps, Cyn. Turquoise to match your eyes. I had them commissioned. Want me to put them on you?"

She nodded, her body hungry, wondering how the naughty but beautiful things would feel. He opened one clasp and clamped it onto her left nipple, letting go to let the jewel dangle down. She whimpered as the weight tugged on her tortured nip. "Oh god, it's better than I imagined."

He chuckled, and picked up the other clamp, toying with her right nipple and attaching it.

Cyn gasped at the pinch and the sweet weight tugging at her as he let go. She gazed down at the dangling jewels, shuddering as she gasped, making her nipples seem to swell and burn while her pussy spasmed. She gasped when his hand went to her hungry sex, his strong arm supporting her wobbly legs. She moaned as he slipped two fingers into her pussy, while his thumb rode her clit.

"That's it, baby, fuck yourself on my hand."

She tightened, arching against him, spasms rippling through her as she came, shouting her triumph into his shirt. She collapsed against him as he held her. Shit, he was still fully dressed. "You're wearing too many clothes, Randal." She murmured against his chest.

"It's Jake or sir, and you can solve that by undressing me," Jake replied, kissing her.

Now there was a brilliant idea. Smiling, wickedly she undid his tie, and pushed his jacket off his broad shoulders. Then she went for his belt and zipper.

"Hey, aren't you forgetting the shirt?" he asked, amused.

"You've got your priorities, I've got mine." She undid his belt wondering if she'd like it across her backside some time. The paddle had been a stinging revelation. That could wait for later. She undid his pants, making him wince when she banged into his hard on.

"Easy, sweet," he gasped, pushing back the dishes to sit her on the edge of the table, and standing up.

He unzipped his pants and let them drop. Her fascinated gaze fell on his erection, hanging huge and hard down his thigh. She was dimly aware of his shucking off his shirt. He opened the love gel and handed it to her. "Enjoy."

She smiled, took him in her hand, and squeezed a good-sized bead on his head, fascinated when he hissed. She flicked her tongue out to taste him, whispering yummy as the mingled flavors of Jake and strawberries burst on her tongue. She took him into her mouth and drew on his hard staff. He jerked and she took him deep down her throat. She gagged a little and he pulled back, but she gripped his hips and sucked him off. He exploded into her mouth as she sucked him dry. She grinned at him. "Now that's dessert."

"Bad girl." He pulled her to her feet and into his arms.

She sighed with pleasure gazing at the sultry look on his handsome face. He could do anything he wanted to her.

"Give me your mouth, Cyn, and wrap your legs around me"

She kissed him and gasped when his stiffening cock impaled her as she wrapped her legs around his waist. He carried her across the floor and outside. She shivered with delight as the evening breeze caressed her bare skin. The sunset was beautiful, and she knew someday she'd have to paint it and him just the way he looked tonight. Bad boy, satyr, sex god, all rolled into one. When he started to walk into the water, she gasped with delight. "You planning on taking me skinny dipping?"

"Oh yeah," he replied, walking into the water. His slid her down onto his rousing cock, and strode deeper, each movement making her gasp. Her sex clutched at him feverishly, her ass rippling on the plug inside her. As waist deep water rushed around them, he cupped her ass, and rode her harder and faster. She moaned, her sex clinging to him as her ass squeezed the butt plug he'd inserted in her. She cried out, coming long and hard. He held her tight, coming inside her.

Chapter 13

Jake woke up the next morning, his mind made up. He was keeping her. He rubbed his rousing cock against Cyn's warm ass, and smiled when she arched against him. He rolled her over and came down on top of her. "Good morning, sugar."

She smiled up at him and raised her leg to open for him fully. "Good morning yourself, sex god."

"So, I'm a sex god, am I?" he asked, pleased.

"In my book, yeah."

He rubbed his cock against her again, and she made yummy noises. "Want breakfast, do you?" he teased.

"I want you."

"Good. Now kneel up on the edge of the bed for your paddling." The startled and excited look she gave him was priceless.

"You mean it?"

"Oh yeah. Move, or I'll take my belt to you."

She smiled and leisurely crawled down to the end of the bed arching her ass up in the air teasingly. "How's this?"

"Tease," he replied with a smile.

"It's good for you." She bit her lip when he picked up the paddle.

He brought it down on her ass, and she moaned, flushing all over.

He started a steady rhythm that had her moaning, his cock twitching as she cried out. Her sex was wet, glistening, and fragrant. Her ass twitching. He was tempted to taste her all over. "Spread your legs, Cyn, I want to spank that bad pussy."

She moaned and spread her legs apart.

Jake caught her mound with flicks of the paddle, and she came with a shriek, her cunt pulsing. He dropped the paddle and brought a lubed vibrator to her ass. She moaned as he slipped the head inside and tightened. He flipped it on vibrate and she shrieked, coming again, loosening up as he slid it home, letting it vibrate inside her as he fucked her ass with it. She moaned grinding against him. He reached out to press her clit, and she came. He gently pulled it out and rolled back on the bed beside her. He didn't want to do anything but pleasure her today. He flipped her around, making her gasp and laugh, reversing positions so that he was on the bottom.

She sat astride him, with a bemused smile. "You used to wrestle, didn't you?"

"I still do," he replied, with a pleased chuckle at the jealous look on her face. Good. Maybe it would keep her from backing away from him.

"I'll have to see for myself how flexible you are," she stated, slipping onto his cock.

Jake hissed with pleasure as she lowered her tight sex onto his cock, barely able to hold him. She sat still for a moment, her eyes closed, a blissful look on her bewitching face, and he couldn't look away. He slid his hands up her body to cup her beautiful breasts, her eyes opened, and she looked down at him with love.

"I'm about to ride you, cowboy," she commented, rocking her hips.

Jake groaned, as she took him, rocking harder, whimpering as her clit brushed against him on the down strokes. He arched up into her making her cry out, her cunt tightening on his dick, milking at him. With a growl, he held her hips to steady her as she rode him, arching up into her again and again, until they were both gasping. His balls tightened. His cock swelled inside her, he was so close, but he was taking her with him. He surged up, tweaking her clit, making her scream as she clutched at him. His other hand reached behind her globes to toy into her anus, and she exploded. Her pussy wringing his cock. He came with a roar as she milked him. Cyn collapsed down on top of him. He pulled her into his arms, their bodies still intimately joined.

"What's the decision, can I still wrestle?"

"Yeah baby, you can wrestle with the best of them."

That afternoon, Cyn put away the lunch dishes and took a minute to gaze fondly at Jake as he wiped up the table. They'd lingered over breakfast in bed, and played around until noon. Now it was time to go back to reality, and a big part of her didn't want to. Things would probably change between them. In a way, this idyll had strengthened their relationship, but it had also created doubts. Jake never talked about himself, his hopes, and his dreams. He'd never even told her that he wanted to continue the affair after he moved out next week.

That left her one short week to get him out of her system.

"Something wrong?" he asked, looking back at her, his stance tense.

"No. I was just thinking about the chores back at the ranch," she lied. "This has been fun, but I need to go back."

"Why? Stay with me another night," he commented, stalking up to her to take the dishes out of her hands and put them on the counter. "I'll make it worth your while, Cyn. S'mores by the campfire, all the strawberry sex gel you can handle, and the paddle."

Cyn leaned into him with a moan, sorely tempted. It wasn't like they'd actually miss her at the ranch. "I don't know." Staying was risky, she'd just crave him more when he left. Besides, she had responsibilities. "I shouldn't."

He gave her a firm look, telling her that he knew what she was thinking. "One more night, do it for me, for us.".

"I'll make a deal with you. You can come back to my apartment. I'll model that naughty underwear, and serve you supper in bed. We'll keep it quiet so as not to blow your cover. We don't want to scare off Hawkins if word got out."

"There's no need to worry about that. Things escalated, and I had to recalculate the odds. I put the word out that I'm back and that arrests are about to take place. It should make the guilty parties run. Then we'll have them. I had to act quickly. Why do you think little sister was all over me? I don't fool myself into thinking it's my good looks."

He was so wrong. He was a total hunk, even if he didn't realize it. "That explains Cordial's cat and mouse game. Maybe she isn't guilty of window peeking." His offhand disclosure could explain Cordial's sudden knowledge of his identity, but not her knowing what they'd done in bed. He should have told her this from the start, and not tried to run the show alone. It was typical of his dominant behavior, and she wouldn't have it outside the bedroom.

"Window peeking?" he asked, his brow arching.

She sighed. "We were watched our night together at the ranch. And when I went out to the mailbox to find the latest obscene note, Cordial came up behind me, confronted me about it, and told me to run while I still could. She knew everything we did and she's not the only one."

"The note?" Jake asked, giving her a probing glance.

"Oh yeah, he must have been watching us. It was pretty sickening."

Jake pulled her into his arms with a groan. "No more playing around. I'm driving you in to the police station right now."

Cyn sighed, leaning into him, his strength restoring her sense of calm. "I know. I already decided that yesterday, and brought the letter along."

Cyn clung to Jake as he drove his Harley around to the rear parking lot at the police station and parked. She'd hesitated to do this, file an official complaint, because she didn't want to make Hawkins think he was getting to her. Thinking if she'd ignored him, he'd eventually give up and go away. It had backfired, he was getting worse. She took off her helmet and handed it to Jake as they dismounted.

"You ready to do this?" he asked, giving her a tender smile.

She nodded. "Thanks for bringing me." She took his hand and walked with him into the rear entrance, strengthened by his presence. "I guess I should have filed a complaint weeks ago," she stated and gave him a puzzled look when he steered her towards the detectives' offices instead of the front lobby. He might be used to special VIP service, but she certainly didn't expect it. "I need to file a report, not go back here."

"No need. I already filed one for you."

Her jaw dropped, as he walked her up to an office door. "You did what?" she asked, her eyes narrowing. How could he have presumed she'd give him permission to do that?

"It needed to be done, sugar," he replied softly. "It was for your own good."

"Don't you *sugar* me," she snapped back at him. "And condescending words like, *it was for your own good*, are guaranteed to get your ass kicked."

"I'll risk it," he murmured grimly, and tapped on the door lettered, *Detective Zane Redcloud* and leaned inside. "Got a minute?"

Zane looked up from his computer. "Sure. Come on in and take a seat. I see you finally brought in the complainant."

Cyn gave Jake an irritated glance, and brushed by him and into the room. She sat gingerly on a stiff backed chair facing Zane's desk, her face heating with embarrassment, when he raked an appreciative glance over her.

"She got another one."

Cyn scowled at Jake. "I do have a voice of my own, you know." She turned back to look at Zane, saying, "I received another of those stupid letters, only this time it's worse. It seems he was watching us." She pulled it out, and handed it over his desk, blushing when he read it.

"I was afraid of this."

"Window peeking?" she asked.

"No, escalation. Stalkers always have to increase their presence to get the same rush."

"Damn sick ass bastard," Jake bit out. "When are you going to arrest him?"

"I thought you wanted me to hold off and wait until your investigation of North Star was complete."

Jake frowned, pinning Zane with a resolved glance. "Not anymore. Some things take precedence."

Cyn took in their man-to-man gaze, and scowled. Detective Redcloud was no doubt used to riding roughshod over suspects, and Jake just plain wanted to smother her with bubble wrap to keep her safe. "Hey boys, a little attention here. I don't appreciate you talking about this over my head." They snapped steely gazes at her, filled with male determination.

Zane arched a brow. "So, you're willing to make out an official complaint?"

"Yes, I am," she stated firmly. "I don't want him bothering me anymore." She smiled when Zane pulled out the paperwork, and turned to see Jake's resolute gaze on her. He'd be more of a challenge. "And as for you, Jake, I won't have you sneaking behind my back, and keeping me in the dark, while trying to protect me."

Jake frowned. "I can't promise you that. Some issues involving Randal Industries are confidential."

"I don't need to know all the business related details. But I do insist on running my own life. You can't protect me by keeping me in the dark."

He frowned. "I'm just trying to help, take some of the burdens off your shoulders."

"I'm a strong woman, Jake," she commented, sighing, when Jake's cell phone rang and he turned his back on her to answer it, talking in low tones. He was doing it again.

Cyn walked away while he was on the phone, exasperated. She headed down the hall to the front door. There had to be some way to convince him to open up and let her in. She wouldn't let him manipulate her this way, and then keep her in the dark. She stepped out the front door, and hurried down the steps. Jake's hand on her arm stopped her when she reached the sidewalk. "Let go," she snapped, turning her head to frown at him.

"Where do you think you're going?"

"Home, alone. I'll call a cab. Until you decide to level with me about what's going on, you're cut off." Jake's stunned expression almost made her smile.

In the coffee shop across the street from the cop shop, he put down his latte and chuckled. And to think he'd only stopped here by chance. Sometimes fate could be a sweet mistress. His plan was working better than he could have imagined. He watched Cynthia Jane say something cutting to the pretty boy, and then stomp away, storming around the corner, Jake following her pleading like a dog.

Good. Soon he'd make them both pay...

Jake tracked Cyn around the corner, exasperated. How could he make her see that he was only trying to shelter her, help her? He could understand her fury, but there was no way he could let her runaway. "Does that mean you don't love me anymore?" he teased, and was gratified to see her stop in her tracks.

She turned to face him, a troubled frown on her face. "I never said I did."

He saw the tender look in her eyes, telling him her repressive frown was a lie, and wanted to shout for joy. Instead, he leaned closer to say, "But you do, don't you?"

"Yeah, cowboy, unfortunately I'm head over heels in love with you. But don't think that cuts you any slack when it comes to this. I won't have you pulling the strings, keeping me in the dark to protect me. I meant what I said. Until you start leveling with me, you're cut off."

He scowled as she turned to go, and grabbed her arm. "You can't go off on your own, sugar, no matter how pissed you are at me. Until this is wrapped up, we're going to be inseparable. You know I'm right about this."

"I'm not a fool, Jake," she replied with a scowl. "Fine, just remember what I want from you. Full disclosure."

"I'll remember," he stated, as they got on his bike. He tensed, not liking her standoffish body language; she deliberately kept space between them, her hands clutching the seat instead of him. Damn. He knew he had some fence mending to do, and that she was right. "We have to stop at Randal Industries. Something's come up."

"I take it your plan to get them running scared worked?" she asked dryly.

"A little too well," he agreed, with a sigh. It had an unexpected effect. Dwain Hawkins was still there. "The forensic audit I ordered is complete along with the investigation I ordered." He was relieved to feel Cyn loosen up behind him, wrapping her hands around his middle.

"Was that so hard?" she teased.

"Yes," he murmured, not wanting her to get involved in the dicey, perhaps dangerous, situation. "You don't have to take on my burdens. You've got enough of your own."

"Remember what you said about burdens, they're easier to bear when they're shared."

He looked over his shoulder at her, noting her pleased smile. "I give up. But let me know if it gets tedious or you get bored."

"It won't happen, I'm not Brandy or Tiffany."

"Thank god for that," he stated, peeling out.

Jake pulled into the Randal Industries nearly full lot, parking next to his father's car. He still wasn't happy that Cyn was involved. It could get nasty, and he didn't want her hurt. Cyn's determined expression, as they walked toward the building, told him she knew what he was thinking. "Thanks for coming, I don't know anyone else who would have worried about me." He reached out to squeeze her hand.

"We're a team." Her hand clung to his.

It was a novel experience, having someone looking after him. He'd been on his own since his late teens. He gave Cyn a smile. "Follow my lead in there, okay?"

"Sure thing. I'm just here to give you moral support."

Shifting back into business mode, he nodded at Tim, as they reached his guard shack.

"Hi Jake, I see you brought some pretty company with you today," Tim commented, giving Cyn a curious smile.

"That's right. Tim meet, Cyn Taylor, my girlfriend."

Tim's eyes widened. "Well, hello, Ms. Taylor. I didn't know it was you. I put the word out for you, by the way, Jake."

Jake nodded. "I heard."

"I hope I did okay." He tilted his head to study Jake's reaction.

"You did a really good job from what I hear," Cyn replied with a kind smile.

"Great," Tim expressed, standing taller. "I'm always glad to help. Randal Industries has been good to me and mine. Your father especially, Jake."

"I know he appreciates your loyalty, as I do." Jake patted him on the arm. "Is Dad in his office?"

"He just went down to the factory floor for a minute. You can wait for him in his office. I'll tell him you're here."

"Thanks." Jake took Cyn through the gate when Tim buzzed them in. Randal Industries employed a lot of good people like Tim, being a major local employer, and he couldn't let them down by allowing the losses to go on.

"He's a nice man," Cyn acknowledged, as they walked down the hall. "But why did you tell him that we're partners?"

"Why not? It's true, isn't it?" he asked, gazing at her. He was relieved when she smiled.

"Yes. It's true, as long as you keep letting me in."

Jake stepped into the anteroom, outside his father's office, and found Maud waiting at the desk, a scowl on her face as she caught sight of him. He gazed back at her fondly; the dynamo had her silver hair pulled back in its usual bun, and was wearing one of her stiff formal suits. She peered out the bottom of her bifocals at him. She'd kept him running on time for years.

"About time you got here, Jacob. Your father's been irate. What do you mean, turning off your cell?"

"I wanted some privacy, for once."

Maud gave Cyn a kindly but curious look. "And who's your lady friend?" she asked, ignoring him.

"Cyn, meet Maud, she's been my nosy, bossy, private secretary for the past seven years, now she's my dad's problem."

"Don't pay any attention to him. I just take an interest in the wastrel's well-being. It's nice to meet you, Cyn. It's about time he got out of the office and had a social life."

He was chagrined to see Cyn grin back at her.

"You don't say. I take it he doesn't date much."

"Are you kidding, he…"

"We'll be waiting inside," Jake interrupted, easing Cyn into the inner office. "Get Bart Donavan on the phone, and ask him to come over."

"I already did, young man. He's on his way."

Jake rolled his eyes, only Maud could make him feel like a kid. He knew Maud had his best interests at heart, but there were things a guy didn't want to talk about in front of the woman he loved.

"Why don't you take a seat, anywhere, sugar," Jake stated, closing the door. He watched her settle into a wing chair in the corner, and paced in front of the desk. He saw Cyn's concerned gaze on him, and stopped. "Drink?" he asked.

"Water would be nice," she replied, with a nod.

He went to the fridge in the wet bar, and got out a bottle of spring water for her. Just then, the door opened, and Silas burst into the room.

"About time you got here, son. Why in blue blazes did you turn off your cell? Maud all but had to send out smoke signals to reach you." He looked at the bottle of water in Jake's hand. "Get me one of those, too, and add some scotch."

"No scotch." Jake handed his father a bottle of water, and carried one over to Cyn. She took it from him, but he noticed her wary gaze remained on his father.

Silas stopped dead in his tracks when he spotted Cyn. He gave her a thoughtful look. "This must be that Taylor girl you've been shacked up with out at the ranch. But what the hell is she doing here? These are crucial times boy, women have no place in business, and besides, she might be a spy."

"Dad, behave…"

"What a crock," Cyn snapped, surging to her feet. "I'm here to support Jake, and under protest, I might add."

"The hell you say." Silas grinned. "You've got spunk. I'll say that for you."

"Same to you, Mister," she commented back, staring him down.

Jake went quiet as they glared at each other, ready to intervene. He wasn't surprised to see his father back down. Cyn could be fierce.

"Well, I'll be damned son. It looks like you picked you a good one."

Silas settled in his desk chair and looked at Cyn. "You're the one who kicked Dwain's ass, and set the dogs on him."

"That's me," Cyn replied with a rebellious grin, adding, "And for the record, it was pygmy goats, not dogs."

"So, you're the scheming redhead that stole him away at the dance."

"I suppose that's verbatim."

"Pretty much, got it from your stepmother. She's at a claw and cackle women's club meeting with my wife, right now."

Maud buzzed, "Bart Donaldson is here to see you."

"Send him in," Silas returned into the intercom.

Jake sat back as the accountant, with a paunch and a comb over, lumbered into the room. Bart gave them all a suspicious glance. Jake sighed; it was going to be a long day.

"Here's the deal. I've pinpointed the losses in the acquisitions department. When I went to confront the culprit, I learned that he hasn't reported for work. The North Star office and his condo have been abandoned, and picked clean of personal items. I was able to recover certain documents. Deeds and land contracts for the properties they took. None of them have been filed, as far as I've been able to ascertain, which leaves Randal Industries in jeopardy." He dumped out a sheaf of documents. The one for the Taylor ranch landed on top.

Cyn gasped.

Jake's gut tightened as he glanced at her shell-shocked expression. "It's not legal." He assured her.

"But damning," she replied, seeing Cordial's signature along with her father's. "It's a forgery, has to be, my dad wouldn't sell, and anyhow, he couldn't. I have power of attorney."

"Durable, or temporary?" Zane asked.

"Temporary," Cyn murmured softly.

"Are there any out clauses?"

"I don't know," she stated, her voice breaking.

"Easy, sugar." Jake took her hand in his. "I'll have my attorney find out exactly what's happening. And Bart..."

"Thank you, but I'll handle it."

Jake watched her shut down right before his eyes, and his gut twisted. Didn't she trust him after all? Her trembling hand, in his, made him furious at Cordial. Damn the scheming bitch. He'd sort this out for Cyn, and she'd come around. "It's time I got you home." Jake stood up. He pulled out Cyn's chair and helped her to her feet. She seemed numb with shock.

"Are you two coming to our party tonight?" Silas asked, rising.

"Party?" Cyn asked in a daze.

"Yeah, the wife is throwing a shindig for our anniversary. I want you two to be there. It would go a-ways in putting down rumors that RI's in trouble."

"We wouldn't want that," Cyn stated sarcastically.

Jake grinned, taking her arm, relieved to see that she was getting her spunk back.

"It'll be good for you too, young lady," Silas commented with a glower. "You still look a little green about the gills."

Cyn laughed. "Thanks, I needed that to snap me out of it. I'm fine, it's just a shock to find out someone you trusted is trying to screw you."

"Ain't it though," he replied with a nod.

"We'll be there, Dad," Jake voiced, steering Cyn toward the door.

Chapter 14

Cyn rode back to the ranch with Jake, her mind in a whirl. How could Cordial have tried to con her this way, or be stupid enough to think she could get away with it? Her father's signature had to be a forgery, at least that thought made her feel a little bit better. Her hand tightened on the copy of the document Jake had given to her.

"I'll get one of my operatives to interview your father about this."

"No." She met his frown with a steady look. He was trying to protect her, in his take-charge way, but she had to handle this on her own. "I don't want to see him hurt. Visiting day is tomorrow. I'll go see him, lay this all out on the table, and get some answers." She watched his jaw set, his hands tighten on the steering wheel, telling her he didn't like it. He probably thought she was being stubborn, but she couldn't help it; she was putting her foot down. A thing like this took tact, and Jake had all the delicacy of a Mack truck. "Don't you see, a shock like this could give him a heart attack or something at his age, this has to be done delicately, and by me."

"And you don't trust me to handle this, right?"

"It's not that, it's just that, it's just that, *hell*...my father thinks my stepmother hung the moon. This is going to come as a big shock to him. He's still crazy in love with her, even though she rarely visits him in

205

prison. Even worse, he trusted me to look after his ranch, Cordial, and their daughters. How can I tell him I've failed?"

"Did you ever think he might have failed you, be conning you?" he shot back, studying her face grimly.

"How dare you infer," she sputtered, knowing deep down her dad had failed her by being a workaholic, absentee, father. But he'd changed for the better after he'd married Cordial. At least she could credit the other woman for that much. "My dad…"

"Left you holding the bag," Jake finished flatly. "Face it, sugar. What kind of father does that?"

"One who's run out of options. He was going to prison, even though it's considered a country club type white-collar crime compound, it's still prison, and he knew they couldn't cope. When he asked for my help, I was touched. He finally needed me. We've always been distant, my father and I," she stated with a sigh.

"I know the feeling," Jake bit out.

Cyn nodded, knowing they'd shared a similar childhood, but at least Jake had grown up with a mother. "Dad was shattered when my mother died, and Pedro and Juanita more or less raised me. They're like second parents to me. But when Cordial came into the picture, it was like he had a new lease on life. I hate to see that spark go out. And when he got in trouble and needed me, I was glad to come back. I love this land, and I can still paint in my spare time."

Jake pulled into the ranch driveway and drove directly to her cabin. "I understand your tender feelings, and respect you for them, but I won't sit idly by and let you get hurt."

"I can't get any more hurt than I already am."

"There are still too many unknown factors for my liking. Dwain Hawkins for instance."

"You heard Zane. The elusive con man has run away. Either way, he's no longer a threat." She opened her door and jumped out before he could get to her, knowing he'd weaken her strong will. She wouldn't let him soften her up with sex.

Jake slammed his door, and walked around to her. "Fine. I'll back off, and give you two days to clear this up. After that, it goes to court with the other pending documents, and Cordial's goose is cooked. The courts take a dim view of forgery."

"I understand, but I want to hear her side of it first. There's the possibility her signature is a forgery, too."

"Right," he whispered, following her to her cabin.

"Where do you think you're going?" she asked, arching a brow.

"You promised to model the undies and feed me supper in bed."

"That was before." She looked at Jake and weakened. "Oh heck, come on in and I'll see what I can whip up."

She turned to look at him once they were inside and she'd bolted the door. She had him all to herself and she wasn't about to let Cordial or the twins intrude on their privacy. "What am I going to do with you?" she mused out loud.

Jake smiled. "How about dinner for starters?"

"Dinner, right." She started toward the kitchen when he stopped her by simply touching her shoulder, coming up behind her. She sighed, leaning into him. "You fight dirty, Jake."

"I fight fire with fire," he commented, nibbling her nape.

Her zipper went down, and she didn't try to stop him. "You expect me to cook naked?"

"Semi-naked," he replied with a chuckle as her dress fell. "You did promise to model these garments."

Cyn blushed as her peek-a-boo undies were revealed. In all the commotion, she'd forgotten she was wearing them. Jake's hands cupped her breasts, his fingertips swirling over her tingling nipples. She moaned. "I never said I was going to sleep with you."

"I didn't have sleeping in mind, sugar. And besides, I've been very good and open, you said so yourself."

She bit back a moan, thrusting herself into his hands. "So, I did." When he stopped playing with her boobs and let go, stepping away, she let out a mew of protest. She needed him, no matter her reservations. He was starting to change, and open up to her, she could see that.

"Let's cook," he stated, taking her hand and pulling her into the kitchen with him.

When he introduced her to chocolate whipped cream shots later, she groaned with ecstasy. "My god, that's good right out of the can."

He smiled. "A perfect guy's dessert. No cooking." He leaned forward to kiss her.

She moaned, opening for him, tasting the best of everything, him and whipped cream. When a fleece lined restraint wrapped around her wrist, she giggled. "Are you planning on tying me up and having your wicked way with me?"

He waggled his eyebrows. "You're onto my evil plan," he replied, boosting her up onto the table.

She smiled at him, bemused.

"Up on your knees darling, legs apart."

She spread herself, the crotchless panties baring her to his hot eyes.

"Now reach behind you and arch your back."

She did and he loosely restrained the other wrist with the cuffs. She felt the restraint inside, her body trembling. She was completely open for him, her breasts thrust out, her nipples hard as jewels, her creamy sex opened for him. He pulled the little flogger out of the *Branded* bag, and she almost came. It had a little leather flap. They hadn't tried that yet. He flicked it at her left nipple, and it made her cry out at the burst of heat. "You are a wicked man, Jake Randal," she murmured with a moan, as he did it again, and then moved on to her other nipple.

"Little old me?" he asked innocently, and aimed it at her clit.

She whimpered, her clit throbbing, her pussy clenching. He kept a driving rhythm, and she came with a shriek, her sex spasming. She was dimly aware of the flogger hitting the table. Jake was on her, pulling her into his arms, kissing her, his hands on her secret wet needy places.

Jake unzipped his pants, groaning when he grasped her hips, and thrust into her wet sex, deep and hard.

Cyn whimpered, her hands still restrained and behind her, her back arched, leaving her totally open to him. He clutched her ass, driving into her, making her tremble, as her sex clung to his hard driving cock. He surged into her, grinding against her clit, and bent to take her nipple into his mouth and suck on it. She shrieked, her sex pulsing as he drew hard on the tender budded point. He pulled her tight to him, his shaft rubbing her clit, and she exploded, fireworks going on behind her closed eyelids, her pussy milking at him.

Jake groaned, and shuddered inside her, his cock plunging into her hard as he came.

He stood in the shadow, his face suffused with rage, as he watched her act like a common whore for Jake Randal. What a bitch. Beating her into submission would be so sweet and satisfying. He groaned, jacking off, his cock red hot. If only she saw what he had, she'd swoon. Randal was probably hung like a mouse like most pretty boys. He couldn't tell with the jerk's cock buried in her snatch.

He came with a roar, spurting against the siding, tripping on her damned sculpture in the flowerbed. He fetched up against her window with a thud, and froze. The morons inside kept on kissing. Soon their time would come...

Up above, Agatha shrieked. "It's him. We've got t...oh wait, he's slinking away like the snake that he is.

Jake left Cyn's hard nipple with a lick that made her wriggle on his cock and sigh with pleasure. He rose up, his cock still buried inside her, to look at the window, the drapes were open a few inches. Damn, he hadn't noticed in his heat to touch her. His senses prickling with danger, he asked, "What was that?"

"I didn't hear anything," Cyn murmured. "It's probably just another incidence of your hyper vigilance; you need to learn to relax, honey."

Jake smiled at her, still arched and restrained, her nipples hard as rubies, a sated look on her beautiful face. "Come on," he stated, pulling her up, and undoing her restraints, earning a moue of protest. He smiled, caressing her face. "Later. I promise."

"I'm going to hold you to that, cowboy."

He drew her off the table, and pulled her robe off the bed, putting it on her. He'd heard someone lurking around outside, and after learning about the Peeping Tom he wasn't taking any chances.

"Stay here." He positioned her by the door and weathered her frown. "I mean it," he demanded, stepping outside. He walked around the cabin in the dark, bright moonlight easing his path. His eyes were accustomed to night vision, and he scanned the area, not seeing a soul. He made his way to the dining room window, where he'd heard the thud. Cyn had a flowerbed planted; he realized when he inhaled the sharp scent of mint. He tensed when he saw the trampled down herbal border, the still wet semen stains on the logs. At least it removed Cordial from suspicion. The peeper was a guy. "Damn," he muttered.

"What is it?" Cyn asked, coming up behind him.

"I thought I told you to stay inside," he replied, turning to pin her with his best repressive frown.

"And I told you I expect full disclosure. Guess which one of us is going to win?" She glanced at the stains, and her eyes widened. "Is that what I think it is?"

"Uh huh. Our Peeping Tom is a guy."

"Yuck. What a sick creep."

"Probably can't get it up otherwise."

Cyn looked at her flowerbed and glared. "Look what he did to my flowers. The pansies are ruined, and the mint will never be the same." She let out a gasp. "Look. He broke my garden sculpture; it was an AB White original. That bastard."

"He probably tripped over it running away. Don't worry, I know where I can get you one wholesale."

"At least this lets two people out of suspicion," she commented, her nose wrinkling as she looked at the stains.

"Two?" he asked, tilting his head.

"Sure, Cordial because she's female, and Dwain Hawkins. Maybe he wasn't guilty of the obscene letters after all. I now feel kind of bad for blaming him, persecuting him."

"Don't, he still could be lurking around."

"That's not very likely according to Zane. It doesn't fit his past M.O."

Chapter 15

Cyn accompanied Jake to his parents' estate, her heart racing. Would his parents accept her? What would the other guests think? It was their first actual public outing as a couple. She'd never worried what others thought of her before, but now she so wanted to make a good impression.

Jake parked his SUV in the driveway. She was glad he'd brought it because she was dressed in her turquoise fairytale gown. Riding on his Harley, dressed for a formal party, would have been difficult, to say the least. She turned to gaze at him; he looked so handsome in his tux. His gaze warmed as it washed over her. When he pulled her into his arms for a kiss, she went with a pleasured sigh. The sensation of his hot lips slanting over hers, his taste, almost succeeded in wiping away her nerves. If he was doing it to distract her, he'd succeeded. She moaned into his mouth, her body aching for him. He cupped her breast through her dress, his palm heating her nipple, making it stiff.

He pulled back to nibble her ear. "Ready to make your entrance?"

She clung to him. "I'm not sure I can do this."

"You can and you will. Sass me and I'll take you up to my room and spank you," he whispered, nipping her lobe.

She gasped with heat, thrilling at his naughty words. "You're a wicked man, Jake Randal."

"And you're a bad girl, Cyn Taylor," Jake replied, letting her go. "That's why you're perfect for me."

It wasn't a declaration of love, but it was close, and she'd take it, she decided, gazing into his eyes. She let Jake help her out of the SUV, her nerves returning. When he reached back to get her wrapped gift, a painting for his parents, she nibbled her lower lip. Would they even like it? "I'm not so sure about this, either."

"They'll love it, and they'll love you, trust me."

She smiled, bemused, when he took her arm, walking her toward the house. She knew it was too late to turn back. Holding his hand, she walked with Jake into the mansion, gazing around at the exquisite interiors, impressed. It was much grander than she'd expected, with antique furniture and a gleaming marble floor. Jake's mother obviously had exquisite taste. There were a few people milling around the foyer, some she recognized. She tensed when the others swept them with curious gazes.

Jake took her elbow, steering her into the living room. She was glad his steady presence was at her side, keeping her calm. At least she was dressed well. She'd gotten her gown back from the cleaners today. Jake's hand, warm and tender on her bare arm, was reassuring, and gave her a boost of confidence, as all eyes seemed to turn to them. *Well, damn, she'd have to get used to being the center of attention if she stayed around Jake.*

"Come. I want you to meet my mother," Jake stated, steering her through the crowd to the petite lady holding court.

Jake's mother, Alice, looked up and beamed when they approached. Her red dress, and sleekly coifed strawberry blonde hair, elegant. Alice's warm gaze lingered on Jake for a moment, before she cast a speculative gaze at Cyn. "Well, son, it's about time you made an appearance. I was starting to wonder if the rumors of your return were just that."

"It's good to see you, too, Mother," Jake commented, giving Cyn's arm a squeeze, before letting go to walk over and give his mother a hug. "I've been rather busy."

"Too busy to visit or were you otherwise more pleasantly occupied?" she asked, her twinkling gaze on Cyn.

"A little of both, but it's good to be home."

"We've missed you. Now I won't have to track you around the country through Maud." She turned to look at Cyn. "And who's your date?"

Jake walked over to Cyn's side, casually looping an arm around her shoulders. "Mom, meet Cynthia Taylor, she lives..."

"At the Taylor ranch these past six months, I know."

Cyn sighed, knowing this was Cordial's doing, preparing for the worst. Lord knows what her stepmother had told Alice about her. She didn't even want to imagine. At least the dragon lady was nowhere in sight. With any luck, she wasn't on the guest list. "I'm please to meet you, Mrs. Randal."

"Call me Alice, dear." With a smile, adding, "You're the reason I haven't seen my son, and that Silas has been so cross."

"Ma'am, I..."

"Don't worry. Anyone who can capture my son's interest and infuriate my stubborn husband is someone I'd like to know better."

Cyn relaxed. "Thanks, I think. I'd like a chance to get to know you better, too."

"So, what have you two got there?" Alice looked at the gift-wrapped package Jake held.

"An anniversary gift." Cyn looked around the exquisitely decorated living room; the wall's hung with original art, some breathtaking AB White sculptures on display, realizing she might have goofed. "On second thought, maybe you'd prefer something else..."

"How can you say that? You're a gifted artist," Jake cut in, and handed the present to his mother.

"Let me see." Alice carefully unwrapped the painting, and set it on a console table along the wall. She looked at it from different angles. "My son is right, you are a gifted artist. Are you showing anywhere at present?"

"Um no. I had to temporarily close my studio in Taos."

"Mom's AB White," Jake stated, with a smile.

"I had no idea," Cyn voiced, stunned.

"I told you I could get you another sculpture wholesale," he teased.

"What's this?" Alice asked.

"Cyn's favorite sculpture, one of your wonderland series, was damaged last night. I told her I could get her a replacement."

"And you didn't tell her I was your mother?" Alice scolded, but smiled. "Jacob, you're as hardheaded as your father."

Cyn smiled, watching their easy affectionate humor. If only she had such a loving family. Being artists, she and Jake's mother did indeed have a lot in common.

"I'm honored that you think so highly of my work. Come into my studio sometime this week, and pick out one of my works. A gift from me for bringing my son home."

"But I didn't..." Cyn started to say when Silas walked up. She and Jake were only temporary lovers. She glanced at Silas, seeing the agitation on his face. More Randal Industries problems, she supposed.

Silas stepped close to Jake. "I need to talk to you, son..."

"Look what Cyn brought us, dear," Alice interrupted his rant.

Silas flicked an interested glance at the landscape. "Nice," he replied gruffly, and turned back to Jake.

"Don't pay him any mind, dear."

"Something's come up, son," Silas stated. "We need to talk."

Cyn was curious to know what it was about, but Silas's closed expression didn't give her a clue. More of the mundane business stuff, maybe. Jake hesitated, giving her a concerned look.

"This shouldn't take long."

She didn't want to stand in his way, and she appreciated his attempts to keep her in the loop. "Go honey, I'll be fine."

"I'll be back, stay by Mother."

Cyn nodded to placate him, knowing he was hyper-vigilant after last night's events. She was on edge herself, wondering when it would come back to hit her. She was standing in a quiet corner when she noticed Cordial and the girls sweep into the room. Cyn let out a groan, making those nearby look at her funny, and making Cordial look her way.

Cordial's scornful glance raked over her gown. "Crap, I thought you burned the thing."

"I tried to Mother, but I couldn't find it," Tiffany hissed back at her.

"Well hell," Cordial muttered.

Cyn watched Jake's mother circulating, approaching Cordial and accepted the inevitable. She headed straight toward the impending collision. She'd be damned if she'd cower in the corner. Eyes narrowed for battle, she watched Cordial speak to Jake's mother, her voice low and intense.

"Well, she's been just wild, carrying on with your son in front of my impressionable daughters. Both of whom have been groomed to take their place in society..."

Cyn rolled her eyes, as she stepped up beside Cordial. "Why don't you just have them show her their teeth, step-mamma, so she can pick out the very best one for her son?"

Cordial jumped, and turned to glare at her as Cyn stared her down. She flicked at glance at Jake's mother and noticed an understanding, and grimly amused, smile playing around Mrs. Randal's mouth. Hooray, the woman saw through Cordial's bluster.

"See what I mean, Mrs. Randal, no class at all. If you'll take my advice," Cordial voiced with a cool smile, warming to the task. "You'll ban her from..."

"It was a pleasure meeting you Ma'am," Cyn cut in, ignoring Cordial's tirade, as she focused on Jake's mother. "I'll look forward to visiting your studio soon. Happy anniversary, and thank you for inviting me."

"Why thank you my dear, you're not going so soon?" Alice shot an irritated glare at Cordial, who gasped.

"I must. I think I'll go check on Jake, and remove myself from certain individuals," she commented, meeting Cordial's glittering gaze.

"I completely understand," Alice replied, with a smile. "And you're welcome to my home anytime. Call me and we'll talk galleries."

Cyn nodded, and walked away, making her way to the den. Heated male voices, one of them Jake's, stopped her in the doorway.

"Blood spatter, you say?" Jake asked. "Are you sure that it's his, Zane?"

"We're running DNA tests now, pal, but they take a while to be read. From the crime scene, it looks like it was a hell of a struggle."

"Or was staged?" Silas cut in. "From what you've said, Dwain Hawkins was a world class con man."

"Warrants from coast to coast," Zane added, "But this time he might have met his match. It looks like one of his victims took the bastard out, permanently."

"I'll believe that when you actually find a body," Jake stated grimly. "Until then, I'm guarding Cyn."

Cyn sucked in a shocked gasp, feeling sickened at the thought of Hawkins being murdered. She'd hated the man, but she didn't want him dead.

"And the deeds?" Silas asked.

"We've turned all the documents over to the DA," Zane replied, "Fraudulently purchased properties will be recompensed."

"All but the Taylor ranch," Jake cut in. "I don't want that released with the other properties."

"You can't wrap her up in tissue paper to keep her safe and out of the mess," Silas bit out.

"Wanna bet?" Jake asked with determination.

So, he hadn't gotten over his overprotecting ways. Cyn stepped into the room drawing all the men's wary glances. Silas reached for his scotch, Zane stifled a grin when he saw her stalking up to Jake, and Jake pinned her with a wary glance.

"Now sugar..."

"Don't, now sugar, me," she snapped, getting in his face. "I thought you were through with this keeping me sheltered, and stupid, overprotective junk."

"He's trying to do you a favor, little girl," Silas commented. "Women are no good at business."

"So, I see," she frowned at the bottle of scotch in his hand, and was relieved to see him put it down, a sheepish look on his face "You men have made a hell of a mess, from my vantage point. I could hardly do worse." She turned to go. "I'll see myself home, gentlemen. Don't want to interfere with your hush–hush business."

Angry and hurt, she hadn't made it to the door when Jake caught up with her. His firm hand on her arm stopped her in her tracks. She gave him a glare over her shoulder. "Let go now, unless you want to get flipped."

"No. I'm taking you home."

"My stepsisters, your would–be harem, are in there waiting for you," she snapped back at him. "I'd hate to see you miss it." She was satisfied to see him grind his teeth with frustration.

"You know better than that," he growled.

"Do I, stud?" She studied his handsome face, wishing he'd learn to trust her to handle things. "If you lied about one thing, what's to say you wouldn't lie about another?" She shrugged out of his grasp and headed for the door, blinking away the tears of frustration misting her eyes. She tried not to let him see her distress, as Jake implacably tracked her out the door. He was holding onto her ranch. A dinky little property like the Double T wouldn't mean a thing to a man of his wealth. He was trying to protect her again. Why didn't he trust her with the cold, hard, facts of life? She wasn't going to go hysterical on him.

Jake made sure Cyn got into the SUV, weathering her scowl of disapproval. She could glare all she wanted, but he wasn't letting her go. He got in, locked the doors, and started the engine. "For the record, I didn't lie."

Cyn smoldered as they pulled up to the ranch. He still didn't get it. She didn't just want him to share good things with her, but real issues too. She wouldn't let him wrap her in cotton wool to keep her safe.

When he parked by her cabin, she opened the door, and leapt out, heading towards her place, disgruntled when he fell into step beside her. The man could move fast, and silent. "Where do you think you're going?" she asked, adding, "I'm not sleeping with you tonight, so go back to bungalow six."

"I'm going with you. I'll sleep on the couch, if you insist. Until this is wrapped up, we do everything together."

"Oh joy," she replied, stomping up on her porch. She arched a wry brow when he pushed her back before she could go inside, and went in on a low crouch to check things out. "Is that really necess..." his glare stopped her in her tracks.

"God damn it," he bit out.

Cyn froze, as she heard a thud, her heart leaping in her throat. If anything happened to him, it would kill her. She rushed inside to help, didn't see him, and tracked the sound to her bedroom. "What is it?"

Jake spun around, a knife in his hand, and scowled when he saw her. "I thought I told you to stay outside."

"I thought you needed me." She watched him smile, relaxing, and felt that electric connection all over again.

He stepped toward her, filling the bedroom doorway. "Maybe you'd better wait in the kitchen while I clean..."

She recognized a delaying tactic when she saw one, and peeked around him at the carnage in her bedroom. Her clothes were tossed everywhere, strewn on the bed, some slashed. Cordial? *We tried, Mom, we couldn't find it.* She glanced at the knife in his hand, recognizing it as one from her kitchen. "Where did you find the knife?"

His eyes narrowed as he gazed at her for a minute. "On your bed."

Cyn closed her eyes with a groan; it was the one answer she'd been afraid of. "Looks like my Peeping Tom stalker, just escalated." Jake's tender touch on her face made her open her eyes. "There's more, isn't there?"

"He left another letter, and pictures taken with a night scope."

"Oh God," she let him pull her into his arms.

"Damn it all, I'm getting you out of here as soon as we call Zane."

"No. I won't let this coward make me run. If you want to put on coffee, I'll see what I can salvage."

"Sorry. It's a crime scene now. You sit down and relax." He walked her toward the sofa. "I'll call Zane's cell."

Jake stalked over to the kitchen, out of earshot and made the call.

Zane answered on the second ring. "What's wrong?"

"He's back, and this time he vandalized Cyn's place, and left a calling card."

"I'll be right over."

Jake pocketed the phone and walked over to the coffeemaker to brew coffee, going through the motions, stifling his rage, for now. He needed to be levelheaded and thinking, to help her. Once he got his hands on the culprit, all bets were off. He glanced at Cyn, she was quiet in shock, and bit out a curse. *Damn it all, where was Zane?* He wanted to get her away from this. Instead, he carried a cup of coffee over to her, and sat down on the sofa next to her. He thrust it in front of her nose and watched her shudder as she took a drink, glad to see her pull out of it. He set the cup down on the coffee table and pulled her into his arms. She went stiffly, and then sagged against him.

"Why won't he leave me alone?"

"Because he's a fucking coward. Don't worry, sugar, we're going to stop him," he replied, holding her. "I'll keep you safe."

"It might have been them," she stated with a sniff.

"Who?"

"Brandy and Tiffany. They were telling Cordial they couldn't find this gown. It's so juvenile, it had to be them."

Jake relaxed his guard a little bit; better them than an unknown threat. Still, he didn't completely buy it. He looked up when Zane knocked, and poked his head around the door. "In there." He shrugged toward the bedroom.

Zane went in, and let out a whistle. He came back out, the knife in an evidence bag. "Did either of you see who did it?"

"No," Cyn commented, pushing away from Jake.

"She heard someone talking about it though," Jake added, as Cyn stiffened beside him. It amazed him that she was still protective of them.

"Tell me?" Zane asked.

"I'd rather not." Cyn bit her lip as she gave Jake a pleading look. "It's a family matter, something I have to take care of myself."

Zane cast a questioning look at Jake. "You okay with this?"

"Yeah, for now. I trust her judgment," he stated, pleased to see Cyn smile at him. "Just do a thorough report in case things go south. Oh, and you're going to find my prints on the knife."

"You know better than to handle evidence."

"He couldn't help it. He thought someone was sneaking up behind him," Cyn cut in, going to his defense.

Zane gave Jake an envious smile. "I'll try to run prints on this," he commented, dangling the knife. "In the meantime, I suggest you leave. The security here is nonexistent."

Cyn frowned at him.

"He's right. Come on," Jake demanded, holding out his hand, and was gratified when she relented, and took his hand without a word. At least she trusted him on some level. He escorted her out to his vehicle and drove her back to the cottage. At least the place had security.

Cyn was shell-shocked as they drove away, feeling like she was abandoning the ranch. When she saw her father, she'd demand some concrete answers. Until then, she'd let her knight in tarnished armor rescue her.

She leaned back and watched Jake lock up and set the alarm system, grateful that she had him. He turned to look at her, the steamy look in his eyes making her a little crazy. The feeling of security when they entered the cottage, and Jake locking the doors and setting the security system, made her let out a sigh of relief. She took in his bad boy smile, and her carefully constructed brick wall disintegrated. She might not completely trust him in the boardroom, but she did in the bedroom. The time out was actually good. She needed to get her head on straight. She needed Jake. She went into his arms, pressing him back against the door, as she hugged him.

He held her, smoothing a stroke down her back. "Easy, sugar, it's the adrenalin kicking in."

"I need you," she murmured, nibbling his ear, not liking her need being reduced to a biological essence.

"Honey, you've got me." He scooped her up in his arms and carried her to the bedroom. "All night long."

"Mmm," she hummed, kissing his jaw. "That sounds great. Why don't you put me down, and get naked for me."

"I'm starting to think you just see me as a sex object," he stated with a grin, as he set her down on the floor.

"Now whatever gave you that idea, stud?" she asked, batting her eyes at him.

"This," he replied, pulling her into his arms.

Cyn let out a sigh of surrender when his mouth came down to claim hers, and melted against him. She kissed him back, her tongue mating with his, and then felt his hand pull down her zipper. She groaned into his mouth when he slid the straps off her shoulders and the dress slipped down between their bodies, hitting the floor. She pulled back to try to frown at him. "You've got to stop doing that."

"Stripping you? Never gonna happen, sugar. I think both of us naked is a great idea."

She smiled, letting him strip her, and then ogled him when he pulled off his clothes. "Very nice," she voiced, eyeing him. She noticed the variety of sex toys on top of the dresser. "I see you've been shopping."

"Uh huh, I believe in being prepared."

"A regular boy scout, aren't you?" She walked over to pick up the tubes of tubes of oral sex gel. The heat in his twinkling eyes made her shiver. "What's your pleasure, strawberry or coconut?"

"My pleasure is you," he replied, stalking up to her, and taking the tubes of gel out of her hands. "You know this lube has another purpose."

She gave him a sly look, intrigued. "Really? Tell me more."

He opened the coconut gel, and smiled, noting her intrigued look.

Cyn's mouth watered in anticipation. Did he want her to go down on him again? The question was answered a moment later when he squeezed a dollop of gel onto her left nipple. The horny, cold-hot feeling, made her moan, shooting straight through her, making her toes curl. He smiled, bending to take her budded nipple into his mouth, as she whimpered. The heat of his mouth\ made her eyes roll back in her head. She let out a cry as he drew hard on her tingling coconut flavored peak. Her knees went weak as she pressed close to his hard body.

Pushing her back against the dresser, Jake let out a macho growl, thrust his thigh up against her sex to brace her in place, and kept on sucking. Grinding her pussy against his hair roughened thigh, Cyn whimpered at the delightful twin arousals. Jake was relentless, drawing harder on her nipple, his rough tongue laving the tortured peak. Her eyes closed, and she completely let herself go. Instantly, a dollop of cold gel covered her other nipple. She moaned, knowing what was coming as Jake gave her throbbing left nipple a last lick.

Stiffening in anticipation, she didn't know if she could handle it without melting into a puddle of need. Her body tightened. The gel-covered right nipple burned with fire and ice as she waited, what seemed like forever, for him to take it in his mouth. Instead, he blew on it. "Oh," she cried as a heat wave drew it tighter, and his mouth closed over it. Little mewling noises poured out of her mouth as her sex went into spasm, flutters tightening her pussy. She gasped, stiffening, crying out Jake's name as she came.

Jake released her nipple with a little kiss on its tip, and pulled her into his arms. "How's that for starters?"

"Delightful, and exhausting," Cyn replied, leaning into his strong embrace, spent, but still hungry. She smiled, nibbling his ear, in love and lust with him. He was all she needed. Jake picked her up, holding her tight, as if she were light as a feather. Cyn hung on tight, wrapping her arms around his neck, while her legs wrapped around his waist. Her sex pressed against his washboard abs, the tingling of arousal returned, and she realized this wasn't over by a long shot.

Jake's hands, cupping her ass, squeezed, and she let out a little giggle.

"Are you fixing to ride me, cowboy?"

"What do you think?" Jake asked, holding her in a secure grip as he carried her to the bed and laid her down. His hot gaze made her burn as he looked down at her. She arched her hips, her legs spreading, silently begging for him. She lay exposed, basking in his obvious delight. It felt so right to have this man think she was special.

"Perfect," he whispered.

Knowing he meant the words opened up a piece of her heart, she'd kept guarded. She watched him pick up the lube and trembled. "Oh, please." She needed him inside her now.

His mouth kicked up in a knowing grin as he squeezed a line of gel onto her bare pussy, putting an extra dollop on her swollen clit. Cyn let out a needy gasp, as Jake knelt between her quivering thighs and flicked a long stroke of his rough tongue up her pussy. Arching toward his tantalizing tongue, she whimpered, her legs shaking, her sex spasming. He sucked the swollen nubbin of her clit into his hot mouth. Her eyes rolled back in her head, as she came, screaming his name.

With a growl, he surged up her trembling body, thrusting into her contracting pussy. He pulled almost out of her and surged back into her, to the hilt. Her hips snapped up to meet his fevered thrusts, her clit rubbing against his rock hard shaft.

He groaned, his hands cupping her ass to hold her closer to him as he thrust harder and deeper.

Cyn cried out, her body shaking, everything tightening inside her. She wrapped her legs around his hips, trapping him to her as her body shook. Deep spasms tugged his hot hard cock, as her pleasure peaked. Waves of orgasm pulsed through her as she exploded, seeing stars behind her closed eyelids. Jake thrusted fiercely into her once more, and went still, coming hard against her cervix.

After a moment, he rolled them over so that her limp body lay atop his, and she was astride him. Cyn sighed with completion, as his big hands stroked her back. Wrapped around him, she felt safe and loved. She wanted to stay that way forever. When she felt his cock stirring again, she raised her head to give him a questioning look. "Again?"

"I'm insatiable when it comes to you, sugar." He chuckled and opened the drawer in the nightstand.

Cyn sat astride him and watched him curiously. "What other tricks do you have up your sleeve, Randal?" She watched him pull the small vibrator out of the drawer and quivered. "Just what do you think you're going to do with that?"

"How about this," he replied, buzzing her left nipple.

Cyn cried out at the pleasure, her head tipping back, as his cock grew harder inside her, driving her crazy.

"I love that sound, sugar," he mumbled with a warm male chuckle, and buzzed the other nipple.

Cyn trembled, moaning; grinding against him, making him groan.

Jake moved the vibrator's tip down to buzz her clit.

Cyn whimpered, lifting up a tiny bit to give him better access. He kept thrusting his cock up into her, rocking into her, as he teased her throbbing clit.

Thrusting harder and deeper, he groaned, "That's it, sugar, take me." Impaled on his once more, hard cock, she trembled, contracting around him, ripples of pleasure fluttering through her sex, as she came.

Grasping her hip tight with one hand, Jake surged up into her, and buzzed her anus. She screamed, her orgasm coming harder, as he slipped the head of the vibrator inside her rippling ass. She whimpered, coming again, sobbing with release as she met his fierce thrusts, her body tugging at his cock.

Jake came with a growl, calling her name.

Cyn collapsed against him, and he held her tight. She felt warmed, bathed in the afterglow, as she sprawled on top of his hard muscular chest listening to his thundering heartbeat slow. She lifted her head and smiled at him. "That was—"

"Hot," he finished, his hand slipping down to cup her ass.

Reveling in the warm feeling, she thought how right it felt to be in his arms.

Chapter 16

Jake escorted Cyn into the minimum-security penitentiary's day room to see her father, despite her objections. After what happened last night, he wasn't about to let her face this alone. He stayed at her side, still not convinced that she was out of danger.

"You don't need to come in with me," she stated, when the guard motioned her to the visitor's room.

"I'm going." He took her elbow, withstanding her frown. He knew she was trying to be strong, and wanted to protect her family, but he wasn't going to step aside.

He walked with her into the large empty room with tables and chairs. Carl Taylor sat at one on the tables, tall and burly with salt and pepper hair, and horn-rimmed glasses. A pleased expression lit the man's gray eyes when he saw Cyn. Then he noticed Jake at her side and his eyes narrowed with suspicion.

"Dad," Cyn voiced with a smile, rushing over to hug her father.

He stood wrapping his arms around her in a bear hug. He looked over her head at Jake. "Is this the dude who's been compromising you?"

Cyn pulled back with a gasp. "Who told you that?" She let out a disgusted groan. "Don't tell me, I already know, Cordial."

"She's your step-momma, honey. She's just looking out for your best interests."

Jake saw Cyn's shattered expression, and felt his gut twist. He took a step forward. "You don't know what you're talking about, mister."

"Like hell," Carl glowered back at him.

Cyn scowled. "Will you two calm down the testosterone display? Dad, this is Jake Randal. He's my, ah...boyfriend. And for the record we're compromising each other."

Jake grinned at Cyn's feisty comeback, relieved that she hadn't tried to deny him, but boyfriend didn't even touch what they shared.

"Silas Randal's boy, the juvenile delinquent who blew town when he turned of age?"

"That's me," Jake replied dryly.

"And just what are your intentions towards my daughter, young man?"

"Dad," Cyn mumbled with a gasp, blushing.

"They're completely honorable, sir, unlike some others I could mention." He watched the older man go stiff, as he digested that information.

"What happened?" he asked.

"Nice way of letting me handle it," Cyn complained, giving him a frown.

Jake met her gaze with a non-repentant stare.

She sighed, and turned back to her father. "The thing is Dad, something has happened, and...."

"Show him the land contract," Jake cut in.

"I was getting to that," she snapped, and pulled out the document. "There's been a swindle going on with Randal Industries expansion plans. They've been scamming properties away from people, while ripping off Jake's dad."

"I didn't sign this." Carl stared at the document.

"I told you so," Cyn stated triumphantly.

Jake saw her pleased glow and waited for the bad news when he saw her father tense. He was damned good at reading people and the man had something to hide.

"But honey, I might have if I'd been presented with this offer. You say it's bogus."

"Phony as the paper it's written on," Jake cut in, meeting the older man's troubled gaze.

"What do you mean you might have taken it?" Cyn asked, her jaw dropping.

Carl took off his glasses, and gave her an apologetic look. "Honey, I'm no rancher, you know that. My stint in this country club with bars proves it. I've been thinking about selling up. I've a job waiting for me in Dallas if I want it. And I'll have the girl's college tuition to front, creditors to pay off, that all takes cash that I don't have. Besides, Cordial isn't happy, as this proves. The signature is hers."

"You'd be willing to testify to that in a court of law?" Jake cut in.

Carl gave him a brittle smile. "Not a chance in hell. I love my wife..."

"But you can't sell," Cyn cut in. "The Double T is in your blood."

"Not mine, honey, maybe yours. It's why I put you in charge; let you get it out of your system. I miscalculated, I'm sorry. Cheer up; when I get out, you can go back to your old life, your studio. I know you miss it, and you're wearing yourself out."

"Who told you that, Cordial?"

"No, Pedro. He's been sending me weekly reports."

Jake smiled, pleased that her father had been proactive in looking after her. "Good thinking."

Cyn flicked him an annoyed glance. "I knew there were spies around the place."

"Yeah, and most of them are on your side. I also heard about the letters."

"Damned blabber mouth."

"I've already gone to the police," Jake cut in. "I've taken steps to keep Cyn safe."

Carl gave him a slow assessing look. "That's not what my wife says, but then she's biased. She's desperate to make good matches for our daughters while she can. Not on my watch."

"Dad, I've never heard you talk this way before."

"I know and it's my fault that we haven't been close. I mean to take steps to rectify that, if you'll let me."

"Of course I will," Cyn put her hand over her dads on the table.

"Take care of her young man," Carl stated, giving Jake a steely look.

"I promise to." Jake took a business card out of his pocket. "Call this number if you want to sell the ranch. I'll see that you get top dollar for it." He saw the realization in the older man's gaze, and despair in Cyn's.

"Time's up." The guard came in.

Cyn was silent on the ride back to the ranch. She couldn't wrap her mind around the fact that her father wanted to sell up, move on. She didn't understand why ranching wasn't in his blood, but now she had to acknowledge it was true. And now Jake was going to be instrumental in the sale. Hell, maybe she could come visit it after he moved in. She didn't know how to feel about that, sad, angry, or glad that it wasn't going to be demolished by Randal Industries.

Jake pulled into the driveway and up to the ranch house. She looked at him questioningly.

"We might as well get this over with."

She nodded, realizing he was right. She had to confront Cordial get it all out into the open, if she was going to survive until her father was released. She got out of the vehicle and made her way up to the front door, walking under the front portico. She wasn't going to slip in the back door like usual. Why should she act like a second-class family member? She frowned when Jake fell into step at her side, but couldn't deny that she drew strength from him.

She rang the doorbell, and Juanita answered it. She swept a glance over them, and smiled, then noticed Cyn's pale face. "Oh my, what happened? It's true that the police were called to your cabin last night?"

"It's true," Jake replied. "Who told you?"

"I heard Cordial and the girls talking. Pedro and I have been worried about you all day."

"I'm sorry," Cyn mumbled, giving her a hug. "I should have realized that you'd fret, and given you a call when we left. Don't worry, I'm fine. We stayed the night out by the lake, and just got back from visiting Dad. I need to see Cordial, is she in?"

"She's in the study."

"Excellent." Cyn walked inside. "This way," she told Jake, leading the way through the foyer, and down the hall to her father's study. "You think you can follow my lead this time?" she asked him, seeing his rueful smile.

"Have at it, sugar. I'm just here as muscle."

Hunky looking muscle she decided, gazing at his sexy body. There was a grimly determined look on his handsome face. The rogue wasn't likely to take a calm, reasonable, tone. "See that you do," she stated in a low tone when they reached the open doorway to the wood paneled study. Jake's Scion headquarters would look right at home in here, she decided with a sigh and focused on Cordial, at the desk, wearing her reading glasses, pouring over some paper. Cyn tapped on the door.

"For the last time, no, you can't go to Europe for the gap season, Tiffany!" Cordial snapped, not bothering to look up.

"It's not Tiffany," Cyn replied, watching Cordial freeze. "And for the record, I told her the same thing when she mentioned the hair-brained scheme."

Cordial opened the desk drawer and quickly slipped the document into it before she shot a worried look up at her. "What are you doing here? And why did you bring him?"

"I came for some answers to some difficult questions," Cyn commented, noting her stepmother's guilty look. "And Jake's just here as backup."

"And muscle," Jake stated with a pirate's grin. "Don't forget muscle."

"If you think you two can come in here and threaten me and my position, you're dead wrong." She glared at the two of them.

"Is that the message you were trying to send when you trashed Cyn's clothes, and left your calling card behind last night?" Jake fixed her with a fierce stare.

Cordial bit her lip. "Calling card?"

"A knife."

"Oh God," Cordial mumbled with a shocked gasp.

Cyn let out a relieved sigh. "You didn't do it."

"Of course, I didn't do it. What do you take me for?"

"A cheat, and a fraud," Jake cut in.

"How dare you?" Her hands shook as she put them in her lap.

Cyn frowned at Jake, silently telling him to back off. "Hell of a job of letting me take charge, honey."

"I won't idly sit by and let that conniving bitch use you anymore."

Cyn couldn't tear her gaze off Jake's sincere one. That he was her champion filled her with joy. She turned to look at Cordial who was glowering at them. "Tell us about your deal with North Star Development," she demanded, and was shocked when Cordial's haughty expression fell.

Her head hanging low, Cordial sniffed back a tear, grumbling, "So he went ahead and ratted me out, damn it. I should have known not to trust him. After all who in their right mind trusts a blackmailer?"

"A blackmailer," Cyn repeated, shocked by the disclosure. It all made sense, her stepmother's sudden change. Cyn laid the land contract on the desk. "Did you sign this?"

"Yes, damn you, I had no choice. He threatened to muddy our good name, make sure the girls didn't make advantageous matches. I had to sign."

"It's okay." Cyn let out a sigh when Cordial burst into tears.

"No, it's not," Jake cut in. "What about the threats you've been receiving."

"Threats?" Cordial looked up, blinking away tears.

"Poison pen letters, slashed clothes. Who's doing it?"

"Dwain of course, I'm sure of it even though he wouldn't admit it. She hurt his pride, you see." Cordial looked at Cyn. "I told you, I didn't want you, hurt, tried to be nasty as I could to you to get you to leave. But you wouldn't, you're just as stubborn as your father, young lady."

Cyn's jaw dropped at the scolding tone, then watched as Cordial burst into noisy sobs.

"It stops as of now," Jake replied grimly.

"But Dwain..."

"Isn't a problem anymore. He's skipped town with the cops tight on his heels. And this land contract you signed is worthless," he stated, picking the document up and tearing it in half.

The next day, Jake knew Cyn was pissed as she rushed the hands through breakfast. The disclosures of the last couple of days had taken their toll on her. She seemed determined to focus on ranch work, to avoid dwelling on her problems, and he admired her for that. The hands seemed to read her edgy mood, and ate up quick, before rushing out to work. Jake wasn't about to leave. He might have overplayed his hand, making an offer for the ranch, and coming down hard on Cordial, but damn it, he was trying to protect her. He wouldn't idly sit by and see her killing herself with work.

He leveled a look at her that made her fall silent. "I know you're mad at me for purchasing the ranch, not to mention grilling Cordial yesterday."

"It's not that," she sighed, "At least, not mostly."

Had he read her wrong? "Then you're not upset that I'm buying the ranch."

"Actually, I'm glad that if my dad's determined to sell, it's going to good hands. Not Randal Industries who'd demolish it. You're not going to, are you?"

"No, I'm not going to."

"And as for Cordial, I'm glad you were there for back up. Something's got to be done about her and the girls."

"Then you don't mind that I threatened her?"

She frowned at him. "Well, you were a little rough on her, but you did it for a good reason. Have the police got a line on Dwain Hawkins yet?"

"They're close. So, what chores shall we do today?"

"I need to move the herd to the south pasture today, and mend some fences in the north pasture. But you don't have to stick around and help me. I know you've got work to do in town."

"I'll help you with your work this morning, and you can go into the office with me this afternoon," Jake stated, lifting her up and setting her on her feet. "I'll buy you a few new toys at *Branded.*"

Cyn gazed at him bemused and flustered, she could hardly wait. His hands were warm, spanning her waist, and his expression determined and sexy. There'd be no gainsaying him and truthfully, she didn't want to. Spending time out on the land with him sounded like heaven. But they'd have to traverse the acreage on horseback. "Do you ride?" she asked, and blushed when he grinned. "Forget I asked."

"Baby, I'm an expert rider," he replied, pressing her against the cabinet, his cock nestling against her crotch. He nuzzled her nape asking. "Don't you think so?"

She moaned, arching against him. "Honey, you can ride me anytime."

Up above, Agatha gasped, calling out, "Red alert ladies, he's back again."

"What a crumb," Imogene grumbled, sniffing back a tear as she glared at Chance sneaking up the staircase. "We should drop a chandelier on him. A big one."

"I've got a better idea," Hilda stated, clapping her hands. A phone suddenly popped into her hand. "We've got a job for you, Eros."

Agatha and Imogene shared a smile. "Excellent," they responded in tandem.

An instant later, a short, bald, ageless man popped into the circle. He hoisted his bow and quiver of arrows higher on his shoulder and smiled. "You rang?"

"We sure did," Hilda whispered, batting her eyes.

He leered up at her. "I'm here to serve, my sweet. What's the job?"

Agatha cleared her throat. "If you'd look down instead of flirting, you'd know. Our fairy goddaughter is in danger."

They watched as Chance crept away from the house and went to get his rifle.

Chapter 17

Jake secured the next stretch of barbed wire, and glanced at Cyn to see how she was doing. Delayed maintenance nothing, the wires had been deliberately cut. It didn't take a genius to figure out why. Somebody wanted to force the sale, and figured losses might do the trick. He wondered if Cordial was in on this part of it. He still didn't buy her tearful repentance, probably never would.

Cyn's troubled gaze made his jaw tighten, as all his protective instincts came out. "Why don't you get us a cold drink? This is thirsty work."

She nodded, pulling off her thick gloves, and walking toward the lone tree where they'd left their horses. "I'll get the lemonade," she replied, heading toward the animals and her pack.

"Sounds good." He wiped his brow. Setting down his hammer, he followed her into the open. A glint of light reflecting off metal was his only warning before a gunshot rang out, hitting the tree next to Cyn.

She gasped, "What the hell!"

Jake tackled her before whoever was gunning for her took another pot shot. He rolled, cushioning her fall, and then lay atop her, protecting her. "Shh," he hissed us another shot pinged out.

A sudden thunder of hooves made Jake smile. He locked gazes with Cyn. "The stampede gives us cover. Roll with me, now," Jake commanded, moving them behind the tree.

Up above, Eros notched two arrows into his bow, taking aim at Chance hiding in the grass with a rifle, and the racing herd. "This is a bit unorthodox, ladies, but it should work." He let the arrows fly, hitting Chance, who yelped and grabbed his butt, and the lead steer. The entire herd turned en masse and headed toward Chance, mooing. Chance let out a wail, jumping up, but they caught him, bringing him to ground as they licked him.

"Well, I'll be damned," Jake stated, as the herd turned, converging on the sniper hiding in the tall grass. Chance jumped up with a panicked cry and tried to run. Jake's eyes narrowed when he put the pieces of the puzzle together, his concern that the North Star had a mole in the ranch confirmed.

Cyn sat up, her jaw dropping when she saw the cattle licking him and mooing. "My god, it was Chance! I can't believe it." Her eyes widened as she saw the cows form a tight circle around him, mooing and licking him like he was a salt lick, rubbing against him. He fell to the ground sobbing. "What's gotten into them? I've never seen them act like that before. It's like they love him."

Jake pulled out his cell phone, pushed the button for 911, and handed it off to Cyn. Her eyes were narrowed on Chance, but she was shaking. He stroked her face, bringing her out of her shock. "Get the cops here, ask for Zane. I'll go take care of this bozo."

"Careful," she requested, looking at the rifle on the ground.

Jake smiled at her. "I don't think he's much of a danger now." He stalked over to Chance, curled on the grass in a fetal position, covered in cow slobber, and picked up the rifle. He carried it back to Cyn. "If he makes a wrong move shoot him."

Chance tried to move, but the cattle wouldn't let him. Jake waded through them, and pulled the slippery bastard to his feet. "Who are you working for, asshole?" he growled as police cars pulled up the road. Chance sobbed, mumbling incoherently. Jake growled with frustration as the police arrived. He let go of Chance, who crumpled to the ground, the cows mobbing him again. He took one look at Zane, striding his way behind the uniformed officers and relaxed his guard.

Zane swept a slow glance at Cyn holding the rifle, to Chance once again mobbed by the herd, and Jake. "What happened?"

Jake stepped aside to let the cattle do their worst. "He took some shots at us; the stampeding herd took him down."

"Jake was a hero."

"Doesn't surprise me one bit," Zane stated with a nod, as the other officers went to extricate the prisoner from the herd. "Who's the sniper?"

"Chance somebody," Jake replied.

"Chance McCall, he signed on a few months ago."

"That name doesn't ring any bells."

"He's new in the area, a friend of my stepmother's..."

"Ah." Zane asked. "Any idea why he came gunning for you?"

"It could have something to do with the fact that my stepmother is being blackmailed by Dwain Hawkins."

"North Star Properties," Zane voiced grimly and turned to Jake. "You didn't tell me this."

"That's my fault," Cyn cut in, putting a hand on Jake's arm. "I asked him to hold off, thought we had things under control. I'm sorry."

Jake pulled her into his arms. "It's okay, sugar, you couldn't have known you had a sniper in your midst."

"I've always thought there was a spy. I just thought it was Cordial. But why?"

"Seems likely he's a confederate of Dwain Hawkins," Zane replied. "Maybe he panicked because he was left holding the bag. Either way, I think we caught our Peeping Tom."

"Slimy bastard." Jake growled as the cops led a sobbing Chance away, the herd following them at close range, mooing.

"You'd better get him over the barbed wire fence, before you're mobbed guys," Zane directed with a chuckle.

"What can I say? My livestock aren't usually this unruly," Cyn commented with a smile. "He seems to be catnip for cows."

Jake held her tight. "I'm not letting you out of my sight."

"Sounds good to me, cowboy." Cyn leaned against him.

Zane cleared his throat. "Hate to interrupt folks, but we need to take this back to the ranch. You want to come with me and send someone back for your mounts?"

"Sounds good," Jake replied, helping Cyn into the jeep.

Cyn tensed as they drove back to the ranch, and saw the shock on Pedro's face, as she got out of the unmarked police car. He took one look at her cut arm and turned to Jake.

"I thought you said you'd keep her safe. What happened out there, Hombre?"

"He did, Pedro," she stated, touching Pedro's arm. "He saved me." She was aware of the other cowboys' troubled gazes. "Chance has been arrested. He tried to kill us."

"He took some pot shots at us from the tall grass," Jake cut in, looping an arm around Cyn's shoulder.

"Then he's the one who was sending you the messages?" Pedro muttered.

"Looks like it," Jake voiced.

"Damn, I knew that kid was wrong, he had a hell of a lot more money than he ought to. God damn it." Pedro took off his hat and slapped it on his leg. "I should' a fired that kid."

"Why didn't you?" Jake asked.

Pedro looked up at the house, "Personal reasons."

Cyn was apprehensive but new it needed to be done. "Let's go talk," she stated, heading for the poolside. They'd be out sunning themselves. Rounding the house, they found the girls lying on chaise lounges, sunning themselves. Cordial sat under an umbrella–covered table, reading a book, a martini at her side. She looked up and did a double take when she saw Cyn's scraped arms.

"What happened?" she asked, making the girls look up.

"Your boyfriend tried to kill her," Jake replied.

The glass slipped out of Cordial's fingers, smashing on the flagstone terrace. "What do you mean tried to kill her? You said Dwain was out of the picture. And I don't have a boyfriend. I'm a happily married woman."

"Coulda fooled me," Cyn grumbled. "You never go visit Dad in prison."

"That's because he asked me not to, he doesn't want me to see him there."

Cyn digested that news, startled, but could tell Cordial was sincere.

"Mom what's going on?" Brandy asked, sitting up.

"CJ claims that Chance tried to kill her."

Brandy scoffed, "How ridiculous, he wouldn't do that, scare her maybe, but never kill her."

"What do you mean, scare her, young lady?" Cordial quipped.

How blind can you be mother?" Tiffany snapped, sitting bolt upright. "She's his lover. They've been carrying on behind your back for weeks. Why do you think she wanted you to hire him?"

Brandy rounded on her with a glare. "Shut your freaking mouth, Tiff, or I'll shut it for you!"

"Oh, I'm scared," Tiffany mocked her. "He's been with me on the side, too."

"Liar!" Brandy screamed, shoving her into the pool.

Tiffany surfaced sputtering. "Slut."

"Silence!" Cordial shouted, rising to her feet. Both girls stared at her in shock, mouths agape.

"The police have taken Chance into custody, for attempted murder. And he's singing like a bird. He was using you two twits, pumping you for information. The police will want to question you," Jake stated, giving the girls a frown that made them fall silent. "It seems he was working for Dwain Hawkins and got nervous when Hawkins skipped town. He decided to take us out, and run."

"Mommy, this can't be true," Brandy wailed.

Tiffany pouted. "He loved me."

"It's true," Cordial snapped. "He was the one who'd pass me the letters to post. But if I'd had any idea, he was sleeping with you two, I'd have killed him."

"What letters?" Brandy asked.

"So, it was you," Cyn mumbled, with a gasp.

"Who else would have easy access to the mailbox?"

"Then you're the one who scrawled messages on the back of some of them."

Cordial shrugged, looking down. "I didn't want you hurt. Please believe me, I had no choice but to cooperate. Otherwise, he'd have..."

"What's going on, Mother?" Tiffany asked.

"I was being blackmailed."

"But..."

"Dwain Hawkins found out that I had a child out of wedlock. My son was born premature, and died. My parents kept it quiet, told everyone I was off to a finishing school. I never told a soul, not even Carl, but somehow Hawkins dug it up, and he's been holding it over me ever since. He wanted a million dollars. I don't have anywhere near that kind of money. He knew it too and said he'd make a deal. If I persuaded my friends that it was a good idea to sell, gave him the ranch, and you too, CJ, we'd be even. He was obsessed with you. I've been going crazy."

"I'll want to talk to you about that," Zane stated, walking up to them. "Our search of Chance's personal affects bore fruit. Chance McCall is an alias; he's a grifter from way back. Worked these scams with Dwain Hawkins for years, usually as the face man, charming the ladies out of their pants for his boss." He scowled when Brandy and Tiffany broke into tears. "I need to take you three downtown for questioning. Get dressed."

"But, Mother," the girls wailed, shooting pleading glances at Cordial.

"Do it," Cordial snapped at them, making Brandy get out of the pool. Both girls wrapped towels around themselves, trembling.

Cordial stood, her shoulders sagging. "I'm actually glad that it's over, and I've come clean. You'd better believe my daughters will be cooperative, or they'll find themselves joining their lover behind bars," Cordial commented, in a firm tone that made the girls sit up straight. "They're going to forget all this boy crazy foolishness, and go back to school this fall, or I'll see they're disinherited." She glanced at Jake. "My husband says that you're going to buy the ranch from him, so that we can get away from here. Is it true?"

Jake nodded. "It's true, Mrs. Taylor. You have my word on it."

"And CJ?" Cordial asked, her concerned gaze going to Cyn.

"Don't worry. I'm going to take care of her," Jake stated, putting his arm around Cyn's shoulders.

Stunned, and equally relieved that it was over, Cyn stood in his embrace feeling strangely disconnected. Shock, she supposed. Cordial had tried to save her; she could hardly wrap her mind around it. All Cordial's sniping, her efforts to get her to leave all took on new meaning now. She might have all the tact of a bulldozer, but she'd mostly meant well. It was a lot to assimilate. "I'm going to be fine," Cyn rushed to reassure her, hoping they could find a way to mend fences. It would be important for her father if they did. "The ranch is going into good hands. Jake will be a good caretaker for the land, and won't let Randal Industries destroy it."

"Good."

Chapter 18

Cyn went back into her cabin that night, alone with Jake, relieved that the worst was behind her. Now she could concentrate on the rest of her life. Now she could concentrate on Jake, and how sexy he made her feel. He walked up behind her after bolting the door, his hand tightening possessively on her shoulders, as he pressed hard and needy against her ass. Her whole body heated, melting into him, and she moaned. God, she needed him, didn't even want to think about the end of the summer, the possible end of their affair. Jake's magic touch was the key to her sexuality. When he was pressed against her like this, she knew she'd never want to stop.

Smiling against her skin, he pressed kisses down her neck. "You are so good for me, sugar," he stated, his erection pressing against her.

She laughed, groaning as he reached around her to cup her breasts, his hands holding her sensitive breasts, squeezing slightly.

"This ranch wouldn't be the same without you. You've got to stay." Unzipping her dress, he peeled it off her in one smooth move.

Sighing, she knew it was almost what she wanted to hear. "Let's talk about this later and let our bodies do the communicating now." She gasped as he tweaked her nipples through her bra.

"You are so right, sugar," he agreed, unhooking her bra. He lowered her panties, asking, "Is it lubed for me, sugar?"

A little fission of excitement and alarm zinged through her as he touched her, cupping the globes of her bottom, rubbing the flesh in between. Her knees wobbled with delight. So far, he'd been nothing but a tease when it came to anal sex. "You know it is," she murmured with a pout. If only he'd stop teasing her about taking her ass. She had kept up her lube and butt plugs, all along, aching for his possession there.

"Step out of the panties, and bend over the back of the sofa, sugar," he demanded with a growl.

Blushing, she did as he said, kicking off her undies, and walking over to the couch. She bent over the padded back, with a gasp. "Are you actually going to claim me?" she asked. "So far you've been nothing but a tease."

He let out a rueful chuckle. "I think it's been the other way around, sugar, and you know it. You make me crazy for you, and for this tight little ass." He teased the lubed opening with a swirl of his fingertip. "I burn to open it with my cock."

She moaned, her ass quivering, her sex pulsing, but he pulled his hand away. Then she saw him pick up the paddle and moaned. He was going to drive her insane with need. He gave her left cheek a rapid smack, and she gasped, stifling her cry against her palm.

"Ass higher," he commanded.

Cyn arched her bottom out, groaning when the paddle came down on her right cheek, gasping as heat flooded her sex. Her ass throbbing, she bit back a moan, trembling as he played the paddle up and down her hot bottom. Spasming, her sex creamed, misting her inner thighs with her juices. She arched her hips out, trying to be good, leaning into the strokes.

"You're mine," he stated with a final smack.

"I'm yours," she sighed. She'd trust him completely. He was her future. When he dropped the paddle, and stepped behind her, unzipping his pants, his stiff cock touching her ass, she gasped with delight.

He nibbled her ear. "God, you're hot, woman, and you're driving me crazy."

She laughed, amused, and bedazzled. "I think I've cornered the market on crazy. Who just got paddled?"

He rocked his cock against her. "I didn't hurt you, did I?"

"No," she insisted, tugging him down again. "I don't think you'd ever hurt me. I trust you completely."

He chuckled. "That's good to hear. We'll have to go paddle shopping, and pick out an assortment."

She laughed at the threat. "That's right, tie me up and spank me, that's the key to my heart," she stated with a hiss, as his cock touched her ass.

"But first, I've got something to give you, if you want it," he teased, his stiff cock pressed against her quivering anus.

Cyn moaned, praying he wasn't toying with her, and pressed back against his teasing cock, so close, but not taking her. "Ah, yes. You know I want it," she replied with a needy groan, as the broad head of his cock eased just inside her ass. She cried out, clinging to him, realizing how big he was. She gasped, adjusting, only wanting him more. Jake held still for a moment, throbbing inside her, stretching her open, as he bent to kiss her nape. Leaning over her back, surrounding her with his heat, his muscular body cradled hers, while her ass rippled on the head of his cock.

"Are you ready for this step, sugar?" he asked, poised to take her, his body tight and tense.

"Oh yes," she murmured, arching her back, pressing against him. She gasped, the breath leaving her as he pressed inside, his cock parting her, until he was buried to the hilt inside her. Cyn moaned helplessly, as her ass rippled, milking his cock at the same time that her pussy quivered.

Jake groaned, lying still inside her. "Easy sugar, just relax and let me love you."

Cyn let out a breath relaxing at his tone as he slowly pulled back and surged back inside her. She gasped, stretched, and was turned on beyond belief.

He rested, kissing her nape. "Is this what you crave, Cyn, this bad boy inside your tight little ass?"

"You know it is," she hissed, arching back to meet his thrusts, gasping as her pussy and ass both clamped down, tugging at him.

"Slowly love," he commented, pulling out to slip back inside.

Moaning, heat surged through her when he did it again, building a driving rhythm that made her cry out. She rocked back against him, his balls slapping into her as he took her harder. He reached down to touch her clit, and she came with a shriek, milking at him.

"That's it, come for me," he demanded, deepening the thrusts.

And she did again, climaxing, her spasms clamping onto him, as he came with a groan, deep and hard inside her.

A few days later, Cyn was working on a commissioned painting in her mini studio area in the cabin. Since the showdown with Cordial and the girls, they'd lived under a quiet truce, and to her pleasure, Jake had stayed with her. They hadn't yet had that talk, but she was hopeful.

She glanced at him with an appreciative smile. He was her prince charming. "I'd like to paint you sometime."

He grinned and sauntered up to her. "I'll pose for you anytime."

"Nude?" she asked, with a grin.

"Any way you want me, sugar."

She sighed with pleasure when Jake stepped up behind her to nuzzle her nape and wrap his arms around her. "I'm so glad that they've got Chance charged."

"Me too," he agreed, his hands slipping up under her blouse to cup her breasts. "Why don't you take a break, and we can..."

"I've got to finish this, honey. Your mom was nice enough to get me the private commission and a showing in Chicago. I can't let her down." The brush shook in her hand as he pinched her nipples with his sexually talented fingers, and she moaned. She could never get enough of him. "Oh, what the hell..."

Jake's cell phone rang. "Hold that thought, sugar," he stated, answering it. "What's up, Zane? Have you got a cold or something, you sound kind of hoarse?"

He cleared his throat. "Nah, too much tequila last night. We found more improprieties at Randal Industries. We need you down here pronto. That Hawkins guy was a real bad ass."

Jake looked at Cyn and sighed. "That's a matter of opinion—a pain in the ass for sure. Can't it wait until later? I'm kind of busy..."

"Sorry," he voiced. "This is urgent."

"Hold on a second," Jake murmured, putting his hand over the receiver. He gazed at Cyn, sexy as hell in shorts and a tank top, a fetching smudge of pink paint on her pretty nose, and fell in love with her all over again. It happened at least five times a day. Even though the thugs had been dealt with, he still felt edgy. "I don't like leaving you alone."

"But you're a smart guy," she stated with a twinkle in her eye, adding, "and you've learned to trust me to take care of myself. Go." Cyn rose up on her tiptoes to give Jake a quick kiss. "I'll be here when you get back, and we can play then. I've got lots of painting to do."

Jake frowned, hesitating. "Are you sure?"

"I'm positive. Dwain is gone, Chance is behind bars, and the girls are leaving me alone. Go, so I can get some work done."

"Fine, I'll be back in an hour. Then I'm taking you out to dinner, we've got lots to talk about." He walked away, putting the phone back up to his lips. "I'm on my way."

Cyn went back to her painting, troubled. What was there to talk about? He was buying the ranch. She was going back to her studio in

Taos, end of story. Maybe they could keep a long-distance relationship, see each other on weekends.

She set down her brush and reached for her pallet knife, when a footstep alerted her that she wasn't alone. Had Jake come back for something? The prickly feeling at her back made her shiver, the hair standing up on the back of her neck. Whoever it was, he was staring at her; the sensation was palpable, hostile. Gripping the pallet knife tighter, she spun around, looking toward the sound in her cluttered studio. Dwain Hawkins stood there, alive and breathing, the clothes hanging on his gaunt frame, a gun in his hand.

"Hello, Cynthia Jane, or should I call you sexy Sin?" he asked with a tight smile. "I bet you didn't expect me to come back for you."

His singsong voice gave her the creeps. "You really aren't stupid enough to think you can get away with this," she spat out, having nothing else to lose. Last time he'd let her get close enough to flip him. This time he'd probably be more cautious.

He glared. "Don't call me stupid, you moron. Your pathetic pretty boy is the dumb one, letting me lure him away like that."

"Then Zane didn't call?"

"Of course not, it's an electronic thing," he replied with a smirk, adding in a superior tone, "Don't rack your weak brain trying to understand, woman."

"And now what?" she demanded, inching closer. "You're going to kill me and run away?"

"Of course not, I want a hell of a lot more than that. I'm going to turn you into my very own sex slave. I'll make Jake Randal pay dearly for exposing me. And I get to have you groveling at my feet at the same time. I can hardly wait."

She glared at him, her skin crawling. "I won't let you touch me."

He laughed. "From what I've seen, Cynthia Jane, you'll let anybody touch you. I've got video proof, in fact. I'll be able to school a bad girl like you to my cock in no time."

"Think again, jerk."

"This is going to be fun," he stated with a smirk. "Payback is sweet."

Cyn got close enough to see the spittle at the corners of his mouth, the cold, insane glint in his pale blue eyes. "Payback you say. What did I ever do to you?" He glared at her, and she gulped. "Oops, forget I asked that."

"It wasn't your lame physical attack. Stupid women like you are a dime a dozen. It's rich boy. He smashed my scheme," Dwain replied with a growl. "He can't be allowed to get away with it, can't possibly compete with a genius like me."

"Wow, that's quite a plan," she commented, trying to humor him, trying to buy time.

He smiled down at her. "I'm glad you realize that. Maybe you're smarter than you look, and I won't have to hurt you so bad."

Jake was cruising down the highway when his cell phone rang. "I'm almost there," he said, seeing Zane's caller ID.

"Almost where?" Zane asked.

"To the station, you called me."

"I didn't call you."

"Crap!" Jake yelled, doing a 360 turn on his Harley. "Send a patrol car to the ranch. I've just been lured away."

Up above, Agatha put down her teacup and scowled. "Red alert ladies!" she shouted.

"Oh, my stars, this is it," Imogene stated.

Hilda scowled. "What a rat."

"This calls for strong medicine, girls. Let's deploy the troops."

They disintegrated like falling stars, setting down like snowflakes outside the cabin.

Agatha looked at the assembled group. "All molecules here, good."

"Imogene, go speed our hero along, or he won't get here in time."

"Right boss," Imogene replied, dematerializing.

"Hilda, go get the goats," Agatha turned to say.

"Will do, Aggie." Hilda vanishing into thin air.

"I'm going in," Agatha voiced, rematerializing inside. Standing at Cyn's elbow, she knew her fairy goddaughter could feel her, even if she couldn't see her. The fool with the gun was too far-gone to even sense her presence. She waved her magic wand, and he gulped, easing back a half step. Agatha grinned, and then whispered, "Be strong Cyn, we're working on your rescue."

Cyn stood a little taller, her chin rising as she glared at him.

Speeding toward the ranch, Jake was praying for greater octane, when suddenly a tailwind caught him, hurtling him so fast the trees were only a blur. He squinted his eyes, lowered his head, and gave it all he had.

The familiar sound of hooves rushing through her lobby made Cyn smile. Dwain didn't know what was coming. She turned to see her wooly rescuers sprint into the room like some invisible force was chasing them.

"What the hell!" Dwain yelled, as the pygmy goats rushed past him. He leveled his gun at them.

That was the last straw. "Don't you dare touch my babies," Cyn shouted, as she lunged at him.

He let out a shriek, tumbling backwards over Curly, the gun going off.

Jake ran into the cabin, his heart in his throat when he heard the gunshot. He took one look at Cyn glaring down at Hawkins, knife in hand, while he sobbed as goats mobbed him, and smiled.

Hawkins saw him, and rolled, scrambling for his gun. Jake went in low and fast, taking him out with a vicious blow. When the man fell unconscious to the floor, Jake pocketed his gun, and went to Cyn. She was standing there looking at him like he was a hero or something.

"My knight in shining armor," she gushed.

He pulled her into his arms, needing to reassure himself that she was in one piece. "Never scare me like that again, Cyn. I couldn't bear to lose you. I love you."

She smiled, reaching up on tiptoes to kiss him, murmuring, "I love you too, Jake."

"Then you'll stay here, and marry me," he pulled back to say. "I bought the ranch for us to share."

"Of course I will, Jake. I thought you'd never ask."

Behind them, the fairies gathered, beaming. "Now that's what I call some fierce fairy action," Hilda whispered.

"It's so romantic," Imogene stated with a sniff.

"All in a day's work, ladies. All in a day's work," Agatha added gently. "In Philadelphia there's a six year-old renting Cinderella."

Cyn opened her eyes and saw her fairy godmothers standing behind Jake. She smiled at them, dazzled when they waved good-bye and vanished. They were real. She'd known it all along.

JULIE CASTLE

Goldie & the 3 Bears

FAIRY TALES REIMAGINED: Goldilocks & the 3 Bears

Tangled Tales Book Three

Chapter 1

Her lips tingled as he gazed masterfully down at her in the moonlight and her nipples budded in the cool night air. She instinctively leaned toward him, creaming, as a sexual energy field snapped between them.

"Who do you belong to, bad girl?" he asked, a sardonic smile curving his handsome face.

"You," she cried out as he slid a hand down the front of her naked body, slowly over her breasts, grazing her nipples until she sucked in a tremulous breath, and his hand slid lower to boldly cup her weeping sex. Everything inside her tightened as he held her in his big, work-roughened, warm hand. She was unable to deny him anything and in exchange he gave her everything. He expertly squeezed her mound, rubbing her clit as he did, and she came with a cry as he held her safe.

Squeak...

Honey Lockwood woke with a snort, sleepily discombobulated but knowing instantly she wasn't alone. Chills went through her as she lifted her head off the overheated laptop keyboard and peered through the golden fringe of her curls that had saddled her with the nickname Goldilocks. The dark recesses of her grandsire's lakeside lair were full of harmless shadows. So why was she shivering? And what had made that noise? It couldn't be one of the Sundowners—roving bands of Werebear males in search of mates. Besides she was immune from the virgin hunt, being a dud DNA wise. Never had she been so happy to be a throwback to the mundane part of her family.

The mating season only served to reinforce her decision to start her own business, leave the clan, and make her life in the human world. If she never saw a macho Werebear again it would suit her just fine. She'd realized how out of her depth she was when she'd caught her sometime beau, Geoff, on his knees pleasuring her Werebear fem cousin, Joelle. The humiliation was enough to make her break away. She'd known then and there that she had to get out. Of course, if she'd been a true blood, she might have found out what it was like to get properly laid.

Instead of being in on the mate hunt, she'd come to this remote cabin alone to regroup before heading off to Chicago and her new life next week. Here she could work on her business plan in private. She'd always had an affinity for numbers, something she and Geoff had once had in common before the mating fever had hit him and he'd lost all sense of reality. Heck, she hadn't even told her family where she was going, not that they cared. She'd fobbed Grandsire off with an explanation that she was off on a singles cruise with her mortal friend, Darla, and he'd been visibly relieved that she was out of the picture. His reaction more than anything emphasized that she had to go back to real life and forget about her clan.

Squeak...

A loose floorboard squeaked in the kitchen again, bringing her wandering thoughts back to danger in a nanosecond. Chills ran up her spine as a sensation of a dark murky aura sent out tentacles toward her and with it came a gasp worthy top note of musky cologne. Damn, the thug had to have bathed in it. Eyes watering, she knew that trouble was on the move, toward her. Her growing ability to read auras, a real non talent in the Were world, was getting stronger. But she rejected the notion that she was cracking up, as Joelle had claimed.

She was as sane as anyone else and she knew she had to move. Unfortunately, her purse, containing her mace, cell phone, and car keys, was in the kitchen where he was. She didn't know how she was certain her nemesis was a he, but considering her luck with men, it had to be some male mortal thug out to do her harm. Probably some mundane out to rob the place although there wasn't much to steal. A blast of crisp night air against her back made her shiver and reminded her that she'd left the patio door open in a last ditch effort to air out the musty fishing shack. If she could quietly make it out the door, she'd stand a chance.

Holding her breath, she eased out of her chair and tugged open the patio doors screen, wincing when it squeaked. Damn, if she lived through this night, she was coming back with a big oil can and oiling the shit out of these hinges. Something crashed in the vicinity of the kitchen and her heart leapt to her throat. Time to get the hell out.

With a gasp, she ran for the safety of the dark woods. It had to be well after midnight and not a creature was stirring, except her. Her crunching footsteps sounded thunderous as she made it to the tree line. She sagged against a tree breathless as the darkness cloaked her. At least whoever had broken into the shack wasn't chasing her. Standing there shaking and feeling like an idiot she wondered if she'd dreamt it after all. No tentacles of evil chased her, not even a mouse sneezed. Maybe her vivid imagination had been working overtime after all. She had been feeling strange lately as her thirtieth birthday approached.

She turned to peer back at the cabin. All the lights were still blazing and just the sight of the light calmed her fears. Given her fear of the dark, she'd brought plenty of nightlights. Everything seemed peaceful. Her belongings, including her brand new laptop, were inside. Could she just abandon them because of a bad dream?

A shot rang out smacking into the tree above her head, splintering the wood. She dropped like a rock, biting back a scream, her arm burning like fire. Oh, my heavens, I didn't imagine it! Then the cabin lights were doused all at once and she knew she was in trouble deep. Fear made her scramble to her feet and run deep into the pitch-dark woods as the overpowering stench of musk pursued her.

Half an hour later, she crested a rise and saw a big lakeside cabin, its light ablaze in the valley below. Lights! Tears of relief sprang to her eyes. Never had a sight seemed more welcoming. She raced toward the house, tripped, tearing the strap on one of her sandals, and hobbled up onto the porch. Breathless, she looked for a doorbell. Not seeing one, she banged on the solid wood door, then reached for the doorknob. The minute she touched it, her palm tingled and she distinctly heard the lock open before it swung open on well-oiled hinges.

Startled, she stood there rubbing her heated palm for a moment as she looked inside the seemingly empty house. Then a rainbow of pleasant auras seemed to bid her into the house. Stunned by her good fortune, she rushed into the house and slammed the door behind her, sagging back against it trembling. As she stood there glancing around the well-appointed but seemingly vacant lodge, a strange feeling of lethargy came over her. The strange auras rubbed against her skin making her tingle. Damn, maybe this was a delayed reaction to shock. She absolutely refused to feel auras on top of seeing them. She couldn't deny the feeling of coming home, but this place was posh compared to her grandsire's rustic compound that she'd grown up on.

As she'd noted from outside, all the lights were on. A fire blazed in the fireplace and something savory simmered in the vicinity of the kitchen. Her stomach grumbled in response, as she hadn't eaten since morning. Nobody seemed to be home. As a matter of fact, the place had a vacant feel, as if it were waiting for its occupants. She rolled her eyes at her vivid imagination and ventured into the empty room looking for a phone.

"Hello," she called out, hearing her tense voice echo through the empty lodge.

Suck it up, Goldilocks, nobody's home so you'll just have to save yourself. She took a step forward and damned near broke her neck when she tripped over her sandal again. With a growl she kicked off the damned things. Then she walked into the living room looking in vain for a phone. Almost out on her feet, she plopped wearily into a huge leather wing chair by the fireplace, smirking when her feet didn't touch the floor. The story of The Three Bears came to mind. This had to be papa bear's chair. The only other furniture in the room were two more leather recliners just as deep, confirming her guess that this was a man cave. Maybe the boys had gone out on a beer run. Some help they'd be.

Fighting her urge to just cuddle up in the chair and go to sleep, she surged to her feet. She had to find a phone...save herself...and get some crazy housebreaker busted. She followed her nose and the delicious smells toward the kitchen. Seemed like a logical place for a phone and she was hungry.

She stopped at the doorway. No phone, but a crock pot on the counter simmered away with what smelled like chili drawing her toward it. Her stomach grumbled again forcefully reminding her that she'd missed dinner. Her mouth watering, she gazed at the three bowls set out next to the crock pot. Shades of The Three Bears again, making her grin. Well, the other Goldilocks had helped herself to some porridge, maybe it was a sign that she should, too.

Before she could censor herself, she ladled a portion of the chili and sat down at the kitchen nook before she fell down. She needed to eat, and she'd pay for the chili when she got her purse back. She took a bite of the spicy concoction, blowing on it when it was too hot, stirring it till it cooled down, and then greedily eating it all when it was just right.

Sitting back, replete, she looked down at her messy clothes and winced. Yikes! She was covered in dirt and leaves from her flight through the woods and tumble down the hill. And there were a few tell-tale drops of chili on her white blouse. The boys would probably think she was crazy looking this way. Hell, she'd be lucky not to get shot at again. She needed to clean up fast.

She stood up on wobbly legs and started down the hall in search of either a bathroom or a phone, whichever came first. Her footsteps faltered when she glanced into the messy den. Up till now everything in this place had been neat as a pin. She smiled when she saw the papers strewn on the oak desktop and tumbling onto the floor. This looked like her office after she'd been on one of her creative streaks.

Then the sound of swirling water caught her attention. Could it possibly be a hot tub? Just the thought made her yearn for warmth. She padded down the hall toward the sound and stepped out into what she could only call a spa. There was a deep Jacuzzi tub and even a sauna. Now this was roughing it in the woods. She gazed longingly at the tub. It was almost calling her name. Should she? A bottle of jasmine bath oil sat on the edge of the tub. Maybe one of the boys had a lover. She didn't know why that thought bothered her more than the prospect of stealing someone's bath. Pushing back those thoughts she poured in the bath oil, stripped, and got in. Sinking down in the water she eased back and closed her eyes with a groan as all her sore muscles tightened a moment before going loose. Drifting away, she sank down in the water, pressure melting away. A few minutes later she woke up in a hurry, coming up sputtering. Damn, she was dead on her feet.

With a wince, she pulled herself out of the tub, her cuts stinging anew. She toweled off and glanced at her trashed clothes, her nose wrinkling. For nothing on earth would she put them back on until she sponged them clean, but she was too tired. Instead, she reached for the white terry cloth robe hanging on the back of the door. It was miles too big for her, but it was warm and enveloping, and she snuggled into it like a security blanket. It smelled of sandalwood and man, obviously a big man, one who could protect her. If only!

Half-asleep, she staggered out of the steamy bathroom into the frigid hallway and shivered, her teeth chattering. Well, hell, she was really out on her feet, maybe in shock. She had to get warm, fast. She headed toward the bedrooms like a guided missile. She'd have a little lie down to regain her equilibrium.

Chapter 2

Cruz Bear walked out of the sky and came to rest next to his lair thanking his lucky stars that he'd kept Lane from meeting his alleged damsel in distress. When he'd gone instead to check on the Were fem who'd texted his techno brother a distress message, he'd been ambushed. The stinky Sundowner who'd jumped him had actually managed to conjure a battle axe out of thin air. He strode toward his cabin wincing as the time jump made his wounds start to knit.

Lane and Tyson probably wouldn't thank him for being sent on a decoy ride but at least they'd come out of it in one piece, he hoped. So, where the hell were they? They should be back by now. Then, his brothers roared into the driveway on their twin vipers, and he relaxed a little. Thank God they hadn't been caught in the same trap. He'd deliberately sent them away, not trusting Lane's source and he'd been right. The question was, had it been a ploy to take his clan down or something more personal?

He was thoughtful as he watched his brothers dismount. Moonlight glinted off Lane's blond hair and Tyson's ebony skin as they strode toward him. Tyson, a telepath, had never been the same since he'd lost his first love, Fleur, in clan warfare three years ago. Now, he looked even more troubled, and Cruz knew he'd instantly noticed his injuries. On the other hand, Lane, being younger and thinking himself half in lust with the alleged damsel in distress, just looked pissed to see him standing there without her. Cruz sighed, preparing to handle another battle. Damn it all, he'd only wanted sanctuary this wild mating week. But clan warfare and designing females were messing with his bliss. "You two run into any trouble?" he asked, thinking of the roving bands of Sundowners that formed over mating season. They'd stop at nothing to get laid.

Tyson's eyes narrowed. "We didn't find jack-shit out in the hinterlands, just like I'm sure you know. Stop worrying about us and tell me what happened to you."

Cruz's jaw tightened as he wiped the blood off of it, sorry that Tyson was so perceptive. Even Lane took a pause from glaring at him. "Not much. I just walked into an ambush, that's all. And after questioning one of Black Jack's sentries, I found out there is no such female."

Lane sucked in a shocked breath. "That can't be true. She's been texting me for weeks, ever since I signed up for weremates.com. It's only lately that she said something bad was going down."

Cruz shook his head wondering if Lane knew how naive he sounded. Exchanging a look with Tyson, who knew women weren't to be trusted, they both frowned. "Yeah, well, it wouldn't be the first time someone's joined the group for cross purposes."

"I refuse to believe that she lied to me. Sheila's not like that, she's..."

Cruz held up his hand to forestall his lament. "Let's take this inside before whoever's behind this manages to break through our shields."

"This conversation isn't over," Lane stated gruffly, and turned to stomp toward the cabin.

Cruz ignored his pissy attitude, knowing that mating fever was making the young bear swain edgy. Hell, he wasn't immune himself, and Tyson, the self-avowed woman hater, still looked at pretty Weres. They were all feeling it and that was the main reason he'd decided to hole up here until the fever was past. He personally had no intention of starting his own line even though it was the very thing Ma insisted on. When the time was right, Tyson and Lane would find mates and he'd be free of responsibilities.

"Come on, baby bear, let's go see what Ma left us to eat." He saw Lane wince at the private nickname and smiled. He'd been dubbed Papa being the oldest, and Tyson much to his chagrin Mama, being a sympathetic telepath. Striding toward the cabin where, as expected, all the lights were lit and smoke was drifting out of the chimney, meaning the fire was lit in the fireplace, he finally started to relax. The spa would be filled and ready for him too. Ma knew he'd be stiff and sore after the supposed peace parlay. After he loosened up, all he'd need was a cold beer and a helping of some of Ma's home cooking, and he'd be back to normal.

"Hold it," Lane said. Lane's tense tone told Cruz something was up. He and Tyson turned to him in unison to see him looking at his diver's watch. If the electronics whiz was worried about one of his sensors something was seriously fucked up.

"What's up?" Cruz looked down at his matching watch to see the luminous dial glowed red, telling them by heat signature that an intruder was inside. Ma would be long gone by now and the cabin locked up tight, so who was inside? Cruz felt his tension shoot up like a Geiger counter.

"I knew these things would come in handy one day," Lane crowed.

At least playing with his gadgets had brought the kid out of his funk. Shit, he couldn't believe that he'd missed the fact that there was an intruder. He glanced Tyson's way and saw the same shocked look on the telepath's face. Knowing Tyson usually sensed danger before they met it didn't make him feel any better. Had the Sundowners broken through the shields after all? He gave hand signals, and the boys took flanking positions, one on either side of him. He stuck his key in the lock braced for an attack. The door popped open before he could turn the key in the lock. Fuck! The damned place was unlocked and the shields were down. Ma wouldn't have left it that way. The dizzying scent of a female Werebear in heat hit him like a brick, making him growl under his breath as his cock stirred. He knew the boys felt it too as they growled low in their throats. Damn! He surveyed the empty room, seeing the shoes by the door, women's sandals, one strap broken. "We've got company," he stated under his breath.

"She smells like heaven," Lane acknowledged, slipping past him and into the room.

Cruz shot his younger brother a wry look. "I thought you were in love."

Lane gave him a chagrinned look. "Sheila hasn't mated me yet. So, I'm still on the marriage mart."

Tyson rolled his eyes. "Don't you know a trap when you see one, cub?"

"Keep it down and watch out for the Sundowner's clan," Cruz cautioned. He didn't feel them. As a matter of fact, all he felt was horny, but he wouldn't be led around by his cock. Cruz moved out without saying a word and the boys joined in on the hunt. Entering the kitchen, he spied a dirty bowl and spoon on the breakfast bar. "Five o'clock," he murmured under his breath and the boys turned toward it. "Someone's been eating my chili."

"Bold housebreaker," Lane commented.

"And hungry," Tyson agreed. "Not your typical bear swain, I think."

Cruz could feel it too. There was something different but tempting about her, like she was a rare hybrid. "Maybe the Sundowners wanted to send us a message. They can get to us anytime. I wonder if she's still here," Cruz wondered, starting a search. He saw one of Ma's prize afghans on the floor next to his leather wing chair.

"Someone's been sitting in my chair," he muttered under his breath.

Tyson chuckled beside him. "Sounds like Goldilocks. I wonder if she's in my bed."

Cruz frowned at the slang term for a mortal woman who threw herself at Werebears because of their sexual prowess. He'd never much liked the way his kind made light of the softer emotions.

"An ugly mug like you couldn't get that lucky," Lane teased.

Moving back out into the hall he picked up her scent mingled with jasmine bath oil. Had she actually stopped to take a bath? He couldn't help smiling at her audacity, but it wouldn't stop him from dropping the hammer on her. His body tightened in anticipation. He stopped short at the bathroom door. The tub was empty, but her clothes were strewn across the floor. A glance took in a mud-stained white blouse with red chili stains and a pair of denim shorts, followed by a matching set of red satin bra and panties.

She was all but leading him by his dick to the bedroom...where she'd no doubt try to blow him away. Anticipation unfurled inside him making him feel alive again when he bent to pick up the red bra. He could swear it still carried her body heat and it smelled like her—strawberries and woman.

"Someone's been using my spa," Cruz chuckled as his hand tightened on the lingerie.

Lane nodded. "It's a little departure from the storybook, but intriguing," he added with a grin.

Tyson winced when he looked at the empty bottle of bath oil. "Shit, she used the last of Carol's jasmine bath oil, big sister's going to kill us."

"Don't sweat it, I ordered another bottle for her birthday." Cruz grinned when he saw his brother's relief. Carol could be hell on wheels, but she was family. "Come on, let's go find her."

They moved silently toward the bedrooms, looking for their naked spy. They walked past Lane's room with its waterbed, empty.

Lane poked his head in the door and grumbled, "Shucks."

Tyson grinned. "Better luck next time, kid," he stated and strode toward his room with its antique sleigh bed. "Damn," he grumbled, finding it empty. Then he turned to look at Cruz. "Only one bed left."

Cruz let out a long, suffering sigh. Shit. This wasn't starting out well, not when the very thought of her had him primed and horny. "That's kind of what I figured."

Tyson smiled. "I'm sure you can handle one little virgin bear."

He surged into the room and froze, taking in a sexy seminude Goldilocks sleeping in his bed. Shit, she was wearing his robe. Someone was playing a warped joke on him. Her golden curls spread out around her head like a halo and her closed eyelashes looked like angel's wings. He gulped. "Goldilocks is sleeping in my bed, it seems."

Tyson grinned. "Someone really wanted to get leverage against you."

Cruz didn't know why she was there, he just knew he needed to get rid of her before he did something really stupid like give in to temptation to fuck her. The front of her robe slipped open to display cleavage voluptuous enough to make a monk horny and he was no monk. His fascinated gaze lingered on the dusky edge of her perfect pink nipples, like ripe strawberries, and his cock came to life. She'd look hotter than hell wearing emerald nipple clamps. He let out another growl, his cock straining at his pants. She wasn't a Sundowner, he recognized all their females.

"Some guys have all the luck," Lane cut in joking. "Care to share, bro? I could help you interrogate her."

Lane knew the rules, whoever made her come the hardest got to keep her. In essence it was up to the female to choose her mates. And despite his earlier feelings, he wanted her more than he could possibly explain. Feeling territorial, Cruz stepped up to her. "She's mine," he blurted out, startling himself. Her eyes popped open, huge, sapphire blue, and shocked. He felt like he'd been sucker punched. Change that to sapphire nipple clamps. He watched her nipples bud.

He watched her mouth drop open in a perfect O of surprise and asked, "Want to tell me what you're doing in my bed, Goldilocks?"

Chapter 3

Honey stared back at Cruz Bear in drowsy wonder. She recognized the leader of a rival pack even though she knew he wouldn't recognize her. She wasn't mating material so why should he? All her erogenous zones sizzled to life as she stared at him, her eyes widening when she detected his aura's glow. Damn, her weird non talent was getting worse. Maybe Jolene was right, and she was losing her mind. On top of that, she was reacting like a dame in heat, but she couldn't be. So why was her body tingling, her nipples stiffening, her pussy creaming? Her hungry gaze latched onto Cruz seeking answers. His aura glowed red hot, the atmosphere crackled around him, and she practically drooled. Yum! Licking her lips, she found her voice. "Maybe I was waiting for you, Papa Bear." The narrowing of Cruz's dark eyes should have given her a clue to his mood, but she was too caught up in fantasyland to notice.

"Were you now?" he asked.

She smiled as he came closer, moving with an aggressive stride that took her breath away. He was close enough to reach out and touch if she dared and her fingers itched to do just that. But she didn't want an audience even if they were part of the dream team. She frowned at Tyson and Lane, and they started to waver before her very eyes. Holy cow was she doing that?

"Just concentrate on me, baby," Cruz demanded gruffly.

Her fascinated gaze flew back to Cruz, her heart doing a little pitter pat as his brothers vanished. She refused to believe that she'd made them poof. More likely they were powerful enough to transport with a thought. Cruz's impatient growl drew her attention away from the puzzle of his vanishing brothers. He towered over her looking like the dangerous predator he was but for some crazy reason she wasn't afraid of him. She'd never heard of him harming an innocent. Somehow, she trusted him not to harm her. He might break her heart, but he wouldn't kill her.

Even from a few inches apart, his body heat rippled through her, making her glow. She could feel her cheeks redden as she focused on his ruggedly handsome face. Then her fascinated gaze traveled down his powerful body to his skintight leather pants, and she gulped. Damn, judging by the bulge, he was huge. In turn his sultry gaze lazily swept down her body making her burn. His hot gaze lingered on her bare breasts and her nipples budded for him. Bare breasts! Gadzooks, she was flashing him. The robe had come open, a provocative, slutty display. Even as she squirmed on the sheets, she didn't move to cover up. "You've got my undivided attention, Papa Bear."

He frowned. "Do I now?"

If she wanted to find out what it was like to get properly laid, he was the ideal candidate. After all, she'd had the hots for him for years. "Of course, you do. It's just like in the fairy tale, don't you see?"

"So, I found you in my bed and now you're mine," he stated, reaching for her.

Honey let out a breathy gasp when his hand closed over her shoulder, sending a zing through her, curling her toes. A force field seemed to snap between them, and she watched his cock actually pop the zipper on his leather pants. She let out a stunned gasp. It was almost like she was drawing power from him, but how?

"Damn," he growled, looking down at his burst zipper for a moment and then looking at her inquisitively.

Honey knew exactly how confused he felt. Then everything seemed to happen at once. He came down on top of her with a throaty growl of satisfaction. She moaned, spreading her legs to make a nest for his rigid cock against her creaming sex.

"I don't care who the fuck sent you to trap me," he states gruffly, gazing down at her. "You're mine, Goldilocks, and I play for keeps."

A thrill went through her at his vow, even though she knew, he wouldn't keep it. It was the answer to her wet dreams, but she knew better than to believe in them. As soon as he took her, he'd realize she was a fraud and dump her, but she wanted a little taste of paradise before it fizzled.

"You talk too much," she grumbled, before kissing his tight jaw.

He groaned in response and pressed her down into the mattress, claiming her with a fierce kiss. She wriggled a little against him, shuddering and kissed him back. Heat and instinct seemed to take over as a fire swept through her. He nipped her lower lip, and she trembled, opening her mouth for him, sizzling when his tongue surged inside, taking her mouth, just like she wanted him to take her sex. He tasted heavenly, like coffee, chocolate, and honey. She let out a little growl of her own, surprising herself. Then his hand slipped down between their bodies to cup her mound, and she gasped.

"Like that, do you, Goldilocks?" he asked, then let out a low masculine chuckle.

She blushed, but couldn't deny she loved it. He stroked her again and she whimpered, pulsing hot and heavy against his hand.

"Tell me," he demanded, pinching her clit a little.

She cried out at the hint of pain and moisture poured out of her pulsing slit. "Yes, I love it. More please," she begged, lifting her ass off the bed to arch toward that teasing hand. She was going to find out if this bear stud was really as big as the rumors had it.

"Good, my naughty Goldilocks," he growled. "Deny me nothing and I'll give you everything." He let out a low growl, pushing back the robe to bare her. She went still.

Honey quivered as he said the magic words from her dream. Damn, was he the phantom lover who'd haunted her dreams? Taking her just so far before fizzling away? Now she knew why the fates had sent her to him. Not that he'd believe it for a minute. She was no beauty, certainly not long-limbed and athletic like her Were counterparts. She was a rounded, softer mortal. But when she saw the look of sultry wonder in his dark swirling eyes, it made her blood heat and melted any doubts. He looked like he wanted to devour her, and it thrilled her to the core.

"Mine," Cruz demanded, cupping her breast and squeezing.

"Yes," she replied with a moan at the display of dominance. She wanted to find out what it would be like to be on the bottom. He pinched her nipples, rolling them between his thumbs and forefingers, tugging on them as she let out an extended whimper of need. She pressed her eager sex to him, dry humping his leg, arching into him, crying out as she exploded.

Chapter 4

Cruz felt the last shred of his self-control crumble as Goldilocks came for him. The mating fever she was exuding washed over him, undeniable and definitely tasty. She was like a gift from the gods and who was he to turn down such splendor? If she brought him to his doom, so be it. For tonight he'd live.

"Spread your legs for me, Goldilocks; show me you really want me." He groaned when she obeyed him, parting her long legs to show him her perfect, pink, wet sex, her swollen clit. God, but he wanted her. His fingers traced a path down her slick sex, to home in on her swollen clit. She cried out, closing her eyes, arching off the bed, as he played with the sensitive nub.

"That's it, love. Go wild for me."

Cruz kept his thumb on her clit, and slipped one finger into her tight wet sheath, before his little finger ghosted her anus. She quivered, as if startled by the dark caress, and then moaned, as he finger-fucked her that way, her body clutching at him. When he couldn't take it anymore, he shed his ripped pants, still amazed that she'd been able to make him pop them freeing the animal in him, and settled between her warm thighs.

He rubbed the tingling head of his cock against her creamy sex, and she lifted her ass off the bed, trying to complete their union, her eyes squeezed shut. Damn it all, he wasn't going to let her reduce him to just some blind, anonymous fuck.

"Tell me your name, Goldilocks," he demanded.

He watched her eyes pop open, and smiled when her steamy, pleading, gaze locked with his, like she really saw him, really wanted him.

"My name is Honey," she answered with a sigh.

He swallowed a hungry groan. Of course, it was. She was so sweet he was tempted to lick her all over. She could have her pick of any stud. Why him? "Do you really want me, Honey?" he questioned, rubbing the head of his swollen cock against her again, teasing her a little, making her hiss with pleasure. The sound sent a shock wave of need through him.

"Oh yes," she replied with a needy moan.

Satisfied for now, he plunged into her and winced when she cried out in pain. Damn, he wasn't used to deflowering virgin bears or whatever the hell she was. He watched her bite her lip and look up at him shamefacedly, like she expected him to reject her. What gives? Then her pulsing cunt milked at his swelling cock, sending tingles through him, and driving him out of his mind, and he stopped thinking. He'd find out her secrets later. Right now, they needed to mate. He rocked into her again and again, drinking in her fevered cries. Feeling himself grow inside her even more to an extent he'd never felt before. It was as if the goddesses were saying this was right. As he neared paradise, he ground against her, wanting to make it good for her. As good as she made him feel. Then she cried out coming, screaming his name. He growled deep, his balls tightening as he shot his load, coming over and over again as he slowly filled her with his seed. She clung to him, her after spasms guiding him as he completed their union. Then he rolled off her, pulling her close to his side as he came back to earth. When she let out a pleasured sigh and cuddled against him, he drank it in as his due.

But lying there in the afterglow as their auras still bathed the room in a rosy glow, he became suddenly wary. Why was she here? He'd been too horny to get the truth out of her a few moments ago. On the bright side, she wasn't turning against him as many Were females would, trying to rip out his jugular or his balls. And her clan wasn't attacking, sensing that he was in a weakened position. It went to support his theory that she was other. Hell, he ought to know about being weird, being an outsider himself. Only Ma knew his true colors. More mystic than true Werebear, he had powers the others didn't know of. But laying here, speculating about her wasn't getting the job done. Now that he'd taken her, it was his job to protect her even if it pissed her off.

He let go of her, smiling at her groan of protest. At least he knew she wasn't lying to him where this was concerned. She'd wanted him as much as he'd wanted her. "Come on," he stated, rolling out of bed. The love-drunk look Honey gave him almost made him relent, climb back into bed, and rock her world again. But he needed to plan, and he sensed that she needed more from him than a roll in the hay. Instead of giving in to his animal urges, he reached out for her hand and tugged the protesting golden-haired beauty out of his bed. Just the sight of her naked curves was enough to stir his senses and jumpstart his cock again.

He groaned as all the blood drew out of his head making it swim and quickly manifested his robe back on her, tying the sash firmly around her waist. He didn't know who he wanted to cover her from more, himself or his lusty brothers. He already knew that if she stayed, she'd have them too, as part of her harem. It was their way, and he accepted it even if the possessive part of him didn't like it one bit. It was one of the main reasons he'd never gone for the mating ritual. He'd seen it turn out tragically. Now he was well and truly stuck. Even as his natural reluctance reasserted itself, her feisty grumbled protest as he covered her made him smile. They were paired if only temporarily and he could handle it.

She cocked her head to look at him. "I wouldn't have thought a big bad bear like you would have a problem with nudity."

He bit back a grin and gave her a stern look, impressed when she met his gaze without blinking. Shit, he'd made lesser Were's pee their pants, but she wasn't a bit intimidated by him. "I don't want you tempting my brothers and getting them in the same trouble you've gotten me into." Her suddenly glum expression troubled him. It was like she thought he was teasing her about being desirable. Nothing could be further from the truth.

She gave him a withering look. "Right, we wouldn't want me, causing trouble."

Cruz didn't like her defeated tone, but he didn't have time to worry about it now. "Come on," he stated, tugging her out of the room. "Let's go find your clothes and get a cup of Tyson's coffee. Something tells me we're going to need it."

He throbbed, his cock hungry for her again as he towed the golden-haired spitfire down the hall. One thing he was almost certain of was that an enemy had put Goldilocks in his bed tonight. The other was that she belonged to him, at least until he wanted to let her go. He'd popped her cherry. In some Were societies, she'd belong to him, body and soul.

Too bad it still wasn't the Stone Age, he'd keep her naked in his bed as one of his concubines. Now it was the females and fates that made the ultimate decision on mates. He decided to set that aside and concentrate on the mystery that was Goldilocks.

Chapter 5

Honey let Cruz escort her down the hall feeling bemused, still horny, and vulnerable. She felt different, changed somehow. Even worse, the mating fever coursing through her veins wasn't letting up. As a matter of fact, it seemed to be building, sharpening her senses, making her tingle. It was shocking she should be feeling this primal need to mate and it was nothing her human mumma had prepared her for. Cruz's strong hand on her arm made her feel both protected and flustered. The macho Werebear had made it clear he thought she was some kind of a siren, luring him to his doom. But the heat he'd released inside her made her want to throw him down on the floor, drizzle honey on him, and lick him all over. A quick glance down at the hard-on that was still stretching his pants made her smile. She'd actually made him pop them before. That was one for her side. Cruz had wanted her too, even though he'd covered her up. At least she wasn't the only one feeling primal.

When they got to the kitchen, she inhaled the heavenly aroma of dark roast coffee and sighed with pleasure, her tension melting away. Tyson could make a mean cup of coffee, and he wasn't transparent and wavery anymore. A glance at him, tall and ebony-skinned, with piercing brown eyes made a shiver of anticipation go through her. If only she were a real Werebear fem she'd be adding him to her harem now. The harems would fuck like mad until their true-life mates were revealed. But she wasn't a pureblood and this strange aberration would pass soon, she was sure. "The coffee smells great, Tyson."

Tyson met her gaze and gave her a thorough once-over.

"Thanks, it's my own special grind. I'll pour you a cup, Miss..."

She could tell by Tyson's reserved glance that he was almost as suspicious of her as Cruz had been. Lane who stopped typing on his PDA to smile at her was more of an open book. Are the Lockwood and Bear clans in conflict now? She didn't know. "My name is Honey," she replied not wanting to reveal her last name just yet.

Lane growled low in his throat. "I really like honey..."

"Let the lady catch her breath," Cruz interrupted in a quietly firm tone. He turned to Tyson. "I could use a cup of that brew, too."

Tyson gave him a look. "I figured as much, big brother, it's coming right up. I figured I'd add a little extra boost of ginseng to yours to build up your..."

"Enough," Cruz murmured wryly.

Honey watched Tyson stir herbs into Cruz's cup feeling the tension in the room. What was the rivalry between them and why did Tyson dislike her so much? Their family dynamics were really none of her business. She was self-protective enough to know that she needed to leave before she fell anymore under Cruz's masculine spell, or did something really stupid like try to bed all three of them. Hell, that's what her kinswomen were doing right now, sampling the cream of the crop so they could choose love mates. Being wooed and screwed. She blushed at the errant thought but couldn't keep heat from blooming inside, and her still pulsing sex from throbbing. As if they could sense her arousal, she felt the three bear boys turn to look at her with awareness in their eyes.

Tyson had a speculative look in his eyes, Lane a big lusty grin, and Cruz just looked pissed, horny but pissed, and her female hormones did a little jig. Is Cruz actually jealous? Her heart leapt at the possibility. But she was too honest to mate them with a lie. She had to tell the three bears the truth about what she was, and the minute she did they wouldn't want her. Hell, she'd found out that bitter truth when Geoff had dumped her to join Joelle's harem. It was better if she walked away. It would hurt less. "Here's the deal. I'm not who or what you think I am."

"Goldilocks," Lane put in with a grin.

She gave him a half-smile back, finding his snarky humor endearing. "No, a proper Were female waiting to bed and wed a mate."

"You mean you're improper?" Tyson asked with a reluctant smile.

Honey felt a quiver of heat burst inside her. She could feel his wall of reserve melting toward her and couldn't understand it. She was a fraud, he should be resenting the hell out of her. Why were they all being so dense? Of course, Cruz had yet to chime in. She turned to frown at him. He was watching her closely but didn't act surprised.

"If you're not a proper Were female waiting to bed and wed a mate, what are you?" Cruz asked, arching a brow.

Well, at least one of them got to the point. Feeling like a specimen under a microscope she met Cruz's eyes squarely. Half-breed or not, she was proud of her heritage. "I'm a throwback. In short, I'm a half-breed, my mother was mortal, and I have no magical talent. So, if you're looking for a whirl on the marriage mart, I'm afraid I won't do..." Why did his eyes twinkle at that statement?

"Then why did you come on to me?" Cruz asked softly.

Honey wanted to cry as her feminine ego crumbled. Come on to him? He was talking like she'd seduced him on purpose, but it hadn't been like that. It had been a mutual ravishment, one she didn't regret despite his boorish attitude. "Believe me, it was nothing personal, Bear. So, you've nothing to fear from me. I'll make no demands on you and you're free to go find an eligible virgin." She saw a nerve in his jaw tighten and wondered why he was so pissed.

"That still doesn't explain how you came to be here," Cruz stated.

"Why am I here?" she parroted back in as snarky a tone as she could manage with her pride in tatters. "It wasn't to mate with a beast like you, that's for sure." She winced when she saw him freeze up at her words, and wanted to call them back. "Sorry. I'm just a little frazzled. In short, I was running away. I'm staying at a nearby cabin. Someone broke in and I ran...end of story."

"The Sundowners," Cruz cut in.

"I admit that I thought so at first, too," she agreed, adding ruefully, "but why would they be after a mundane like me? Everyone knows I'm not eligible."

"Easy, sugar," Tyson stated, handing her a cup of coffee.

She gasped when their fingers touched, and his aura flared with a golden snap making her tingle all over.

Tyson let out a gasp. "Damn, sugar. How the hell are you doing that?"

Honey trembled when his hot pink aura layered itself up her arm and over her skin making her tingle and the whole room smell like cherry blossoms as his wistful thoughts of Fleur made her ache for his loss. The reason for his former standoffishness became painfully clear. How in the hell was she doing this? Speechless for a moment, all she could think was that Cruz had somehow short-circuited her meager powers. "I'm not sure. Weird things have been happening to me lately. But not this weird."

Cruz grumbled, "I can think of at least one reason for them to be after you."

Honey flashed him a puzzled glance. "Why?"

"Have you ever glowed before?" he asked dryly.

She looked at the pink sheen on her skin and shook her head. "No, but I've never seen auras before either. It must be something you did to me." She heard Cruz mutter something but then Lane stepped closer, drawing her attention. His blue aura was pulsing with excitement, and it sent a corresponding zing through her senses.

"Do me next," Lane stated and reached to hand her some honey.

Honey let go of Tyson to take the tupelo honey Lane handed her and giggled when his blue aura snapped, instantly layering itself on her skin. "Good gravy," she murmured under her breath.

Chapter 6

Cruz sat there frozen with frustration and jealousy as his brothers lit his woman up and knew he was in trouble, deep. She'd said she was staying in a nearby place and that could only mean one thing. She was part of the Lockwood clan. "The only place nearby is the old Lockwood place five miles away, and Black Jack doesn't come up here too often anymore," he stated, gauging her reaction. The sudden intake of her breath told him everything.

Honey bit her lip. "Nobody's supposed to know about Grandpa's private fishing hole."

Cruz's gut tightened and he saw equally wary looks come into his brother's eyes temporarily throwing cold water over their mating fever. Black Jack Lockwood was the powerful leader of a large clan. Usually, they were in alignment but given the fact that they'd tried to kill him, Cruz knew the peace pact was over. Was sending Honey to tempt him the first step in an attack? Looking at the troubled look in her big blue eyes, he rejected it.

"Black Jack and I have worked together from time to time." He looked at her curiously, trying to place her from the females he'd seen in the Lockwood compound. "Funny, I don't remember you."

"You wouldn't. I'm half-human. I lived in the real world with my mom until she was killed in a car accident when I was fourteen. It was only after that that I came to live on the compound. I do remember seeing you there once or twice. And no, you never noticed me."

How the hell could he have overlooked someone as precious as her? "So why were you hiding out at the fishing shack?" he asked a little roughly. He knew the minute she glared at him that he'd hit the target. She had been hiding out, but why?

"If you must know, my boyfriend just dumped me. I needed to get out of the compound. Besides, I was upset over my cousins bragging about the mate hunt to come, and needed some quiet time before I made the move to Chicago. I was just in the way anyhow."

A wave of jealousy came over him at the mention of her boyfriend, even though he knew he had no right to feel that way. "Who was he?"

"Just another mundane like me. Geoff and I kind of went together like peanut butter and jelly. Anyhow, it doesn't matter now that he's joined Joelle's harem."

He remembered the slinky Joelle very well, but seeing Honey's baleful look, kept it to himself. It was the pain in her eyes that got to him. He wanted to put a big hurt on stupid Geoff and anyone who'd dared to hurt her. She hadn't been well treated in the Lockwood clan. He could read between the lines. And he of all Were's knew the stigma of being different. "Tell me about the break-in," he asked, wanting to change the subject.

She sighed. "I was sleeping over a hot keyboard. Something woke me up, the sound of a loose floorboard. I thought maybe I'd dreamed it. I tend to get a little carried away when I'm working on my business plan. But then I heard it again. Someone was creeping through the shack, toward me. So, I ran."

"That's it?"

"Not quite. Once I got to the woods, and nobody gave chase, I thought maybe I had dreamed it after all. I turned back in time to see the lights doused. Then the jerk took a potshot at me."

"Son of a bitch," Cruz bit out. A traditional Were wouldn't use bullets to take her out. But there were other much scarier creatures that might. Whether they wanted to capture or kill her, he didn't know, but he vowed then and there to protect her.

"Well, that's my story. I ran through the woods, saw your lights, and the rest you know."

"How many were they?" Lane asked, pulling out his PDA.

"I can't be sure. Like I said, they cut the lights. I'm guessing, based on the fact that they didn't come after me, it was just some teens looking for a place to party."

Cruz was hoping the same thing, but he knew better than to count on it. "Shit, I'll talk to Black Jack right away."

"Don't you dare," she stated with a gasp.

Her shocked reaction made him hesitate.

"Please promise me that you won't," she requested softly.

It went against his instincts, but he found himself inclining his head. "You'll need to stay here until the danger is over," he demanded and watched her chin rise defiantly. "Please," he added softly and relaxed when she nodded. He met his brothers' gazes and saw the same all-for-one instinct in their eyes. Hell, they were all rejects in one way or another, maybe the fates had intended this. "Besides, you don't have to go out looking for mates. You've got a built-in harem here," he added, seeing first Lane and then Tyson nod. He knew what a stretch it was for Tyson to trust anyone, and it only confirmed his instinct that Honey was a trustworthy Goldilocks.

"Damn right," Tyson chimed in.

"Boy howdy," Lane added with a grin.

Cruz watched the startled look of wonder on her face as her gaze roved over them. A mingled blend of feminine maidenly modesty and sexual heat warred within her. He could feel it. He knew heat had won when her eyes locked with his, and he felt his formerly hardened heart open while his senses stirred. A sensual spell seemed to be upon them and he, for one, didn't want to fight it.

"You're all mine," she replied with a cautious smile.

He couldn't help smiling at the greedy, playful gleam in her blue eyes. She was going to lead them on a merry chase. Heat flared between them as he reached out to touch her and the snap sent a shock wave down to his stirring cock, making him crazy as his red aura washed over her making her glow. Damn. It was the most beautiful sight he'd ever seen. He swept her into his arms and swore in his heart to protect what was his. He shouldered his way into the bedroom and kicked the door shut behind them and the walls glowed with their mingled red and gold auras. Damn it was enough to make him drunk with heat.

Chapter 7

Honey tingled when Cruz set her down on the floor in front of the bed and just looked at her like he wanted to eat her up. She instinctively picked him, knowing that it was right. He was going to make her his, and she welcomed it. When he flicked her robe off her shoulders and it dropped to the carpet with a swish, she shivered with delight. "You've been a very bad girl, Goldilocks," he stated teasingly, walking around her.

She shivered with delight and a little trepidation at his masterful tone. How did he know this was one of her fantasies? "Have I now?" she asked, playing along.

"You know that you have," he replied, one corner of his mouth kicking up. "And you've got to be punished."

A sensual shock wave went through her at the word punished. Would he really punish her? Nobody, certainly not her parents, had ever even spanked her. "What did you have in mind, a time-out?" she teased, pushing her luck. Then she saw the matching flare in his eyes and heat flared through her, making her toes curl in the thick carpet.

"No, something a little more primitive than that, I think," he muttered, picking up a hairbrush off the dresser and sitting down on a bedside chair. He patted his lap. "I think over my knee would be the best way to start. We'll take you through the basics first before I introduce the paddle and bondage."

She gulped, her pussy fluttering wildly at his words. She looked deep into his swirling amber eyes. Mystical and sultry, oh my, and he really meant it. At first, she stood frozen. Then she found herself moving toward him as if propelled by his will and her secret desires to be dominated. "I'm not sure if I..."

Then he snagged her wrist, toppling her onto his lap and she went with an inelegant oof. Landing on top of him, her ass in the air, she felt a blush cover her from head to toe. Good grief, she felt like a naughty concubine. "Hey!" she yelled just as the hairbrush came down on her ass, startling her. She let out a yelp as a heat wave washed through her and her pussy pulsed. "I wasn't ready."

"I was," he stated, raising the brush.

She tightened, waiting for it. "Please," she whispered.

"Oh, baby, I will. Now ask me to discipline you or you won't get fucked."

She shuddered at the threat and her sex clenched emptily waiting for the brush to fall, waiting for his touch. "Please discipline me, sir."

"Better," he commented, smacking the paddle down on her other cheek, making her squirm with the sting and the heat. Then he spanked her, slow at first and then building up harder and faster, until she didn't know when to expect them and she was laying over his knee sobbing and giddy with need. When they were done, he spun her to sit astride him facing him and kissed the tears off her cheeks. "That brands you as mine, love. You will obey me in this room, or I will tie you up and take my belt to your sweet ass," he commanded. "Understand?"

She shuddered at the command and her willingness to go along with that. "That's primitive even for a Were," she groused, leaning lazily against him. Hearing the beat of his heart, feeling the ridge of his cock pressed against her.

"I've never been a very progressive kind of Were," he replied, bending to kiss her.

She kissed him back, loving the feel of him against her, rocking against him, dry humping him because his damned clothes were in the way. And then he growled as she felt his surging cock break his zipper again and she giggled. She wasn't the only one feeling primitive. And then she lifted up a little to hop on his cock and they both groaned in unison.

"Little queen," he groaned, slamming into her.

She sobbed, rocking against him, seeing stars as her pussy tightened around him. And then she rode him hard, taking him deeper. He clutched her ass, surging into her driving her over the edge. And they came with a shout clinging to one another.

Chapter 8

At sunrise Cruz woke up pressed against Honey's ass, feeling warm, languid, satisfied, and strangely energized even though she'd worn him out throughout the night. He cupped her left breast, feeling the strawberry pink nipple bud against his palm. She was so exquisitely responsive, it was hard for him to concentrate on the task ahead—bearding her grandfather in his own den. Knowing he might not come back alive he wanted one more taste of paradise. His aching cock nestled between the sexy globes of her rounded ass, and he rubbed it against her, smiling when he heard her sleepy murmur of pleasure. He rolled her onto her back and kissed her. She moaned under him, kissing him back. He thrust his tongue into her mouth, his arousal building as he felt heat build inside her. His hand cupped her breast, rolling the nipples as he drank in her breathy gasp. He reveled in his ability to excite her as her nipple jutted out harder. Then he rolled onto his back taking her with him and loved the feel of her warm body sprawled atop him. He put his hands on her waist, and effortlessly pulled her up so he could suck on her nipples. Her breasts dangled like ripe fruit for his voracious mouth.

As his hot mouth closed over her right nipple, he felt a shiver of delight go through her. And then he was lost, sucking on her nipple, his cock rising to the occasion. She spread her legs and rubbed her creaming pussy against the ridge of his erection, torturing him too. He growled, making her giggle. He smiled against her honeyed skin and arched against her, driving her wild as he moved on to suck her other nipple. She let out a cry, riding against him. When he was satisfied and so horny he could stand it no more, he released her nipple and she let out a murmur of protest. He ignored her and lifted her higher so that he could taste her sweeter fruit.

She seemed flustered but when his tongue flicked out to lick her pussy she moaned and stopped struggling. He savored her, licking her labia and sucking it into his mouth until she was thrusting against him. Then he let her go to lap at her clit and she screamed with pleasure. He flicked against her again and again until she was sobbing and arching against his teasing tongue. His hands tightened on her hips, holding her captive, as he pleasured her with his mouth. He sucked on her clit, drawing it into his hungry mouth, nursing at it. And then as she was shuddering, his tongue slipped into her pussy. Her body went spasmodic for him as she came, her pussy rippling on his tongue as he drew her pleasure out.

Cruz was dazzled by her response, his heart open for her, his cock hard enough to break off. But he wanted to brand her as his and make it last. When he finally eased her down to lie beside him, she was limp. He kissed her, and she opened for him. He knew she tasted her essence on his tongue as she purred for him.

Honey wrapped her arms around Cruz, kissing him back, feeling dazzled. Oral sex—wow! It was the most forbidden, erotic, experience so far. Somehow Cruz always managed to up the ante every time he took her. Now in the afterglow, she was suddenly bit by the notion to do the same thing to Cruz. How she'd love to rock his world. She slipped her hand down his toned body to reach for his erection. She could hardly wrap her hand around his hot pulsing staff, confirming her thought that it got bigger the more they touched. He growled as she fisted him and then bent to taste him. She looked up at him. The burning look in his eyes and the rigid set of his body told her he was holding back, waiting for her to make the next move. The sense of feminine power that filled her at that moment spurred her on.

She watched a nerve in his tight jaw pulse, made a yummy noise, and focused on his cock. It was hard, bobbing in front of her face. She experimentally flicked her tongue out to taste him. Salty, sweet, and all man...hers. A drop of pre–cum glistened on his slit and she lapped it up, stealing it. He growled in response, making her quiver, emboldening her. She smiled, swirling her tongue around his hot cock's velvety head and then opened her mouth to take him in. His groan excited her, made her suck on him hard, trying to take more of him in. He tastes like honey!

"Enough," he gritted, his hands on her shoulders

Honey gave him a frown, her lips still holding him trapped, not wanting to give him up. But his demanding, if tender, look made her stop. She let him slip from her mouth and left him with a kiss and a promise. She wanted more. When Cruz pulled her up his body and then flipped her over onto her back, she went with a giggle. Then his mouth crushed hers with a kiss and she stopped giggling to moan. She kissed him ravenously knowing he tasted his essence on her tongue, reveling in it.

He broke the kiss to gaze down at her, his eyes glittering with banked fires. "Reach out for the bedposts."

Shivering with anticipation, she did as he said and by magic soft fur restraints snuggled around her wrists. Her back arched a little, as she let out a little gasp of surprise. Feeling his hot gaze on her made her nipples harden to tingling points as he gazed at every inch of her breasts. She felt as if he were touching her. Tremulous, she gasped for breath as if she had run a marathon. He moved closer and reached out to touch her. His fingertips brushed over her nipples, making them jut out harder, just begging for his attention. She hoped he'd make good on his seduction and wasn't just teasing her.

"More," she begged, arching out for him.

"Be good and you'll get fucked," he promised hotly, skimming his hand over her once more.

"Yes, sir," she stated with a gasp.

He chuckled and bent to lick her nipple

She bit back a scream of pleasure when his rough tongue rasped over her. Damn, but the bear could lick. Then her eyes rolled back in her head when he sucked on her. She went wild, arching off the bed, crying out. And in a flash, he was lying on top of her, pressing her into the bed. She tried to put her arms around him and grumbled when she realized she couldn't. He laughed and she fumed.

"Wrap your legs around my waist, Honey," he demanded.

She didn't need more encouragement and flowed around him wrapping her legs around his body. His cock scraped against her sensitized pussy, and she cried out with need. He growled and thrust into her, his hands cupping her ass. She cried out, her cunt milking at him instantly as he deepened his thrusts. He growled, muttering passionate words in a different language that she didn't know but felt to the bottom of her heart. Then she stopped thinking as he fucked her harder than ever before.

She clung to him, never wanting to let go. It was at that moment that she promised herself that she'd fight to keep him. Then he kissed her, driving high and hard inside her, driving all rational thought from her head. It pushed her over the top and her orgasm rocked through her like a shock wave. Her last conscious thought was of his growl as he emptied his essence into her.

"Honey!" he shouted, coming high and hard inside her.

She drifted back to earth listening to him whispering sweet, soothing sounds into her ear as her restraints magically vanished. There were definite perks to sleeping with a strong Were talent. Then he eased back up beside her, rolled onto his back, breathing hard, pulled her into his arms and she melted against him. Bathed in afterglow, she reveled in the feel of being in his arms.

"Sleep now, sweetheart," he commanded, stroking her hair.

"I'm not going to let you play those Werebear mind-meld tricks on me," she replied with a yawn, her eyes drifting shut.

<h1 style="text-align:center">Chapter 9</h1>

Cruz smiled, kissing the top of her head as she drifted off to dreamland. He waited until she was sleeping deeply and then rolled out of bed. It took all his strength to leave her, but he had a job to do. Dressed, he walked down the hall to the kitchen where Tyson and Lane were talking. The concerned looks they gave him told him they were on the same wavelength. There was trouble coming but they'd protect what was theirs. "Watch over her for me, will you?"

Tyson nodded. "You want backup at the Lockwood Camp? I can call in a few of our warriors to babysit and accompany you."

Cruz winced they all knew that Black Jack wouldn't take well to that. He'd just have to take his chances solo. He shook his head. He also knew what Tyson wasn't saying, he didn't want to let another woman that close. They'd just all have to get over their hang-ups if this was going to work. "No. We all know she'll need you both here. Besides, I don't want to go in all gangbusters to the Lockwood Camp. It'd break more treaties than we can count."

Tyson let out a sigh and looked toward the bedrooms. "You're probably right. She knows what you're up to?"

"No. And I wouldn't advise telling her. She'd kick my Werebear uss," he stated with self-mockery.

Tyson's eyes twinkled at that last statement. "The lady does sound interesting."

Cruz did his damndest to quash the jealous feelings inside him. "She is." He turned to Lane. "How about you, junior, you ready to stand and deliver?"

Lane smirked at him. "I've never had any complaints," he quipped, adding solemnly, "If you're going to be so bonehead stubborn as to go in with no backup, at least take this new data–port I designed," he suggested, thrusting a handheld device in Cruz's direction.

Cruz looked down at the matte black device in his hand. "What does it do beside text and send tweets?" he asked, thinking of the kid's latest love. Of course, looking at the strong set of Lane's body, he knew he wasn't really a kid.

"Well," Lane replied with a grin. "The redial is a panic button. Hit it, and our clan warriors will get the Bear signal."

Cruz groaned at the batman reference. The kid also liked comic books. "Yeah, I'll be sure not to push that one."

"Also, type in 911, and it'll pack a punch to knock anyone on their ass..."

"Sounds interesting," he intervened, pocketing the device. "I'll see you when I see you," he stated, starting to teleport.

"And make sure you're in a clearing when you set off the bomb. It's star six nine."

Chapter 10

Honey woke later that morning feeling blissfully sated but alone. She didn't need to reach for Cruz to know he was gone. Maybe Cruz had gone for some of Tyson's yummy coffee. They could both use the caffeine buzz after the night they'd spent. Being ravished by a hunky Werebear stud could wear a girl out. She smiled and snuggled under the covers. No wonder her Bear sisters indulged in harems. She was still tingling. And best of all, after last night, she knew that she wasn't such a flop in the mating department. She might not have a harem, but she could handle one man. The only troubling thing was that she still didn't have a handle on her emerging powers, even if they were insignificant.

She sighed, tossing and turning as she waited impatiently for Cruz to return. After a while she came to the painful realization that he wasn't coming back. Some lover she was if she couldn't hold on to him all night. With a grumble she rolled out of bed. She'd just have to track him down and find out exactly where she stood. After Geoff's desertion, she was through being laid-back. As she moved, feminine muscles she wasn't aware of spasmed in protest. A hot shower just might make her feel human again and ready to face the world. She still didn't know where Cruz was, but she knew he wouldn't be paying that call on her grandsire. After all, he'd promised.

Well, actually, he'd just nodded but she'd taken it as a promise.

Stepping under the steaming shower, she let out a groan of relief as all her knotted muscles unraveled, loosened. Then she reached for Cruz's sandalwood body wash, realizing that it smelled like him. Lathering up, she indulged in a few fantasies as she scrubbed herself clean. It was time to come up with a game plan. First, she'd track down Cruz and say her goodbyes on her terms. Then she'd go assess and repair the damage on her grandsire's fishing shack. After that, she'd get on with the rest of her life. It might be loveless, but at least she'd had her taste of bliss.

Out of the shower, she noticed the clothes she'd worn last night freshly washed and folded on the dresser. How thoughtful. Cruz and she had been too occupied last night for her to even think of it. She'd bet it was Tyson.

She walked out of the bedroom, fully clothed and feeling as pulled together as she was going to be. Determined to be as sophisticated about this mating game as her Were-sisters were, she moved purposefully down the hall. Drawing in a steady breath, she took in the heady aromas coming from the kitchen and headed there like a beeline, her stomach grumbling. She was famished and hopefully Cruz would be there. She had to admit to herself that she was in danger of falling hopelessly in love with him, but she'd never let him know. She was determined not to fall for Tyson or Lane's charms either, no matter what her natural inclinations were.

She turned the corner, feeling Tyson's gentle pink aura before she saw him and noticed a difference. It was somehow warmer, less guarded. As she walked into the room, Tyson turned to smile at her and she couldn't help responding in kind. He wasn't hostile today. What had made him soften toward her? The hot pink aura around him practically glowed, telling her how comforting it would be to touch him. She blushed at the errant thought.

"Pull up a seat, my lady. I've got your breakfast ready. I scented you the minute you left the bedroom," he added with a grin.

His answer confirmed that he was very powerful. "You saying that I smell funny?" she teased back, looking around the room for signs of Cruz. Where the blazes did he disappear to?

"No, you smell like a woman should smell," Tyson replied, giving her an approving once-over. "Feminine, intoxicating."

The breath caught in Honey's throat and her captive gaze flashed back at him. Damn, he was attractive in a rough-around-the-edges way, but she couldn't afford to get involved with him. She had to keep her mind on her to-do list. Find Cruz and say goodbye.

"Can I tempt you?" he asked, pouring her a cup of coffee.

She bit her lip as the heat rose inside her. Damn. She needed to cut the sensually charged flow between them like yesterday. She had a list. Oh yeah. "Where's Cruz? I need to say..."

"Cruz is gone, love," Tyson cut in while carefully watching her reaction.

Honey blinked back tears of humiliation that sprung to her eyes. Damn it, she wouldn't be a weak female.

Tyson added gently. "Don't take it so hard, love. Cruz had some important business to take care of in town. Otherwise, he wouldn't have left. He told me to take extra special care of you."

She took in the way the swarthy bear stud said 'care of you,' and blushed down to her toes. He was reporting for harem duty. So why was she flustered? Because you're not trained to handle a harem, stupid. It was the opportunity of a lifetime. Not that she was considering it, her nerve endings tingled. Still, it was a comfort to her wounded pride that Tyson was hanging in there for her. But she couldn't take him up on it.

"No thanks, I need to get going."

He moved so fast he was a blur one instant and holding her hand the next.

"You can't leave."

Her natural feistiness kicked in. She was tired of being told what to do. Just what kind of game were he and Cruz playing? "Don't even think you can order me around."

"Now calm down, sugar. I didn't mean to rile you up. Of course, you're in control of this harem."

Somehow, she didn't believe him, but she found herself softening toward him just by his force of will. She licked her dry lips, her gaze drifting over her would–be harem mate. Tyson was drop–dead gorgeous if one liked ebony gods, and she did. Strong, glittering eyes, luscious lips, tall and powerful with a sensual look in his eyes that told her he knew what she was thinking. And he had a swagger she knew was probably earned. She looked at him seeing the sincerity there, shocked that she could read him that clearly. He wanted her, needed her to heal him emotionally. It shocked her that she could pick that up.

Tyson broke eye contact to look down and pull out a chair for her. "Have a seat at the breakfast bar. I'm dying for you to sample my latest creation."

Honey could feel that he'd allowed her past his defenses to show her that he trusted her, and she felt honored. Her heart went out to him along with her lust. Damn, this was getting complicated. She stopped trying to fight it and dropped onto the chair. Her to–do list could wait until she figured this out. "Thanks. I really am starving and that smells divine," she replied, feeling shy.

He smiled. "I need an honest opinion from someone with good taste."

She couldn't help beaming at his compliment. He slid the platter of silver dollar pancakes in front of her and added a small, heated pitcher of syrup.

"They're purple raspberry with homemade syrup."

She took in a heady whiff. "They smell heavenly and look almost too good to eat."

"I'm told they taste even better. Although the boys will say shoe leather tastes good if I keep on doing the cooking."

She felt herself warming to his seductive smile. Tyson had a smooth line, and she couldn't help responding a little bit. To demonstrate, he picked up a tiny cake, dipped it in the syrup and pressed it to her lips. She felt a bit flustered as she took a bite, her lips brushing his blunt-tipped fingers. She groaned with bliss as the summer flavors burst on her tongue. It was better than she'd imagined. Then, Tyson grinned and leaned forward, and she knew the time had come for her to make a decision. Give in to her raging hormones, her destiny, or run away.

"Let me have a taste."

She leaned forward, trembling on the brink, knowing that there was no way she was backing away from the challenge. Then his mouth brushed over hers, his aura mingled with hers, and she closed her eyes and kissed him back. He was different than Cruz, a little more tentative, but nice. When he pulled back to gaze into her eyes, she was breathless. Tyson's grin told her he read her mood. His flaming gaze passed over her breasts and her nipples budded hard while her sex was suddenly drenched. Damn!

A tingle of anticipation made her heart race. Tyson seemed to read the surrender in her eyes, muttered something that sounded like thank you and leaned in to kiss her again. She bit back a growl as his hot mouth slanted over hers. Damn, the hunky Werebear could kiss. Then he pulled her into his arms. Her budded nipples brushed against his chest and a jolt went through her.

"Nice," he stated, sitting down and lifting her onto his lap. "Don't let it throw you, love. It's your choice and I want you, too."

A blush heated her all over as her sensitized sex pressed against his growing erection. She tried her best not to squirm and drive them both insane. Well, that had firmly put the ball in her corner. "I'll do my best, but I'm kind of new at this. I've never been trained to handle a harem."

Tyson grinned. "I think you're a natural, sugar. How about you consider me your test subject?"

Honey bit her lip, more tempted than she wanted to admit. What the hell, she'd let nature take its course. "I do have this seduction theory I'd like to test out."

"I think I can tick off a few of your boxes, sugar," Tyson replied with a slow smile. "You've got yourself a new addition to your harem, Goldilocks."

Emboldened as the fever hit her, she leaned forward the few inches it took to kiss him. His husky growl thrilled her.

She broke the kiss to nibble his jaw.

"What's next?" he asked, groaning.

"Now we see if I can seduce you," she answered, looking up at the gleam in his dark eyes.

"Sugar, I'm seduced," Tyson groaned.

Encouraged as she felt the sexual tension build, she smiled, adding, "With your pants on."

"Not fair," he complained with a husky laugh as she shimmied off his lap to tongue his flat nipple through his white tee-shirt, making it hard.

He let out a growl.

Honey smiled against his moist skin. If she didn't undress him, he wouldn't know how inept she was at this. She scattered kisses down his washboard abs, feeling them contract under her mouth as he hardened and groaned under her ministrations. Then she was over the hardness of his cock. It jutted out for her practically jumping under her ministrations as she knelt on the floor. Her lips skimmed over the hard ridge under his chinos, and she ached to really taste him. Instead, she settled for pressing her tongue flat against his cock and stroking up. His cock grew so stiff, his snaps popped, and he let out a pained growl.

"Have mercy and let me loose before I get a case of blue balls that cripples me."

"So, you're really seduced," she asked, before licking up his shaft, pleased that she'd gotten such a fevered response from him.

"Totally, little queen," he replied with a growl. "Please."

She gave him another lick, craving his taste and his cock popped out hard, ebony black, and pulsing with life. She took a moment to admire it for a moment and he groaned. It wasn't as long as Cruz's, but it was bigger around. A drop of pre-cum glistened on the tip as if drawing her and she leaned in to lap it off, bringing a groan from both of them. Then she swirled her tongue around his cock head, flicking against the flap before opening up to take him in. She savored the taste of him, like honey and man drawing on him until he was bucking under her, his balls drawing tight to his body, and then he howled, coming with a blast. She drank down every drop, her pussy pulsing along with his coming.

Then, in a move so fast, it made her head spin, he picked her up and reversed their positions so she was perched on the stool and he stood before her, smiling, a sensual promise in his eyes.

She smiled at him. "I did it. I seduced you."

"Um hum," he stated, leaning forward to kiss her.

"You don't have to," she murmured with a gasp as he kissed his way down her body, giving her a taste of her own medicine. After all, he'd volunteered to be a test subject, he didn't have to reciprocate. She groaned, arching toward him.

"Oh no, sugar," he replied then chuckled. "I'm not the only one who's going to be tortured." He flicked his tongue over her nipple inside her bra.

When his teeth scraped against her tingling peak, it drove her wild. She cried out, everything inside her contracting. Her pussy clenched, going soaking wet in an instant. It was like he was drawing out the animal side of her.

He moved down to kiss her bared abdomen when her clothes slipped up. Just the feel of his hot wet tongue on her belly button was enough to drive her mad. She had turned from a sex-starved spinster into a sex maniac overnight. It was enough to make a girl dizzy. Then he pulled her shorts off and laid his tongue flat against her clit, wetting her panties and the sensitive woman flesh beneath. She screamed with bliss, her breath catching in her throat. He sucked her through the cotton, and she came, her eyes rolling back in her head. Her panties dissolved, and he proceeded to drive her mad. She whimpered as he lapped at her with his rough tongue, seeming to savor her juices.

"That's it, sugar, cream for me," he murmured.

His tongue stroked up her wet slit, making her shudder again and again until she was weeping with ecstasy. Then he sucked on her clit drawing hard on it, nipping it as his fingers thrust into her cunt and she came with a scream. When she drifted back to earth she was sitting astride him again, this time bare sex to his rampant cock, her budding nipples tingling as they rubbed against his chest, and she was gone. She whimpered, unable to stop herself from rolling her hips as he thrust into her. She gazed deep into Tyson's dark and stormy eyes. He was watching her, enjoying her enjoying him. "What are you doing to me, you bad bear?" she asked.

"Pleasuring my little queen," he replied, leaning forward to nibble her nape as his arms wrapped around her.

Honey trembled at his words, he really meant them. Her hands clutching his shoulders because he made her feel dizzy with desire, she stuttered, "Don't make promises you can't keep. The fates will never make a match for me."

"Why don't you let us worry about that?" he asked with a sad smile.

She watched his eyes darken in response and trembled. They'd risk their necks for her. She wouldn't allow that, but she could live in the moment for now. "Okay," she whispered and watched his satisfied masculine grin. Then he rocked against her, bumping her clit and her eyes rolled back in her head. Frantic for more, she arched her hips, taking him deeper, her passion-swollen clit pressing against him, and cried out in pleasure. He was holding back, trying to be gentle, but she wanted all his Werebear strength

"Easy, love," he stated, holding her tight to him as he thrust deeper up into her.

"No," she sobbed, crying out her pleasure as he controlled the thrusts. "More please," she demanded. Then he surged harder, and she cried out. She kissed him then, their mouths joined as their bodies were. Tyson's tongue thrust into her mouth in tandem with his thrusts into her pussy, and she dissolved around him into a puddle of need. His shaft rubbed against her G-spot, and she started to quiver, waves of orgasm starting as a ripple and then completely overtaking her.

He stiffened, his thrusts harder, fiercer, and came high and hard inside her. Honey clung to him as she came back to earth and then snuggled against him. Tyson smoothed a hand up and down her spine, and then held her tight. Wrapped in the warm cocoon of his arms, she closed her eyes, feeling sated and protected, and curiously sleepy.

"That's right, sugar, trust me to take care of you," Tyson murmured as he listened to a gentle snore come from his little queen. He smiled sadly. She was right, he wouldn't get to keep her, but she'd helped him open his heart and he hadn't thought any woman could do that. After losing Fleur, he'd vowed never to risk his heart again but now he felt healed.

Chapter 11

Cruz came down inside the gates of the Lockwood compound. Honey's grandfather, Black Jack, liked things old school, thus the rugged setting. If the gruff old Bear had his way, they'd all be living in caves. After sleeping with Honey last night, Cruz had known he'd have to settle this with the old bastard to keep her safe. He'd left her in the care of his brothers, partly because he didn't want to see her mate them, but also because he knew that he could trust them to keep her safe.

He walked down the path, feeling spying eyes on him, but kept loose. As expected, when he stepped toward the council fire, Black Jack's guards shambled out of the mist and flanked him. He cast an eye over the motley older crew guarding the place. Obviously the young Werebear warriors and females were out in the mate hunt making it a vulnerable time for all concerned. He was surprised that Black Jack had allowed his numbers to be so weakened. Cruz kept a tighter rein on his own people.

Black Jack arched a wooly brow as he cast a surly glance his way. "Heard you tried to invade our territory the other day, boy. You've got a hell of a nerve coming back here."

"I was here on a rescue mission," Cruz stated, grimly impatient that his mission was delayed by this old news. "One of your women sent out a distress call. I came to check it out."

"What kind of distress call?" the old man demanded.

"She texted my brother that she needed help," he admitted, seeing the older man frown even though he rolled his eyes at the text reference.

"I haven't heard of anyone in trouble. Who was it?"

Cruz hesitated. If the distress call had been genuine, it might be a mistake to say her name but everything in him said it had been a ruse to pull Lane into danger.

Black Jack saw his hesitation and waved his guards back so they couldn't overhear.

Cruz gave him a nod. "She said she was Sheila."

"You sure about that, boy? There is no Sheila in our clan."

"I figured that out, once I got jumped," Cruz replied wryly.

"Didn't stop you from injuring one of my sentries," Black Jack muttered with a growl.

Cruz remembered the sentry who'd challenged him while he was limping back to the exit portal. "Sorry about that. I couldn't tell if he was in league with the smelly bastard who jumped me."

"So, what are you doing back here? There were some who said your clan wanted war."

Cruz stepped closer to the man. "And there are some from my camp who think you want war. We both know it's bullshit. We have more personal matters to discuss." He stepped closer, stopped masking, and knew the instant the old man sensed Honey's essence on him. He'd wear her brand until he was either chosen or eliminated by the fates.

Black Jack let out a low growl of outrage when he looked at him and sniffed the air, then he waved his guards away. "What the blazes have you been doing with my Honey child?" he demanded in a low tone.

Cruz froze, feeling all attention on them from the hangers-on in the camp. Black Jack was too irate to carefully choose his words, and Cruz didn't want Honey to suffer because of it. "Why don't we take this inside?" he asked, not wanting to volley Honey's name around the campfire.

Black Jack waved his hand, and they zapped into his den. Cruz found himself sitting in a leather wing chair across from Black Jack, who was seated behind his big mahogany desk.

"Talk fast," Black Jack stated, adding in a surly tone, "They may be your last words."

Just how much of the truth could he trust the patriarch with? Outside of the ambush and the attack on Honey, the Lockwood clan had been peaceable. Sure, they'd had their share of power struggles and intrigue but that was true for all of their kind. "Who would want to hurt Honey?" he asked watching the old man turn somber.

"Hurt Honey, what are you saying?"

"Did you know she was holed up at your fishing shack?"

"No. She said she was going off on a cruise with her girlfriend before she moves to Chicago. I figured after the way things turned out, it would be good for her to get away."

"Yeah, she said her stupid clod of a boyfriend joined someone else's harem." He knew the old man picked up on his jealousy when he gave him a thoughtful look.

"What happened?" he asked, crushing the pen.

"The shack was invaded, some fool took a potshot at her, and she came running to me." He watched the old man absorb what he said and frown at the last part. "I take it you didn't send her to lure me." But he already knew that it wasn't true.

Black Jack's eyes glittered. "Give me a little more credit than that. My granddaughter doesn't have any powers."

He read past the old bear's cagey expression. "Bullshit," Cruz belted out flatly. "I'm sure you must have sensed her latent powers."

Black Jack scowled. "I couldn't be sure. Besides I never wanted this life for her. She deserves a safe human life. Anyway, her powers wouldn't have been released if you hadn't touched her."

Cruz held steady, waiting for retribution. "Someone else must have known or guessed her powers. We can't let them get to her."

"I'll send my guard to..."

"She'll never agree to that. She made me promise not to tell you."

Black Jack gave him a smile. "She's going to kick your ass, boy."

"No doubt," he replied, picturing her outrage. "You sure did raise a stubborn granddaughter."

"She gets it from her mama who, even though she was mortal, lured her own harem and pair-bonded with my son Seth. After they died, I did my best to raise her as human. I didn't want her to face the danger of a guardian. If you've brought danger to her, I'll..."

"I have a plan to keep her safe." Black Jack's words had given him hope that he might get to keep her. Her mother had been mortal, and the fates had pair bonded them. "After the heat is over, I'll set her free."

Chapter 12

Honey yawned as she slowly came awake in a strange bed, feeling more than a little confused. Where was she? And then it all came back to her...the break-in at the shack, her coming into heat and sexual awakening at the hands of first Cruz and then Tyson Bear. She blushed, tingling all over, and sat up. This antique sleigh bed wasn't Cruz's four-poster. Her last memory was of falling asleep on Tyson's lap after he'd made her come like a screaming banshee. By the process of elimination, this had to be his bedroom.

She cast a fascinated glance around the room feeling Tyson's vibes come off every inch of the elegantly decorated place. Black leather and erotic art. Then she saw the painting on the wall, a beautiful dusky woman and knew in an instant it was the love that he'd lost. Fleur, he'd called her. Feeling in kin with the image, she whispered softly, "I think I helped him heal."

She pushed back the covers, amused to see that she was fully dressed. Tyson was a gentleman. But where was he? This was the second Bear brother who'd run out on her after sleeping with her. It wasn't a good track record for a harem mistress. She forced back her desire to fall back asleep and rolled out of bed, wincing when her knees wobbled. She gripped the headboard, stifling a yawn. Why was she so sleepy? The clock on the wall said it was midafternoon.

Perhaps they really were using some kind of weird sleep spell on her. She vaguely recalled warning Cruz about that before she'd zonked out. Damn it all, she had to take charge of her harem now and set down some ground rules.

She opened the bedroom door to find Lane standing there as if waiting for her or standing guard. She rocked back on her heels startled and he reached out to steady her. The heartbreaker's grin he flashed her was enough to make her steps falter and her heart go pitty-pat. His very real delight at seeing her was enough to disarm her.

"Thanks," she stuttered, standing on her own two feet and gently disengaging from his grip.

"You're welcome, love," he replied with a little pout of disappointment as she pulled away.

She would not be deflected by him or the sensual heat blooming inside her. "Were you waiting for me?" she asked sharply, knowing she desperately needed to regain control.

"Of course I was. I wanted to make sure that you were okay. After your fright at the shack, I knew you might need me."

He said it with such sincerity that she felt like an ingrate for doubting him. "Thank you," she stated, knowing that it was inadequate. At the flicker of pleasure and something else in his eyes she wondered yet anew if she was being manipulated. "Is Cruz back?" she asked and saw deception flick in his eyes for a moment before he shook his head.

"Not yet. I'm sure he'll give me a call soon if he needs help..."

Her attention piqued at his words. "Help with what?"

"Um, a few boring business details. Don't worry your pretty little head about them."

"Listen, Bear, don't bullshit me. I've got my MBA. Cracks like that will not get you where you want to go." Now why did she say that? She wasn't actually going to sleep with him, was she?

The twinkle in Lane's eyes said he thought she was. "I'm sorry. I didn't mean to patronize you. I just didn't want you to worry."

She felt mollified by the sincerity in his words and reached out to pat his arm. "Don't worry about it. I tend to overreact when big bad male Bears underestimate me."

He grinned. "Believe me, I won't make that mistake again."

"How about Tyson?"

Lane shook his head. "He had some business to take care of too."

Her shoulders slumped. Boy, sleep with them and she sent them running. She was two for two. "Figures," she muttered. "Well, it's been fun, but I've got to go..."

Lane moved to block her path. "Please don't go. I know they'll be back soon. Tyson wouldn't leave if he didn't have important business."

"What important business?" she demanded.

"He wanted to check out the shack before you left us," he stated with a shrug.

She was actually relieved by that revelation. "Oh, okay."

"Good. Come on, you don't want to go yet," Lane murmured in a playful tone. "You haven't seen me do my stuff yet."

She knew he was eager to join her harem and deep down, she wanted him, too. "Just what stuff is that?" she asked, thinking of Tyson's amazing oral technique

"Surfing," he replied with a playful grin, adding, "Get your mind out of the bedroom, love."

"Surfing in Wisconsin?" she asked, amused.

"Come on, surf's up."

"I don't have a swimsuit," she commented, grinning. She'd recalled seeing a surfboard leaning against his wall in his bedroom. She'd thought it was just decoration. Who knew he actually used it? But he didn't stop to grab the board, just towed her out the back door.

"Neither do I, sugar," he stated with a playful leer as he rushed her down to the beach.

She laughed when suddenly his clothes vanished, then he grinned.

"But as a consideration to you, I'll add these."

She smiled when he blinked board shorts onto himself. "You Bears have powers I've only heard rumors of."

"You ain't seen nothin' yet, love," he replied, leaning in to kiss her.

She let out a gasp as his playful blue aura mingled with hers and then she kissed him back. Her body heated up along with her mind. He was her final harem mate, and she wanted him.

He broke the kiss to murmur, "Now you?"

She nodded and he gazed at her clothes making them vanish. She blushed, feeling excited and proud when his fascinated gaze lingered on her curves. He liked what he saw. Then a string bikini covered her naughty parts, making her smile. "I like your taste in swimwear," she murmured then chuckled.

"Thanks," he stated, tugging her out the back door. "No need to worry about attack. I've got the property covered with a security bubble."

She relaxed and gazed out at the beautiful private lake. The water was smooth as glass. "I don't think you're going to be doing any surfing in that."

"Watch," he voiced, snapping his fingers and waves suddenly lapped against the shore.

"Wow. Color me impressed."

"Good," he replied, towing her into the surf.

She giggled, a little scared. "I don't surf."

"Trust me?" he asked, holding out his hand.

She made a decision, and put her hand in his. It seemed to mean a lot to him that she trusted him and his hand tightened on hers. Then she found herself on the surfboard with him. She laughed, startled when they rushed through the surf, getting a thrill that raised her heartbeat and her arousal. Damn. Lane pressed up against her back, his erection pressing against her ass. "This ought to be illegal. It's too damned fun," she giggled out with a smile.

"Ready to get wet?" he whispered into her ear.

She purred. "You bet." Then she looked up, saw the playful twinkle in his eyes and sputtered, "Don't you dare," a moment before the surfboard vanished and they both dropped into the water. She went under with a splash and came up laughing and Lane wrapped his arms around her, holding her afloat. They clung together, wet and wild.

"Okay if we get naked?"

She nodded, and their swimsuits vanished. She floated against him in the water, reveling in the free feeling. Then he bent to kiss her, and she stopped thinking as his hair-roughened chest brushed against her nipples, driving her wild. Her mound brushed up against his hard cock and she moaned. He drove into her, and she wrapped her legs around him, taking him deep inside as the water around them sparkled pink. Then, she closed her eyes as he rocked into her and came with a scream.

Chapter 13

Honey yawned and came groggily awake. Rolling over, she let out a startled gasp when waves rippled under her body and grabbed the covers for purchase. Swaying with the waves, sweet memories of surfing with Lane and the sexy aftermath came to her. At least after this seduction, she had immediate recall. She sat up in bed, feeling bemused and took a good look around his room, trying to ground herself.

Lane's surfboards were once more hung on his wall, confirming her memory that he had zapped them away. Her last memory was of lying on the beach with him in afterglow. Now, she was in bed alone. She looked down at his king-sized waterbed and smiled. Somehow it fit her water-loving lover. She was even lying on aqua blue silk sheets. Lane was totally a water element.

She moved toward that edge of the bed and once again felt the bed move under her. The waterbed's ripples only partially accounted for her feeling still at sea, but there was something else going on with her. She yawned, knowing her sleepiness was out of character for her. Her last words to Cruz this morning played back at her. I'm not going to let you put me under one of your, *'Were sleeping spells'* echoed back across her consciousness.

Shit, she knew in an instant that it was true and a little piece of her heart broke. She'd trusted them, given herself to them, and they were playing some kind of game with her. They were animals at heart, and she should have expected it. The Bear boys were slipping her mental Mickeys, and she didn't like it one bit. But maybe there were extenuating circumstances. They might be trying to help her. She just had to find out why they were doing it. It smacked of Were trickery and she didn't want any part of it. Her soft human heart wanted to give them a noble reason for keeping her cossetted this way, but having been raised around their kind, she wasn't so sure.

She pulled herself together and tiptoed down the hall, trying her hardest to sneak up on them, not an easy task when she had no magic tricks of her own. She sensed Lane's aura in the great room before she was halfway down the hall and knew he was alone. Cruz hadn't returned yet. She couldn't believe how let down she felt. She told herself to cut the pity party and keep going. Lane would have to answer her questions.

Then she felt the atmosphere change and picked up a new aura approaching from the west. An air sign. Then a warm pink aura washed toward her as Tyson walked into the building and she smiled. Tyson was here. At least he hadn't stayed away after she'd claimed him. She listened to the door click behind him and heard his greeting.

"Lane, I'm back."

She was pleased with herself that she'd guessed his identity when he wasn't within visual sight. At least one part of her was getting stronger since mating.

"Took you long enough," Lane stated.

"Patience, cub. I was using your new thingamajig to scan the shack. Took a little time to get it working."

"Tell me you didn't break my new diagnostic scanner," Lane demanded with a grumble.

"Relax, it's still in one piece."

"So. What did you find? Is everything okay back at the shack?"

"Inconclusive. It picked up a Were presence but that could have been a remnant from the owners. It also picked up some human out-of-control vibes. Whoever did this was just out to cause damage. They trashed the place but funny enough, they didn't steal anything. I stashed her laptop and purse in the trunk of her car and drove it over here." Honey's body tightened. How dare he!

"Shit, I hope you weren't boneheaded enough to leave her car where she can find it. Cruz will have both our asses if she escapes."

"I'm not stupid. I parked it behind the shed and her purse, laptop, and keys are securely locked in the trunk. Even if she spots the car, she won't be able to start it. I can always say I had it towed here if she challenges me. Our main job is to keep her satisfied and sleepy so that Cruz can do his thing. Which brings to mind, is everything going okay here?"

"Things are going swimmingly. Our girl is sleeping like a baby in my bed right now," Lane stated with pride.

"So, she recruited you for her harem," Tyson asked dryly.

"She wasn't going to at first. She wanted to leave, as a matter of fact."

"Shit, we can't let that happen."

"Relax. I managed to distract her, and she was none the wiser that I did a mental push on her."

Honey tensed as the reason for her sudden change of mind became clear. It was worse than sleeping spells, they were using mind control.

"Is Cruz back yet?"

"What do you think? Black Jack isn't known for quick negotiations. It'll be a while yet before he returns. You didn't put her out too deep, did you? She's starting to get suspicious.

Honey stood there frozen, her heart breaking. Cruz had flat-out lied to her. He'd promised he wouldn't tell her grandsire. If this prompted Black Jack into a heart attack, she'd kill Cruz herself. He'd been playing games with her, manipulating her. It just proved what a human fool she was to fall for him. Now her only way to get out of this unscathed was to harden her heart, be just as sneaky as he was. Well, the Bear brothers didn't have to worry about taking care of her anymore.

The first thing she needed to do was get away unnoticed. She quietly turned on her heels and tiptoed down the hall to the back door. Luckily, she'd seen how Lane turned off the alarm earlier. When she got to it, she punched in the series of numbers, glad of her affinity for numbers. At least she could get out of this quietly. Then when she was safely outside, she made a dash for the shed which was cloaked by a thick stand of pine trees. If she made it there, they probably wouldn't notice her even if they looked this way.

She rounded the corner to see her car parked right where Tyson had said it would be. She winced when she saw the graffiti spray-painted on it. Damn, those teens must have been really angry. She approached the car anyway, determined to put the Bear brothers behind her. Now she had to get her keys out of the trunk, but how? Angrily she banged on the trunk with her fist. I wish to hell I could do magic like the Bears. At the thought, her trunk popped wide open. She stood there for a moment startled. How in the hell did that happen? Unless she'd picked up some enhanced powers from the Bears. She'd heard rumors of exchanges if the mating was true. Is it possible? It didn't really matter. She was through with love, and Cruz. And she had no time to ponder her good luck.

Quickly, she grabbed her purse and fished for her keys. After she quietly shut the trunk, she ran to the front of the car and used her remote to unlock its doors. Soon she was driving away, putting the lodge in her rearview mirror. How long would it be before they discovered her missing? It didn't really matter. She wasn't bound to any of them, and this really wasn't running away, she was running toward her future. So why did she feel so forlorn?

At least Tyson had done her the favor of checking out the shack. It was safe to go back and clean up the damage. She was a mature woman and she could clean up her own mess. She'd put things right, pack up, and head out to her new life in the morning.

Cruz walked out of the Lockwood Camp feeling better than he had in a long time. He and Black Jack had come to a compromise of sorts. The old Bear would trust Cruz to be Honey's guide through the season. Then when it was over and they remained unmarked, as the odds said they would, he would let her go. It was bliss, at least temporarily, and he intended to make the most of it.

At the edge of the Lockwood Camp, he neared the exit portal back to his own realm. The PDA Lane had insisted he take remained firmly in his pocket. He hadn't needed rescuing, after all. As he got to the clearing an itchy feeling between his shoulder blades told him he was being watched. Reminders of the ambush yesterday flashed through his mind. He covertly reached for Lane's device while scenting the air for the smelly Sundowner who'd gotten the drop on him. Instead of funky musk, a cloyingly sweet scent he remembered all too well wrapped around him. Joelle! He frowned as he turned to see Honey's half–cousin, Joelle, slink into the clearing. This was a complication he hadn't anticipated and didn't want. Honey had said Joelle had already formed her harem, even going so far as to steal Honey's former beau, thank the gods. He owed her for that. He didn't feel the threat coming from the powerful Were fem but there was a sultry smile on her lips that he didn't like. Shit!

"Did you miss me, lover?"

Cruz tensed at her teasing words. "For the record, we've never been lovers."

Joelle made a show of sniffing him and rolling her eyes scornfully. "Hmm, I can smell that you haven't missed someone else. I'm surprised at an elite like you scraping the bottom of the barrel with that little commoner."

He ignored Joelle's snide comment, tensing as she stepped into his personal space. He raked a disinterested gaze down her lanky body. She was all smooth lined and powerful angles and the skimpy outfit she wore, a leather top and skirt, barely kept her covered. As he watched, one strap casually slipped off her shoulder, baring one breast for him. In the Were community she'd be considered the most beautiful, but he found Honey's warmth much more alluring. "What do you want from me, Joelle?"

"Guess," she stated, reaching out for him.

"Not interested," he replied as she splayed a hand on his chest, her long fingernails digging into him. Apparently, she was out to expand her harem. Of course, she always had been greedy. She wanted to bag herself a clan leader and move up in the Were hierarchy, but she left him ice-cold. Ignoring her obvious come-on, he looked for minions behind her, feeling wary. He sensed a trap, and somehow, he read the insincere vibes coming off her loud and clear. Surprised at the new gift he wondered if he'd gotten that enhanced power from Honey? He smiled at the thought, wondering what she might have gotten from him. It was a good sign.

"Stop thinking about that usurper and pay attention to me!" Joelle shrieked as she dug her nails in.

Cruz winced as she scratched him, effectively tearing his thoughts away from Honey. He scowled down at her, the rage in her eyes startling him. She was out of control. Had she been behind his attack yesterday? It seemed pretty damned likely, but why? One thing was becoming crystal clear, she hated Honey. "How long have you been jealous of your cousin?" He knew he'd hit a sore spot when she flushed.

"Jealous? Don't make me laugh," she stated, pushing him away. "That freak is no kin of mine."

He teleported from the scene, grateful for the reprieve as she stood glaring at him. Somehow, he knew this wouldn't be the end of her interference. It had hurt her pride that he'd turned her down and she'd do her best to make him pay. But as he went, the musky smell of the Sundowner filled his nostrils.

Chapter 14

Honey pulled her car up behind her grandsire's fishing shack. Two could play the hide-the-car game. Her fingers trembled as she pulled the key from the ignition and gazed at the dilapidated shack. What a disaster her life had become. She was running away from the only men who'd made her feel like a woman and toward a future she wasn't certain of. Would Cruz come after her? Not bloody likely, he was too busy making deals with her grandsire. Well, she refused to be a pawn in Were politics anymore. Thank goodness she had found out that he was playing games before she made the mistake of falling even more in love with him.

Grandsire would probably kick his lying ass for losing her and it served him right. With a sigh she walked up the rutted path, key in her hand. She tried to open herself up to any hostile Were vibes that might be lingering from the break-in. Tyson had said it was human, but could she trust him and Lane's crazy diagnostic tools? When nothing concrete came through the ether but petty childish anger, she decided that Tyson was right. This was the work of some mundane teens with a severe case of teenage angst. She sympathized as she felt their pain, knowing how hard it was to be an outsider and opened the door.

Cruz teleported back to his lodge, putting the weird meeting with Joelle behind him. He actually felt happier than he had in a long time knowing that warm and sexy Honey was waiting for him. He and Black Jack had come to a deal. The old man would trust him to protect her and guide her through the mating fever. But they both knew that in the end he wouldn't get to keep her. Still, he felt lucky for the hand that fate had dealt him. He couldn't wait to get back into her arms and into his bed. In the meantime, the old man was instituting an intertribal hunt for the thugs who'd threatened her.

He popped into the house and felt a little let down when he didn't see her or feel her aura. He grinned, realizing that he'd picked up more from Honey than he'd realized. Tyson was busy in the kitchen and Lane was out back. He could feel their essences, their auras. And they were happy. It meant that everything was as it should be at home. Then he heard Tyson whistle as he cooked supper and grinned. Hey, he was getting pretty good at this. If his grouchy woman–hater brother was this happy, Honey must have worked her magic on him. The pain he carried over losing Fleur was diminished. Honey's touch must have done it. He waited for the pangs of jealousy to bloom inside him and instead felt an enhanced contentment. This was the way it should be. He strode into the kitchen saying, "I'm home. How's it going, bro?"

Tyson looked over at him and smiled. "For the record I felt you before I saw you."

"So, you got some of her talent too," Cruz stated with a nod. "Uh huh. Don't worry, bro, I know she isn't mine."

Cruz didn't know what to say to that. They both knew that the fates wouldn't choose either of them.

Tyson didn't give him a chance to talk, adding quickly, "And to answer your question things are fine here. Seeing that you're back in one piece, Black Jack must have spared your balls."

"Shh," he hissed, looking around to make sure Honey wasn't within earshot.

"Don't worry, we didn't tell her," Tyson muttered dryly. "And she's asleep, so she didn't just overhear this."

Cruz heard the reproach in his brother's voice. "I did it for her own good. She'll understand after the danger is passed."

"You think so, do you? Well, let me tell you that lady had been pushed around by, 'snarling growling Bears', her words, so much that she's going to push back."

Cruz winced at the words. She'd spat at him that she was sick of dealing with overly macho Bears and now he could understand it better. But damn it, he had no other choice than to go to her grandsire. He'd just have to convince her of that. "I'll deal with her," he stated firmly. "And the good news is that Black Jack and I have come to an understanding."

"Hot damn, that is good news," Lane commented, coming into the room.

"Keep it down, junior," Cruz cautioned, looking toward the bedrooms. He didn't want Honey rudely awakened until he'd figured out what to say to her.

"Don't worry, she'll be asleep in my bed for a long spell. Surfing can wear you out if you're not used to it," Lane replied.

Tyson turned to say to Cruz, "I scanned the fishing shack."

"Anything turn up?"

"Nothing solid, just some muddled essences I found troubling. At any rate Lane is running some diagnostics on my specimens. And I made necessary repairs and brought back her things."

"They didn't steal, her stuff?"

"I know, I was just as surprised. I drove back her car with her purse and laptop stowed in the trunk."

"I didn't see them out front."

"I hid them behind the barn. I figured you'd want them out of sight."

Cruz nodded, glad that his brother was so farsighted. He wouldn't rest easy until mating season was over. "Good. I should go wake Honey up."

Lane shook his head. "I'd wait a while if I were you. She needs to sleep it off."

Tyson scowled at him. "What do you mean sleep it off? I thought you said she was just normally sleepy. You didn't put a spell on her?"

Lane flushed and looked away. "Well, she was getting ready to leave after we surfed. I had to do something."

"Shit," Cruz and Tyson grumbled in unison.

"She said something about sleeping spells and I panicked," Lane muttered out.

Tyson growled. "She said something about that after my time with her after breakfast."

"I'm just as guilty, she did the same with me in bed this morning. When she wakes up, she's going to kick all our asses," Cruz replied with a growl. He turned and strode down the hall to Lane's bedroom. How in blazes was he going to sweettalk her into staying and giving him another chance? Tension built as he opened the door and stepped into the room. Then he focused on the empty waterbed and his heart sank.

Honey was gone. He didn't have to search the lodge to know it. He felt it deep inside. It felt like a punch in the gut. She didn't want an animal like him. She'd made that perfectly clear before, but he'd been too in lust with her to listen. The animal side of him said let her go, but his newly discovered heart said, '*hell no*'. Besides, he had promises to keep. Damn it all, how was he supposed to protect her when she shut him out?

Chapter 15

Honey walked through the shack, her can of mace in her hand in case the teenage vandals came back. Tyson had actually done a fine job replacing the broken window and zapping out what she was pretty sure were dirty words on the paneled walls. The place was actually rather pristine, which was creepy in itself. At least he'd been as good as his word, which was more than she could say for Cruz. She sighed, feeling too demoralized to be scared. How could she have given her heart to Werebear? A lying, stinking overly macho Werebear. Having grown up around the species, one would think she would know better.

And then a sound behind her made her realize she wasn't alone. The world seemed to slip into slow motion as her heart pounded. Chills shot up her spine. Damn it, the vandals were back, and she was through playing nice. Growling, she spun around aiming the can of mace toward the sound and pushed the plunger hitting Cruz straight in the eyes.

He coughed, waving the mist away and she gasped when it back-washed her way, making her eyes sting. "Here, give me this before you hurt someone," he stated, snatching the can out of her hand.

She glared at him, brushing the tears off her cheeks. The fact that he wasn't even crying spoke volumes. "How the hell did you get in here, Bear? My door was locked," she demanded even though she knew the truth. He was a powerful Were and locks couldn't keep him out.

"A five year-old could have jimmied that flimsy lock, but we both know I wouldn't have to bother with the mechanics," he replied with a rueful smile. "You shouldn't be here alone, Honey."

Was he really worried about her? The sincerity in his voice told her yes. And it was enough to temper her ire. "I'm fine. So, you don't have to worry about babysitting me anymore."

Cruz winced. "Which one of my blockhead brothers said that?"

She noticed his discomfort but also that he didn't bother to deny it. "Does it really matter? I won't be a pawn in this power game you're playing. I'm sick and tired of warring Werebears and their lying ways."

"I didn't lie to you, Honey," Cruz commented, closing in on her.

"You didn't tell me the truth." He hadn't actually lied but he'd deliberately misled her. It amounted to that same thing, didn't it? Part of her said no. Maybe he was trying to protect her. She wanted to fight him, but her heart didn't. "I've got protection against the burglars," she added, reaching for the gun she'd liberated from her granddad's gun safe. The approval she saw in his eyes made her feel better.

"Good," he stated, stepping closer. "But do you have protection against the fire between us? I know I don't."

Startled by his blunt words, she stood there, hesitating. It wasn't the most gallant come-on, but it sent a quiver of need through her. "No," she replied and could have bitten her tongue over the admission. His eyes glittered sultry fire as he closed the distance between them. Heat rushed through her, pooling in her sex and she knew then and there that she couldn't deny him.

"You want this?" he asked, standing still.

She nodded, aching for his touch. When he didn't move, she walked into his arms, nestling against his hard body. "More than you know." Smoothing a hand over his rippling forearm, she peered up at him, seeing the banked passion smoldering in his eyes. Her being quivered with excitement as she came to a decision. She reached up on her tiptoes and kissed him. He went still for a moment and then kissed her back with a hunger that made her tremble. Her body melted as he pulled her to him. He kissed her like he wanted to consume her, like he couldn't get enough of her, and she felt the same.

He broke the kiss to murmur, "Are you sure it's me you want, Goldilocks?"

"Yes," she replied, nibbling his neck and hearing him growl in response. His animal passion thrilled her, making her tremble. Her hands roved over him as he picked her up and carried her into the bedroom. He was everything she wanted.

And then he was standing with her next to the bed. Her knees buckled when he nuzzled her neck while unbuttoning her top. His hot lips skimmed along her neck, his hand cupped her breast, and she moaned, sagging against him. He peeled it off, stripped off the rest of her clothing, and laid her on the bed. Honey lay back, eyes shining as she watched him shed his clothes.

Then he came down on the bed on top of her. One of his big legs rested over hers, holding her still while his hand slicked down to toy with her pussy. His big fingers rubbed her labia, teasing her stiff clit, sending sparks of pleasure through her. She whimpered as he pressed her clit, her pussy flooding with moisture. He was slipping his fingers inside her, one, then two, stretching her. She touched his cock, feeling the surging heat of him, testing him. He groaned, rippling against her.

He gave her a stinging spank. "Stop that or I won't be able to wait."

"I don't want you to wait. I need you, Cruz." She gasped as he played with her clit. "Oh yes, there." He growled, teasing her.

"Yes," she whispered, before kissing his neck, even more turned on by his reckless passion. He wanted her so badly, he was shaking; she could feel the tremors coursing through his body. She was on fire, hot for him, but he seemed to delight in making her wait. Playing with her breasts, he tasted her, sucking on her nipples, making her arch against his hungry mouth, seeking more. "Oh, please, please."

"Soon," he stated, moving onto the other peak, drawing hard on her nipple, licking it with his raspy tongue until she was quivering with pleasure. She now knew the meaning of domination; he was in charge. Two could play the teasing game. She reached down for his rampant cock. He jerked in her hand, growing to an enormous size, hot and steely. With a groan, he slipped from her grasp and pressed a string of kisses down her body, stopping to lick her navel and then lower to her pussy. She cried out when his rough tongue licked her there, her head thrashing on the pillow. When he sucked on her swollen clit, she screamed, ripples of orgasm sweeping through her.

He made a place between her legs and surged into her.

Honey sucked in a gasp, amazed by the sheer size of him. "You're so big."

"We're made for each other, Goldilocks, you're perfect for me."

He thrust inside her and she cried out in bliss. Then he started moving in and out of her, a rocking motion that made her crazy. Honey moaned, meeting his thrusts, seeing stars behind her closed eyes. Her pleasure built, waves of ripples increasing where they met. If anything, he seemed to be getting bigger inside her. She didn't understand it as she gasped, her body pulsing as their bodies joined. Then he reversed their positions so that she was sitting astride him.

"Ride me, Goldilocks," he gritted out.

"Yes!" she cried, loving the sensation of being on top.

He grasped her hips controlling her movements as she went wild. He filled her deeper and harder as she rode him, quickening her pace. Pressure built inside her as her pussy milked him and then she screamed as orgasmic spasms overtook her, clamping down on him, making him growl. He stiffened, coming with a growl, emptying inside her. Just then, she felt a searing pain above her right breast, and she heard Cruz suck in an equally pained breath beneath her. She looked at the expression on his face worried that she'd hurt him. But he didn't look hurt, he looked stunned as he stared at the location of her burn. Only then did she look down and take in the mating symbol now tattooed above her right breast. A Celtic blending of their two tribal marks. Then she glanced at the tandem mark on his chest and gasped in shock. She wobbled atop him, and he reached out to steady her.

"This wasn't supposed to happen." Cruz's continued silence told her what she needed to know. He didn't want this.

"I didn't anticipate it, either," Cruz confessed after a moment.

She didn't know what to make of his gruff admission, but his troubled expression made her crumble inside. She tried to get off him only to have him hold her tight. "Damn it all, let me go."

"No. We need to talk."

"Not now," she demanded, feeling hurt. "Now let me loose."

She wanted to call back the hurtful words and would have, but the next moment a bullet hit the headboard right over her head. In a move that took her breath away, Cruz rolled them both off the bed and hit the floor covering her with his body.

"Oh my god, the housebreakers are back."

"Shit," Cruz muttered softly

Honey trembled under him as bullets exploded around them. As she gazed up at him her fears eased. She wasn't alone anymore. When Cruz's eyes glittered back at her she knew he cared even if he wouldn't admit it.

"My cell is in my purse," she whispered. "If I can get out there, I can call for help."

"I've got something better," Cruz stated manifesting a PDA out of midair.

"What the heck is that?" she asked, hopefully gazing at the strange-looking device

"The Bear signal," he replied with a wry twist of his lips.

"Just like Batman, huh?" she commented wryly. "This must be one of Lanes inventions."

Cruz nodded. "It should bring help," he added, pressing a fast kiss on her lips.

She gasped when she heard glass break in the living room. "They're coming in. We've got to go."

"Correction, you've got to vanish'"

She didn't like his determined tone. "And let you take a bullet for me, I don't think so. We're in this together, mate."

"I can take care of myself and look at it this way, if I go our mating marks won't be binding," he murmured in a soft tone.

He meant if he died. The comment really made her see red while scaring the shit out of her. Did he really think that she'd rather see him gone than be mated to him? "Don't even say anything like that."

"I'm an animal, Goldilocks, it's the way I think. Be good," he replied and stretched, turning into a bear.

She knew he was doing it to make a point. "If you think that's going to make me run..." she started to say and then felt her world spin. A moment later she found herself standing in Cruz's lodge bedroom all alone. "Darn it all, he can't do this to me." She sputtered and looked around the empty room.

"Lane, Tyson," she called out but got no answer. Of course they were out helping him. While she stood here useless. And this was all her fault. If he got hurt, she'd never forgive herself. She knew then that she could never walk away from their binding, no matter what.

She looked around the room feeling his hot aura. It felt alive, like part of him. If only she could get to him. As she gazed at the spot in the corner where she'd touched down, she saw a slight difference in the atmosphere. That was the portal. Could it work both ways? There was only one way to find out. She walked over to the spot, held her breath and concentrated hard. Nothing happened. Not so much as a molecule moved. Shit. Then she spotted one of Cruz's PDAs on the dresser. It had to be one of Lane's gadgets. He'd said they had supernatural powers. Could it beam her back?

The moment her hand closed over it she felt Cruz's vibes strongly, and his pain. Damn it, someone was hurting him. Concentrating anew, she felt the world spin and suddenly she was standing inside her grandsire's fishing shack. She took in the fight in a worried glance taking in the wounded Werebears lying crumpled on the floor. She let out a horrified gasp as one of them died flickering back and forth from Were to man, wondering how she was going to tell the good bears from the bad.

Cruz spun to look at her at that moment and growled. "I told you to stay away." He let down his guard, changing back to human.

"I don't listen very well," she replied, hurting for him when she saw his wounds. He had a wicked gash on his side oozing blood. She saw his eyes narrow, as he picked up his PDA, knew he was going to send her away, and glared back at him. "Don't you dare, or I won't bond with you," she demanded, pulling the threat out of her ass. She was shocked when it worked, and he hesitated. Did he really want to bond with her? Then she recognized a foul odor from the night the shack was broken into and cried out as she saw a motley Werebear sneak up on Cruz with a battle axe. "Look out behind you. It's the stinky bastard who broke in here the other night."

Cruz was already turning, parrying the bear's moves. "I smell him," he commented, making his opponent growl angrily.

She knew Cruz was pissing the other bear off to throw him off-balance, make him reckless. She picked up the mace she'd left on the coffee table and moved in. The white bear snarled, going for Cruz's throat raking him with a vicious swipe. Cruz feinted away and then moved in to bring him down with a blow. The dying Werebear flickered back and forth to a raggedly dressed Sundowner.

She sagged with relief as the battle suddenly ended around her. It was over. And then someone grabbed her from behind. A hand wrapped ruthlessly in her hair as a gun was thrust against her spine. "Move and I'll kill you, mutant bitch."

"Joelle!" Honey grumbled. "Damn, I should have smelled your perfume a mile away. Did you make the Sundowner stay extra stinky to cover your traces?"

The victorious Werebears having returned to human turned and looked their way. Honey saw tears in her grandsire's eyes as he looked at her, and fury in Lane and Tyson's. But the cold retribution she saw in Cruz's eyes almost made her feel sorry for her half-cousin.

"Joelle, girl, let Honey go," Black Jack insisted, stomping their way.

"One more step, you, old fart," Joelle snapped. "And you'll be scraping your Honey child off the floor."

Honey realized at that moment just how crazy Joelle was. And how much she hated her, but why? She was no threat to her.

Black Jack glowered back at her but his eyes were worried. "So, this is how you repay my kindnesses."

"Kindnesses, my ass. I'm your rightful heir, not this freak," she stated, tightening her hand in Honey's hair.

Honey winced but kept eye contact with Cruz. Whatever went down, she wanted him to know that she loved him with all her heart. "Have you lost what's left of your mind, Joelle? I'm not Grandsire's heir. In fact, I'm leaving the pack, and you know it."

"Ask him," Joelle spat.

Honey winced as her hand tightened in her hair. "Tell her it's not true, Grandsire. And we can all get back to reality." The sad look on Black Jack's face told her shockingly that it was.

"You were the chosen one."

"Chosen one?" she asked startled. "I can't be. I'm only half-Were."

"See even the freak knows the truth," Joelle crowed.

"Bite me," Honey whispered under her breath

"Don't tempt me, you stupid little commoner!" Joelle shrieked.

"Hurt my mate and you know I'll destroy you, Joelle," Cruz stated in a deceptively calm voice.

Honey shot a shocked glance his way as her heart warmed. He was claiming her publicly.

"Don't get your balls in an uproar, Cruz lover," Joelle replied. "Be a good little Bear and I might even let you fuck us both."

Honey burned at the insinuation. Cruz told her he'd never touched Joelle, and she believed him. "Lay one skanky finger on my mate, and I'll scratch your crazy eyes out."

"Ooh, big talk from the freak," Joelle mocked. "Now, listen up, old man, you are going to abdicate and name me as your replacement..."

Honey literally saw red as Joelle dictated her terms and felt Cruz's aura reach hers. She glanced at Lane and Tyson, and they nodded, latching on. Then, the room began to glow, making Joelle let out a gasp. "Police lights. What idiot called out the mundane police?"

Honey knew she'd never get a better opportunity. She shook off Joelle's grip, spun, and blasted her in the face with the mace. Joelle cried out, trying to cover her eyes. The gun fell out of her grip. Honey kicked it away and sent her angry vibes Joelle's way making her scream and drop to the floor.

"I told you she was the chosen one," Grandsire stated dryly before his guard took Joelle away.

Honey rushed into Cruz's arms, trembling in the aftermath. She wasn't so sure about being a chosen anything, she just knew she was where she belonged. In Cruz's arms.

"What the hell do you think you were doing?"

She looked up at his glittering eyes and knew he was feeling the same thing she did. They belonged together. "Covering your back. Isn't it about time someone did?" The startled look on his face was priceless.

"My god, I thought I was going to lose you," Cruz stuttered, holding her tight. "Promise me that you won't ever scare me like that again."

She pulled back to look deep into his dark eyes. "It's a deal if you promise not to be so bossy and stubborn for the rest of our lives." She saw the hope spring in his eyes.

"Will you bind with me, my feisty rescuer?"

She nodded, overcome with emotion. "Oh yes. I'm not letting you get away again."

Chapter 16

Honey stood at the entrance to the Lockwood courtyard under starlight. She only wished that her parents could have lived to see her wed to a member of the badass Bear clan. Her mother would have smiled, having had a wild side herself. And now that she'd grilled Grandsire about being the chosen one, she knew that her mother had been a seer which gave her other powers. That's why she'd never fit in with her clan. But now Cruz was helping her develop them and had put her in contact with his clan's seer. Members of both clans were gathered in the garden for the binding ceremony. Now that mating fever was over and Joelle's cohorts had been rounded up, peace once again reigned.

She smiled as Tyson and Lane walked up to the flower strewn arbor. They weren't really part of her harem anymore, Cruz becoming a harem of one, but she was delighted that they remained close. Then Cruz walked up to the head of the aisle and took her breath away. He looked drop-dead gorgeous in his tux.

"You ready to marry that wild Bear?" Black Jack asked with a smile as he took her hand.

Honey nodded. "I think it always had to be him." She took a deep breath as her grandsire proudly walked her down the path. The guests turned to look at her, but she only had eyes for Cruz. When she looked into his eyes, all else faded away.

The official looked at the wedding guests. "Is there any objection from either clan to this match?"

Honey turned to give the guests a forbidding scowl, and they erupted in laughter.

Cruz took her hand, turning her around. "Easy, Honey. Don't zap them with your auras."

"I wouldn't dream of it," she replied with a smile, thinking of the blanket of rage she'd draped over Joelle. She hadn't known that she'd had it in her.

"There is no objection," Black Jack stated. "I give my granddaughter to the Werebear Clan.

Honey smiled at him, and he leaned over and kissed her cheek.

"Be happy," he commanded, before placing her hand in Cruz's.

"I now pronounce you bound together. What has been brought together this evening, let no creature put asunder."

Cruz scooped Honey up in his free arm, holding her close. Cruz didn't slow down until he had them in their binding chamber. He'd stolen his Goldilocks's heart and he wasn't giving her up. He bolted the door and then set her down, gazing at her in wonder. He could still hardly believe it, that this vision of loveliness wanted him.

"Come here, mate," Honey demanded, crooking a finger at him. Cruz stepped toward her, suddenly feeling unprepared. Mating he knew; binding was another story. He pulled her into his arms and kissed her. She kissed him back, melting into his embrace; her stiff nipples rubbing against him through her gown drove him crazy. He touched her gown, and it fell off her so that she was suddenly naked, shivering with excitement in his arms.

"You've got to teach me how to do that!" she exclaimed, stepping out of her gown.

"All in good time, Honey," he replied, picking her up and carrying her to bed. "You've got a lifetime to learn all my tricks."

She nibbled on his ear, making him hiss with pleasure.

"Sounds delightful, but you're wearing too many clothes, Mr. Bear."

Cruz groaned as she reached down to cup his growing erection.

"Pants be gone," she murmured, then giggled when he burst out of them. "At least I have one power."

"Always did," he stated with a growl, his stiff cock rubbing tantalizingly against her warm thigh. "Honey, you've got all the powers you'll ever need inside you."

She smiled, opening her legs. "Take me, my mate."

Cruz settled against her warm, welcoming body, her pussy wetting the head of his cock. "No more harems for you."

"Not even a little one?" she teased.

He let out a growl frowning down at her. "What do you think?"

"No harems, but remember that goes both ways," she agreed with a smile.

He nodded. "You have my word." He looked down at her. "Ready?" He didn't miss the sudden, expressive longing in her big blue eyes. "Yes."

He took her hand. "Our hands are bound, our bodies joined as one," he voiced in a low rumble, surging into her. "I take you as my one true mate, Honey."

Honey cried out, her pussy clutching his cock as her body and soul claimed him as her own. "Our hands are bound, our bodies joined." She gasped with pleasure, wrapping her legs around him as he took her to orgasm. "I take you as my one true mate, Cruz."

She arched into his touch, his needy heat. Her ability to bring him to a fever peak still astonished him. His hardness slipped inside her joining them physically.

"I'm going to bite you now. I promise not to take too much blood. You'll know what to do if it's right. Let your heart be your guide."

He bit her, feeling her orgasm and his own. Tasting her sweet nectar, he felt connected with her body and soul.

Honey gasped when the fleeting pain from his bite turned into pleasure. She rocked with it and could hardly believe it when her canines grew long and sharp. Instinctively, she let go of her inhibitions. She bit Cruz on the neck, gently sinking her incisors into his flesh. Instead of being scared, she was enthralled. She felt all he was, all he'd experienced, and knew she was giving him the same gift. His blood tasted like the finest wine. She felt them become one. The connection rocked her to her soul. She snapped into another orgasm and felt him thunder against her cervix harder, longer, as they rocked together.

Finally, she fell away with a stunned cry, missing the connection.

Outside, a cry of celebration rang out. "What on earth is that shout?"

"Our family crest lit up the night sky announcing to my people that we are one."

Honey snuggled at his side content. "Then that means…"

"That we are true life mates. How does it feel?"

"I'll tell you in about a century," she replied then laughed, wrapping her hand around his hardening erection.

"Ah, my demanding little queen. As always, your wish is my command."

JULIE CASTLE
Knock Three Times
FAIRY TALES REIMAGINED: Aladdin's Wonderful Lamp
Tangled Tales Book Four

Chapter 1

Chemise Logan tucked a wisp of strawberry blonde hair behind her ear as she fumbled with the old freestanding safe's dial. Trust her eccentric aunt Betty to leave the combination in a cryptic note, along with the deed to the antique shop, when she'd decided to go off on an extended adventure in Egypt. The note stating that she'd find her life's greatest treasure inside this monstrosity had been intriguing, but she wasn't getting her hopes up.

This was just not Chemise's day, or even her month for that matter. In fact, her life had become a series of disasters of late. The first and most devastating was that she'd been fired from her job at the museum after the scroll she was conserving spontaneously combusted as she was working on it. She knew there had to be a logical scientific explanation for the fire, but she hadn't come up with it yet.

Then on top of that Barry Lattimer, her fellow conservator and some-times beau, had put the blame on her before publicly dumping her. She'd always known that he was ambitious, but she hadn't realized what a craven coward he was until they were confronted by the outraged museum director Dr. Edwards. Barry had crumpled like a wet paper bag in the face of his wrath and left her to take the heat.

Now she faced the possibility of criminal charges while Dr. Edwards tried to prove that she'd been negligent, and no doubt collect big time from the museum's insurance policy. Her girlfriend, Miko, suggested that the scroll had burst into flames because of a curse still made her smile. She didn't believe in all that hocus pocus nonsense. She was a scientist and she knew she hadn't been careless. There had to be a logical explanation. But living under a cloud of suspicion sucked, big time.

If that trio of disasters wasn't bad enough, she now had her thirtieth birthday party to get through tonight...dateless. She wasn't quite sure she was ready to face the glam squad, her sure to be pitying ex-coworkers, yet. Not with her future in jeopardy. Gritting her teeth she gave the stubborn safe's dial a hard twist and to her shock it loosened with an audible click that echoed through the deserted shop. Halleluiah! She let out a relieved sigh. At least something was going right.

Auntie had been so protective of this safe—paranoid, even—when she'd tried to peek inside it as a child. So consequently, the safe's contents had to be interesting, maybe even valuable, at least she hoped so. Going through the mystery goods would keep her occupied until Janelle, the glammest of all her old work buddies, came to pick her up for the party at Charlie's Bar and Grille.

The safe's heavy door swung open with an audible creak that made her shiver. It was like something out of an old spook movie. But she didn't believe in ghosts, she told herself firmly. Brimming with excitement, Chemise bent down to cautiously peer inside the old freestanding safe and saw exactly nothing. Letting out a disappointed groan, she scanned the big safe's nearly empty shelves. Some treasure!

Had Betty sold everything to keep this rat trap afloat, or maybe there had been nothing here in the first place. She felt a twinge of sympathy for her eccentric aunt, the proud woman who'd left her the antique shop and told herself to suck it up. Aunt Betty would hate being pitied as much as she did.

Then a glint of gold from an object tucked way back on the safe's top shelf caught her eye. Pay dirt! She reached inside and drew out a jeweled pendant, knowing instinctively that it was solid gold. Drawing it into the light she gazed down at the image of Isis, Egyptian goddess of love, fascinated. Wow! It was exquisite. Her hand's trembled a little as she held the necklace feeling its antiquity. It couldn't be real, Aunt Betty wasn't likely to have a genuine artifact, but it was precious to her just that same.

The pendant had to be part of the Egyptian tourist junk that had flooded the market after Lord Canarvon unearthed King Tut, but it was expertly done. She slipped the exquisite necklace on, thinking it the perfect accessory to set off her plain turquoise dress, and felt a sense of warmth overcome her as it nestled in her overly plump cleavage.

It was then that she spotted another metallic object tucked away in the back on the same shelf...it was too big to be another pendant...a priceless statue perhaps? Yeah, and pigs would fly sometime soon, there was no way that her luck would turn from bad to good that fast. Still the treasure hunt was fun, not to mention distracting.

Her heart raced as she reached into the safe and wrapped her fingers around a warm metallic object. Strange she'd expect the metal to be cool to the touch not warm. Intrigued, she pulled her curious find out into the light and gazed down at an ancient Egyptian oil lamp. Now *this* was the real thing. She could feel the item's antiquity; the former curator in her was as excited as a schoolgirl. It didn't matter if she made a dime from this shop when she got to touch beauty like this.

Why had Auntie stuck this treasure away? It belonged in a museum. Cartouches decorating the artifact told her it had belonged to some-one important. Roughly translated, they read, '*Knock three times*'. She smiled and did just that, rapping three times on the table.

The lamp warmed even more vibrating under her fingers and thun-der clapped outside rattling the floorboards of the old building and her along with them. Letting out a cry of alarm Chemise fell back against a dusty fainting couch as a long trail of steam escaped the lamp with a hiss. Watching in disbelief she saw the mist instantly solidify into solid male perfection before her eyes. Naked male perfection, she amended, looking at miles of tanned skin. Good golly, she was obviously hallucinating, but what a sexy way to go crazy. She must have hit her head when she landed and was now unconscious...yes, that made sense. But staring at him she couldn't work up any regret. Woohoo, happy birthday to me! When she went off the deep end, she did so with gusto, dreaming up her very own private love genie. But at least she'd picked a dream lover who couldn't give her away. She watched his glare focus on the lamp still clutched in her right hand.

Her fascinated gaze swept over the phantom genie she'd dreamed up, focusing on his stirring cock. Wow, what a package, and it was all hers. His body heat, his very presence wrapped around her, making her blush. She gulped and managed to tear her eyes off his truly impressive manhood, not that she'd seen that many others to compare him to.

Her stunned gaze traveled up, past six-pack abs and broad shoulders, and finally focused on his handsome, scowling face. Why was he scowl-ing at her? As their eyes met, an unexpected wave of lust hit her, taking her breath away, and making her stop thinking. He was irritated and sexy as hell, and his whiskey brown eyes seemed to read her thoughts. He was wearing a pendant just like the one she'd found in the safe which was now nestled between her breasts. At the thought of it, the pendant seemed to heat up in her cleavage.

When his hot gaze ghosted over her breasts, she felt it like a stroke. Chemise's sex grew wet and her nipples budded tight as if he'd touched them. How was he doing it she wondered her lips tingling along with the rest of her as she stared at his sensual mouth? It didn't really matter how he worked his sexual tricks as long as he satisfied her. He was everything her wet dreams could have conjured up and obviously her mixed up mind knew she needed to get laid to get over the traumas of late.

He frowned and ripped his pendant off. "If she sent you to fetch me, vixen, tell her to screw herself."

Vixen? She'd never thought of herself as a vixen. She watched in shock as he opened his palm, and the pendant he'd torn off vanished into thin air. Of course, he'd speak English—she'd dreamed him up—but his British accent coupled with his fury took her by surprise. She pushed away from the fainting couch and her knees buckled. His hand instantly shot out to steady her, catching her before she could fall. When his warm strong hand wrapped around her forearm, she let out a sensual whimper as a jolt went through her making her sex spasm, and blushed. No wonder the lamp had felt hot with him inside it. It brought up the wild question of how he'd feel inside her. When she glanced at him his smirk told her he read her errant thoughts. Well hell, he ought to come wrapped in asbestos.

"She chose well," he stated, tugging her toward him.

Chemise couldn't help being entranced by the brooding hunk even as he handled her like she weighed nothing more than a rag doll. Barry's ending shot that she was fat and frumpy echoed through her mind making her feel the humiliation all over again. But the genie's hold tightened on her arm as if he sensed her mind wasn't on him, and it snapped her back to him leaving Barry in the dust where he belonged.

She locked gazes with her sexy genie. A fine tremor going through her as every sexual circuit in her body turned on, responded to him even though he wasn't actually doing her. His body heat transferred to her as he relentlessly drew her to him. She licked her lip and watched his eyes darken at the action. *Ooh nice*, thought, creaming. She'd always dreamed of a demanding lover, not that she'd ever had the guts to admit it. She only dated safe men like Barry, who couldn't see past her dowdy image. And sex, there was precious little of that in her life up to now but in a moment that would change.

This was different. The sexy genie now turning her into a puddle of mush was only a fantasy. Even she could come to a fantasy, she assured herself. Then they collided and she let out a moan, pressing against him like he was a magnet.

"Holy moly," she blurted out flicking her tongue out to taste him. She took a little lap at his nipple and listened to him groan as it stiffened under her tongue. His cock jerked as he rubbed it against her. She was actually seducing him.

"No," he gritted, pushing her away.

She glared back at him. Well hell, he certainly wasn't acting like a dream lover now.

Barry's words, *You're fat and frumpy, and no man would want to sleep with you,* played across her mind, making her sigh.

The genie stared at her, hard. "What does she want?"

The question tore her mind off the sad state of her love life. Bewildered by the sexy genie's aggressive tone, she asked, "She?"

The way he rolled his eyes told her he thought she was lying. What the heck?

"The goddess you serve. Isis." He focused pointedly at her pendant displayed in her open cleavage.

Isis! Her breath caught in her throat as his hot gaze ghosted over her cleavage once more. It was then that she noticed that three of the top buttons had come undone on her sundress and her curves were practically tumbling out of the garment. Her nipples jutted out stiffening diamond hard as his appreciative gaze lingered on them. What was he some kind of sexual catnip? This was *so* not the sophisticated way she wanted this to play out. Her chin rose mutinously as she tried to get her racing hormones under control. "Goddess, I serve?"

His eyes narrowed. "Don't lie to me, vixen. I will not tolerate it."

The implied threat made her angry and she glared back at him. She would have to dream up a nut to sexually satisfy her. "I serve no goddess, only myself."

"You wear her image."

"So did you."

His expression turned remote at her words, and she wondered why. She could feel his suspicion, his anger, as he focused on the pendant she wore. It was obvious that there was no love lost between him and the goddess. What would engender such antipathy? She studied him seeing a nerve pulse in his tight jaw. Then he looked at her and she saw the pain in his eyes. He was hurting for some reason and he needed her.

She sighed, feeling responsible for him. It wasn't his fault he was mentally off-kilter. Everything she touched lately was a little off, especially the scroll she'd somehow destroyed. The loss of the ancient book of spells that'd combusted before her eyes still pained her. Why should the genie she'd dreamed up be any different? "Should I call you Genie?" She watched the corners of his sultry mouth turn up with reluctant humor, and she relaxed.

Now that was more like it. The smile made him approachable—yummy, even. Her lips tingled as she stared at his sultry mouth. She *so* wanted a big bite of him. She knew she was desperate for sex when her urge to jump her hallucination was almost irresistible.

"Why should you call me Genie? My name is Lucien."

She savored the name thinking it fit him but couldn't resist teasing him, "I thought all men who emerged from magical lamps were genies."

"Not if they had the job foisted on them by an unscrupulous evil genie. I was working on a dig in the Valley of the Kings when Zander captured me to serve out the needs of his mistress, Isis."

She watched him turn from seductive to ice cold in the blink of an eye as he turned away from her. It didn't stop her from studying him curiously. She tried to keep her gaze above the waist, but it was hard to miss his still rampant cock. So, he was an Egyptologist who'd been the love slave of a goddess. Now *that* back story she would have dreamed up, seeing that her passion was Egyptian antiquities.

He gazed around her shop. "What kind of rubbish shop is this?"

Rubbish shop. She glanced at the cluttered shelves filled with assorted dusty collectables and sighed understanding his comment. Her former co-workers had voiced similar opinions, putting her on the defensive. That was another reason she wasn't looking forward to her birthday bash. Aunt Betty's tastes had certainly been eclectic, but she'd had a good eye.

"This is Aunt Betty's Antique Shop." Her chin rose as her pride kicked in. "I sell old things, like you, hot stuff."

He turned to focus on her, his eyes narrowing. "I am not for sale, Aunt Betty..."

It was almost like he was used to being tricked. "I'm not Aunt Betty, so you've nothing to fear from me on that score," she commented with a smile hoping to reassure him. "I inherited the shop from her. I'm Chemise. *Miss* Chemise Lawson." She held her hand out to him and time seemed to stand still as he hesitated, making her wonder if he'd play nice. She looked into his stormy eyes and almost regretted her friendly gesture. This fantasy could prove dangerous, she knew.

Then he took her hand, and she felt a pull as old as time. His fingers wrapped around hers, hot and work roughened, and like a moth to the flame she couldn't stop herself from leaning into him, feeling his potent strength. She bit her lip, holding back a moan as his stiff cock pressed against her hip and something forbidden opened deep inside her psyche. Nestled close against his tempting hot body she closed her eyes, embarrassed by her primal reaction, as he bit out a low curse.

"Hell, I've no time for this," Lucien muttered, but he bent to nuzzle the nape of her neck anyway.

Great, leave it to her to conjure up a reluctant genie. Panting, almost swooning in his arms, she stiffened, prepared to reject him first. She wasn't some charity case. If he didn't want her, he could just poof back into the lamp and she'd get on with her life. She pulled back to tell him so, then hesitated when she saw the sweat on his brow. He was fighting his desire for her. It was a balm for her wounded pride.

When Lucien's smoldering gaze swept over her breasts, she arched toward him knowing she needed to make the first move, to free him from what she didn't know. His tactile gaze touched her just like before and she could swear she felt him touch her there. Her nipples budded tighter as she pressed against him, aching to have him inside her. Her clit tingled and her sex grew creamy as her arousal grew exponentially.

His sultry smile said he knew how she was feeling even if he wasn't happy about giving in to both their desires. Hell, he was probably a mind reader too. He couldn't just cut and run on her; she'd dreamed him up, damn it! "You can't go," she demanded. "You owe me three wishes."

He reached out to gently tug the lamp out of her hand. "You've been reading too many fables, my lady. You're mistaken. I owe you nothing."

She frowned as he stole her lamp right out of her hand, his fingertips caressing hers as he pulled away. "Wrong, I know the fairytale as well as you do, buster. I release you and you grant me three wishes."

The corners of his mouth quirked up in a half smile at her fierce demand. "You don't have the power to truly release me, Vixen." His expression sobered as he reached out a hand to cup her cheek. "Zander will soon learn of my escape and come for me. I must go. A gentleman does not put a lady in jeopardy."

Well, that just tore it, he was going to cut and run. Only she would dream up a reluctant genie. She pulled back breaking contact from his hand stroking her face and looked away to hide the tears of frustration misting her eyes. "Go then if you don't want me. I've got a hot date coming to pick me up in a few minutes anyway."

"Hot date?" Lucien asked, puzzled.

"In your lingo a beau, an escort, you know a man." She cringed inside as she told the bald faced lie but couldn't take it back. Why she cared what a fantasy man thought of her she couldn't say. She swore she could hear him gnash his teeth in aggravation and when she turned to look at him, she could see fury in his eyes. Was he really jealous? The possibility stunned her. And then he reached out to snag her pulling her hard into his aroused body and she stopped thinking.

Lucien let out a growl. "Don't be daft, woman. How can you say I don't want you?"

Chemise picked up his masculine outrage loud and clear as he tested his throbbing erection against her hip. Damn but she wanted a small taste of that. She let out a murmur of surrender, wrapping her arms around his neck. Shaking with need, she melted against him in a big puddle of lust, aching for him to possess her. And when his mouth slanted over hers with fierce demand, she knew she'd found paradise.

Chapter 2

Sir Lucien Darby's head swirled with doubt as he kissed his sexy little summoner. She was wearing Isis's symbol of protection, but she was a far cry from the simpering handmaidens Isis always sent to fetch him. Even if he hadn't had her strange provocative dress and language for clues, Chemise's feisty attitude would have told him she was different.

She sounded nothing slightly reminiscent of the woman who'd spoken to him through the safe all these years telling him that she was probably telling him the truth. His daily visits with his hostess as she liked to call herself had kept him up with modern times and given him hope that he'd someday be free. But could he trust the sultry maiden who'd summoned him?

He knew that the pendant the temptress wore was chillingly real because he possessed an identical talisman. It was his last link with the goddess, and he'd sworn he'd never use it. He'd expected one of Isis's tricks when he was summoned, not an unconventional tease that made him hard with one glance from her wide turquoise blue eyes.

He nipped her lush lower lip in retribution, and she moaned opening her mouth for him driving him mad with desire. Did she have any idea what she was doing to him? He thrust his tongue into her sweet mouth demanding her surrender and she gave way. She kissed him back her tongue tangling with his in unvarnished sexual demand. He didn't know how long he'd languished in his lamp, but he knew he couldn't put his overwhelming sexual urge down to simple arousal. The sex kitten in his arms called to him like no other.

He was a man out of time, but he didn't care. Time ceased to Matter when Chemise kissed him. He found her spellbinding, arousing. Chemise was built for love, for him, but who the hell was she really? His beloved?

Nonsense, he wasn't falling for that fairytale again. Isis had had an astrological chart made for him. Oswald had assured him that someday his beloved would release him from captivity. Three signs would mark her. She'd trust him for no reason, she'd risk her life for him, and she'd bear a heart-shaped beauty mark on her left breast. He'd been fool enough to believe the prophecy, thinking Isis was the promised one. It'd all been a trick and after he'd uncovered her deception, she'd banished him to his lamp.

Who Chemise was, and what she wanted he'd find out later. Right now, he had a century long need to slake and he couldn't help sensing her deep feminine desire. Someone had hurt her badly and she wanted to use him for her own purposes. Hell, he ought to be used to it by now. And he really didn't mind being used by her he decided with a wry smile as she shivered against him. Knowing he was a lust drunk fool he tested his stiff cock against Chemise's soft womanly body again.

Chemise whimpered, rubbing her hard nipples against his chest, and he forgot all about the past. He'd never felt such warmth. He could tell she was hesitant, untried in the art of seduction, but her instincts were good. When she tumbled him down onto the couch, he acquiesced with a grunt, pulling her atop him, even though he knew he should hurry. The urge to be with her was just too strong to resist.

Sprawled atop him, she froze for a moment as if shocked by her own boldness, and he stifled a groan. If she stopped now, it would kill him and anyway, he couldn't bear to let her go. He smoothed a hand down her spine, and her clothes magically vanished in his hand's wake. It was one of the tricks Isis had taught him, the better to service her, but he didn't want to think about that heartless bitch now. Instead, he focused on the goddess who he was with as she blushed atop him her soft nude body now pressing against him. It was pure torture, but he was no rouge to take her by force. She would have to show him that she really wanted this. He waited breathlessly for her reaction. Would she play the shy maiden, or would she keep ravishing him? Her big blue eyes widened in surprise, and he watched, bemused, as a blush spread from her face to her delectably curved ass. He watched its motion with avid interest. He had plans for that saucy bottom and every other inch of her, too.

"How did you do that?" she asked with a sultry smile.

"Magic," he replied, gazing at her through a haze of desire. His cock was so hard he thought it might burst at any moment. Damn, he wasn't going to last long. It had been so long, centuries probably, and he'd never been near anyone like her. She wriggled against him, and he bit back a moan as it bucked growing even harder as she moved. A sexy innocent who threatened to unman him with a twitch of her hips.

"Oh Lord, Barry was right. I suck at this." She let out a distressed gasp. "Did I hurt you?"

He pulled her closer, looping an arm around her waist when she tried to move away. She dared to make eye contact with him, her blue eyes smoldering with desire, and he felt like he could gladly drown in their turquoise pools. *Who the devil was Barry,* he wondered, outraged, but when she blanched at his scowl, he schooled his expression into one less fierce. "On the contrary, you're too good at it. That's why I was groaning." He saw a flush of pleasure light her face, and was glad that he'd put it there. Then she gently moved on him again and he gritted his teeth forcing himself not to grab her and take her.

Let the innocent seduce him, he decided in a heated rush as his cock twitched in response. Knowing that she wanted this as much as he did help keep him sane. When she bent to lap at his nipple, he let out a hiss, as his blood sizzled. His sex starved body was rousing to painful proportions under her tender ministrations. He thought that he might not be able to handle it for a moment. That he might turn into a ravening beast just like Isis had claimed that he would, but sheer willpower kept him from acting on his impulse. He could control himself, he realized as heat tempered with reserve rushed through him! It came as a shock to him. So, Isis had lied to him about this too. Why should he be surprised? The bitch goddess would use any trick in the book to keep her love slaves in line. When Chemise moved onto the torture his other nipple thoughts of Isis faded into oblivion. He only wanted to concentrate on the fascinating creature he was with. The link to the goddess was gone. He lay back with a blissful laugh, letting Chemise ravish him to her hearts delight.

She raised her head, shooting him a troubled frown as she stopped seducing him. "Are you laughing at me?"

His body throbbed, unsatisfied beneath her tempting curvaceous body, and he cursed himself for making her stop. "I wouldn't dream of it, my lovely," he responded.

He could see that his response startled her. She wasn't used to being called lovely, but he found her full curves and guileless ways utterly charming. Should he perhaps recite a sonnet to tell her how desirable she was? As he considered it, she gave him a tender smile and shimmied down his overly aroused body inch by torturous inch to dip her tongue inside his naval. Heat scalded through him a red haze covering him as he lost all rational thought.

"Good," she stated, swirling her tongue inside his navel. Then she left his belly with a kiss to slip down even lower to fit between his legs.

He froze guessing her intentions a moment before her hot tongue flicked out to taste his cock. He let out a groan, his body jerking in response.

"I don't think I could take it if you laughed at me," she murmured a moment before she swirled her tongue around the head of his cock.

Lucian groaned stunned by her disclosure and sincerity as she licked the throbbing head of his cock like it was a sweet. He lay back for a moment reveling in the sensation of being taken by this innocent as she opened up and took him as deep into her mouth as she could. His cock pulsed as she drew on him and then pulled back to tease the vein under his cock's head. He let out a growl, cock twitching as his balls tightened and his body prepared to explode. Knowing he couldn't last much longer before the bewitching innocent unmanned him, he reached down for her.

"Enough," he commanded.

She gave him a mew of disappointment, her sultry lips still wrapped around him, and he lost a little piece of his heart. She was his if only temporarily. His very own love slave if you like. And he needed to be inside her now.

"Give it up or I'll paddle your sweet ass," he demanded giving her an imperious look.

"Meany," she said letting him go.

But he didn't miss the excitement in her eyes. The minx wanted to be disciplined by him. It made his cock even harder. He pulled her up his body and they both hissed with pleasure as she rubbed sensually against him.

"Would you really spank me?" she asked, her eyes widening.

"Count on it," Lucian affirmed watching a telling blush turn Chemise a delightful rosy color. It was only when he drew her higher, dangling her generous breasts over him like ripe fruit he wanted to devour, that he saw the heart-shaped mark on the curve of her right breast. His heart almost stopped beating as he gazed at the mark that told him that fate was smiling on him again. Oswald's prediction had come true. His beloved had truly set him free, but at what cost. She wasn't of his time, would never believe the prophecy if he told her of it. Maybe fate was laughing at him instead, giving him one taste of bliss, before sending him back.

"What's wrong?" Chemise frowned down at him freezing up. She looked away. "If you've changed your mind and don't want me, take your bloody hands off me."

Her pain broke through his self-pity. Some bastard had obviously convinced her that she wasn't desirable. At least he could fix that before he was re-consigned to the lamp. "You, silly woman," he replied in a teasing tone that had her looking at him again. He deliberately rubbed his erection against her mound making her gasp and quiver against him. He could feel the heat in her creamy mound. "How can you even think that I don't want you, Chemise?"

"Well," she whispered with a blush. "I guess I've got your hard on to prove it. It is kind of hard to deny."

So that's what they were calling erections now. He flicked his tongue out to taste one of Chemise's sweet strawberry peaks and her nipple puckered turning ruby hard under his tongue.

She moaned, "Lucien."

Needing no further encouragement, he sucked her nipple into his mouth rolling it around his tongue, nipping it, making her quiver and cry out as he tested his cock against the soft wet heat of the curls shielding her feminine secrets. He let out a growl and captured her other tit in his mouth as she frantically rubbed her mound against him, trying to hurry him. But he had no intention of rushing, wanting to enjoy her. He drew back one hand to give her sexy ass a smack making her squeal. "Behave yourself."

"No," she moaned her eyes twinkling as she rubbed against him again.

He gave her another spank making them both moan as his balls tightened and his cock bucked against her. So much for his futile attempts to slow things down...they were both too hungry to wait...but he had to be sure of her. He'd once been a gentleman after all and even though he knew he was less than that now some essences died hard. He slid between the folds of her creamy sex wetting the head of his dick on her nectar and watched her turquoise eyes grow soft with passion. "Do you want this, Chemise?"

"More than you could possibly know."

Her honey voiced surrender succeeded in pushing him over the edge. "Oh, I think I've got a good idea," he gritted out as he pressed against the entrance to her tunnel of love. With a groan of need, he pressed against her creamy barrier, and it gave way as he began to enter her tight wet sheath. Her sex spasmed in reaction to his invasion, clamping down on him, forcing him to gasp with mixed pleasure and pain.

"You're too big," she stated with a cry, going still.

Feeling her shut down on him fucked with his mind but he strove to be calm and reassuring even though he felt consumed with fear. That she'd reject him, and most of all that it wasn't to be, she'd never be his. "No, beloved. It will be perfect," he crooned, his words coming out a little gruffer than he intended. Knowing he was close to disaster he decided that she needed action more than words. His hand slicked down between their bodies to find and play with her with her stiff little clit. She jerked as if a live wire had touched her and shuddered as her cunt relaxed around him and her juices coated him. Groaning at the hot velvety cage she made around him he thrust the rest of the way inside her warmth until she took him all and they were both trembling.

"Oh my, I had no idea," Chemise whimpered, rocking against him.

"That's it," he praised, his cock throbbing as her sheath rippled over him threatening to end him before it had even started. It was a perfect fit, the fates had chosen well to make her his beloved. Gripping her hips, he pulled halfway out of her to thrust up into her hard making her cry out. Kittenish noises poured out of her mouth. He gazed up at her in wonder, stunned that he'd finally found her, that she was real. A wave of tenderness came over him as he looked at her slightly crooked smile, her wide set cat's eyes, her lush curves. He supposed she wasn't traditionally beautiful, but he found her fascinating. Then her sheath rippled on his and he forgot all about thinking as he fucked her harder.

"Ride me my beloved," he gritted out as he urged her to sit astride him. Without any more urging she ground against him moaning.

Lucian's hands tightened on her sexy hips as he pulsed inside her thrusting deeper until they were both gasping. Knowing he couldn't hang on much longer, he arched his thrust to brush against her g spot while reaching for the sentient nub of her clit. She came apart in his hands, screaming his name, and he jerked joining her in bliss as he came with a roar against her cervix. Wave after wave of cum poured out of him as she milked at him. Her blissful cries music to his ears. It was oh so satisfying to know that she was with him all the way. When it was over and he was finally sated, he pulled her down on top of him the intimate skin on skin contact, almost as satisfying as the sex. He reveled in the sensation as her scent, her essence, wrapped around him. The room smelled like sex, like her, and he knew he'd never forget her. Too bad he couldn't keep her without bringing her danger. She settled against him with a sigh of pleasure, and he held her tight, knowing he'd found a treasure.

Cradling her in his arms, Lucien held her as if he never wanted to let her go savoring the stolen moment of bliss. If history repeated itself, Zander would have sensed his escape by now. It was only a matter of time before his nemesis hunted him down to try to force him back into captivity. It was the only way for Zander to roam free and wreak havoc on society. But this time would be different Lucian vowed. After their previous conflicts he knew a few of the evil genie's weaknesses like a few lines from the spell that would send him back into captivity. It was what he'd been working on all those centuries ago that had gotten him trapped in the first place.

"What's wrong?" Chemise asked, raising her head to look at him.

Lucian cursed himself for letting his worries about Zander intrude on this moment of bliss. His sweet beloved was perceptive he thought meeting her troubled gaze, but his sweet shopkeeper would have no idea about what it took to defeat Zander. Much as it went against his newly born tender feelings for her, he knew that he had to leave her for her own good. Taking a moment to make love to her might have been foolish but he couldn't regret it. "There's nothing wrong Chemise," he replied pulling her back down atop him.

She sprawled across him boneless once more as he stroked her back until she all but purred. When she was relaxed, he cast a sleeping spell on her and felt her go under as she went limp. He held her tight for a moment, placing a kiss on the top of her fiery head. Then he forced himself to let her go, wasting some of his magic to reverse their positions so that she was lying on her back on the couch.

He felt cold and bereft as he gazed down at her preparing to leave her. She'd hate him for it but losing her was the price he had to pay to keep her alive. Chemise murmured in her sleep and curled up a little more on the couch sound asleep. He gazed down at her longingly for another foolish moment, wishing things were different, that he could stay and claim what was his. But Zander would stop at nothing to destroy Chemise, a mere mortal who'd had the temerity to summon him.

The still gallant part of him knew that he needed to draw danger away from Chemise tonight and fast. In the past it hadn't taken Zander long to get a bead on his location. This time he'd be ready for combat. And who knows maybe sex with his beloved would somehow give him extra ammunition against the evil genie. As he thought it, he felt a tingle surge through him and smirked at his wishful thinking. After all these years you wouldn't think he'd have any innocence left. He had to follow the plan he'd been concocting since their last encounter. Fight it out, trick Zander into revealing the rest of the spell, and then put the evil genie back in the lamp where he couldn't victimize others. Sever his last tie with Isis, and then what...die...maybe. Right now, he didn't care. Going back to the half existence he'd led before Chemise had summoned him was unthinkable.

She shivered as if she'd sensed the direction of his thoughts. Was that part of Osmond's prediction true as well? Were their thoughts linked? It was a painful thought. He'd know when she woke to find herself alone and cursed him out, but he'd also know if Zander came for her. He blinked Chemise's clothes back onto her, shielding her from his hungry gaze in an attempt to get on with what he had to do. He couldn't give in to temptation and fuck the sexy shopkeeper again, he had to save her. With a grumble of self-reproach at his weakness for her, he dressed himself in a flash and bent to pick up his lamp from the floor where it had fallen when they were trysting. This he had to take care of first. He couldn't very well walk about the city with the key to their survival in tow.

Remembering Chemise's mention of the safe, he glanced around the cluttered room for the vault and saw it standing in a dark corner of the room, the door ajar. Perfect! He carried the lamp to the open safe and thrust it inside, knowing instinctively that this was where he'd resided for years. Quiet, secure, with just a hint of a lavender scent that he'd found relaxing. Strange he even semi recalled an old woman stroking his lamp and murmuring soothing sounds he hadn't understood. Aunt Betty? He glanced at Chemise in questing and saw her smiling in her sleep.

The women in her family were definitely different, and he thanked his lucky stars that they apparently, liked old things like him. He left the lamp in the far left corner of the safe and firmly closed the door, spinning the lock and taking the precaution of putting a blocking spell on the safe to prevent it from opening. He could just as easily block Chemise's mind from remembering the combination, but looking at her he couldn't do that to her. This would just have to be good enough. And he'd have to finally trust someone. It wasn't easy but he knew that he had to take a chance on Chemise.

He walked away from the safe, hoping that the vault's heavy metal casing would block its location from Zander. After all he'd lied undisturbed there for years and that wasn't Isis's style. Her parting words that he'd have to come crawling back to her to beg her forgiveness when he decided to be a good bed slave echoed through his mind. He sneered, like he wanted an icy piece of ass that bad. The imperious goddess could go to hell if she wasn't there already. *Isis must have truly forgotten him*, he decided with a feeling of relief. At least he'd only have one otherworldly creature to battle.

He pulled his mind off Isis and gazed back at Chemise, still dazzled by her tender and genuine reactions as he'd made love to her. He'd never experienced anything like it. He gave his beloved one final, hungry glance before he strode from the shop. Her sleeping spell would be wearing off soon and from what she'd said her hot date would be coming for her. Every jealous bone in his body came alive at the thought of her being with another man. She still contained his scent, his essences, she was his damn it. And you can't afford to keep her, he told himself with self-mockery. It's better if she goes with another, forgets you. Yeah, so why did the primitive part of him want to kill? Because he was a fool, that was why. At least she wouldn't be alone tonight.

He forced himself to leave the shop his mind clouded with pain and ran smack dab into a tall blonde woman in a short red dress. He eased back before they actually touched wanting no other female's scent on him that would block Chemise's essence. He found it comforting and he wouldn't lose it. Who the whorishly dressed blonde was, he didn't know, but when he saw her eyes narrow with suspicion on him, he felt like the guilty bastard she thought him to be.

"Not so fast buster." She glanced at the shop's closed sign and scowled. "What the fuck do you think you're doing sneaking out of Chemise's shop?"

"She summoned me," he replied dryly and watched her eyes narrow in doubt.

"Yeah right," she muttered. "If you've touched her, I'll...,"

"And who are you to be lurking outside my beloved...that is Chemise's shop?" he demanded, turning the tables on her. He watched a speculative look come over her face as her fear dissolved.

"I'm here to pick her up for her birthday party. And your 'beloved' better be as untouched as you claim she is or you're going to be in a world of hurt buster. Where the fuck is she?" She pushed past him.

He stepped aside, letting her pass him. The woman's accusatory tone fit because he had harmed Chemise. He'd taken her innocence and left her marked for death. Yeah, he was a gallant gentleman alright, he thought with self-reproach. But at least this wasn't another man picking her up as Chemise had claimed. It was enough to brighten his night. He was glad to know that Chemise had a champion. She'd lied about a man picking her up. It wouldn't be the first time a female had deceived him, but this time he was glad. Maybe she was trying to make him jealous. He couldn't help smiling at the thought. "You must be the hot date she mentioned."

"Hot date," the blonde parroted startled.

"Never mind," he stated as he stepped around her satisfied that she'd confirmed his thoughts. Chemise wouldn't be in another man's arms tonight. "She's inside, waiting for you and I don't think you should keep her waiting."

Chapter 3

Chemise drifted awake knowing that something inside her had changed. Her heartbeat was racing, and her quivering body tingled sensually, while her mind drifted in a pink orgasmic fog. She started to move her legs together and her sex throbbed; rippling on the verge of an orgasm that had her gasping with surprise. Holy cow! It was like she'd been ridden hard by a phantom lover. Burry, her drip of an ex, could never be this potent she thought wryly coming out of her haze.

She was lying on the old fainting couch in her aunt's shop, she realized, looking around her cluttered surroundings in what could only be described as wild sexual abandon. Her legs were spread, her dress hiked up high on her thighs. What's more her dress was unbuttoned leaving the upper curves of her heaving breasts exposed. She smoothed a hand over her wrinkled dress wondering what the hell had hit her, and then it came back to her in vivid color. Lucien! She'd found the lamp, produced her sexy genie lover, Lucian, seduced him, and then poof, he'd vanished, and she'd woken up with a hell of a hangover.

She shook her head and winced when it ached with the movement. Shit, she must have hit her head and imagined it all...but it had seemed so real. Lucien had felt so real in her arms, and between her legs. Her face heated at the randy thought as she reluctantly relegated her perfect lover to fantasy land. At least she had the find of the Egyptian lamp to console her...wherever it was. She looked around in horror to find that that was missing too. She couldn't have fantasized the lamp...it'd happened before she'd hit her head. So where was it? A glance at the safe showed her that it was locked up tight...weird she'd been sure that she'd left it open. Oh lord had she dreamt that part up too? Maybe Barry was right, she was losing it, making critical mistakes.

Her shoulders sagged at the realization that it'd all been a sexy dream. Still, she couldn't help glancing around the vacant shop for signs that Lucien did exist. There were no indications that he'd been there except for the throbbing between her legs and the ache in her heart. Of course, he wasn't there, he wasn't real and she had to accept that fact or lose it completely. It was time to get back to grim reality even if her heart wasn't in it. There were the accusations she had to weather, her career to try to salvage, and her thirtieth birthday party to endure. Life was not looking up. Bells tinkled as the shop's front door opened.

"Chemise, are you okay?" Janelle called out from the front of the shop.

Chemise sat up with a mortified groan as the head glamazon called out for her, her voice sharp and panicked, her high heeled shoes clicking rapidly on the worn linoleum as she raced toward her. Oh no! What the hell. Panic was not in Janelle's vocabulary.

Damn! Brushing the hair out of her eyes Chemise tried to pull herself together and grimaced as she sat up on the fainting couch and tried to straighten her mussed clothes. She looked as disheveled as if she really had spent the afternoon seducing a genie. The crumpled dress combined with her shaking fingers didn't make it easy to pull herself together. Thank goodness Janelle hadn't walked in on...what? A weird sex dream that her warped brain had conjured up? Nothing had happened, so she had nothing to be embarrassed about.

"I'm in the back room," she called out, picking up on her friend's worried tone. When Janelle burst into the back room and then screeched to a halt her mouth forming an O of surprise Chemise's face heated with embarrassment. Chemise saw the startled look in her friend's perfectly made-up blue eyes and cringed. Did her wicked fantasy show? The change from fear to amusement on Janelle's pretty face made Chemise wince inwardly. This was so going to be embarrassing. Chemise ruefully met her gaze, taking in her usual sleek appearance a far cry from her rumpled self. "What's the Matter?"

"I could ask you the same thing, girlfriend," Janelle replied looking pointedly at the front of Chemise's turquoise sundress.

It was only then that Chemise looked down and saw that it was unbuttoned. Lord, she looked like a slut...a freshly satisfied slut. A blush heated her face as she nimbly blushed and quickly did up the buttons.

"I'm just getting dressed," she murmured and froze stunned when her fingers brushed against the Isis pendant nestled in her cleavage. My god it was real. She hadn't fantasized that part. The knowledge made her tremble, making her wonder what else might be real.

"That leaves the question of who undressed you," Janelle teased. "And here I thought you were moping over Barry. Who knew you had some action on the side."

Bemused by that fact that at least one of her finds was real, she stroked the exquisitely carved pendant reverently, feeling a strange beam of heat rush through her. Too bad she couldn't say the same for her sexy genie.

"Who knew you had some action on the side. Good for you. I saw him, he was sexy as hell."

Chemise barely paid any attention to the head of the glam squad but the words, "action on the side" made her look up with foolish hope. "What did you say?"

"Who's the hunk?"

"What hunk?" Her heart started to pound. It couldn't be true. She told herself to calm down. "Hunk?" Good grief was her psychosis contagious or what. She couldn't let Janelle succumb to the vapors, too. Chemise gulped as she stared at her drop–dead gorgeous friend. The museum's donations coordinator was as exquisitely dressed as usual, tonight in a red dress that showed off her model thin body. The knowing twinkle in her glamorous friend's eyes made Chemise blush anew. There was no way on earth Janelle could know the naughty fantasies she'd been indulging in.

Janelle nodded. "Yeah, hunk. Tall, dark, and handsome, if you like them brooding, which apparently you do."

That described Lucien to a T, but she wouldn't let herself go there, she couldn't afford to go there and lose her grip on reality. Chemise shook her head, avoiding Janelle's incisive gaze. She *so* didn't want to talk about her dream lover with her slinky pal who made her feel like a frump. Even so her body tingled at the thought of her private genie. "I wish," she stated, moving off the couch and trying not to wince when her body unaccustomed to sexual activity, even the imaginary kind, gave a twinge of protest. Ignoring the sensual tenderness, she turned away to pick up her purse off the counter and reach for her keys. "Come on let's go get this over with."

Lucien winced when he mentally heard Chemise dismiss him as only a fantasy and told himself to let her go as he slipped into the back of the Blue Tropical bar. He'd managed to walk past two muscle bound doorkeepers by fogging their minds. The moment he'd walked away from Chemise's shop he'd felt the spook hubs other worldly pull. Here he should be able to acquire information about Zander, maybe even track the bastard down. One thing was for sure, he'd rather go down fighting than be trapped again. If he was correct, the evil genie would be in reach of his lamp just in case.

He stood in the back of the room taking in the tropical theme. The name Blue Tropical was illuminated in neon above the bar. He halted in the shadows his eyes adjusting to the dim lighting as a thudding tune vibrated through him and gave only a brief glance at the blonde seminude woman dancing on a stage. Her scrawny charms couldn't compare to Chemise's soft curves. Thinking of her made his cock swell and he willed the hard on away.

He turned to survey the pub's customers, looking for his target, but didn't spy Zander. His gaze swept over several other leather-clad men playing billiards who were laughing and gesturing rudely. As if they felt his stare, they turned to glower at him. Their threatening looks said that they would welcome violence, but they didn't spark his ire. He wasn't after such stupid prey. When he met their glares with a steady look they shrugged and went back to their game. It was a stand down of sorts and he'd take it.

He turned to the left feeling a tingle of Zander's tendrils of power draw him toward the bar. There was some tinge of his spore in the atmosphere. Then a tinkle of light female laughter halted his steps. He knew that laugh…Isis's favorite handmaiden Jasmine. The goddess probably sensed his hard-on for Chemise and sent her to try to keep him in line, he thought ruefully. Shit he didn't want Isis interfering in this.

He spun to see a woman moving toward the back entrance her laughter tinkling like water in her wake and started after her.

"Hold it," a man called out harshly.

He turned expecting to face a biker and instead saw the bartender glaring at him. Could he possibly be under Zander's influence? He almost felt sorry for the erstwhile lad. "You don't want any part of this boy."

"That's where you're wrong," the bartender stated and then looked toward the back of the room. "Mack, Chris, escort this customer out. And make sure he doesn't come back."

Lucien was aware of concerned gasps and the crowd clearing as the thugs reached for him. Shit, he could play it two ways: fight back and cause more collateral damage or take it outside. "I'm going," he replied holding his open hands up in a sign of surrender and heading for the back door with his escorts in tow.

"Don't try anything funny, asshole," the younger thug murmured.

"Shut up, Chris," the older one demanded in an irked tone.

They weren't getting along, excellent. "In case it escaped your notice, I haven't done anything wrong."

"Can it, buddy. If Jeremy says you're trouble, we believe him," the older thug replied.

"Yeah," Chris joined in. "He knows spooky stuff. Besides, you were eyeing his girl. Big mistake."

Mack let out a growl. "Shut your mouth, Chris."

Shit, the bartender had power and Jasmine a dangerous combination, but where did Zander fit into the picture. He stepped into the cool night air knowing the dark would give him the advantage. Lucien stepped away from the light spilling out of the building and sensed a motion behind him as Mack swung at him and lunged to the side going out of range and then going in for the kill. He had Mack down before he could recover and groaned when Chris kicked at him. He grunted as the man connected with his ribs and waved his hand putting them both under his spell. As they collapsed and snored, he heard running high heeled footsteps and then a woman screech.

The familiar scent of rose attar wafted his way making his eyes water as he turned to look at Jasmine. She was standing in the shadows, hands on her hips, as she glared at him in outrage. "What the hell did you do to my friends?"

He could only shake his head at her as he took in her presence. Jasmine was dressed in modern day clothes, of a mini skirt and skimpy top, her makeup heavy, gold bracelets adorning her arms. But he could also feel Zander's mark on her. How had that happened and why?

"I see you've lost none of your lethal charm after all these years, Lucien." She stepped closer.

He spared a sympathetic glance for her friends. "You know they'll come out of his sleeper hold none the worse for wear."

"You'd better be right," she spat.

"Why the concern for the mortals? It's not like the selfish Jasmine I used to know. As a matter of fact, you used to refer to us as toys." He watched her eyes lower as something close to remorse crossed her pretty face, and he was stunned.

"My reasons are none of your business. Tell me what the hell are you doing here, anyway, and out..."

"Out of the bottle," he filled in closing in on her. A few sleepy groans behind him told him Mack and Chris were rousing but he didn't spare them a glance. Instead, he focused on Jasmine as she seemed to finally grasp his fury and stepped back a pace. He snagged her arm before she could succeed in transporting and escape him. Zander's essence rolled off her as he touched her making him smile with victory. It would be over soon. "Where is he?"

She glared at him for a moment, and then rolled her eyes. "What difference does it make to you bed slave. If you have an ounce of sense, you'll run away and enjoy a few moments of freedom while you still can. Find a woman. Get lucky." And then her eyes widened as she looked at him. "Ooh. You already did, didn't you?"

Shit, did his besotted expression show? "Just tell me what I want to know."

"I'd tell you if I knew just to see the pissed off look on his icy face," she replied, rubbing her arms as if chilled. "The truth is I don't know where he is right now. He's mostly left me to my own devices since he talked me into helping him escape her wrath. He only pops in when he wants something, like he did about an hour ago."

"That explains his taint on you."

"His what?" Her brow wrinkled.

"It doesn't matter." Shit, he'd just missed him. If he'd come here instead of making Chemise, his beloved, he would have found him. But he couldn't regret that no matter what. The fact that Zander had made an appearance about the time he'd escaped proved he still guarded the lamp. "What did he say?"

"He did seem agitated talking about some female he scented. I told him to get lost, and he left talking about tracking her to some party..."

Chemise! Lucian's blood turned cold. Damn it he should have known that Zander would play dirty. He turned to leave.

"Hey, where are you going?" Jasmine yelled.

He spared her a glance. "To rescue a damsel in distress," he replied with a grim smile when she rolled her eyes. "I'm through running."

Chapter 4

Chemise smiled warmly at her three friends and former coworkers as Janelle led her toward a back booth at Charlie's Bar and Grill. Only a few miles from the museum, it'd become a special hang out place for them over the years, whether they were celebrating, commiserating, or man hunting. Of course, she was the one they were usually trying to fix up with a blind date. After her imagined flirtation with Lucien, she just wasn't in the mood for any of their well-meaning hookups.

Amber Black, a flirtatious brunette, was an I.T. specialist who worked in the business office, was dressed in a sexy little black dress complete with pearls. "Hey how's it hanging, girlfriend," she stated hoisting her chocolate martini in salute.

Miko Kawasaki, a petite Asian doll of a woman in a scarlet sheath dress, was a conservator like Chemise had once been before the disaster, only she worked on textiles. Miko wiggled her fingers in a wave. "Happy birthday, Chemise."

"Thanks." Chemise smiled in response to Miko's sweet expression. They had been especially close, working in the same department. Except Miko was still working Chemise thought wryly.

"Shove over and pour me a cold one," Janelle demanded, sliding into the banquette. She lifted a martini glass to her lips and took an appreciative sip. "Ambrosia."

Chemise grinned at her antics, losing the rest of the anticipatory stress she'd been carrying. This party was just what she needed to get over her troubles. She took her place at the table. "Give me some of that heavenly concoction, too."

Tonight, she wouldn't even think about the calories, she decided. She barely noticed her friends give each other relieved looks and realized that they'd been worried about her. It was touching really, even though she didn't like to worry anyone. She self-consciously lifted her glass.

"Thanks for being here for me, guys."

"And where else would the glam squad be?" Janelle asked.

Chemise smiled as tears of gratitude misted her eyes. She blinked them away not wanting to give them more reason to worry about her. Through the years, they'd all bonded over coffee breaks against the sexist politics at play in the museum. The director and all the department heads were male and indirectly chauvinistic. The fact that the glam squad had stuck by her after she'd been fired, unlike Barry, the faithless rat, meant a lot.

"Damn right," Miko and Amber replied in unison, lifting their glasses.

"Thanks," she stated swallowing the lump in her throat.

"Happy birthday!" they screamed in tandem, toasting her with chocolate martinis.

"Thanks."

She slid into the booth and wrapped her fingers around the chilled stem of the martini glass deciding to enjoy herself...or at least try to. Feeling their sympathetic glances on her, she raised her glass and smiled, meeting their gaze.

"Cheers," she murmured clicking glasses with them her fingers wrapped around the martini glass's chilled stem. She was going to enjoy herself tonight and worry about her troubles tomorrow. Then she took a bracing sip of the frosty concoction while the others drank, savoring the blissfully decadent taste as she thought about what to say. Knowing that she needed to face facts she carefully set the glass down on the table.

"So, how are things going at the museum?" Might as well get the awkward subject out of the way while hopefully putting everyone else at ease.

Miko shook her head and set down her drink. "Not good."

Chemise braced herself going still, she couldn't help it. And then she saw her friends exchange concerned looks, and told herself to cool it.

"I didn't mean to say that it was bad..." Miko amended.

Chemise reached out to touch Miko's hand. "It's okay Miko. Tell me."

Amanda shook her head. "What she's trying to say is that the, the director hired a special investigative consultant to look into things."

Oh Lord, the director hadn't been making idle threats when he said he was going to nail her hide to the wall. He must have brought in some heavy hitter to take her down. The thought of being the subject of a criminal investigation was enough to make her dizzy. She, who'd never had so much as a parking ticket, it should have been laughable, but it scared her to death. It wasn't fair. Yeah, well who said life was fair. She'd dreamed up a lover only to have him vaporize on her.

Janelle winced as she watched Chemise freeze up. "Um, maybe we ought to change the subject ladies."

Chemise forced herself to relax. "It's okay. I need to know what I'm up against. Who's investigating things, someone from the FBI? Should I expect a G-Man at my door?"

Janelle rolled her eyes. "You know the director doesn't want that kind of official scrutiny. It would be bad for his career. He went private sector, some snooty broad who insists on being called Dr. Amelia January."

Chemise absorbed the information not sure if she should be happy or not. At least she wasn't under arrest...yet! The feds weren't after her, but she'd never heard of this Dr. January. What kind of expertise might she have? "So, you say she isn't making much progress."

"Oh, she's making progress all right," Miko muttered wryly with a shake of her head.

If mild mannered Miko was irked, it had to be serious. "What kind of progress is she making?" Chemise asked, picking up on the disapproving looks in her friend's eyes. They were pissed, too.

"She's making progress with Barry," Miko stated while the others nodded in sympathy.

Janelle rolled her eyes. "That's an understatement. To put it plainly she's got the brownnosing creep wrapped around her little finger," Janelle muttered.

Amber nodded. "But despite his attempts to throw you under the bus, they aren't making much progress."

"Who is she?" Chemise asked with an inward wince figuring the director would bring in some heavy hitter in the industry.

"Some snooty bitch," Janelle replied with a shrug. "And so far, the high-priced snob hasn't been able to come up with an explanation for the..."

"Inferno," Chemise cut in sourly.

"Accident," Miko corrected gently while the others nodded.

It wasn't a vindication, but maybe it was the best she could expect. She knew they couldn't prove her guilty, she hadn't done anything wrong.

Perhaps they'd just let the subject drop. With the museum's budget stretched tight, how hard would the board of directors look? They'd simply continue to quietly lay the blame at her door, effectively black-balling her within the industry. Then they'd move on, especially if the museum's insurance paid up, leaving her to pick up the pieces of her life. She sighed, demoralized. At least things couldn't get much worse.

Amber let out a horrified gasp, her eyes going wide as she stared at the club's front door. "Oh Lord, speak of the devil."

Cripe, she had to stop the proclamations. Knowing it was bad, she nevertheless turned to see what other disaster was coming her way, and caught sight of Barry the rat with another woman on his arm. Her censuring gaze swept over his less than thrilling form, sandy brown hair, cool and calculating light blue eyes behind horn rimmed glasses, and a superior attitude, and she felt nothing but scorn. The fact that she didn't feel any lovelorn twinges she put down to Lucien's sexual healing. The knowledge that she was well and truly over him was satisfying. Having put Barry in his proper place in her life, the past, she turned her attention to his date. The lady was willowy, dark, and exotic looking female who was dressed to the nines in a business suit that must have cost a fortune. The hired consultant?

Janelle leaned in to mutter, "Shit, honey, we had no idea he'd show up here."

"Don't worry about it, I'm not," Chemise hurried to reassure her.

"Talk about lack of class," Miko muttered glaring at the pair. "It was known around the museum staff that we were having your party here. I can't believe he forgot..."

"He didn't forget," Chemise replied as Barry's gaze fell on her. "He came here on purpose to flaunt her in my face. She's the high-priced consultant I take it."

Amber nodded. "That's her all right. Oh blast, they're coming our way. Come on ladies, let's move..."

"You go ahead. I'm not running," Chemise interrupted when the others started to rise.

Her friends all sat back down sticking with her to the bitter end, and she gave them a grateful smile. As Barry and Dr. Amelia January moved in on her, she studied their purposeful strides. Barry was looking a little stressed around the edges, his tweed suit rumpled, pinched lines of stress around his mouth and eyes. On the other hand, Dr. January looked triumphant. The good doctor didn't do subtle worth a damn. They weren't even pretending that this was an accidental meeting. The realization gave her pause. Dr. January, however, had the determined look of a bloodhound on the scent of its prey. The problem was that the prey happened to be her.

"Chemise, we want a word with you," Barry stated, stopping at their table.

Chemise gave him a cool look. "I don't want to talk to you. Go away."

"Now, babe, don't take that attitude. If you'd use your brain instead of your emotions, you'd see that I'm only trying to help."

She gave him an icy look that could have frozen water, objecting to the pet name and the jerk's condescending attitude, ever conscious of his companion studying her. "Care to introduce me to your little helper?" she asked, ignoring his comment and stabbing the woman with a pointed look.

"Dr. Amelia January," the woman replied, pulling a card out of her pocket and tossing it on the table in front of her. "And it's not a request for an interview, it's a demand."

Barry sighed and touched Amelia's arm. "Now, honey, you'll get farther with her if you..."

She shook off his touch, which made him pout and then smiled at him which made him relax again. "Let me handle this, love..."

"Love," Chemise repeated under her breath in shock, meeting her friends' equally stunned gazes. Talk about unprofessional behavior. She cleared her throat to gain their attention. When Barry and Amelia looked down at her, she gave them a firm look back. "If you really want to question me..." She started watching Barry nod and Amelia's focus shift completely to her. "You will do it in the proper way. Call my attorney to set up an appointment tomorrow. Tonight, I'm here to celebrate my birthday with my real friends, and I won't have it spoiled by the likes of you."

Amelia gave her a frosty, chilling stare while Barry just looked wounded. Tough. He'd shown where his loyalties lay, and she wouldn't have him back on a bet.

"You'll regret this," Amelia stated with a hiss.

Chemise had about enough of her snide comments. "Leave before I call a cop and have you arrested for harassment."

She surged to her feet intending to throw them out if necessary and blushed when the movement made her dress slip off one shoulder, baring an expanse of her cleavage, and her dress slipped off her shoulder, going south. How humiliating. Still, she fought back a blush and glared at the two of them. Barry's eyes were practically popping out of his head us he ogled her. When he saw her glare, he gulped and took a hasty step back out of slapping range.

Smart man, she thought baring her teeth in a parody of a smile. With him quelled she refocused on Dr January. Amelia stayed put unafraid but there was a new cautious look in her eyes as she stared at Chemise's partially bared cleavage, her eyes widening with astonishment. Shit, was the woman bi? Feeling exposed, Chemise looked down to see exactly how much skin she was flashing and noticed that the pendant had slipped out of its place of concealment. So that's what Dr. January was looking at with lust. No way was she giving it up to her rival. The woman might steal her job, not to mention her ex, but she couldn't have the jewel. Feeling very possessive of her new pendant, Chemise carefully tucked it back into her cleavage.

"Who are you?" Amelia demanded.

The other woman's strident tone made Chemise jump. *What the hell?* She glanced up to see the lust-filled look turn to fear. A new wariness appeared in her rival's eyes as she backed up. Relief surged through Chemise as her enemy retreated. She wasn't sure that she'd actually have the power to toss them out on their ears, but she wasn't going to let them see her doubt. Instead, she raised her head high and gave Amelia the same fuck off smile. "I'm your worst enemy," she replied quoting one of her favorite movie lines. To her astonishment Amelia actually blanched suddenly looking older and took another step back, before turning and walking away. *Cool, who knew she could scare anyone.*

"Well, cheer up, girlfriend, you certainly sent her packing," Janelle commented in stunned approval.

Just as shocked by her easy victory Chemise nodded. "Thank heavens for that."

"The fact that they came here sniffing around means they can't find anything. There's still a good chance you'll be cleared and get your old job back. They haven't hired your replacement yet." Amber let Chemise know.

Her old job back. They should have been satisfying words but left her vaguely unsatisfied. Did she even want her old job back? Deep inside she ached for more. Like your sexy genie a wicked voice in her head said tormenting her, making her pulse speed up as she thought of Lucian. He had been fascinating not to mention sexy as hell and even as a fantasy more man than Barry could ever hope to be.

"And if they don't take you back, the hell with them," Janelle cut in. "You've got other things to think about, like that hunk you were canoodling with."

Chemise swallowed a groan as the others' eyes lit up with curiosity and the naughty fantasy, she was weaving about being spanked and ravished by the brooding genie hunk vaporized. They were constantly trying to fix her up, but there was no way they could match-make with a mirage. "I told you there *is* no guy. It must have been a lost guy you bumped into."

"What guy?" Amanda asked, shooting them a curious glance.

"There's a guy. More proof that she really is over Barry. Hooray!" Miko excitedly pumped her fist.

Chemise stifled a groan. She should have known Janelle wouldn't let this juicy piece of gossip drop and the glam squad would run with it. The other girls were constantly trying to fix her up which was one reason she'd glommed onto Barry as a convenient escort, but there was no way they could match-make with a mirage like Lucien. "I told you there *is* no guy. It must have been a lost guy you bumped into on my doorstep." She watched her friend's excitement simmer down as they bought her assertion and relaxed.

"Too bad," Janelle stated with a sigh. "He was red hot."

Chemise gave the matchmaking trio a firm gazes even as foolish hope filled her. She firmly squelched it knowing that it couldn't be true. Whoever Janelle had encountered couldn't be half as hot as Lucien was. And after her fantasy tryst she wasn't in the mood to be fixed up with any of their cast-off dates. She had to make that clear to her friends or she'd be up to her ears in nerds. "I'm not interested in dating right now."

"But it's your birthday," Miko protested with a pout.

Chemise watched them exchange troubled glances and got a very bad feeling that she was about to be ambushed by three glamazon cupids. "You idiots didn't set me up with a blind date tonight, did you?" Their guilty looks made her shoulders slump. Of course, they had. And here she'd thought she was in for a fun girl's night out. After her tryst with Lucien, she wasn't in the mood to dance with some awkward stranger.

Miko shrugged. "We may have mentioned your party to a few eligible men."

"Oh Lord, a nerd lineup," Chemise murmured.

"Maybe she could find her own guy before they get here," Miko offered with a hopeful smile.

"Not bloody likely," Chemise mumbled into her chocolate martini as she took a bracing sip for strength.

Amber sat up straighter and stared toward the bar. "Don't worry, Chemise, it looks like you won't lack for male companionship after all. Get a load of the stud at the bar, and the way he's staring at you. Seems like your birthday is looking up, girlfriend."

Stud at the bar! Lucien? Chemise's breath caught as the wishful thought passed through her warped brain and her blood sizzled in response. He was the only hunk she knew. After Janelle's continued assertion about seeing him leave her shop, she was starting to believe, even though she knew it couldn't be true. Still her needy gaze snapped up to the bar as she looked for him in vain. He wasn't there, of course, because he wasn't real. She let out a crestfallen sigh when she locked gazes with the strange man watching her. He was good-looking in a cold way, but she wouldn't call him a hunk. Cold, she thought, shivering. His, with coal-black hair and intense icy gray eyes seemed to focus on her, but he who stared at her wasn't Lucien.

"I'm not interested in him."

"Told you she wasn't up to this," Miko stated quietly to Amber.

Chemise winced at Miko's pitying words and felt her friends, feeling their sympathetic glances on her. If they thought she was this fragile after being fired, they'd really think she was nuts for dreaming up Lucien. It wasn't in her to make them worry. Crap, she needed to convince them that she was okay pronto. She took a calming breath coming up with plan B on the fly. She'd dance with the devil if it meant defusing the situation she found herself in.

"I'm fine, really," she added at their doubtful looks.

When the man with the ice-cold eyes started walking toward her, she tried to relax and smile at him even though all her fight and flight instincts screamed. She bit back a groan, fighting the strangest urge to run. Her fingers tightened on her glass, going white, and she had to force herself to let go before she broke the stem. Crap, it was true...she was cracking up if a mere stranger made her want to flee. The guy closing in on her. He looked perfectly nice in a remote, cool way. He was even dressed like a businessman in a tailored suit. There was nothing to be afraid of, she told herself as he stopped in front of her. Still, she couldn't help herself from sucking in a panicked breath. What the hell was wrong with her?

He smiled, his mouth curving into a satisfied smile as he took in her reaction. "Dance with me."

Did he like scaring women or what? Put off by the seeming order and his victorious demeanor like he'd won some contest she didn't know about, she frowned up at him, ignoring the hand he held out. He was a jerk, and she didn't want to dance with a jerk, she'd just wait for the blind date lineup. The very thought made her wince, but she didn't take well to being ordered about, and this iceman was putting her back up big time. The iceman. He seemed to slowly pick up on her hostile reaction and his smirk eased into a genuine smile as he lost some of his stiff formality. She let out a sigh, realizing she'd overreacted. It seemed that he wasn't such an ogre after all. If she danced with him, her friends would stop worrying. She smiled and took the hand he extended. "Love to."

"Good," Miko muttered.

Amber nodded. "I'll say. Go get him, girl."

Chemise tried to ignore the high fives behind her, pasted on a smile, and hoped this icy lothario wouldn't notice them as he led her out onto the dance floor. Shit he'd probably think she needed a team of matchmakers to get laid. Although when the man took her in his stiff arms sex was the last thing that came to mind. A tremor went through her as a chill breeze swirled around them. She gazed up at him to ask him if he was cold too and was taken aback by the probing look, he was giving her. It was as if he were trying to analyze her. Weird. Her heart raced, and her breath caught in her throat. Dizzy, she tried to back away as far as his arms would let her go, needing breathing space. Breathing deep, to quell her incipient panic attack she told herself to go through the motions of dancing. Still, she instinctively backed off, leaving plenty of space between them. *It's only a delayed reaction to my hallucination bothering me, this man has been nothing but polite.* So why did she want to call a cop? She gazed at his pleasant expression.

"You dance well," he observed, whirling her across the dance floor.

"Um, so do you," she replied, almost missing a step, which made her stumble and crash into him again feeling as ungainly as an elephant. "Sorry," she murmured and tried to make space between them again. This time his arm at the small of her back tightened, keeping her pinned to him. Then she looked around the dance floor and she realized that he'd managed to dance her into a dark corner. What the hell? How had she missed that? Other dancers swung by paying them no attention. It was as if the other dancers were separated by a force field. Boy, her imagination was running wild, she thought with a roll of her eyes. The iceman was just an ordinary run-of-the-mill pervert, and she knew how to take care of them. Stomp on his instep and then rack him hard. Him holding her so close would be his undoing. She stopped dancing and glared up at him, noticing that his pleasant mask had slipped. The fury she saw in his icy gaze stunned her. She was glad she was close enough to knee him in the groin if he tried anything. Tensing, as fight or flight instinct kicked in, she felt physically assaulted by his glare.

"He must find your fierceness amusing," he stated, his probing gaze raking her face before dropping lower to linger on her cleavage all but tumbling out of her dress because of her struggles.

His interest was cold, clinical, leaving her chilled inside. He wasn't a pervert, he was a nut job. There was no he in her life unless he meant...

"He?"

"Lucien," he bit out.

Her jaw dropped as fantasy and reality made her head swim again. Had he really said Lucien's name? She tried to steady herself. It couldn't be real…she was hearing things. Or maybe she was still dreaming, and this was part of the fantasy. As she thought it, he pinched her hard on the arm and she yelped.

"No, you're not dreaming."

What the hell. Now Mr. Frosty was reading her mind.

"Stop that," she hissed, pulling her arm away from his bruising fingers.

He let out a pleased chuckle. "You're feisty. I like that in a bed slave."

His frosty smile told her he knew what she was thinking, feeling. "I'm nobody's slave," she hissed.

"Well certainly not a very well trained one," he agreed. "But I'll soon train you properly."

Shivering at his matter of fact tone, she knew that she was up against a powerful force. He might be crazy, but he was strong crazy. She cast a panicked glance back at her friends still laughing and having a good time at their table. But instead of sensing her need, they stared right through her and totally ignored her predicament.

"Don't bother. They can't see or hear us."

He could only be one person. "Zander," she whispered in disbelief as she tried to rack him. He thrust his leg between hers, preventing her move, and bent her arm back until she cried out.

"How nice, he told you my name," Zander replied. "Where is my other slave? My magical lamp. My personal property."

She recoiled in horror as he bit out each statement in cold fury, but then outrage overwhelmed her fear and she gave him a shove, catching him by surprise, saying, "Lucien isn't your slave anymore, you washed out loser. I freed him."

Zander stumbled back and jerked her with him. His grip on her tightened making her gasp in pain, and then he blanched for a minute. Smirking, he said, "You stupid mortal bitch. You don't have the power or the authority to release him."

It echoed Lucien's own sentiments but she couldn't accept that. There had to be some way to keep this arrogant asshole away from him. Then she recalled the pendant that Lucien had torn off himself, the twin of the one now secretly nestled in her cleavage. How did the goddess play into this whole scenario? "Who does, the bitch goddess you serve?" she snapped and watched Zander's gloating smile falter. *Was Lucien correct about Zander no longer having Isis' protection? Zander's reaction seemed to confirm it.* Flashing the pendant to her other foes had made them leave. Would it work on this jerk she wondered wincing when his fingers dug into her arms. Her tingling senses alerted her to Lucien's presence, and a sense of relief made her stop struggling.

Zander's eyes narrowed as he took in her new meek change of demeanor. "So, you realize the futility of your struggle," he crowed.

She smiled at him. With the pendant's powers and Lucien in the vicinity for backup she could take this icy jerk. "Something like that."

"Good," he replied stroking a hand down her arm. "In reward, I will let you live. I could make use of a pretty slave like you."

Her skin crawled as he touched her, and she fought not to show it. She had to time this right. She didn't want any bystanders to get hurt. When the rock music changed to a slow dance, she swayed with the music brushing against him and saw his eyes flash with lust. She glanced at a couple dancing by, her mind screaming *notice me*, and damned if they didn't turn to look. Wow, now that was interesting. Was it pendant power or Lucien's interference? It didn't matter it would give her the edge she needed. If she could just get Zander to let her loose a little bit, she could pounce. "Let's dance, we're attracting attention."

"I told you, they can't..." He looked at the dancers who had stopped to stare at them, and frowned. "What do you think you're about?" he demanded.

"I didn't do it." She shrugged feigning innocence. "After all, I'm just a mortal slave girl. You don't need to be afraid of me."

He nodded, seeming to regain his composure.

"Afraid of you," he parroted with a smirk. "I don't think so."

"So, dance or are you chicken," she taunted feeling his hands tighten on her in retribution. But she refused to be cowed.

"Blast," he muttered swinging her onto the dance floor.

Chemise breathed a sigh of relief as he waltzed her toward the club's back door and Lucien's vibes only got stronger. Zander meant to steal her away and it would be his last mistake. She played dumb as he danced her toward the door and the Lucien tingles going through her strengthened making her gasp and Zander look at her curiously. When he faltered, she used that opportunity to tug the pendant out of hiding, flash it at him making him shrink back, and then kneed him hard in the balls. He let out a bellow as Lucien popped up on Zander's left seeming to come out of nowhere. When Lucien's concerned glance focused on her ignoring Zander, she scowled back at him. Why had he come back after leaving her? She didn't want his pity. She wanted him to love her, she realized, appalled. The thought only made her madder.

"Took you long enough to get here, stud, but as you see, I can take care of myself."

"Now, beloved," Lucien murmured reaching out to take her arm before she could run away.

"Don't call me that! You fucked me and left me, there was nothing loving about it," she stated watching him give her a relentless gaze in return. It made her want to kick in the balls too. Then the hand holding her fast gentled his fingers caressing her needy flesh and she all but turned into a big puddle of Chemise goo for a moment. The sound of Zander sobbing and cupping his balls faded into the background as she gazed into Lucien's sexy eyes. Did he really care for her? Could she risk it? "You've got a lot of explaining to do..." Lucien's glance of concern before Zander became aware of him. Zander let out a snarl as Lucien tore him away from Chemise.

Zander laughed and launched himself at Lucien, getting in a punch to his ribs. "You think you can protect her, fool?"

Lucien pushed Chemise behind him gritting out, "Leave. Go back to your friends."

He was trying to save her, she wasn't just a casual lay for him. Her whole body rejoiced at the realization. Instead of obeying Lucien and taking the easy way out, she stepped out beside him facing Zander, earning Lucien's frown. So, she wasn't very biddable, she had a personal interest to protect. Damned if she was going to let him hurt her boyfriend.

"He doesn't have Isis' protection," she stated flashing her pendant once more and making Zander wince and back away a pace. "See," Chemise called out, and she saw Lucien smile as Zander glared at her.

Lucien smiled and stepped toward Zander. "Interesting. There must have been a power struggle of epic proportions."

Zander's eyes narrowed. "What would you know of this?"

"I know that you're whoring Jasmine out in town. That really is low even for the likes of you."

Jasmine! Just hearing the gentle way Lucien said the other woman's name told her they had a past history. Chemise frowned at the men as they circled each other like gladiators. "Who the hell is Jasmine and what did you do to her, you icy asshole?"

"You dare to speak to me as such," Zander snapped flashing a glare Chemise's way.

"I dare plenty, bub," she muttered glancing pointedly at his injured balls.

Zander let out a growl advancing on her and Lucien grunted and landed a solid punch to his midsection.

Reeling back, Zander glared at him, conjured a gun out of midair, and aimed it at Chemise. "Touch me again and she dies."

Lucien stepped in front of her, blocking Zander's aim, and the Isis pendant appeared in his hand. "You'll have to take me out first."

Zander froze, his eyes narrowing. "Where did you get that? he asked with a smile and pulled the trigger.

Chemise's heart stopped as Lucien let out an oof in front of her indicating that he'd been hit but resolutely stood his ground. She stepped out from behind the protection of Lucien's broad back to level a glare at Zander. His hand was shaking and there was a feverish look in his cold eyes. She lifted the pendant. "Be gone before I use this to blast you into ice cubes."

With a muttered oath, Zander disappeared into thin air.

Chemise watched him go, bemused. The most unbelievable things kept happening to her, and they were real. Trembling with shock, she turned to look at Lucien. He was leaning against the wall, a stunned look on his face as he gazed at her. He couldn't believe what she'd done either. Then she lowered her gaze to look at the bleeding gash in his arm and winced. He had been hit trying to save her and he was real.

"Are you alright?" he asked, pushing away from the wall as he approached her.

She nodded and took in his masculine scent as he closed the gap between them, breathing in his manly spices. He looked like a wounded warrior, a nerve pulsed in his jaw, and his mouth was a firm line. He was obviously feeling the same surge of adrenaline she did, but he was better at controlling it.

"I'm fine, thanks to you," she responded, trying to be strong. She winced when she noticed the bleeding knuckles on his clenched fist. "You're the one who's hurt. My God, he shot you. We've got to get you to the hospital."

"It's nothing. I'll heal, besides, we don't have the time to play doctor," he stated wiggling his eyebrows suggestively.

How could he be so blasé at a time like this? "Like hell, it's nothing. You could have been killed."

Lucien shook his head and pulled her into his arms. "No, he only wanted to injure me. Zander will only kill me as a last resort. He wants me back in the lamp so he can continue his attacks on humanity."

Chemise nestled in Lucien's strong embrace, feeling him stiffen when her hands accidently brushed against his injured arm. It might not have been a fatal injury, but it still hurt. She pulled away, not wanting to hurt him more. *Had Zander broken his ribs?*

"Wait. So, if you remain out of the lamp, there's a way you can send him back?"

"We don't have time to discuss it," he replied, taking Chemise by the arm and moving her toward the exit. "You were really worried about me?" he asked softly.

"Of course, I was," she stuttered. *Still am.* His surprise told her just how badly he'd been hurt over his years of captivity. "Obviously, being the object of concern is a new experience for you, but you'll just have to get used to it with me." She watched his slow smile emerge.

"Hurry, we must leave."

She got the picture. Zander would be back. From what Lucien had told her, the evil genie wouldn't give up this easily. She shivered, understanding the need to rush. But her friends would worry if she just disappeared on them. So, she stopped in her tracks, halting their retreat.

"I can't just leave. My friends will worry."

He sighed, his irritated gaze instantly flicking over to Janelle. "Fine. Say your goodbyes to your friends."

So, Janelle and Lucien really had met outside the shop, and he didn't give any indication of being besotted by the glamazon. Wonders would never cease. Chemise gave Lucien a bright apologetic smile making him look back at her with surprise. "I'll be right back."

"No," he murmured taking her arm. "We need to stay together tonight."

Heat rushed through her from the touch of his hand, and she gazed up at him feeling totally besotted by the sexy genie. She wanted nothing more than to spend the rest of the night with him. She'd worry about tomorrow later. "Okay," she replied feeling a blush cover her face.

"Good," he commented easing his grip on her.

Chemise felt a tremor go through her when he caressed her arm not quite letting her go. It was as if he was as afraid to lose her as she was to lose him. It was still hard to wrap her head around the fact that she could attract a stud like him, but she was going to enjoy him to the hilt. "You might as well come with me then," she commanded turning to lead the way back to the girls' table with Lucien following closely at her heels. She watched the other's startled reactions as they caught sight of her and vowed to get this over with quick. Her friends' admiring and curious glances at Lucien made her blush. She'd gone onto the dance floor with one man and come back with another. Such goings-on were so unlike her usual dull self, she'd just have to brazen it through.

"Ladies, meet Lucien..." She turned to look at her genie, not sure of his last name. Oh my, she'd slept with him and she knew nothing about him.

"Lord Lucien Darby," he continued with a little bow.

Chemise stared at him fascinated hearing the girls *oh* and *ah* behind her. He was a British Lord, how perfect. But it shouldn't have been a surprise. In his day only the wealthy and well connected were archeologists. She managed to tear her gaze off of him to look back at her beaming friends. They were born matchmakers, but she wasn't letting them meddle with this.

"We're going. I've got to leave, girls."

"I can see why," Amber agreed with a grin. "You know Lucien I'm having a cocktail party this weekend. Why don't you and Chemise attend?" She batted her eyes at Lucien.

"He's the one from the shop," Janelle muttered.

"Excellent," Miko stated, her gaze running him up and down him. "He's worth hiding. I can see why you were keeping him a secret."

Chemise blushed, wishing they would stop talking as Lucien looked at her studying her uncomfortable reaction. It was true—and she wasn't about to share him —now that she knew he was real, she had to hustle him out of here before they tipped him off to what a dating reject she was.

"Bye," she stammered, turning away.

"I'm having a party tomorrow night. Why don't you and Chemise attend. I'm sure she'd be happy to give you directions." Janelle turned her attention to Chemise and winked.

Chemise groaned at the blatant fib. There was no party, but Janelle would throw an impromptu one to insure, that Chemise had a second date. And then Amber and Miko would get in on the act and she'd be booked solid. She turned to shoot her friends a quelling look and they just gave her bright smiles in return.

"I would be happy to escort Chemise if I'm still here," Lucien replied with a nod of his head as Chemise grumbled. "But now, we really must fly."

"Have a happy birthday," they called as Lucien took her arm and rushed her out of the building.

She breathed a sigh of relief as they made a getaway even as out on the sidewalk, he turned to look at her. "Your conveyance. Where is it?"

"Um...I rode over with Janelle. Sorry. We can call a cab."

"No time," he stated, grimly.

"My cousin Jeremy is working at a bar only a few blocks away. We could walk there and then I'm sure he'd give a ride home."

Lucien shook his head, limping a little as he pulled her toward the alley, "We can't chance being seen." Once they stepped into the shelter of the alleyway, he swept her into his arms.

Her heart twisted at the sign that he was so badly hurt, and she looped an arm around his waist to steady him. The scary part was that he let her. "Let me call for an ambulance," she requested her hand slipping into her clutch purse for her cell phone.

"No doctors," he confirmed with a firm shake of his head.

She frowned at him. "Don't be such a negative Nellie, you need medical assistance."

His soft smile as he pulled her into his arms made her heart trip and she pressed against him reassured by the steady beat of his heart. Maybe genies couldn't die. It was a thought to cling to. And then she felt him place a gentle kiss on the top of her head.

"You're the only thing I need to heal me," he gritted, his arms tightening around her. "Just hang on to me, beloved, and don't let go."

"Just what kind of kinky healing do you have in mind?" she teased, gazing up at him, feeling bemused as she took in the heat in his eyes. Her lips tingled as she gazed at him, feeling sure that he was going to kiss her. He kept calling her his beloved, an endearing old-fashioned pet name and she was starting to like it a lot.

"Just think of your boudoir and you'll find out," he replied.

Her thoughts drifted to the double bed in her above the shop flat. Then his eyes darkened and he bent to kiss her, his hot mouth slanting over hers, and she opened for him, letting out a sigh. She kissed him back melting against him and then her world suddenly seemed to spin away, as the earth left her feet, making her dizzy like she was hanging in space. She opened her eyes and only saw a blur of light and motion and the feeling of flying through the air intensified. She let out a gasp squeezing her eyes shut as she gripped his shoulders tight and fought to regain her equilibrium. And then, suddenly, they were in the shop, close to the stairs leading up to her living area. She blinked up at her sexy genie in amazement at a loss for words.

She'd captured her genie. Now she just had to try to keep him. His body heated as he followed her up the stairs, making her sizzle, and she deliberately tried to slow down her racing hormones. She wanted to take her time taste him thoroughly this time around.

Chapter 5

Lucien looked around, fascinated by Chemise's charming bedroom, thinking the bright jewel tones fit her perfectly. The soft quilt covered bed gave him ideas of tumbling her onto it and taking her until they both were spent. He ached to really be able to stay with her. If he defeated Zander, and if Isis didn't pull one of her tricks, maybe it could happen. But he wasn't fooling himself that it would be easy or quick. Instead, he'd just live for today, for this woman. He turned to gaze at Chemise, sucking in a breath at the burning ache in his side and trying to conceal his pain. Instead, he decided to focus on Chemise in her natural setting and found her watching him cautiously. She'd been bold forcing his hand and her feisty attitude made him want her all the more.

He knew he was hurt, and that he should leave while he still could. But somehow, he couldn't make himself go just yet. *Hold steady, you fool.* He needed to touch her once more. He stepped toward her, and she held up her palm for him to stop. Disappointed, he froze, feeling like the fool he'd called himself, part of him dying inside. Had he misinterpreted her desire for him?

He shoved his hands in his pockets to keep from touching her and bowed stiffly. "Very well. I will not touch you."

"No, silly," she stated rolling her eyes. "I just want to remind you that we have all night and I'm not about to be rushed like I was this afternoon."

So, the little minx wanted to taste him again. Her words made all his blood surge to his groin, making him shake a little. Lord, she was going to kill him before the night was through. Death by a hard-on, he thought with a rueful twist of his mouth. Knowing it was suicide he gave her a bold look and watched a charming blush cover her as her nipples tightened under her dress. He sucked in a pained breath as his cock twitched while his head spun. Hell, it wasn't a bad way to go out. Zander would never find him here, his form would turn to dust, and Chemise would be safe.

"I'm yours to command, my lady," he managed to grit out, meaning every word. It was a line he'd learned to say for Isis, but this time, he really meant it.

"Would you like a drink?" she asked, looking toward the kitchen.

"You wouldn't have any port, would you?" he questioned, wistfully thinking of a drink he hadn't tasted in centuries. It would dull his pain, too.

"As a matter of fact," she replied with a bright smile. "Aunt Betsy sent me a bottle. Coincidence, huh." She picked up a bottle.

Lucien knew it was more than that but kept mute as she poured them each a drink of the smoky liquor. He remembered the essence of it as Betsy read to him, keeping him content over the years. This all had the makings of a great cosmic jest.

When Chemise walked up to him and handed him a glass, his fingers brushed over hers, and he watched her shudder. It set off an equal tidal wave through him. He wanted her, but he'd let her set the pace. He hoisted the glass toasting her and then took a sip savoring the flavor and warm glow it left. She was watching him so hungrily that it made him even shakier than the loss of blood. Instead, he held out the glass to her lips and she took a sip sighing.

He gazed at her lush mouth wanting to taste her charms. Then he moved toward her, felt his strength ebbing, and clutched the doorway. Fuck. He was weaker than he realized. He summoned the last of his powers to stand straight before her worried eyes and give her a regretful smile. He couldn't stay and have her go through his death. He would have to leave. "I must go, my sweet summoner."

Chemise flushed at his words and reached out to grab his arm. "Not so fast, buster."

Lucian froze, tormented by her tender touch fighting both of them. He forced himself to turn around and look at her. "Yes? Was there something else you wanted?"

"*You*, damn it!" she shouted.

He couldn't help smiling at her sassy reply, which only made her scowl at him harder. He wanted her just as much, but he balled his hands at his sides to keep from touching her.

"I didn't give you permission to leave," she stated rashly then bit her lip.

The command went through him like a shock wave, hardening his heart a little, transporting him back to his days as Isis's plaything. Then he saw her bite her lip, pain in her eyes, and relaxed. Chemise was nothing like the imperious goddess.

He smiled and reached out to gently stroke her face. Every movement was hell, but he forced himself to do it. These may be his last moments, and he wanted to enjoy them. "Know that I want nothing more than to stay, but I will not bring you danger again, beloved. I've blocked the lamp from Zander so he will not follow you here," he murmured, breaking away. "I must lead him away from you..." His head swam as he took two steps from her, and his world started to go black. "Fustian," he growled and collapsed.

Chemise let out a cry of alarm, grabbing Lucian's arm. All she got was his leather jacket as he slipped out of her grasp and crumpled to the floor. Now that he wasn't wearing his coat she could see a bleeding wound on his side through his torn tee shirt. Terrified she fell to her knees beside him her heart breaking. Damn it all, he was hurt all this time, and he'd tried to keep it from her. And stupid her she'd been too blind to notice. She tugged his shirt up to bare his wound and her stomach tightened as she saw blood oozing thickly from a hole. That bastard had shot him, but at least he was still breathing...still alive. She looked at the steady rise and fall of his chest for reassurance. Then she took in his pale face and her gut twisted. This was so not good. She couldn't lose him now.

She reached for her phone to call 911 and her hand hesitated as Lucian's words came back to her. *Modern medicine will do me more harm than good, beloved.* Was it true? Maybe there was something different about him. He needed help...now...but she didn't want to risk his life. *Jeremy!* Her wacky cousin was a part time med tech who used herbs and right about now he'd be stripping at Blue Tropical which was nearby. He'd help, she knew he would, and he was good at keeping secrets. She punched in his number on speed dial, and he picked up on the second ring.

"Hey there, Shimmy, need some cheering up?" Jeremy asked.

She smiled at her childhood nickname. "No, I need some help at my place, and bring your first aid kit."

"Lord, Shimmy, what are you getting me into now?"

"You'll see when you get here. Please hurry...it's urgent," she replied, hanging up. Then she raced to the bathroom and got a clean folded towel. Kneeling next to her unconscious lover she pressed the towel to his wound hoping to staunch the bleeding. He let out a groan in his sleep and she winced knowing she was hurting him, but she didn't let up the pressure. It was the only way she knew to save him. She didn't know how much time had gone by when she heard Jeremy's familiar tread racing up the back stairs to her.

She turned to see her six four, blond, blue eyed drop–dead gorgeous cousin race into the room dressed in a Hawaiian shirt and shorts from his bartending gig at Blue Tropical.

He dropped down on his knees at her side yanking open his medical kit. Then he gently moved her hands aside so he could check Lucien's wounds. He pulled back the towel and let out a low whistle. "Damn, cuz. This is the dude I tossed out of Blue Tropical earlier tonight. Did he bother you, too? Did you shoot him?"

She gave him a shocked look. "Of course, I didn't shoot him. How could you say..."

"It brought you out of shock, didn't it?" he asked sassily, giving her a quick grin.

And then his words hit her. "What do you mean you kicked him out of that dive you work in?" She gave him a stern look visually warning him not to lie to her. "What the blazes was he doing there?"

"Tailing my girl," he replied with a frown. "At least, I thought he was. I had Mack and Chris toss him out."

"Dumb and dumber," she muttered, remembering yelling at them for talking Jeremy into working at the seedy dive. As far as she was concerned, he was wasting his potential.

"Hey, they're not so bad," he stated with a shrug. "Anyway, when I went out to look for them, I found them sleeping in the alley and Jasmine was gone."

"Jasmine," she speculated seeing Jeremy's face flush.

"So, what happened to him?" he asked, ripping open Lucien's torn shirt and then rolling him to look for an exit wound.

She let him avoid the question, wondering where Jasmine fit into this and irked that Lucien had been chasing her. No doubt the other woman was drop dead gorgeous so why was he wasting his time with her? She put that question aside as Jeremy rolled Lucien to the side exposing a gaping wound. She winced when she saw the bulging blister on Lucian's back. The skin was actually white around the blood red center.

"What the hell?" Jeremy asked, probing it. "This looks like frost bite."

It fit with Zander's icy vibes. Could the man have actually used some kind of otherworldly weapon? She watched as the blister popped open as Jeremy poked at it, and an oblong sphere of ice dropped into Jeremy's hand followed by a trickle of blood.

"Now I've seen everything," he stated shaking his head. "An ice bullet."

Chemise gazed at it in disbelief as he held it in his hand. That just wasn't possible, but seeing...then again Lucien was from another time. The room began to spin as she looked from the ice bullet to Lucien's oozing wound. My god, no wonder he'd been cold. She thought she was going to faint for a moment as her head swam.

Jeremy gave her a look. "If you're going to puke, go in the bathroom."

She shook her head, steadying her breathing as she braced herself against the foot of the bed. "No. I'm fine."

"So, what happened?" Jeremy asked.

She saw the curiosity on her cousin's face and wondered how much to divulge. It was up to her to keep Lucien's secrets while he was unconscious. As close to the truth as possible was probably the best bet. Less chance of getting confused that way. She took a deep breath. "We were at the bar, and someone took a pot shot at him. I didn't know he was hurt until he collapsed on me."

"So that's why you didn't call 911?" he questioned. "But why didn't you when you realized he was hurt?" He looked suspicious.

Hearing his doubtful tone, she had to force herself not to look away. Jeremy could handle the truth. Hell, he believed in weirder stuff than she did, but she couldn't tell him. "Right." She hoped he'd let the subject drop.

"And the frozen bullet?" he asked, his eyebrow arching with doubt.

"Who knows," she stated defensively. "I didn't shoot it. Maybe it's some new kind of weapon."

He let out a snort as he reached for some gauze. "Yeah, right. If it was a silver bullet I'd have guessed werewolf. But that's not it." He pressed the gauze against Lucien's wound and gave her a probing look. "What the heck is he, Chemise? And how much trouble are you in?"

Well, hell, she didn't need or appreciate that 'how much trouble' crack. It wasn't like she asked him to help her that often. Yeah, she'd rescued a few lost souls, animal and human, that she'd asked him to treat for free, but she hadn't done any lately. "Who says I'm in trouble?" she shot back.

"Then why all the secrecy and the blackout curtains? I know you like to take moon baths."

She looked at the closed drapes and frowned. She should have known he'd pick up on that. She could fob him off with a lie, but it stuck on her tongue. She might need someone in her corner just in case and Jeremy was her closest confidante. She'd just have to trust him with the truth. "I'm not sure how much trouble we're in."

His gaze sharpened. "Okay…" he started slowly. "Tell me the rest… who or what is this?"

She hated the concern she'd put in Jeremy's eyes. The last thing she wanted to do was to worry him, or have him call her overprotective parents. They'd be over here in a shot, and then what would happen to Lucien? Her fond gaze lingered on Lucien, and she sighed. "And he's a genie."

"Shit no wonder he was after Jasmine."

She felt shaken as she looked at his grim expression. Something told her she wasn't going to like what he had to say. "Why do you say that?"

"She's from his time."

She gulped. "You mean a female genie. I didn't know there were any."

He shook his head. "No, she's one of Isis's fallen handmaidens."

"Then they knew each other…"

"Maybe intimately," Jeremy filled in grimly.

She heard his jealous tone and felt it, too, but she knew that any other man she dated would have a past. She had Barry to live down. She couldn't blame Lucien for his indiscretions. "I'm sure they're both facing difficult circumstances we can't even comprehend. Are you going to be okay?" she asked Jeremy.

He nodded. "Yeah. I'll suck it up as usual. I don't know why she won't tell me all her secrets."

"Give her time," Chemise replied looking fondly at Lucien.

"I'm not sure what kind of metabolism he has so his treatment will have to be a bit touch and go," Jeremy said as he started to tend to Lucien's wound.

"Do you think he's going to be okay?" she asked worriedly.

He looked up and gave her a rueful smile. "Don't worry, I'm not going to try to kill off my competition."

She blushed feeling flustered. "I didn't mean to imply."

He chuckled. "Got you. You can feel his aura as well as I can. You two are meant to be together."

Now it was her turn to give him doubtful eyes. "Come again? Since when can either of us feel auras?"

He shook his head. "It runs in the blood, Shimmy. Why do you think Aunt Betty left you this crumbling edifice?"

"I was her favorite niece," she replied feeling doubtful. She and Betty had always both loved old things, in fact they seemed to have a lot in common.

"You've got to let go and open yourself up to your potential," Jeremy stated going back to work on Lucien.

"Now you're starting to sound like a high school guidance counselor," she added with a wry smile. "Mine told me to be a teacher if I remember correctly."

"It's good advice, but not a schoolteacher. Maybe a psychic mentor."

"So, now you believe in all the woo-woo otherworldly junk?" she asked, and the look in his eyes said yes. "You do." Maybe he was right. She hadn't believed in genies before today and now she was in love with one.

"Come on help me get him warm," he stated reaching for the covers.

She helped him tuck Lucien into her bed and then turned to Jeremy. "He's shivering."

"He's cold and getting colder by the minute," Jeremy added. "And I'm not sure how to treat this. The best thing you can do is to keep him warm. The rest is up to fate, and you," he commented looking into her eyes.

She felt the truth in his words. "How?"

"I'd suggest shared bodily warmth, for starters," he replied with a wink.

"Great," she murmured as he turned to go.

"You want me to send down some bouncers from the club to stand guard outside the building?" he offered.

The thought of the muscle bound bouncers guarding an antique shop was almost comical until she thought of them scaring off her customers. And Lucien had said that Zander couldn't track them here. Something about his lamp being hidden. "I don't think so. Just lock up on your way out and the first-class alarm system aunt Betty installed should do the rest."

"You sure about that?" he asked.

She knew he wanted to protect her, but she didn't want this precious time alone with Lucien to be interrupted by bouncers. "I'll be fine."

"If you insist," he stated after a moment. "I'll lock up on my way out but call me right away if anything goes wrong."

After Jeremy's footsteps faded, she gazed down at Lucien sensing that she was his only hope of survival. Jeremy's words of shared bodily warmth echoed through her mind. Was it really so simple? Without hesitation she shed her clothes and pulled back the covers. Her fascinated gaze couldn't help traveling up his nude body, admiring him. If anyone told her yesterday that she'd have a hunk like this in her bed tonight she'd have laughed at them. Things like this didn't happen to her.

Then she saw Lucien shiver and panicked. Was he getting colder? She reached out to touch his forehead and he grabbed her hand in a blur and jerked her across him. She landed with a startled gasp, sprawled across his hard chilled body. Hearing his teeth chattering her heart went out to him. But then a glance at his face contorted with rage alarmed her. A moment later, he rolled them over, pinning her beneath him, his hands gripping her arms with a bruising force. Damn he was having a nightmare and didn't know what he was doing.

"Damn you, goddess. I'll not be your chew toy."

She let out a shocked gasp when his thigh thrust between her legs. She winced, realizing he thought she was Isis. A surge of jealousy swept through her. Was this just a preliminary to their usual sex games? She'd give herself to him but not under the guise of another woman, goddess or not. It hurt that he didn't instinctively know her.

"No, damn you," he growled eyes squeezed tight.

He was fighting Isis off in his own way. That thought made Chemise relax and smile but that didn't make this any less a nightmare for Lucien. She had to get through to him, relax him. She managed to raise one arm up as he loosened his grip and rubbed it gently down his back. "It's Chemise, Lucien," she crooned softly. "You're safe." She felt him shudder, his skin warming a little under her palm and to her relief he went limp, relaxing as he rolled off her. *Thank heavens!*

But in the next moment he was shivering again, his teeth chattering again, as the cold resumed. She could feel the sheets grow ice cold around them. Well hell! Zander was trickier than she'd figured. *Shared bodily warmth, stupid. Do it!* She snuggled close to him covering him with her own body trying to warm him. His arms wrapped around her holding her fast, making her breasts rub against his chest and warming her from the inside out. Pressed against him she absorbed his scent, his aura, trying to open herself up to the powers Jeremy claimed they shared. Warmth and light seemed to surround them in a pink haze, and she smiled. Even if it was only her vivid imagination, she liked it. She laid her head against his shoulder hearing his beating heart, trying her best to memorize her sexy genie. For all she knew he'd make good on his threat to leave her come sunrise. And even though she didn't want to do it, she knew she'd have to let him go. She wasn't a user like Isis, and she wasn't going to treat him like a plaything.

She felt his cock start to stir against her abdomen and smiled. At least one part of him responded to her instinctively. She doubted he got that rock hard for the imperious goddess. She rubbed her leg over it and felt a wave of warmth go through both of them. From chest to groin he actually seemed to glow. Wow! Was that just her imagination? She tried it again just to be sure and he let out a sexy grumble, welcome heat surging through him. Was this what he meant by her being the medicine he needed to heal him? No doubt it was part of the spell Isis had put him under. That thought was enough to make her frown, and she stopped. He immediately started to shiver again.

Damn, she could save him, but it would mean sexually using him the way the goddess had done. She couldn't do that, could she? *Am I really using him, since I care for him?*

"Please," he moaned in his sleep.

Instantly, she flowed over him again with her body, then her hand slipped down between them to cover his straining cock with her hand. He pulsed to life under her touch, and she planted a gentle kiss on his still unresponsive mouth and the cold from his breath almost took hers away. Still, it didn't deter her. Then his mouth softened just a little under hers like a marble statue coming to life, his breath warming. Having thawed him out she started to kiss her way down his body. She scattered butterfly kissed over his chest and stopped to lap at first one flat male nipple and then the other making him groan a little under his breath.

Satisfied she dipped down, licking his washboard abs until she came to his belly button. Then she dipped her tongue inside, tasting his earthy flavor and he muttered incoherently, his hips flexing off the mattress and surge of heat going through him. It was working.

With a grateful smile she moved south, skipping the part that was straining for her, ignoring his bobbing red cock to instead kiss his feet. He wriggled his toes as if ticklish and she smiled. Then she tongued her way up his muscled calves heat following in her wake. She stopped to pay special attention to the tender curve at the back of his knees, making his legs twitch. Feeling naughty she made her way to his inner thighs tracing damp shapes with her tongue that made him shake and his cock jerk and pump in the air. Only then, when his heat was rising did she shimmy up his straining body to suck the head of his cock into her mouth like a lollypop. His hips lifted off the bed as a groan tore out of him, and his hands went to tangle in her hair. That roused him a little.

She pulled back to tease at the tendon under the head of his cock and then suck his balls. When she finished teasing him, she licked the drop of pre cum off his slit and then opened wide to take him in. Savoring him she made gentle love to him with her mouth, feeling him flame with heat. Taking him even deeper into her mouth, she forced herself to breathe deeper and relax as she tried to deep-throat him. He pulsed like life itself in her mouth as she bobbed wetly up and down his purple veined shaft throbbing in her. It was like fucking him with her mouth and she did a thorough job of it, drawing every ounce of essence out of him. The room seemed to glow alabaster pink around them as their aura's blended and he jerked in her mouth. Every pulse made her pussy quiver, her honey wetting the sheets.

Feeling closer than ever to him, like they were cosmically linked, she cupped his balls, squeezing a little as she took him deeper. He groaned jerking, his balls drawing up, and her sex rippled with pre orgasm. What the heck, what she did to him made her twice as horny. Deciding not to question it she drew harder on him, feeling his cock spasm as he spurted into her mouth and an orgasm tore through her at the same time. Stunned, she drank down every drop of tribute that Lucien's body gave her and then surged up his body to cuddle his now warm body.

He turned to her, cocooning her in his warmth, and they slept.

Chapter 6

Someone lying on her doorbell woke Chemise with a start the next morning. Her bleary eyes stung in the bright morning light when she opened them. Good grief, how late had she slept in? Then she remembered the events of last night. Lucien! The ice bullet. The way she'd pleasured both of them with her mouth. Lying still she tried to come to terms with all that had occurred. The comforting feel of Lucien's warm body spooned against her ass told her he was fine. Actually, the heat and feel of his morning erection pressing against her bottom was enough to make her blush and press back against him, her mood brightening. She hadn't dreamt that up. She'd really ravaged a genie to save him. Then the moron on the doorbell gave it another extended poke, and she groaned. Seduction would have to wait until later. It could be Jeremy, but he probably would have called, and anyway, he knew where she hid the key.

Whoever the ringer was, he was determined. The fact that the racket didn't rouse Lucien was worrying. She rolled over to look at him and saw that he was sleeping deeply, a mysterious smile on his face. "Wonder who he's dreaming about," she grumbled to herself, rolling out of bed. The thought that it better be her was petty, but she couldn't help it. The cool morning air hit her warm skin and goosebumps broke out. Shivering, she reached for her old terry cloth robe tying it tightly around her waist. The first item on her to do list was to get rid of the pest at the doorbell, the second was to wake up Lucien with a little morning delight and then fix them both a nourishing breakfast.

She padded down the stairs, her head aching, when the pest kept ringing the doorbell. Then he pounded on the door, and she grumbled under her breath. *Whoever this is, is dead meat.* She reached for her back door and tore it open, determined to give the pest a piece of her mind and froze when she saw Barry standing on her doorstep in the rain, looking rather dashing in his trench coat and carefully styled hair. Image was everything to the snob. The mocking gaze Barry raked over her sleep rumpled appearance clearly said he thought she was a slob, and it pissed her off. She knew damned well he slept in cowboy jammies and a hair wrap, so his do wouldn't get mussed.

"Nice try," Barry stated snidely flicking an amused glance at her robe. "But I'm not likely to be swayed from my mission by that get up."

Her chin rose at his insulting words even though she knew she probably looked like hell. Who the hell did he think he was to be talking to her that way? "What the hell do you want, Barry?"

"My things," he replied trying to step past her and into the building.

She quickly moved to block his entry and saw him scowl. His things added up to a toothbrush and a change of clothes both of which he'd left here a year ago. Was that panic she saw on his face? "Go away, I have company."

"Don't give me that," he spat back, reaching out to shove her away. "Nobody's going to shack up with you. Not since I spread the word around that you're frigid."

She knew he was deliberately trying to throw her off her game, and she refused to give him the satisfaction. "I don't give a damn what you think. Leave before I have you thrown out."

"By whom?" he asked with a smirk.

"Me," Lucien cut in from the stairway.

Chemise watched Barry's eyes widen with shock and she winced. She really didn't need these kinds of complications. She turned to tell Lucien so and gulped when she saw he only wore a towel wrapped around his hips. The bulge of his manhood was clear as he descended the stairs toward them. She watched him, fascinated, and Barry faded into oblivion.

"Chemise," Barry hissed. "What the hell do you think you're playing at? If you hired this impotent gigolo to make me jealous, you wasted your money."

Chemise watched Lucien's furious reaction to the statement. It was a cruel reminder of what he'd been to Isis. She whirled on Barry, her outrage erupting. "Lucien is more man than you could ever hope to be, you asshole. Now get out of here before I try my new Judo moves on you."

"Bitch," he hissed drawing back his hand to slap her.

Chemise was so startled by the violent action, she hesitated for a moment. Then she turned the tables on him, grabbing his hand and tugging him off balance so that he fell on his face. Then Lucien was there in the blink of an eye.

He growled, picking Barry up by the scruff of his neck and threw him out the door.

Barry landed on the alley's wet concrete with an *oof*. "I'll sue you both."

"Touch Chemise again, and you will die," Lucien stated with grim promise.

Chemise watched Barry pale in reaction. He knew Lucien meant it. She picked up the briefcase that Barry had dropped in her doorway and tossed it at him. "And take your things with you."

He tried to reach for it, and it popped open, documents from the collection they'd been working on fluttering to the wet pavement with a thud.

"What in the hell are you doing with these?" she asked, and Barry glowered at her in reply. She saw the guilty look on his face, and it came to her. "You were going to plant these in my place," she stated and smiled when his shifty eyes looked away.

"You can't prove a damned thing, bitch," he grumbled gathering the papers and shoving them back in the briefcase.

"You will not speak to her as such," Lucien commanded stepping into the alley in only the towel.

Barry jumped to his feet and turned to run, smacking into a wall instead. "What the fuck are you doing to me?" he wailed.

Lucien grabbed his shoulder, pulling him around to face them. "You will apologize."

Barry's face was red, mutinous, but as he looked at Lucien he calmed. Then he glanced at Chemise and sighed. "I'm sorry Chemise. I didn't have any choice."

Chemise took in his abrupt change in amazement. It had to be something about Lucien's power that made him cooperate against his will. "Just don't try it again," she answered, puzzled.

"Be gone," Lucien stated snapping his fingers.

Barry blinked as if waking from a trance and looked at the two of them in confusion. "What just happened?"

"You decided to play fair and stop trying to throw me under the bus," she replied wryly.

Barry frowned at her. "It doesn't sound like me."

Then Lucien waved his hand and Barry vanished.

Chemise gasped and turned to look at Lucien. "What did you do to him?"

"Sent him home."

She relaxed a little knowing that he hadn't killed Barry. He might be an ass, but he didn't deserve to die. "Good."

Lucien stood there looking back at her, chilled by more than the morning wind. Did she care that much about her first love? Was he too late? "Don't worry, I won't hurt your boyfriend," he stated dryly and saw her sudden scowl in reaction. It made him feel better, but he needed the words.

"Then get out of the wind before you catch pneumonia," she demanded stepping up to him and placing her hand on his chest. "Because *you're* my boyfriend."

He groaned when she cupped him with her hand and squeezed. "Am I?"

"You know it, stud," she replied with a smile. "And if you say Barry's my boyfriend anymore, you won't get tasted."

"Like you did last night?" he asked, surging into her hand. Her fingers hesitated for a moment as if she was embarrassed, and he watched a blush cover her face.

"You remember that?".

"Don't think I'll ever forget it," he commented with a grin. "That is not unless you do an even better job of it now."

"Bad man," she stated squeezing him in punishment.

"Very," he agreed scooping her up in his arms. "What say we get out of these wet things and into a warm bed?"

She clung to him. "Should you be exerting yourself after your injury?"

He smiled down at her as he carried her up the stairs. He'd never felt better, and it was because of her. "I'll let you know if you need to take over," he teased. "After the way you tossed Barry, I see that you can take care of yourself."

"Thanks," she replied with a smile.

He watched her flush with pride and knew that he'd found his love prize. Then the air conditioning kicked in and she shivered in his arms in her wet robe. He cursed himself for being an insensitive prick and bypassed the bed heading into the bathroom instead.

"Hey, where are you going?" she protested, glancing longingly at the bed. "I was going to taste you."

He shouldered his way into the bathroom and turned on the shower. "First things first," he replied, standing her on her feet. She wobbled a little and gazed up at him with adoration in her eyes. He felt honored as he slid the robe off her body baring her curves. She blushed again, trembling a little and he knew it wasn't from the cold. He felt the same call of lust. He shed his towel and quirked a finger saying, "Come here, Chemise."

She walked into his arms, and he held her tight enjoying the feel of her soft skin tucked tight against his body. He was still shaken by finding her in danger. He held her close, feeling possessive.

Her breasts tantalized him, the nipples hardening, rubbing against his chest, and making his mouth water with the need to taste her sexy strawberry tits. Hell, she tasted sweet all over, he knew, and the knowledge of what she'd done to save him made him even more determined never to let her go. He luxuriated in the sensual feel of Chemise in his arms, as water cascaded over and around them. She closed her eyes in seeming bliss, pressing closer and he responded, his cock going rigid against her hot body. He bit back a groan knowing that he would never get enough of this redheaded siren. Then he oh–so–slowly let her slide down his damp body, hearing her whimper with need before she stood on wobbly legs in front of him. He smiled down at her as she moaned.

"You're a tease, Lucien," she commented, rubbing her nipples across his chest.

"Takes one to know one," he replied with a groan spreading his feet a shoulders length apart so that he could pull her hot wet curves firmly against him.

"Yes," she cried grinding against him.

He let her get away with it for a moment of ecstasy before he gazed down at her masterfully, and gave her saucy bottom a sharp wet smack. Only one of them could be master.

"Ouch," she mumbled coyly and grinned up at him.

He watched a blush cover her body and knew that he was going down...on her...but first, he had a few rules to enforce. "Behave yourself, my lady."

She smiled. "I'm not sure I can do that. You seem to have brought out the temptress in me."

He smiled back knowing that it was true. Her lush lips were tempting him, begging him to kiss her. He had a maniacal genie after him, and a pissed off goddess who'd like to see him dead and he didn't care. All he wanted to do was make Chemise his. He was in trouble, deep.

"So, what are you waiting for?" she asked pertly.

He shook his head. She was begging for a spanking, but he had other things to accomplish first. "Patience is a virtue," he replied reaching for a soapy sponge. He swirled it over Chemise's lovely body, paying special attention to her tempting tits, watching them tremble in his wake as she inhaled a shaky breath. The scent of strawberries filled the room, and he smiled. He'd never eat a strawberry again without picturing her. He rubbed the sponge over her nipples again slowly watching them bead as her pulse kicked up a beat. And then his beloved's knees wobbled, and she let out a cry, leaning into him.

"Oh, baby, do that again."

"Soon," he stated swirling it down around her belly and lower. She let out a moan as he dropped the sponge and combed his fingers through her sex, tweaking her clit. She gasped, her body glowing as her cunt tightened around his fingers. He held her tight until she came back to earth.

Chemise came back to earth in Lucien's arms as the shower pounded down on her. She turned to lay her head on Lucien's shoulder, enjoying his touch, the slippery feel of his body against hers. She'd wanted a dream lover, but he was way beyond her expectations. "That was..."

"Sexy," he filled in.

"Earth shattering." She lapped at his nipples, drinking a droplet of water off his skin. His cock pressed hot, and hard, against her slick thigh. "It's your turn," she replied stepping close enough to let his erection slip between her thighs. It rubbed hot and tantalizing against her. She wrapped both hands around his hot cock to hold him. Chemise sank down to capture him in her mouth. She drew on him, taking it deeper in her mouth. She sucked, breathing deep, and felt him tremble and give her everything he had. She drew on him, draining him, and licking him clean. She looked up to find Lucien looking at her with wonder.

He pulled her to her feet. "It's just like you did me last night."

"You remember that?" she asked with a gasp. He'd been unconscious. How could he remember anything? But they did share a special bond. The knowing masculine look on his face made her blush.

He nodded. "I remember every exquisite moment. Where did you learn the technique?"

She blushed at the question, but answered. "My personal library. You're the first chance I've have to put it into practice." His gaze smoldered at the last statement.

"And I'd better be the only."

His possessive statement thrilled her, but she wasn't sure he was here for the long haul. After all he'd talked about leaving her last night. She saw his displeased expression and knew her silence bugged him. Good. It might be smart to keep him guessing. Her eyes widened when he slapped off the shower, growled, and bodily pulled her out of the shower.

"Now get this, Chemise. I won't share you with anyone. You're mine," he insisted, bending to kiss her.

"I'm yours," Chemise replied with a sigh, as his mouth claimed hers. She rubbed her tingling nipples against him, drawn into his possessive embrace. His tongue swept into her mouth mating with hers as his hands swept down her slick back to cup her ass and squeeze. She moaned, pressing tight to him, her sex throbbing as his cock stirred.

He broke the kiss to rub his manhood against her. "You belong to me, Chemise, say it," he hissed.

"I belong to you," she agreed, with a pleasured whimper, rocking against him watching his whiskey eyes darken.

Then he walked over to a chair by the window, sat down, and quirked his finger. "Come here, beloved."

She knew in a heartbeat that he meant to spank her, and her heart raced. Did she want him to discipline her? A big part of her said *hell, yeah.*

He sat there quietly, waiting for her, his eyes eating her up. With a sigh of surrender, she walked toward him looking deep into his eyes. Then she was there, his body heat warming her as they touched, and he took her wrist tugging her gently over his lap.

"You'll take it over my knee."

Her tummy quivered as she sprawled across his hard lap, and she felt the insistent throb of his hard cock pressed against her thigh. Her already creamy pussy clenched knowing he was so near yet so far away. She wanted him...bad. "But I wanted to taste you," she protested in vain, embarrassed because she knew it was a delaying tactic.

"All in good time, Chemise," he stated rubbing his hand over her bottom. "You placed yourself in my hands, and you're going to get it."

Chemise felt a flutter of excitement and alarm, at the size of his reach, as the heat of his huge hand just lying across her ass. She trembled, her nipples budding, achingly hard, her stiff clit jutting out, throbbing. She moaned as it pressed against his thigh. When Lucien raised his palm and gave her a quick smack, she whimpered at the sting and speed. "But I wasn't ready..."

He swatted her again, this time a little harder. "Ready now?" he teased.

Chemise's sex creamed. "Oh my God, yes," she gasped.

She trembled as he rained teasing blows across her bottom and arched, hoping for more. He was toying with her, making her ache for a harder paddling. "Please," she wailed. He stopped, and she let out a sob of frustration.

"Want more?" he asked.

She wriggled, trying to inflame him, and nodded.

"Say it," he demanded.

"Please, I want more."

"More, what?" He caressed a scorch path over her stinging ass with his fingertips. "Do you require a proper spanking, Chemise?"

"Oh, yes," she replied arching into his touch. "Spank me properly."

"Excellent." He drew back his hand.

Her sex wept for him, trembling as he spanked her harder. She whimpered with need and arched up for him, taking them as foreplay. He caught her on the bottom of her ass with his open palm, driving her into his thigh. She cried out with delight. Her stiff clit rubbing against his hard thigh, making her hungry sex spasm.

"Like that, do you?" he asked, pleased, doing it again.

She shrieked with pleasure. "Yes," she admitted, shuddering, the contact with her clit increasing.

"Now, be a good girl, and reach down and play with your clit, Chemise. I want you to come while I spank you."

Embarrassed by the sultry command, she hesitated, even while she ached to obey.

"Now," he commanded, his open swat catching the bottom of her ass harder, driving her higher.

She gasped and did as he said, her hand rushing to her clit, while he heated up the spanking, catching the bottom of her ass over and over again, making her moan. Her body tightened, and her sex spasmed, her ass throbbing as she came with a shriek. Her hand fell away from her clit. Lucien's hand replaced it, his rough fingertip pressing her clit, his fingers filling her cunt, his little finger dipping into her juices and pressing into her anus. She gasped, as he loved her in his hot kinky way, wringing out and extended orgasm, which tore through her until she was limp.

When it was over, she lay across his lap, totally drained.

Lucien pulled her up, taking her into his arms, rocking her. "We have to set a few ground rules, Chemise."

Chemise leaned against him, loving the low rumble of his voice, his racing heartbeat, and his manly essence. His cock was still rock hard under her hot ass, reminding her of what they'd just done, and what was to come. "Rules?"

His hand cupped her breast. "Un huh, three little rules. First, I want you naked and ready for me when I say so."

Her nipple beaded as he fanned a fingertip over the tingling peak, making her gasp. They were still fully dressed, if you didn't count her panties about her ankles and she was putty in his hands, and she wouldn't have it any other way. Nibbling his ear as he gave her nipple a little pinch, she complained. "In essence, your own love slave."

He smiled. "I've never had one before. Do you mind?"

"No, baby," she replied, with a tender smile hoping to heal him.

"It's Lucien or sir when I'm disciplining you. When we have our sessions, you'll comply."

She didn't quite like his pleasure with giving orders. "Or?"

"You'll get lots more spankings."

Chemise's bare bottom burned against his lap. "Like that's much of a threat. I loved it, and you know it." She snuggled closer. "I've got a demand of my own."

"Such as?" he asked.

"I get to taste you soon, and then as much as I want."

He groaned, his hand slipping between her legs to touch her wet sex.

Chemise cried out when Lucien's index finger homed in on her stiff clit. He pressed the sensitized nub, and she moaned, instantly throbbing with arousal again. He tweaked it, and she muffled her cries against his broad chest, as she came. When she recovered, she peered up at him. "If this is how you conduct your negotiations, no wonder you get your own way."

He chuckled. "I'm a man who knows what he wants." He kissed her. "Next, you'll be bare and open for me when I need you."

Her eyes widened as she gazed at him. He wasn't kidding. "Another stone age thing?"

"You got it, beloved." He spread her legs his little finger probing her ass. "Oh, and fourth, we need to keep your tight little rosebud lubed for my cock."

Her breath caught as both her ass and pussy quivered. She'd been afraid the prospect of anal sex would turn him off. It was in chapter six of the book she was reading. "We do?"

"I'll insist on it," he demanded, kissing her hard.

Chemise gave herself to him, kissing him back. His tongue slipped inside her mouth to mate with hers. She was secretly thrilled by his primitive demands. A hot and heavy affair was just what she needed.

"I think that's a yes," he stated with a laugh, his arms going around her.

"Oh yeah," she mumbled, against him, listening to his heartbeat race. At least she knew she wasn't the only one affected by this lust.

"One more thing, if Zander comes back, you will do as I say and be exiled for your own good."

Her heart chilled at the casual way he said it. Zander had almost succeeded in killing him. That couldn't be allowed to happen again. "And let you fight this battle alone. I don't think so."

He frowned. "I knew you were going to be difficult. I can't fight him if I'm worried about protecting you."

She let out a sigh, relenting...a little. "Fine."

"Good," he replied.

She relaxed seeing that he'd bought her demure act. "So, what's next?"

He smiled, and ran a hand down her body. "Some things are better taken slowly."

Chemise burned for him. "But not me," she complained.

He smiled. "Show me what you want."

It was all she needed to hear. She wriggled on his lap reaching for him and accidentally pressed his groin earning a pained groan.

"Easy, love," he murmured, reaching out to steady her.

"You wouldn't have spanked me so hard if you wanted easy." She burned, slipping off his lap. Feeling like a predator, she raked a hungry glance over him.

"In a hurry, are you?" he teased.

"You ought to know, you started the fire." His well-defined muscles, tight male nipples, and six pack abs were irresistible. She leaned forward to lap at one flat brown disc, and it beaded under her tongue. Yum, he was delicious.

She licked a path to his other nipple, and then sunk down to taste his six-pack, and dip her tongue inside his naval. She swirled it around making him growl and jerk. He was ticklish there, excellent. She did it again. His growl made her glance up at him for approval. The heat in his gaze made her cream, then she looked down at his cock.

Chemise gazed at his cock for a heartbeat, admiring it. It was huge, long, thick, and heavy enough to hang down at his thigh. The red head was blunt and mushroom shaped. Her cool fingers ran down the hot silky length of him, and he hissed, his cock's head rising up. A drop of precum beaded on the slit. She leaned forward to lap at it and sighed with pleasure, feeling Lucien shudder. Suddenly, she found her female power again. She lapped at his slit again, loving the salty male taste of him, as he leaked more cum, making him groan.

"Lick the head," Lucien ordered.

She didn't need further urging as she swirled her tongue around his cock's hot velvety head, stealing another drop of cum off the slit.

"Shit," he bit out trembling. "Suck on the head."

After another lick, she opened her mouth and took him inside, only able to contain a little. The erotic feel of his hard throbbing cock her mouth was addictive. She sucked, and both her hands wrapped firmly around his shaft. He hissed, his cock twitching under her ministrations. She could feel him tightening getting ready to come, and her pussy quivered with excitement. She wanted it all.

"That's it, beloved, give it up now."

She gave him a mew of disappointment, her mouth still keeping him. He gently rubbed his thumb over her cheek. "Now," he commanded gently.

Reluctantly, she let the head slip out of her mouth, giving his cock a final lick of departure. He drew her to her feet, and pulled her into his arms. Chemise went with a hunger, burning as his mouth claimed hers. Then, he was carrying her across the room to place her on the bed. He came down on top of her, and she welcomed his weight, the promise of his possession.

He broke the kiss to string a line of kisses down her throat, over her collarbone, to one hard nipple. He took the bud into his hot mouth drawing on it, making her squirm with need as she felt the pull deep inside her. Then he moved onto the other, teasing her to distraction, drawing the sensitive bud hard into his mouth, making her cry out. Arching up, into his hot mouth, she ran her hands over his hot back.

He moved on to scatter kissed down her abdomen, and she burned. When he moved down, settling between her spread legs, she couldn't help blushing. Her breath caught in her throat, and she tried to pull him up, to no avail, Lucien would not be moved.

"Let me," he whispered.

When his hot tongue rested against her swollen clit, Chemise's eyes rolled back in her head, and she let out a shriek. It was that earth shattering. Pushing her hungry sex against his mouth, she was lost to ecstasy. Lucien began to lap at her, his tongue teasing her, before pressing into her quivering pussy. She rolled on the bed, but his hands reached up to hold her hips fast. There was no getting away from the pleasure he was making her feel, and she didn't want to escape as she throbbed with arousal under his rough and talented tongue.

He'd already made her come so many times, but she felt the pressure build inside her again. Then he took the bud of her clit into his mouth, and drew on it. Chemise exploded, her sex convulsing empty. Lucien surged up her body and thrust into her in one quick motion. Chemise cried out at the invasion as he finished taking her virginity, and Lucien sealed her mouth with his, silencing her cry.

He lay still, breathing hard on top of her, his body tense as he waited for her newly opened pussy to become accustomed to him. She closed her eyes, feeling stunned by the sensation of his huge cock filling her. Her after-spasms rippled at them, making her gasp, and him growl. She smiled up at him and rocked against him, only to feel his huge cock delve deeper inside.

"Easy, babe, take it slow." He slowly started to withdraw, and then rock back into her.

Chemise arched up to meet his strokes, taking more of him. He was huge. Her eyes widened with surprise. "More," she moaned, as his hot cock filled her. He rocked into her, harder and deeper, until they both gasped. "Oh yes." She wrapped her legs around him, forcing him deeper, and winced, but didn't let him go.

He lost control, surging into her, again and again, until she tightened coming, shouting his name. He surged into her once more and exploded, coming hard and fast tight against her cervix. When Lucien eased off of her and pulled her close, Chemise snuggled against him, sated and dazzled. It was everything she'd dreamed of.

Amelia January paced her office in frustration as Barry, her slave, sat there shaken and damp after his encounter with Chemise. He'd failed her and she was this close to killing him, but she knew she needed to use restraint. She turned to glare at the sniveling pretty boy. "Are you telling me that she was with a man?"

"I'd never lie to you, Amelia," he stated, gazing up at her with adoration.

She basked in the glow of his unconditional adoration. And why shouldn't he idolize her? Soon, others would when she toppled Isis from her throne and took her rightful place in the heavens. "Of course, you wouldn't," she replied softening her tone just for him and he relaxed. The look of fear vanishing from his face. "Did he recognize you?"

"How could he? I've never seen him before."

"That's odd. From what you said, our Chemise doesn't date much."

He smirked. "She's the original old maid."

"Yet you saw a naked man in her house."

He nodded. "Well, he was actually wearing a towel."

The knowledge that Chemise wasn't alone coupled with Isis's protection couldn't be good. Could Isis have sent one of her soldiers to guard the girl? "Describe him."

He frowned. "I'd rather not, it was very embarrassing."

Her hands balled into fists at his whiny answer, but she forced herself not to hit him. Instead, she walked up next to him pressing her body against his still damp one. "Please."

He heaved a heavy sigh. "Okay. He was tall with dark hair and brown eyes. And he talked with a British accent."

A shock went through her as she heard Lucien's description. Fuck. Not one of Isis's guards, but her sexual plaything, her genie. If they were together with a direct conduit to Isis, she was lost. Unless...

"You're dismissed," she commanded, stepping away from Barry. "Go get yourself cleaned up." She ignored the wounded look he gave her and walked to the bar to pour herself a stiff drink.

Chapter 7

Lucien was working in the back of Chemise's shop trying to help her sort inventory while contemplating his next move. Chemise was occupied with customers in the next room giving him plenty of time to think. It all came back to defeating Zander. It was the only way he could find to a happy ending. He heard Chemise's voice as she talked excitedly about an antiquity and smiled. Lucky for him she liked old things. Then he sighed and hefted another dusty box of Aunt Betty's finds. According to Chemise they'd been gathering dust for decades in storeroom. What he gathered, although Chemise would never tell him so, was that she couldn't afford to pay the storeroom's rent any longer. If only he were still wealthy. As the heir to the Duke of Lundy he once had a fortune. But he didn't regret losing what he'd once had. All he wanted to hang onto was Chemise.

The fact that Zander had been so put off by the Isis pendant made him wonder. Perhaps he could conjure his own and use it to lure the bastard out and kill him. He twisted to set down the box in an area that Chemise had cleared and stifled a groan as his newly mended wound reopened. Damnation. His hand went to his side to check and came away with a few streaks of blood. Suddenly ice seemed to surround him as the world darkened. He heard Chemise talking to another man, but couldn't quite make out their voices.

"How's the patient...?" he asked.

"Trying to prove he's a superman."

"I'll see to him."

"Do that. See if you can talk some sense into him. He can't leave yet and go off on some crazy mission."

Lucien managed to open his eyes and see the other man walking into the back room. There was something familiar about him. Longish dirty blond hair, wearing a colorful shirt and short pants. As their eyes met, the other man rolled his dramatically. The bartender who'd thrown him out of Blue Tropical yesterday. Shit, could things get any worse?

"Don't zap me with an ice bullet," he commented raising his hands in surrender. "I'm Chemise's cousin, Jeremy. I'm not here to mess with either of you."

Lucien looked back at the smiling man's bare hands and open expression and relaxed. Leaning against the wall before he fell down, he suddenly made the connection. That voice, he recognized it. "You're the man who saved my life."

Jeremy shook his head. "Much as I'd like to take credit, I can't. I'm the guy that patched you up, Chemise is the one who saved you."

Lucien inclined his head. "I stand corrected," he stated, pushing away from the wall a bit unsteadily.

"I'd suggest you better sit down instead," Jeremy muttered, looking at his unsteady movement.

Wanting to argue but knowing it was futile, Lucien sank down on the fainting couch he'd tumbled Chemise on yesterday. Just the memory was enough to jump start him into a hard on making his head swim. As long as Chemise didn't know he was still hurting, he was content.

"Let me see how bad this is," Jeremy suggested, checking the wound. "Luckily, it's just a tear. Take it easy for a few days and you'll heal."

"I don't have the luxury of that much time." Lucien saw Jeremy's troubled expression. "You don't need to tell her about this. I don't want Chemise to worry, but I will do what I need to in order to protect her."

"That's kind of what I figured."

Pleased by the other man's reasonable attitude, Lucien watched as Jeremy looked over his shoulder to make sure they were alone, and then turned back to him. "I want you to make sure that Chemise is taken care of if I don't make it back." He conjured the safety deposit key out of midair and handed it to the other man. "Give her this after I've gone."

"Fuck that. Shimmy doesn't want your money, she wants you. If she knew I let you walk into battle alone, she'd kill me. I'm coming with you."

Lucien shook his head. "We can't leave her alone."

"I can send Mack and Chris over to look after her," Jeremy stated with a grin.

"That is not going to make her happy," Lucien mused aloud.

"No but I'd trust them with my back of hers," Jeremy replied.

Lucien nodded. He'd find a way to make it work. It would be good to have back up even of the mortal kind and Chemise still wore Isis's amulet of protection. The two should be enough. He'd just have to find a way to get around her objections. Make love to her until she couldn't say no. He smiled thinking of thrusting into her until they were both spent. And the way Jeremy accepted him as real was telling. "What is your connection to ancient Egypt?"

"Would you believe Aunt Betty?" Jeremy offered.

"Not quite," he countered seeing the other man's reaction. "There's something else."

"My girlfriend is one of you," he muttered with a shrug. "But don't ask me who, cause I'm not naming names."

And then it all came together. The bar where he'd scented Zander and missed him. "Jasmine." The other man flushed and looked uncomfortable telling him it was true.

"How in the hell did you know?" he asked, astounded, and then shook his head, a look of jealousy on his face. "Don't tell me you and she…"

"Nothing like that. We knew each other because she was one of Isis's favorite handmaidens. Then Zander lured her away…"

Jeremy sneered. "That asshole. I gave him a beat down last week that I thought would keep him away, but the bastard still comes around to try and tempt her."

"You actually touched him," Lucien interrupted, startled that a human could hurt him.

"Did more than touch him," Jeremy admitted with a smirk. "I laid the bastard out cold."

"How?" he asked, and Jeremy gave him a chagrinned smile.

"The slimy jerk's allergic to gin. I wasn't aware of that until he rushed me in the bar, got some spilled on him, and started to sneeze and shiver. The guy's got a glass jaw. I connected with his chin, and he was out cold. But before the cops could get there and arrest him, he vanished." Jeremy's eyes widened. "Don't tell me he's your rogue genie."

Lucien nodded. "One and the same. We must speak to Jasmine about this. If we can elicit her cooperation, we can set a trap for him."

Jeremy frowned. "No. I don't want her involved. I won't let her get hurt."

Lucien clapped him on the shoulder. "Nor I. But you say he's after her. Ridding her of him is that best way to keep her safe."

Jeremy nodded grimly. "I don't like it but you're probably right. Come to the club tonight and we can talk, but I can't promise you she'll see it your way."

"I'll be there," Lucien agreed grudgingly. "And you'll send friends to watch over Chemise."

"Consider it done."

Chemise locked the door to the shop and put out the closed sign and turned to look at Lucien. He was leaning against the shelves in her back room watching her like he wanted to ravish her. He'd been acting different since he and Jeremy had talked. It was as if they were planning something and didn't want to tell her. She walked over to Lucien as he was sweeping up and put her arms around him. "What are you thinking about?"

"You," he replied bending to brush a brief teasing kiss on her lips. "Us."

Chemise leaned into his strength growing wet and needy for him. She wanted to tumble him again on the fainting couch, but the good head gel was still upstairs in the bedroom. Even as she thought it, he opened the drawer to pull out a tube of strawberry gel. "You think of everything, lover," she commented with a giggle.

"I try," he gritted.

She wondered if it was genie magic as Lucien's hands stroked down her back shaping her form, and squeezed her ass. She rocked against the solid brand of his cock catching fire for him. "Oh please," she whispered when he pulled back.

"Beloved," he growled picking her up and carrying her to the fainting couch.

She giggled and reached a hand down to grope him making him groan. He sank down onto the couch with her on his lap astride him. She cried out as her bare pussy pressed against his soft washed jeans. Now she understood why he'd forbidden her to wear underwear.

She couldn't stop herself from rubbing her love swollen clit against the hard ridge of his cock. When she did so, her budding nipples rubbed against his chest making her whimper. She hissed at the waves of pleasure building in her, zinging through her sensitized clit, and gazed at him through love drunk eyes. He was watching her, enjoying her enjoying him. It undid her last bit of restraint. "What are you doing to me, Lucien?"

"Granting your fondest wish as any good genie would do," he teased, his hand cupping her ass and squeezing.

Chemise trembled, sagging against him, her hands clutching his shoulders because he made her feel dizzy with desire. He was growing bigger, harder against her sensitive pussy, making her tremble. "Thank you." She rolled her hips again, gasping at the pure pleasure as her bare pubes pressed against his soft washed jeans, and the throbbing hard-on inside them. She watched his eyes darken in response.

He smiled, his hands slipping down to grip her bare bottom, holding her still against him. "So did you fantasize about me today, too?"

"Yes," she blurted out, burned by the fire in his eyes. So, he'd ached for her as well, it was a balm for her raging hormones. He was just barely keeping it under control. His cock growing stiffer against her, beads of sweat breaking out on his brow. She leaned forward to lap at the steady pulse beat in his throat, tasting his salty skin, hearing him groan she murmured her confession against him, "It was hard to wait on customers knowing that you were back here waiting to be ravished by me."

"I was just as frustrated," he stated wryly as his hands went to the straps of her sundress. He gave them a poke, and first one and then the other skittered off her shoulders.

Chemise shivered with desire as they fell, and his hungry glance ate her up. Then his hands covered her breasts, and she gasped. His heat surrounded her as her nipples budded against his hot palms. Then he began to pluck at them drawing them out harder.

"Yes," she cried, her head rolling back, her eyes closed. He took advantage of the situation to nibble her ear, suck on her neck and then drop down to capture her nipple in his hot mouth. "Oh my," she whimpered as he drew hard on it while his hand slipped between her legs to touch her creamy sex. He teased her clit with his rough fingertip, and she started to spasm.

"That's it beloved, go wild for me," he groaned.

She reached down to unzip his pants with trembling fingers and gasped when he sprang out hard and ready against her. It was enough to drive her into another orgasm as his hot cock thumped against her quivering pussy. And then he picked her up so that she was perched atop his hard-on.

"Yes?" he asked for permission.

Chemise trembled, as she looked deep into his passionate dark eyes. "Oh yes." She whimpered as he eased her onto his erection, sinking inch by inch onto his rampant cock until he filled her completely. When they were fully joined, she sighed with pleasure, her heart racing even though so far, he was doing all the work. Frantic for more, she arched her hips, taking him deeper, her passion–swollen clit pressing against him, and cried out in pleasure. He was holding back, trying to be gentle, but she wanted all his wild passion.

"Slowly," he murmured holding her tight to him as he thrust deeper up into her.

Impaled, she could only sob her pleasure as he controlled the thrusts. She was amazed at the strength that took as he held her pressed to him, and thrust up into her again and again. "Oh my," she voiced, clutching his shoulders tight. She kissed him then, their mouths joined as their bodies were. Lucien's tongue thrust into her mouth in tandem with his cock's thrusts into her pussy and she dissolved around him into a puddle of need. His shaft rubbed against her G–spot, and she started to quiver, waves of orgasm starting as a ripple and then completely overtaking her.

He stiffened, his thrusts harder, fiercer, and came high and hard inside her. Chemise clung to him as she came back to earth and then snuggled against him. Lucien smoothed a hand up and down her spine, then held her tight. Wrapped in the warm cocoon of his arms she closed her eyes, feeling sated and protected, a sleepless night caught up with her.

Lucien listened to a gentle snoring come from the woman wrapped around him and smiled. A fellow might think he'd bored her to sleep, but he knew he'd wished the slumber on her. The growing darkness outside told him it was almost time to go. He gently separated himself from her straightening her clothing and tucked a blanket around her. Just then he heard a tapping on the door and turned to see two burly bouncers from the club enter the room. He eyed the one that had threatened to throw him out of the club and the other man had the grace to look chagrinned.

"We're here like you asked. What's the job?"

"You mean Jeremy didn't tell you?" he asked, stepping toward them. He watched them look past him to Chemise sleeping on the couch and wince.

Chris winced. "Oh, shit if we knew it was her, we wouldn't have come..."

"Shut your stupid mouth," Mack warned him, and Chris piped down.

"So, you've had run–ins with Chemise before, I take it," Lucien stated dryly.

Chris smirked. "She tried to kick our asses when Jeremy left med school to work at the club. Called us bad influences."

"So, what's the plan?" Mack asked, ignoring him.

Lucien put on his leather jacket and headed for the door. "Lock the door after me and don't let anyone else in."

Mack nodded. "You can count on us."

Lucien went out the door, hoping that he could keep his promise to return.

Chapter 8

Amelia January stood in the midst of the oak grove in the park...mag ical ground. She closed her eyes and willed the servant to her. A startled hiss told her that he was near and shocked that she'd summoned him at will. She opened her eyes to see Zander, the servant genie, standing there glaring at her. The urge to blast him into nothingness ran through her but she needed him.

"How?" Zander demanded, stalking up to her.

She smiled coldly back at him, and he stopped in his tracks as he ought to. Enjoying his discomfiture she let a few seconds of tension go by. He deserved to squirm. The servant had plenty to be worried about. "You dare question me, worm."

Almost unwillingly, he bowed his obeisance to her. "Goddess."

Inhaling a deep breath as she was finally called by her rightful title, she drew herself up straighter as she stared down at the top of his bowed head. "That's better," she stated giving him a smile when he straightened up. "I have summoned you here for a purpose, Zander."

He nodded, his face flushing.

The flush on his face told her he remembered being the court's sexual plaything, not that she'd ever wanted him. "Not that. I've no need of your dubious sexual prowess. If I recall correctly, Lucien was always far better in bed than you were. It was the reason that Isis helped you trick him so that you could go free, was it not?" She saw the suspicious glance he shot her and smiled.

"If you know all this then why send for me?" he snapped.

She wanted to slap him for his petulant tone, but restrained herself. She could destroy him at her leisure after she got her way. "Because we can do each other a favor."

"A favor?" he asked, drawing closer.

He was curious. She had him where she wanted him. "How would you like to know where Lucien is?"

He stepped even closer. "You know this, or are you just toying with me?"

She saw his greed and anger, but most of all his jealousy of Lucien and knew she could use his evil feelings to her own advantage. She also read his fear of her. Good, he knew just how powerful she was. "Of course, I know this. I will tell you, you will kill him, and bring me back my prize."

"Prize?".

The fool didn't even have a clue to the value of what she was seeking. "The Isis pendant that Chemise wears."

He winced. "It's cursed to me. You know I am not allowed to touch…"

She sighed. Why were all men that served her such fools? "I will go with you. You can capture Lucien, and I will take possession of it."

Chemise was laying in a blissful slumber, her body still warm and tingling from her orgasm. She snuggled under the covers alone. *Alone!*

Then the sound of gruff male voices arguing nearby drew her out of her slumber. It took work to actually open her eyes, but she eventually did it. Damn it all, Lucien must have used another one of his sleeping spells on her. She was going to break him of that habit if it was the last thing she did.

When her sleep-heavy gaze could focus on the men she let out a mortified groan. Mack and Chris, the two thick headed Neanderthals she'd taken to task for Jeremy being a stripper/bartender. They both spun toward her at her sound of dismay, both going for weapons. Good grief, if Lucien must have left her with these muscle-bound babysitters, things were bad.

"Shit, she's awake," Chris stuttered slipping his knife into its sheath.

"Shut up," Mack murmured under his breath while putting away his gun.

"But he said she wouldn't wake up for hours," Chris whined cracking another pistachio and popping it into his mouth.

She narrowed her eyes as she saw him eating what was left of her precious bag of nuts. "He did, did he," she grumbled, pushing back the covers and sitting up. It was only then she remembered how nude she and Lucien had been. Blushing, she looked down to make sure she was covered and sighed with relief. At least he'd dressed her before he *poofed* this time. It was an improvement. Maybe Lucien could be trained, after all. "Tell me, gentlemen," she stated as she watched them actually step back. She managed to sit up, no thanks to them, demanding, "Where did he go?"

"Now lady, don't get excited," Chris stammered backing up.

Mack merely rolled his eyes in disgust as he slashed the other man a longsuffering look. "Just shut the fuck up and go stand in the other room before she clobbers you."

"Don't think running away is going to save your stinky hide," she replied, watching Chris hightail it into her shop's kitchenette. Surging to her feet, she let out a groan when her legs wobbled, and Mack lunged forward to grab her before she hit the floor.

Mortified, she bit back a grumble as she steadied herself. Lucien's spells packed a hell of a wallop. All things considered, the men in her life had a lot to answer for. She stiffened her rubber band legs, pulled her arm out of Mack's grasp. "Tell me what I want to know. Where's Lucien and how much trouble is he in?"

"Don't you see, sweetie, he doesn't want you to get hurt."

Shit, it was worse than she feared, and her babysitter wasn't talking. She reared back her foot to kick him when suddenly there was an explosion that knocked them both off their feet. She let out a groan as Mack fell on top of her, pressing her into the floor. She tried to breathe under his heavy body and realized when she tried to push him off her and he didn't move that he was stunned. What the hell had happened? Maybe a gas line explosion. Then she heard familiar voices.

"So, where the hell is she?" Dr. Amelia January asked.

Chemise stifled a gasp as the pendant she was wearing seemed to heat up, almost burning her cleavage. Shit did that mean that the bad doctor had Zander genie in tow? It was just the way it had acted last night. She had her answer in a moment when he grumbled.

"I do not know," Zander hissed. "I sense her presence nearby, but…"

"You're useless," Amelia interrupted. "Like all men."

"How dare you speak to me as such. I'm not a mere mortal like your love slave, Barry. She's nearby but her presence is blocked," he stated.

"No wonder with all this collateral damage you caused," Amelia blurted out.

Chemise winced when Mack was kicked on top of her and let out a groan.

"Fool. Can't you see that he doesn't move. He's dead," Amelia complained. "Now, search for the woman and pendant immediately."

Chemise huddled under Mack's unmoving bulk as she heard her shop being torn apart. She had to bite her lip to keep from telling them off, but she knew she had to keep quiet to stay safe. She wouldn't put anything past these two fiends.

"I found another," Zander called out from a distance away.

Oh no, the other bouncer he'd gone into her shop's kitchen to get more nibbles. Then she heard a groan and a slap.

"Where is she?" Zander demanded.

"Dunno," came the pained and slow response.

Then a siren sounded in the distance, and she had hope. Someone had reported the explosion. Help was on the way.

"Hurry," Amelia rushed out. "Mortals are on their way."

"Tell me," Zander insisted.

She struggled to get out from under Mack so that she could help him as the sirens grew louder.

"Don't fight us," Amelia murmured with a feline purr. "It can be so much more pleasurable if we work together."

"Ahhhh," Scott moaned with a sigh. "I suppose she went to the club to help her boyfriend, Lucien."

Chemise heard running footsteps coming her way and struggled all the harder. She should have guessed that Lucien was going to the club. The only reason she hadn't was the spell he'd put her under.

"There's a victim," a man called out.

"Make that two," she stated as she felt Mack being gently rolled off of her.

She looked up at the paramedic and gave him a weak smile. "Thanks, he weighs a ton."

Then he concentrated on her while Mack was tended to.

"I'm okay," she voiced trying to brush him off. She shot a worried glance at Mack. "How about him."

"Slight concussion. He should be fine," the paramedic explained. "Let's concentrate on you."

"There's another man in the mini kitchen in back. You might want to check on..."

"Found him," another fireman yelled. "He seems to be covered in frostbite, but he's smiling."

"Thank goodness for that," Chemise murmured. Now all she had to do was warn Lucien and rescue him.

Lucien stood outside the club waiting for Jeremy and Jasmine to appear. He could picture Chemise sleeping and sexy as he'd left her and itched to get back to her. But first, he had to take care of business. At least she had Mack and Chris to keep watch over her. Hopefully she'd sleep through the night until he returned and be none the wiser. Footsteps behind him made him spin around. His eyes narrowed when he watched Jeremy sidle up to him with Jasmine in tow. The scowl on her face spoke volumes. She didn't want to be here. Was she just frightened of Zander or was she his minion, a love slave that would do his bidding.

A glance at Jeremy told him that the boy was infatuated with Isis's former handmaiden. Was it a love spell or was it true? Time would tell. "I see you finally got here."

"This is stupid," Jasmine hissed looking around her for trouble.

He saw her nervous glance, felt her fearful vibrations, and knew that it was real. "The only way for either of us to be truly free is to defeat him. Surely, you can see that."

Her sharp gaze flashed back to him. "So you say, but we both know that he cannot be beat. As I remember, you've tried and failed before."

He winced, his mind going back to the beatings he'd taken in the past only to be forced back into the lamp and imprisoned. This time would be different, he finally had something to live for. "But this time we've got Jeremy on our side," he stated with a smile.

Jasmine put a hand on Jeremy's arm. "You keep him out of this. I will not see him hurt."

He knew just how she felt. It was the way he felt about Chemise. "Agreed."

"Now wait a doggone minute," Jeremy cut in. "I'm not going to be pushed aside like a kid."

"Of course, you're not," Jasmine crooned running a soft hand down his arm.

Lucien watched as his eyes became all dreamy and soft as he calmed down. Jasmine had him under a spell of sorts. He waited until she turned back to him to say, "Take the whammy off the kid."

Chapter 9

Half an hour later, Chemise made her way into the club. The vibration of the music pulsed through her as she surveyed the crowd looking for her man. Then she saw Lucien in a back booth with a slinky brunette pawing him. Irate, she stomped his way.

"Take your hands off him, lady, he's taken."

The brunette turned to look at her flashing an outraged glare but the tears in her eyes make Chemise wonder.

Lucien pulled her down beside him. "What are you doing here?" he demanded.

"I came to warn you," she replied stung by his annoyed tone. If he didn't want her help fine.

"Where are Mack and Chris?" the brunette asked.

"On their way to the hospital," Chemise stated seeing the look of fear in the other woman's eyes. "And just what do you have to do with this mess?"

The brunette turned to look at Lucien. "I told you he was too powerful. If you know what's good for you, you'll run and leave this mortal to her own devices."

Chemise resented her dismissive tone and her words. "Now, you just hold on a minute."

Lucien put a hand on Chemises arm. "Chemise meet Jasmine, a former member of Isis's court and a direct conduit to Zander."

Chemise got was he was saying. Don't piss off the bitch still she eyed her rival with irritation. Then she put herself in the other woman's shoes. She'd obviously run off from said royal court and gotten mixed up with the frost king. No wonder she was so moody.

"Hello."

Jasmine gave her a curt nod and then turned to Lucien. "You're running out of time."

"So are you," Chemise cut in. "Zander is on his way and he's not alone."

Jasmines eyes narrowed. "You lie."

"Why would I?" Chemise shot back.

"To make yourself important and to make me betray him."

"Haven't you already accomplished that with my cousin Jeremy?" Chemise asked, flashing a worried look at her blissfully lovesick cousin. She reached out to touch his hand and he just smiled at her. "What the hell did you do to him anyway?"

"This is none of your concern," Jasmine replied, pulling his hand away from Chemises grasp.

"Bull..."

"Ladies," Lucien cut in. "You said he had a person with him, beloved, who is he?"

"She," Chemise stated sourly.

"Oh no, Isis," Jasmine murmured with a horrified gasp.

"Not likely," Lucien voiced focusing on Chemise.

"Maybe it's just an alias but she calls herself Dr. Amelia January. She's the investigator looking into the fire and she's powerful."

"Black hair, piercing blue eyes, and a superior attitude," Jasmine guessed.

"Who is she?" Lucien demanded.

"That's right you probably never met her because Isis didn't like to share. She was a minor goddess and if she's with Zander, that's trouble."

"Take your lover and go," Lucien muttered indicating Jeremy.

Jasmine stood and pulled Jeremy out of the booth with her.

Chemise let out a startled gasp when Lucien whisked her out of the booth, too, and headed outside. "Where are we...?"

"No time to talk. You'll just have to trust me."

She did, but she didn't think he'd believe that now.

Then he swept her into his arms, and they moved away in a dizzying blur.

Chapter 10

Suddenly, they touched down, and she opened her eyes to see a strange room. The alabaster walls seemed to glow with an inner light. She looked around, fascinated. Silk wall hangings framed opulent furnishings and a large bed. It was like an *Arabian Nights* fantasy bedroom. Were they in the lamp?

"Where are we?"

"Some place safe."

She glanced over at him, hearing his confident tone. He was watching her like *she* was the most exotic thing in the room. His sultry smile made her blush, and a heat wave rushed through her. "Are you sure about that?" she asked to change the subject.

"For the moment, yes," he replied, stepping toward her.

Chemise instinctively backed away, feeling vulnerable. She'd had the courage to ravish him before. This time, she'd play it cool. She'd be aloof, seductive, and exotic, not out of control. So why did she want to tear his clothes off and taste him?

"How can you be sure?" she shot back at him, watching the corners of his mouth kick up in a smile. He knew exactly how he was affecting her, damn it all.

"It's inside your safe."

His words confirmed her guess. "We're in your lamp."

He nodded.

"Can we get out again?" she asked, recalling that he'd been imprisoned.

"Yes. If I entrench myself here, I can come and go as I please. But if I'm trapped—that's a different story."

She wouldn't mind being trapped with him for, say, one hundred and one sexy nights. Her heated gaze moved from his captivating face to the bulging erection inside his pants. "But what about me?" she asked.

"As my guest..."

"Captive," she corrected. His wicked smile made her heart trip, and her sex grow creamy. Damn it all, there went her hard-to-get act.

"As my guest, I can pop you in and out at my will."

"Then you can pop me back to my place?" His hard smile told her it wasn't going to be that easy.

"I can, but I won't."

The disclosure made her shiver with delight. "Then I am your prisoner."

"Would you like to be?" he asked, intrigued.

It was too close to the truth for comfort, but she confessed. "Maybe."

"That's no answer."

His bad boy smile was maddening and arousing. It made her want to tumble him onto the bed and have her way with him. Her body still tingled from their last coupling, and she wanted more. But tonight, the equation had shifted, *he* was in charge. She bit her lip, trying to hide how vulnerable she was. "This place is like an Aladdin's treasure chest of goodies."

He looked around the plush surroundings and shrugged. "My mistress presented me with many gifts."

"Isis." Her jaw tightened as she spoke her rival's name. Jealousy was petty and unbecoming, but she couldn't help it. She must be dull compared to a goddess, but there was no way she wanted to share her man with that bitch.

He shrugged. "At one time, she teased me with promises of freedom. She taught me that women lie." He came up behind her, bending to nibble the nape of her neck.

"I don't," she stated with a gasp, she leaned into him, her body on fire.

"You already did. You told me a beau was picking you up."

Her knees wobbled as he nipped her earlobe, and she recalled her fib she'd told him about a boyfriend picking her up. "Sorry about that. It was a white lie. I wanted to make you jealous."

"You did," he replied, his hands cupping her breasts as his fingertips fanned her nipples.

Whimpering, she thrust her bosom more firmly into his talented hands. "Really?" she questioned, astounded.

"Yes, really," he assured her with a chuckle.

Emboldened, she asked, "Would you like to carry on where we left off, Lucien?"

Chapter 11

"Do you mean you're going to attack me again?" he asked, teasing her.

"I didn't exactly *attack* you." Her face heated even as she pressed her ass against the tempting bulge of his cock.

"Near enough. Don't worry, I'm used to it."

"I'm not Isis," she stated, offended that he would make the comparison.

"Well, I know it. You're more passionate and tender."

She melted at his words. "Thank you. But I think I'd rather *be* attacked." She moaned as he pinched her nipples. "Oh yeah, that's it."

"Do you know what you're asking?"

"Uh huh," she murmured, her body aflame. She looked over her shoulder, locking gazes with Lucien, excited by the heat in his dark eyes. She knew he'd be masterful, sexually demanding, and she craved it. "I'm yours."

He nodded and let her go, stepping back. "Prove it."

She stood immobile for a moment, startled by the daring demand. How could she prove it? She reached back to unzip her dress, shrugging it off her shoulders, and let it drop to pool at her feet. Lucien's hungry gaze made her body quiver. She gave him a teasing smile, noting the heavy beat of his pulse in his throat. Emboldened, she reached back to unhook her bra and let it slowly slide off, revealing her breasts an inch at a time. The flare of heat in his gaze made her sex wet and her nipples tight. Her hands shaking with need, she peeled down her panties and stood before him, unashamedly naked.

"Very good," he appraised, reaching out to tweak one nipple.

She gasped with pleasure, but he dropped his hand, making her pout. "Your turn," she demanded, breathlessly.

He closed his eyes, and his clothes vanished. "No fair!" she exclaimed. "How did you do that?"

"It goes with the job."

"What else can you do?" she asked, intrigued. She watched his mouth kick up into a wicked smile. Then she let out a gasp as she felt unseen hands caress her, touching her nipples, her sex. "That's cheating," she whispered, panting for breath.

"So, who said I play fair?" he countered, quirking an eyebrow. "If you want to be my love slave, go to the chest and pull out the red velvet pouch."

Gasping as she fought to control her arousal, she made her way to the heavy oak chest and opened the lid. She pulled out the red bag. It was larger than she'd expected and filled with something hard. Intrigued, she carried it back to Lucien.

"Open it and see your toys," he demanded with a smile.

She laid the bag on the bed, pulled the drawstring, and poured out two white marble phalluses—one large, one small as her little finger. Did he mean to use them on her? Her body clenched at the exciting thought. She gazed at them, imagining how it would feel if he teased her with them. Her sex pulsed. Intrigued, she gazed up at Lucien, her hand tightening on the large one.

His eyes twinkled. "Show me how you'd like to pleasure me."

Her lips tingled as she stared at his sultry mouth. She brought the marble phallus to her mouth, swirling her tongue around its cool head. It warmed to her touch. Her eyes met Lucien's as she sucked on it, and she saw his eyes darken. He was just as turned on as she was, but he was better at concealing his emotions. She groaned and sucked harder, her pussy quivering with each stroke. This was what she'd wanted to do to him earlier—what she still wanted to do to him.

"Come here," Lucien commanded, sitting on the edge of the bed.

She walked toward him on unsteady legs, still mouthing the dildo, the hot look in Lucien's eyes driving her on. He smiled and reached out to tumble her across his lap. She acquiesced with a muffled gasp of shock and delight.

"Does my naughty slave girl need a spanking?" he asked as his big hand spread across her bottom.

Her buttocks heated as his hand lay above them, and she nodded. "If you say so," she replied, pulling the dildo out of her mouth and placing a kiss on its bulbous head.

"Good answer," he stated, his hand coming down on her bottom with a smack.

She gasped as heat moved through her bottom, making her pussy quiver. He was going to make her come if he kept that up.

"Keep sucking," he demanded, accompanying his words with short, quick spanks.

She moaned around the phallus as he caught her by surprise, setting up a steady pace. Her clit brushed against his leg, making her gasp. Tightening as the ripples took her over, she let out a cry as she began to come.

Next, Lucien gently took the phallus out of Chemise's greedy mouth and slipped it into her creamy pussy. She moaned helplessly, her spasming walls clamping down on the object as he nested it deep inside her. He eased the smaller phallus into her ass, and she gasped in surprise, her body rippling on the device. He began to spank her again, making the marble shafts vibrate inside her as her body clamped down on them. With a final, hard smack to her mound, he pushed her over the edge until she cried out as she came.

When it was over, she hung breathless and limp over his lap. Lucien picked her up and placed her on her back on the bed. She moaned as her hot bottom hit the cool sheets, her pussy and ass rippling with after spasms. The shock of being turned over Lucien's knee still made her senses reel. She gazed up at his handsome face through an orgasmic fog as he stood over her. "More, please," she begged with a sigh.

His eyes twinkled. "Spread your legs, Chemise. Let me see your treasures."

Her legs parted at his command, and she couldn't help blushing as he gazed hotly at her bared pussy. She knew she was wet and pink, the dildos still clenched by her hungry body. He smiled and reached down to stroke her labia, tracing maddening circles around the two dildos. She cried out, arching her hips off the bed.

"Play with yourself, beloved. Show me how you like to be touched."

At his urging, one of her hands went to her clit while the other plucked at her stiff nipples. His smile made her crazy. She bit back a moan and reached for the phallus in her pussy, fucking herself with it. She desperately wanted the real thing, but she had a feeling he wouldn't be rushed.

"Is that how you'd like to be fucked?" he asked, sitting beside her. He cupped her breast, bringing the nipple to hardness again while she let out a needy whimper.

"Reach up and grab the headboard," he commanded. "Don't let go until I tell you to."

Her hands shook as she reluctantly released her hold on the dildo. She was achingly close to coming, and he knew it. Her ass was still hot from her spanking. She gazed deep into his eyes, telegraphing her need, and reached up for the spindles of the headboard.

The breath whooshed out of her lungs as he knelt between her trembling thighs and touched his tongue to her clit. The wet heat almost pushed her over the edge. He sucked her clit into his mouth, nipping it, and she came, her eyes rolling back in her head. He surged up her body, pulled the dildo from her pussy, and settled between her warm thighs. His throbbing cock rubbed against her creamy sex, and she arched up, trying to complete their union, still clutching the headboard.

He backed off an inch, hesitating. "Look at me, Chemise," he demanded.

Her eyes popped open at his demand. His intense look made her want to hold him. He'd suffered so many betrayals, but she was different. She loved him. The thought came as no surprise.

"Do you want this, Chemise?" he asked.

The swollen cock rubbed against her clit, and she hissed with pleasure.

"Yes," she replied with a needy moan, and gasping when he began to enter her. Her ass rippled on the small dildo, and she moaned. She murmured and gave herself over completely, melting around him. His huge cock filled her completely and he lay still inside her, letting her get used to his size and to the double invasion. She moaned, luxuriating in the sense of being claimed completely.

As he began to piston in and out of her, Chemise met his thrusts, quivering, gasping for breath as he drove deeper. The tingling pleasure swept from the point of their joining until it filled her entire body, and the rest of the world seemed to fall away. She closed her eyes and gave herself over to the sensations, tightening and convulsing around his driving cock. Lucien stiffened, coming hard against her cervix.

When it was over, he rolled to the side and held her close. Almost immediately, Chemise fell into an exhausted sleep, feeling Lucien holding her tight.

An hour later, Lucien went to his crystal ball. He didn't want to leave Chemise, but he knew he had to locate Zander. Zander's reaction to Isis' emblem had been telling. Zander really wasn't under her protection anymore. Lucien would use that to his advantage. He gazed deep into the swirling clouds inside the orb, seeking out his nemesis, and ground his jaw with frustration when Zander stayed out of sight. The evil genie was powerful and crafty. Lucien couldn't afford to underestimate him.

Chemise sighed in her sleep, and Lucien turned to gaze possessively at her. She was his very own sex slave. She hadn't expected the dominance, but she'd enjoyed it. He sat down with his quill and parchment and began to plan.

A few moments later, he sensed her presence and looked to see Chemise standing next to him. It didn't say much for his defensive instincts that he hadn't sensed her movement. And in that instant, he acknowledged that his odds weren't good. Zander was powerful, even without Isis' protection. Still Lucien focused on Chemise, dazzled by her beauty. He wrapped an arm around her naked waist, drawing her close to him.

Her fascinated gaze was focused on his crystal ball. "Is that what I think it is?" She peered into the orb's cloudy depths.

He smiled loving her inquisitive nature. "It's a crystal gazing ball."

"How does it work?"

"Concentrate on what you want to see, and it may appear."

"How about my office...or ex-office, I should say."

The anger in her tone made him wonder. "You lost your position?"

He watched her blush, and he wanted to hurt the one who'd wronged her. Whatever had caused her dismissal both angered and embarrassed her.

"Yes," she answered with a sigh.

They gazed into the ball as a cluttered office came into view. The top of her desk held a wilting plant and stacks of papers.

"Why that bastard. He told me my things were being shipped to me."

"He?"

"Yes—my boss, Dr. Edwards. And he let my plant die. What a jerk."

"Tell me about it," he offered, hoping to unburden her.

"A scroll I was working on suddenly burst into flames for no reason. I know I didn't do anything wrong, but it pains me that the ancient text was lost."

"You are an archivist?" he asked, shocked they had so much in common.

She smiled sadly. "I was." She glanced at the parchment he'd been writing. "Actually, part of the text was exactly like this—the calligraphy was just the same."

He went still as a sense of destiny passed through him. She was his beloved, and these events were fated. He knew it.

She picked up the illuminated page reverently. "Did you copy this? The calligraphy is outstanding, nothing like my scribbled notes."

"You have notes?" he asked sharply.

"Yes. Why?"

"The complete spell is what I need to defeat Zander. It will send him back into the lamp permanently. I've been trying to recall parts of it."

She looked up at him in wonder. "That's impossible. Things don't fall together for me like this."

He pulled her closer. "I have a story to tell you. When I'm done you may be a believer."

"Tell me."

"After I was captured, I refused to do Isis' bidding, so she had a gift made for me...an astrological chart that showed that a woman would set me free. I'd know her by three signs. She would give her life for me, she would trust me when she had no reason to, and she would have a heart-shaped beauty mark on her left breast. At the time, I was fooled into believing Isis was the woman. Now I know better."

She gazed at him in wonder. "And she'd be called your beloved."

He nodded.

She frowned. "Then you've known our destiny all along...and didn't tell me."

He could feel her hurt. "Would you have believed me?"

"No," she admitted with a sigh. And then she met his eyes.

"You thought it was a trick, didn't you?"

He wanted to deny it, but she was too smart for that. "At first."

"How could you be so..."

"Suspicious. You were wearing Isis' protection."

"That's true," she replied grudgingly.

"She doesn't just hand those pendants out to anyone." He glanced at the pendant still nestled in her décolletage. "How did you..."

"I found it in the safe, along with your lamp. Aunt Betty left them to me in her will. People always said she was psychic. I wonder if she knew?"

He smiled, relieved that she seemed to forgive him. "Sometimes, it's better not to question fate."

"Right, let's get back to Zander. Have you tried to trap him in the past?" Chemise asked.

"Yes. I only had a brief look at the scroll and didn't know the complete spell, so my efforts didn't work. They will this time, thanks to you."

"My notes are complete," she explained, smiling. "All we have to do is pop over to my office and get them."

His jaw tightened at her excited tone. There was no way he'd expose her to danger. "Just tell me where to go." Her stubborn frown made him even more determined to keep her out of it. She'd throw herself in the path of danger if he allowed it.

"Impossible. The museum is like a maze. I'd have to show you."

He captured her chin to force her to look at him. "No. Zander already tried to kill you once, and I won't make the same mistake twice."

"He won't hurt me with you around."

"I'm not taking that chance," Lucien defended flatly.

She glared at him. "You can't stop me. I know my way around the museum, and you don't. I'm going."

He shook his head.

"Look at it this way. If you get worried, you can pop me back in the lamp."

"No." He pulled her astride his lap, smiling at her outraged shriek. Then they both gasped as he entered her. It was a dirty way to win an argument, but he didn't care. "Don't fight me on this," he scolded, nibbling the nape of her neck.

She moaned, rubbing her stiff nipples against his chest. "You're a stubborn man, Lucien."

"Now you *are* sounding like Isis."

"Bringing her name up at a time like this isn't a smart move, stud." She nipped his earlobe.

"Sorry," he answered as her honey walls rippled on his throbbing erection.

Chemise ground against him making them both gasp. "So, she accused you of being stubborn?"

Lucien groaned and thrust up into her. "I wouldn't bend to her will. She left me with one final chance to call to her. I haven't used it. You feel so damned good wrapped around me, beloved."

"Oh, yes," she moaned.

"I heard it's your birthday."

She whimpered as she ground against him. "Um hum. I'm turning the dreaded three-o. And I can't think of a better way to celebrate it."

He pulled the ring off his little finger. It had been in his family for centuries, and he wanted to bind himself to his lover. He slipped the ring onto Chemise's finger, smiling at her gasp of surprise. "Happy birthday, Chemise."

She looked at the gold ring, touched. "I can't accept..."

"Would you like to go over my knee instead?" he warned, his eyes twinkling.

She grinned and nodded. "I think I'd like that."

He rolled his eyes. "I think I've created a monster. Take my ring." Lucien's hands stroked down her back, tracing her form, and squeezed her bottom. He growled, smacking her ass playfully.

"What are you doing to me, Lucien?" she murmured.

"Playing with my love slave," he replied, spanking her again.

"You're driving me crazy," she muttered with a gasp.

"Good. It's mutual."

"I remember when I thought you weren't real."

"How about now?" he asked, surging into her.

"Oh yeah," she murmured. "You're the real deal."

He thrust into her a final time as her orgasm pushed him over the edge.

Lucien held her tight as their heartbeats slowed in tandem. Though he knew she'd hate him for it, he willed her into a deep sleep, his body still joined intimately with her. He'd put Chemise in a safe place while he dealt with Zander. He'd protect her at all costs. He sighed and did the one thing he'd vowed never to do...he called in his last favor with the goddess.

He conjured his pendant out of midair and scooped Chemise into his arms as he stood. He dressed them with a blink and thought of Isis. Moments later, they were standing in the audience room of her palace. As usual, his clothes vanished, and he felt the chill of the cold marble floor.

Isis, seated on her throne, glared down at Lucien with Chemise in his arms. Isis always stripped him when he appeared before her; that was just one of her ways of humbling him. He stood before her without bowing. "I need your protection."

The air around Lucien crackled with her outrage. She glowered imperiously down at Chemise in his arms. He noticed her furtive glance around the empty hall as her servants retreated. She was afraid of being caught with her secret plaything.

"How dare you bring this mortal before me, *slave*."

"I'm calling in my last favor." He watched her eyes narrow with calculation and was repulsed. How could he ever have found her attractive? He much preferred the warm and tender woman in his arms.

"What will you give me?"

His mouth quirked into a sarcastic smile. She always demanded her pound of flesh. He held out his hand, and her pendant appeared in his grasp. "I'll give you back your love gift. You wouldn't want Ra to know you gave it to a mere mortal."

She sucked in a breath. "You dare to threaten me."

Hell, he didn't have time to argue with her. "No. I'm just stating a fact." Chemise stirred in his arms, and he stroked her back, renewing the sleeping spell.

"What do you want from me?" she asked, intrigued.

"Protect my beloved while I battle Zander. And give me your word that after it's over, she will be safe."

"That bastard—I was forced to banish him."

"Let me guess, he was starting fires again."

"I should have killed him," Isis replied bitterly.

"But that would have attracted too much attention."

She arched a raven brow. "You ask so little. You do not even beg for your life?"

He held Chemise tighter. "She is my life." He watched her roll her eyes at the sentiment. He knew she would never understand.

"What do I care? You'll destroy each other, and I'll be rid of you both." She regally inclined her head. "I'll protect your plaything while you go on your fool's quest."

Chemise woke in a strange bed. She looked around at the thick lime-stone walls in shock. Where was she? And more importantly, where was Lucien? Had Zander found a way to separate them?

"You're awake," a woman stated from a dark corner of the room.

Chemise peered into the shadows, and her jaw dropped when she saw the goddess walking toward her. After conserving so many man-uscripts, she'd recognize Isis anywhere. Isis looked remarkably like her pictures and the image on the pendant nestled between her breasts. "Lucien will be furious when he learns that you kidnapped me."

Isis laughed. "Do not presume so much, foolish mortal. You are be-neath my notice."

"Then why am I here?"

"He gave you to me, fool." She flashed a cruel smile.

Chemise burned. That had to be a lie. "It's not true," she blurted out, but the goddess' smug smile made her doubt herself. She glanced down at Lucien's ring on her finger and her confidence returned. Lucien would only hand her over to the woman he hated for one reason...her protection. He was going after Zander alone, and he'd called in that last favor he'd talked about. Her steady gaze flashed back to the goddess. "You can't let him fight Zander alone."

Isis's eyes narrowed. "You're very perceptive for a mortal. He made his choice," she replied sourly, raking Chemise with an annoyed gaze. "There is nothing I can do for him."

"Choice?" Chemise asked, picking up on Isis' envy. To think a goddess would be envious of her seemed ludicrous, but it was true.

"His life or yours. He chose poorly." Isis turned to leave.

Chemise bolted from the bed. "Bullshit. You caused all this just because you had an itch that needed scratching." She froze while Isis glared back at her. A heartbeat later, Chemise gasped as she was flung back against a wall.

Isis smiled. "I promised to keep you safe. I didn't say how."

Chemise glared back at her, refusing to cower despite Isis' threats. "If you won't help him, I'll leave and do it myself."

Isis laughed. "You will remain here."

"The hell, I will." Chemise lifted the pendant from her chest, acting on a hunch, and watched Isis' smug smile falter.

"Where did you get that?" Isis hissed.

"From my aunt," she replied, rubbing the pendant. Apparently, it had power. Now if she could just get it to work. She thought of Lucien and felt her body tingle.

"Stupid fool. If you go back, you forgo my protection."

Chapter 12

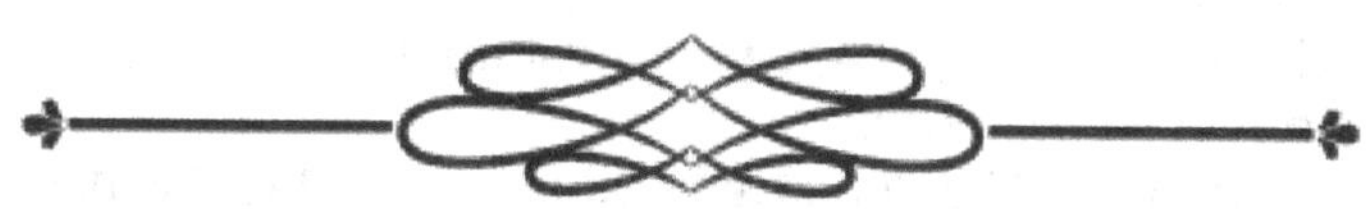

Chemise felt the world spin away and touched down in her office at the museum. It was dark, still evening, so not much time had passed. She stepped toward the light switch, but the night watchman's plodding footsteps made her freeze. It wouldn't do to have him catch her in the act of stealing back her notes.

After his footfalls faded into the distance, she dared to switch on the lights, then ran to her desk. She'd left the notes in her top drawer. If she was lucky, they'd still be there. She pulled open the drawer and found her notes on top. She let out a sigh of relief, but the sound of her office door opening made her look up in a panic. Zander stepped into the office and shut the door. His searching gaze scanned the room, and she noticed the lamp in his hand. Was Lucien trapped inside? Her senses told her he wasn't. She would have felt his vibrations.

"Where is he?" Zander asked.

"You're still asking the same stupid questions." She watched his eyes ice over at the jibe and she pulled her notes out of the drawer. She only knew one way to fight him. "I'd worry more about me, not him," she stated.

He laughed as he saw the notes in her hand. His gaze made the edges of the paper singe.

She patted out the fire. "You. You're the one who burned the scroll and got me fired."

He grinned. "It's one of my favorite tricks."

He wasn't just nuts—he was a firebug. She clasped her notes tight, chanting, "Genie from…"

Zander stopped in his tracks and threw her a glare. "Stupid mortal. You cannot defeat me."

But she sensed his doubt—it was why he'd destroyed the scroll. This was fate. "I wouldn't be so sure of that. I have Isis' protection," she voiced to distract him, and she watched his mocking smile.

"You would be at her palace if that was so."

"I was. I left."

He shook his head. "That was your first mistake."

"Why aren't you with her?"

His eyes narrowed. "I don't have to explain myself to the likes of you."

He raised the lamp, and she fell silent at the threat. If he smashed the lamp, Lucien might be injured or killed.

"That's better. Shut up and sit in your chair. I'll deal with you at my leisure."

She sank into her chair and gasped when she heard Lucien's steady treads heading their way. The cold smile on Zander's face chilled her. She reached for her wilted plant. When Lucien opened the door, she lobbed the pot straight at Zander's head. It bounced off his head with a thud, and he groaned, crashing into the wall.

"Why, you, stupid bitch!" he yelled as he set her chair on fire.

"Don't touch her," Lucien ordered with a deadly growl, taking Zander to the ground with a flying tackle.

Chemise's heart lodged in her throat as she watched the men roll across the floor, fighting for supremacy. Lightning and thunder flashed inside the room. She had to stop this craziness before Lucien was killed.

She began to chant the spell again, "Zander, Genie from Below, go back from whence you came. Set your captive free."

Zander let out a howl of pain, his body turning transparent. In a whoosh, he was sucked into the lamp.

Chemise gazed at Lucien, praying he was alright, terrified she might lose him.

He picked himself off the floor with a wince. "You saved me again. It's getting to be a habit with you."

"Do you mind?" she teased, relaxing when he smiled.

"Not a bit," he assured her, pulling her into his arms.

She nestled against him, feeling the rightness of his embrace. Were the fates smiling down at them? "Where do we go from here?"

"How about back to bed?" he suggested.

"Now that I like," she responded, and she began to kiss him passionately. She broke the kiss to gaze up at him. She had so many questions that needed answering. Like, would he stay with her?

Was he still a genie? His lamp or her apartment? Frankly, she didn't care as long as it had a bed. "Does that mean I get to keep you?" she asked, her body melting into his as his cock throbbed against her.

"I don't know," he teased, one of his hands cupping her breast, his fingertips fanning the nipple to attention. "That wasn't one of your three wishes."

"Hah," Chemise shrieked. "Those don't count. I didn't know you were real at the time."

"And now?" he asked, studying her reaction.

"You're very real." She moaned when his hand slipped down to possessively cup her mound and pressed closer to him. "I don't care if we have to find another bottle to live in. I'm keeping you."

"And you wouldn't miss this place or your shop?" he asked, wrapping an arm around her waist.

He was a bit worried about her decision. The realization warmed her heart even as it firmed her resolve. "Not a bit. I've found an antiquity that interests me a lot more than anything in the museum."

"Nice to know I'm appreciated," he replied with a grin. "And you'd go back to my time with me?"

"In a heartbeat," Chemise agreed, wrapping her arms around his neck as he played with her.

"We could be bi-coastal," he offered. "Time jump so you could study your favorite time period up close and personal."

"Lucien, lover, the only thing I want to get up close and personal with is you," she stated, melting against him as her sex quivered. The sultry look in Lucien's eyes told her he'd found his home, and it was in her arms, wherever they chose to go. "Now, about those three wishes..."

CHECK OUT MORE GREAT READS FROM ROWAN PROSE!

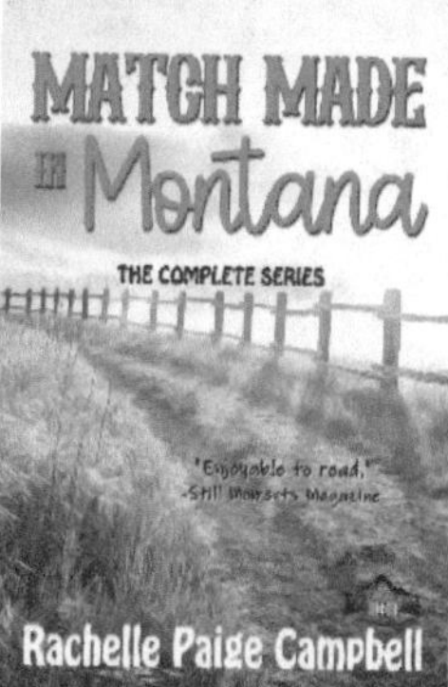

Julie Castle is a natural-born romantic with a modicum of artistic talent inherited from her mom and a love for telling tall tales she got from her dad. That set her up for being a starving artist, the biggest fibber in the world, or a romance author. She's so glad she chose the latter. She's always had a love affair with the written word. As a child growing up in a small town, she loved visiting the local library, a converted gilded age mansion, and getting lost between the pages of a book. The drafty old mansion could be a spooky place, but she still loved it. She enjoyed poking into behind the scenes areas she wasn't supposed to venture into. She's still the same way, which is why she loves writing romance with an edge, paranormal, suspenseful, super sexy, or just laugh your pants off funny. She resides in Wisconsin with her family.